WEBS *of* PERCEPTION

WEBS *of* PERCEPTION

A NOVEL

DARLENE QUINN

GREENLEAF
BOOK GROUP PRESS

From chocolate and coffee to skin cream, every purchase matters. To improve lives, protect the environment, and invest in the future, look for the Fairtrade mark. Please visit fairtradeamerica.org to discover how you can become a conscious consumer and make a positive difference in the world.

This book is a work of fiction. Names, characters, businesses, organizations, places, events, and incidents are either a product of the author's imagination or are used fictitiously. Any resemblance to actual persons, living or dead, events, or locales is entirely coincidental.

Published by Greenleaf Book Group Press
Austin, Texas
www.gbgpress.com

Copyright ©2018 Darlene Quinn

All rights reserved.

Thank you for purchasing an authorized edition of this book and for complying with copyright law. No part of this book may be reproduced, stored in a retrieval system, or transmitted by any means, electronic, mechanical, photocopying, recording, or otherwise, without written permission from the copyright holder.

Distributed by Greenleaf Book Group

For ordering information or special discounts for bulk purchases, please contact Greenleaf Book Group at PO Box 91869, Austin, TX 78709, 512.891.6100.

Design and composition by Greenleaf Book Group
Cover design by Greenleaf Book Group
Cover images used under license from ©Shutterstock.com/ESB Professional; ©Shutterstock.com/EpicStockMedia; ©Shutterstock.com/Alita Xander; ©Shutterstock.com/Ronald Sumners

Publisher's Cataloging-in-Publication data is available.

Print ISBN: 978-1-62634-566-9

eBook ISBN: 978-1-62634-573-7

Part of the Tree Neutral® program, which offsets the number of trees consumed in the production and printing of this book by taking proactive steps, such as planting trees in direct proportion to the number of trees used: www.treeneutral.com

Printed in the United States of America on acid-free paper

18 19 20 21 22 23   10 9 8 7 6 5 4 3 2 1

First Edition

Dedication

To Jack, my loving husband—who always has my back

Acknowledgments

Without the aid of the many dedicated professionals who generously shared vital information, it would not have been possible to create the true-to-life drama and realistic settings that have become the hallmark of the Webs series.

Maintaining accuracy and authenticity—not only in the world of fashion and retail but in all areas—is important to me. This novel required in-depth research into some new topics, such as the functions of the brain, semester-at-sea programs, the aftermath of rogue waves, and the state of retail—online vs. brick-and-mortar stores—in our world today. (However, I never allow the facts to get in the way of page-turning suspense!) To this end, I owe a great deal to many people, including the following individuals:

As always, I owe my firsthand retail education and the ring of truth that reverberates throughout this work of fiction to the former executives and the sales and sales-support associates of Bullock's/Bullocks Wilshire. Also, I must again express my gratitude to Allen Questrom, master of merchandising, retail, and company turnarounds, who led Federated Department Stores out of bankruptcy and on to the acquisition of The Broadway/Emporium Stores and R. H. Macy & Company, Inc. Likewise, I am eternally grateful to Terry Lundgren, the former chairman, president, and CEO of Macy's, Inc., under whose leadership Macy's has become a national brand, blanketing our nation with more than eight hundred Macy's department stores and forty Bloomingdale's stores under the Macy's umbrella. After handing over the reins, Terry remains as executive chairman of the department store company.

Of assistance in researching this novel was Dr. Kenneth Martinez, neurologist, to whom I am grateful for his generous gift of expertise. He took time out of his busy day to meet me for coffee—and even brought with him a plastic model of the brain to illustrate its various functions and to discuss the possible effects of a blow to the head. Any amnesia-related errors that appear in this novel are mine alone. Selina Anderson also generously shared her unique experience being on a semester-at-sea program and answered all my many questions.

For my questions regarding the consequences of a disaster at sea, I would like to thank the following individuals aboard the Princess Cruise Lines: Kyler Mann, onboard sales manager; Dusko Babic, assistant purser; and from the Philippines—Joyri Ismael, waiter; Arnaldo Longalang, assistant waiter; and Von Kevin Aranas, junior waiter. From Cunard Cruise Holidays, I wish to thank Kevin M. Grubb, Acc., cruise travel specialist. I would also like to thank my granddaughter Jamie Weeks for filling me in on what I needed to know about California State University, Long Beach.

I extend my thanks to my wonderful review committee members: Nanci Gee, Barbee Heiny, Peggy Kuntzelman, Barbara McClaskey, Mike McNeff, Dolores Ayotte, Jon Batson, Brenda Minor, Stefanie Jackson, Kevin Keeny, Toni Rakestraw, Sue Senden, Kami Weeks, Samantha Noelle Golt, Karen Sherman Grisham, Sandra Hicks, Sally Fritch, and Lisa de Vincint. And a special thanks to Ginnie Wilcox, who volunteered to proofread the manuscript prior to the printing of my advance reader's copies, giving me the advantage of an additional check for accuracy and readability.

I couldn't do without the folks at News and Experts: Marsha Friedman, Steve Friedman, Jay York, and Miguel Lantigua. It's a joy to work with this savvy group of publicists, all of whom are dedicated professionals with a great sense of humor.

I must also thank Greenleaf Book Group, particularly Justin Branch, director of consulting; Dan Pederson, project manager; Neil Gonzalez, the very best cover designer extraordinaire; Carrie Jones, director of production; Corrin Foster, marketing manager; Steve Elizalde, distribution account executive; Lindsey Clark, staff editor; my incredible editor, Linda O'Doughda, who shapes my stories and makes them so much better; and freelance copy editor Amy D. McIlwaine, for assuring accuracy and order with her fabulous sense of time and place. Your collective enthusiasm and dedication have not only enhanced this work of fiction but also made the journey to publication an exciting and enjoyable adventure.

Thanks also to my creative webmaster, Eddie Velez, who publishes my biweekly newsletters with increadibly creative graphic designs, and Michael Stephen Gregory at Random Cove, who produces my amazing book trailers.

And finally, a special thanks to my fantastic administrative assistant, Kathy Porter, the award-winning author of the Gray Guardians series and an invaluable part of my team. And most of all, thanks to my awesome husband, Jack Quinn, who makes my writing life possible, before and after publication.

Part One

May 14–19

Chapter 1

My eyes shot open. A cold, biting breeze brushed my cheek, and I shivered at the dampness seeping into my skin. My heart pounded in my ears. My body shook, and my breath escaped in gasps.

Where am I? The question drifted through my foggy brain, my aching head.

The cramped space reeked of salt water. The floor rocked unsteadily beneath me. I blinked and tried to focus, unable to wrap my mind around my surroundings. *Why am I on the floor?*

I blinked again. The slightest movement hurt.

Still on the floor, I leaned on my elbows and pushed myself to an upright position. Then, lifting my hand to my head, I felt for the spot where it throbbed. My fingertips moved gingerly. The right side of my forehead, near my hairline, was sensitive and sticky.

Faint light shimmered through a shattered, rain-spattered window, dimly illuminating the area. Vague shapes surrounded me. I had no depth perception. Nothing made sense. I stared at my fingers, and though I saw no color, I knew the sticky substance must be blood.

I shook uncontrollably. My mouth was dry, and I felt nauseous. *What happened to me?*

Forcing myself to focus, I took a physical inventory. I was between two single beds, their soggy spreads dripping onto the floor. I was fully dressed, wearing a pair of jeans, a lightweight T-shirt, and a hoodie. With this grasp of the basics, my initial panic subsided a fraction. In its place came a more rational fear. *Something really bad has happened.*

I needed more light. Cautiously pushing myself to my feet, I peered into the gloom, stretching my arms in front of me to feel for unseen obstacles. I moved slowly, my hands sliding along the wall.

At last, my fingertips touched a switch. I flipped it on. Bright lights flooded the small room.

I was on a boat. But why? I concentrated hard. *What happened to put me in this place?* No longer able to keep hysteria at bay, I realized I couldn't answer that simple question. I couldn't remember anything at all.

Thundering footsteps and loud voices vibrated through my throbbing head. I felt faint, but I knew I must not give in to weakness. I just wanted to go home.

With that thought, I sank down onto one of the soggy beds with a renewed sense of horror. I didn't know who I was, or where I was, and I had no idea where home might be.

CHAPTER

2

Thursday, May 14, 10:15 p.m.—Manhattan, New York

Ashleigh Taylor gasped as an inexplicable pain sliced through her heart, constricting her chest. Slowly taking a deep breath, she straightened her posture and glanced at Conrad, seated to her left in their box seats, hoping she hadn't disturbed him. She needn't have worried. Having spoken of nothing but *Hamilton* in recent weeks, he was leaning forward, totally absorbed by the riveting performance.

Ashleigh had not shared the strange sense of foreboding that had overcome her shortly before they'd entered the Richard Rodgers Theater. *What is there to tell? How can I put such a hollow feeling into words?* But here it was again—that nearly imperceptible knowledge that something wasn't right. Ashleigh closed her eyes, and gradually her breathing returned to normal. She did her best to brush apprehension aside, but even so, she willed the final curtain call to come soon.

In the lobby, as Conrad explained why "History Has Its Eyes on You" was his favorite song, Ashleigh nodded and powered on her iPhone. "That's strange," she said, staring down at the screen.

Conrad fell silent and raised a questioning brow.

"Four calls from April since intermission," Ashleigh went on.

They continued to weave seamlessly through the throng of theatergoers toward the exit.

Times Square, as always, was buzzing with activity. Conrad spotted their limo to the left of the theater's entrance, and he motioned for David to remain behind the wheel while he helped Ashleigh inside. Once they were both settled, he pulled out his BlackBerry.

"Whoa. I've had a couple calls from April, too." Conrad shook his head. "What could be so urgent at this hour?"

Ashleigh looked at her iPhone display. April's first call had come in at eight forty-two. Before calling back, she checked for voice messages. There was only one.

She hit play.

"Where are you, Aunt Ashleigh?" There was a moment's pause before April continued. "Sorry. I'm a bit rattled. Please call as soon as you get this message."

A lump formed in Ashleigh's throat. She heard the anxiety in April's voice. Gripping the phone, she punched in the number.

It rang only once before April picked up. Not bothering with a greeting, she asked, "Have you heard from the girls?"

"Not since they left Southampton." *Why would we?* Ashleigh thought. *They're somewhere in the mid-Atlantic.* "What's wrong?"

As she heard her own words, a sinking sensation settled in the pit of her stomach. They had known Paige and Mark Toddman's daughter since she was four years old. April was a mature young woman who seldom came across as rattled.

"You haven't heard? The rogue wave." Following a quick intake of breath, April continued, "It's all over the news . . ."

As April began to rush through the details, Ashleigh pressed the speaker button on her iPhone.

"Hold on," Conrad broke in. His tone was calm, his words measured. "You say a rogue wave hit the *Rising Star*?"

Ashleigh frowned. Placing her hand on Conrad's arm, she whispered, "Rogue wave?"

"At about six thirty our time, CNN reported a seven-story wave hit the *Rising Star*. There are broken windows, an inch or two of water in many cabins . . ."

Ashleigh's throat constricted as April detailed the damage. All she cared about was the safety of their daughters. "How about the passengers?" Ashleigh blurted out.

"Thank God, there have been no deaths reported. Some passengers have minor injuries. Mostly from falls, or being hit by flying furniture and glass. The ship wasn't disabled. They think it will arrive a day late, but at least it's sailing under its own power." April fell silent for a brief moment. "When I couldn't reach you, I called my parents right away. They suggested I keep trying to get in touch."

Pulling Ashleigh close, Conrad said, "Thank you, April. We have the emergency numbers for the ship. And there may already be a message on our home line. We'll let you know as soon as we receive any news."

Ashleigh ended the call and leaned into her husband, grateful for his warm, strong body enfolding hers.

"Love," Conrad said, "all I know about rogue waves is that they're also called monster waves, which makes sense because they're huge and unpredictable—caused by some combination of undersea currents and high winds." He flipped on the TV screen. "The experts will have far more reliable information."

Scanning channels, Conrad found what he was looking for on NBC, when a news reporter appeared on the small screen, her face frowning in concern. "In the high drama of the high seas, an eighty-foot rogue wave broadsided the *Rising Star*, four days out of the English port of Southampton, turning a luxury study cruise for college students into a nightmare. Now, you may have heard of this type of phenomenon as a freak wave, an extreme wave, a killer wave, a monster wave, or just an abnormal wave. Whatever you might call it, these are spontaneous, colossal waves on the ocean's surface. They occur far out at sea and are a threat to even the largest of ships and ocean liners. Unfortunately, these sea-serpent-like swells are not as rare as one might think . . ."

The reporter glanced down. "The seven-story wave hit the port side of the *Rising Star* between six and seven o'clock local time, knocking out the windows of the ship's restaurants and shattering several balcony doors. The floors of more than twenty cabins were left in a foot of water. Several students and crew members sustained minor injuries. However, no fatalities were reported . . ."

Conrad smiled and kissed Ashleigh on the forehead. "Be strong, love. You know our girls. They're survivors, like their mother. They're sure to make the best of the situation and come away with a boatload of stories to tell—no pun intended. Marnie is most likely taking notes for her next short story as we speak."

Ashleigh leaned over and kissed his smiling lips. Tension eased from her shoulders. *If anything bad happened to any of my girls, I would know.* But the newscaster's next words sent her reeling.

CHAPTER
3

Somewhere in the Mid-Atlantic Ocean

The bright overhead lights stung my eyes.

How long has it been since this nightmare began? How long have I been here, wrapped in these thin, heated blankets? Through snatches of murmured conversations, coming from every direction, I began to piece together the here and now.

I was on a ship. As I'd been carried down to this sick bay, I'd noticed more college-aged young people than older adults. But since I hadn't had much of a view outside, I couldn't guess the time of day, much less the time of year. Or what year it even was.

The only memory I could conjure up was of the cabin where I'd awakened, but I still didn't know *why* I was on this ship.

Images came back to me sporadically, of soaking wet shoes and soggy magazines scattered across the floor of the cabin. There'd been a cacophony of voices outside my room. From their urgency, I'd known I had to get out, no matter how much my head ached. But when I took a step toward the door, the room began to spin. Too weak to stand, I'd groped for something to hold on to, but only managed to plunk down onto the closest sodden bed.

The next thing I remembered was a gentle voice, and when I opened my eyes, two crewmen were beside my bed with a stretcher, clad in tall rubber boots, damp navy trousers, and white shirts embossed with navy and gold emblems. It was like a scene from the movie *Titanic*.

I felt the sickening swaying motion of the stretcher balanced between the crewmen as they carried it down a long corridor toward an elevator.

I caught glimpses of passengers in life vests. Some were huddled together and talked softly, while others cried hysterically.

The sounds echoed again now through my aching head.

I tried to orient myself, but I couldn't concentrate. My head pounded so loudly the entire band of seventy-six trombone players from *The Music Man* seemed to be marching through my skull.

I felt a gentle touch on my arm. "Marnie," a voice said, "I'm Dr. Pearson. You've had a nasty fall." A small, balding man clad in blue scrubs bent over me.

"You know me?" I asked. *Marnie*. The name did not ring any bells, but at least *someone* knew who I was. An overwhelming sense of relief shot through my veins.

He nodded. "I met you and your sister at the captain's table shortly after we began the voyage, and I saw your sister in my office just the other day. A great many people are concerned about your welfare."

It was true that several people had run up to me on the stretcher, asking if I was okay, but I had no idea who they were.

"Questions regarding the well-being of you and your sister have inundated—"

"My sister? I have a sister?"

"You don't remember?" the doctor asked. He sounded concerned but not shocked. "Given the blow you received to your head, it's not unusual for you to experience memory loss." He held up a wrinkled hand. "I'm no expert on amnesia, but I don't believe there's any cause for alarm. It's most likely temporary. Things may remain a bit hazy for a short period. I know of athletes who report being unable to recall incidents leading up to their injury, yet all their other memories remain intact."

"You said I had a sister. And she's on this ship?"

The doctor smiled patiently. "You do indeed. And without having seen your driver's license and passport, I would be in the dark as to which—"

"Where is my sister?"

The doctor's gaze dropped to the floor. "The ship's staff and crew are searching for your twin. So far, aside from her and a missing waiter, everyone else is accounted for." He paused, gesturing to the bedside table where an oversized signature Michael Kors handbag sat. "I'm sorry, Marnie, but we had to open your handbag for identification."

I have a twin? My stomach tightened. I prayed for my sister's safety. Hopefully, when they found her, she wouldn't have a knot the size of a golf ball on her temple, nor a fuzzy brain. I threw in another quick prayer: that my memory would return quickly.

Here in the hospital area, the faint scent of disinfectant did little to mask the strong scent of seawater. "What happened to this ship? Why are people in life jackets sloshing through the flooded corridors?"

Dr. Pearson filled me in with a few broad strokes. Then he focused on me once more. "Your head injury should be examined by a neurologist, but the *Rising Star*'s sick bay lacks proper medical staff and equipment. The ship never lost power during the disaster, but we still have two more days at sea before we reach port. Search and rescue has been called. Luckily, there is a Coast Guard ship only a few hundred miles from here. They have a helicopter that will airlift you to New York–Presbyterian Hospital. Your writing coach has contacted your parents."

Writing coach? Parents? I felt as if I'd fallen down the rabbit hole. I couldn't conjure up an image of parents, nor did I know how a writing coach fit in. *I'll think about that later.* My hand unconsciously drifted to the bandaged right side of my head, which throbbed with pain. Strips of gauze ran under my chin and encircled my head like a doughnut ring. The bandages had already begun to itch.

I hoped Dr. Pearson was right and my amnesia was temporary. Short-circuiting any hope of relief, my mind began to reel. Why is it I understood the meaning of amnesia, and recalled an old Hollywood movie, when I couldn't remember my name or anything about my life before waking up on the damp floor just a few hours earlier?

"Dr. Pearson," I called out as I saw him turn to leave. "I know you are not an expert on memory, and I agree that I should see a neurologist—"

"And I am going to suggest a psychiatrist as well."

"You think I'm crazy?"

"Not at all. Last week at dinner I found you and your sister quite intelligent and utterly enchanting. But until you regain your full memory, you are sure to experience periods of confusion and loss. A qualified psychiatrist can help get you through the rough spots."

I nodded, sending a jarring spiral of pain through my head. I gulped in a couple of breaths and said, "I don't understand why I can't remember my sister or my parents, or even my name, but—"

The expression on the doctor's weathered face was grave. He looked exhausted. "Marnie—"

"Wait. I'm not delusional. I understand amnesia has temporarily erased those memories. What I don't understand is why I can remember random things like a Broadway song, and what a Michael Kors handbag is, and even the rabbit hole from *Alice in Wonderland*."

He nodded sympathetically. "The brain is a very complicated mechanism. Even neurologists don't know all its complexities. What I do know is that there are different parts of the brain, and each store different kinds of information. So, for example, you may forget certain things while at the same time you remember others."

The ship captain's voice blared over the loudspeaker. To my relief, Dr. Pearson instantly stepped away and turned down the volume to a tolerable level.

The captain apologized for the unavoidable conditions and thanked the passengers for their cooperation and tolerance, and the crew for its diligence and hard work. He then announced, "To complete repairs in a timely manner, we have altered our course. The *Rising Star* will now dock in Charleston, South Carolina. For those who are anxious to get home but have no one available to pick you up, we will provide transportation. The other alternative is to await repairs and then return to Brooklyn as planned on board the *Rising Star*—albeit a few days later than originally scheduled."

Was I anxious to get home? Would someone be there to pick me up? I had no clue.

"We'll arrive at the Charleston terminal before noon on Sunday," the captain went on. "After repairs are completed, the ship is scheduled to arrive at the Brooklyn terminal at five p.m. on Tuesday. In the meantime, the crew and I will make every effort to see that you're as comfortable as possible."

There was a long silence before the captain resumed. "Unfortunately, I now have some very sad news. Our competent safety team has spent hours searching every inch of the ship, but there is no longer any doubt. Two individuals were washed overboard by the rogue wave. God rest their souls."

I closed my eyes and felt Dr. Pearson gently squeeze my hand.

Chapter

4

Thursday, May 14, 11:40 p.m.—Manhattan, New York

As the limo sailed north along the Henry Hudson Parkway, Conrad switched the TV channel. The news that one student and one *Rising Star* staff member were unaccounted for sent Ashleigh's mind into overdrive. "I—I must call Elizabeth," she stammered. "She'll be out of her mind with worry."

Elizabeth had been a trusted and much-loved treasure in Ashleigh's life for as long as she could remember. She'd met the kindly nurse in the home of her surrogate grandfather. She had been a friend and perfect companion for the iconic Charles Stuart in his late eighties and had been by his side to navigate the troubled waters of his daughter's mental illness. As the grandmotherly presence in the Taylors' Greenwich home since shortly before the birth of Juliana, she had supported and cared for the Taylors through many dramatic moments, from the kidnapping of Marnie as an infant, to her return at age eight to her biological family. Little had Elizabeth known the significant role she would play in the family—with Charles and his unstable daughter, Caroline, and with his "granddaughter" Ashleigh and her children—for decades to come.

In the limo, Conrad ran his fingers through his thick, dark, silver-streaked hair, deep creases forming on his brow. "Hopefully Elizabeth has not yet heard the news. She may not have turned on a TV or radio this evening. Otherwise, we'd have heard from her by now."

Ashleigh considered his words. "Good point. But even more reason to reach her as soon as possible."

Elizabeth's cell phone went straight to voice mail. Rather than leave a message, Ashleigh pressed END. Almost immediately, her iPhone rang. Glancing down at the caller ID, she saw it was Elizabeth and hit TALK. "I just called your—"

"Oh, Ashleigh." Elizabeth's voice was whisper-thin. "I crawled into bed early and must have nodded off. I just turned on the TV."

"We just heard it ourselves."

"Are the girls safe?"

"I'm sure Callie and Marnie are making the best of it."

"You've not been contacted yet?" Elizabeth said, her soft voice full of concern.

"We're headed straight home to check for a message. The *Rising Star* has a swift emergency communication system in place." Ashleigh withheld the news of the missing student.

"That's good," Elizabeth said. "Please wake me with any news, no matter how late. I'm praying for their safety."

When Ashleigh ended the call, a thought flashed in her head. "Remote code," she said, and began scrolling through the notes on her iPhone.

It took Conrad no more than a fraction of a second to grasp her meaning. "Do you have it?"

She nodded. "One, seven, zero, three."

Conrad punched in their home number and then the code. It had been a long time since they'd needed to access voice messages on their landline remotely.

In the next moment, Conrad's grip on the BlackBerry tightened and the color drained from his face.

Chapter 5

Thursday, May 14, Midnight—Bronx, New York

Conrad's organized mind faltered. *What about Callie?* He needed more information. He needed to form a rational plan. *No time for delay.*

"Love, there were two calls from aboard the *Rising Star*. They were both about Marnie." Feeling Ashleigh's body stiffen beside him, he quickly added, "She's safe. She was knocked off her feet when the ship was hit and received a blow to her head." He rushed on, sensing Ashleigh's mind was traveling the same path as his. "The first call was from the ship's administration office, and the second from Marnie's creative writing teacher—a Professor Frank Gaspar." He paused. "Neither left word of Callie."

"Callie wouldn't have been one of Gaspar's students," Ashleigh pointed out. "But the main office should have relayed news of the safety of both girls."

Conrad nodded. "My thoughts as well." His gut tightened another notch. "Gaspar confirmed the ship is en route, traveling under its own steam. It will dock in Charleston, however, not Brooklyn. And not for another three days. So the ship's doctor contacted the Coast Guard and arranged for a medevac transport for Marnie."

Ashleigh's face turned ashen.

Conrad held up a hand. "Gaspar said there's no cause for alarm, but particularly since Marnie has medevac insurance, the doctor felt it best to get her examined by a neurologist sooner rather than later. He wants to rule out any chance of swelling or bleeding in her brain."

Ashleigh's eyes closed. "Swelling or bleeding—"

Conrad hurried on. "Apparently, Marnie has a good-sized gash at her hairline, but the doctor stitched her wound, and all her vital signs are strong. Gaspar said they're just being extra cautious. Marnie will be taken directly to New York–Presbyterian Hospital. Barring complications, she should arrive tomorrow morning."

Conrad reached for Ashleigh's hand. "Love, Marnie is also experiencing signs of amnesia. Gaspar said the doctor felt the condition was only temporary, but Marnie should see a neurologist. As well as a psychiatrist."

Ashleigh straightened her posture and lifted her chin. Neither spoke for what felt like a very long time.

"That seems like a lot to leave in a phone message," Ashleigh continued, "and yet it's not enough. Did Gaspar leave a phone number? Can we even reach the ship?"

"No, he didn't. But the number should be on caller ID." Conrad drew in a breath and gazed out the window as if there were answers written in the stars. "In the meantime, we need to confirm that Callie is safe." Shaking his head, he began to punch a fist into his open palm. He felt . . . powerless.

"How about Allison?" Ashleigh said. "Maybe we can contact her?"

When Callie had danced on the high school competition team, Allison Dee had been one of her teachers. Callie had bonded with the talented young woman, and Allison had since become like a member of the Taylors' extended family. Allison now headed the master dance program on board the *Rising Star* and had been the catalyst for Callie applying for the semester-at-sea program in their senior year at university in Southern California.

"Terrific idea. Though it's unlikely we'll get through." Conrad instantly shifted their focus to something positive, saying, "We'll get Pocino on board. He has the wherewithal to cover more ground in half the time."

Ashleigh nodded, hoping they could enlist the help of their friend and investigator-at-large. "But if he's not in New York—"

"He is." Conrad squeezed her hand. "He's dealing with an internal situation at Jordon's headquarters. He was still wrapping up loose ends when I left the store this afternoon—which feels like ages ago."

Though her eyes were moist, Ashleigh forced a smile. "Since their years of dancing together, the girls have grown apart . . . their interests, their chosen careers. But they love and care about each other, and . . ." She wiped her cheek with the back of her hand. "Marnie is hurt. Callie should be with her."

"Perhaps she is with her, love. Pocino will cut through the red tape. Even in the best-case scenario, there'll be no shortage of *that*."

12:15 a.m.—Queens, New York

Dead tired, with boarding pass in hand, Ross Pocino lumbered toward Gate 55A. Once seated on his flight, he planned to order a scotch on the rocks and doze off till touchdown at LAX.

His cell phone vibrated in his jacket pocket, and he was tempted to let it go straight to voice mail. But ignoring a call just wasn't in him. Compulsively, he pulled out the BlackBerry.

Reading CONRAD TAYLOR on the caller ID, he punched TALK. "Pocino," he answered, raising his voice above the clamor of conversation and rolling luggage wheels all around him. Then he listened.

"Holy shit. No, I had no idea that was the ship the twins are on . . . Yes, at JFK . . . Just tell me what you need. I'll do an about-face, call in a few favors, and head to Brooklyn . . . Right, but no point in taking off for Charleston now. The main offices and communication hub are here in New York."

Pocino headed out of the airport terminal to catch the Avis shuttle, surprised by the turn of events but determined to get to the bottom of things. Yet one fact that Conrad had shared chilled him to the bone: There had been no communication about Callie.

Chapter 6

Friday, May 15, 3:25 a.m.—Aboard the Rising Star

Neither asleep nor fully awake, I was unable to move. My arms were wrapped snug against me, as though plastered to my sides. I heard the scrape of metal on metal. Opening my eyes, I saw my body was wrapped in layers of blankets, tightening around me, holding me in place. Bound like a mummy, I felt like I'd awakened on the set of a horror film.

Pushing down the scream lodged in my throat, I took in the scene around me. From among the voices, I recognized Dr. Pearson's husky tones. He stood outside my line of sight. Within my peripheral view, I could just see a trim, dark-haired man looking down on me with a worried expression on his unshaven face.

"Did you reach Marnie's parents?" Dr. Pearson asked the other man.

"No one answered at the Taylors' home, but I left a message," he replied.

"Did you leave the ship's medical call-in number?"

"Damn . . . should have thought of that." Then, turning his gaze on me, he said, "Oh, you're awake."

As far as I was concerned, that was still up for debate.

"Marnie, I'm Frank Gaspar," he continued gently. "I replaced Professor Bradford for this leg of the trip. I was looking forward to meeting and working with you. Professor Bradford's notes indicate you had made amazing strides in developing emotional depth for your characters . . ."

Professor Bradford? Strides in emotional depth? What is he talking about?

"... such a shame you and your sister came down with the flu in Southampton—"

"Professor Bradford was your creative writing instructor through most of the semester," Dr. Pearson broke in, answering my unasked question. "He provides a much sought-after summer workshop for a select group of budding writers in London. Therefore, he could not be with us on the final leg of the journey back to New York. Professor Gaspar took over his master class."

Uncomfortable on this hard, unyielding surface, and unable to string things together, I just wanted to crawl into a nice soft bed. But the doctor was still talking.

"... but let's not worry about that now. The helicopter has reached the ship, and the lines have been secured to assure a safe transfer."

"Doctor, why am I bundled so tight and belted to this ... this ... whatever is beneath me?"

"Oh, I'm sorry, Marnie. I began to explain the medevac procedure before you fell asleep. Apparently, you're sensitive to the medication. This is a scoop stretcher—it's more substantial and versatile than canvas. The helicopter is unable to land on the ship, so a basket supported by sturdy cables will be lowered to the foredeck. Medevac crew members will make sure you are safe and secure before the basket is hoisted up into the helicopter. You will be in this contraption a very short time, then transferred to a regular gurney aboard the helicopter. A nurse will take care of your every need." His eyes glistened. "Soon you will be with your family."

Family? The air whooshed out of my body. I had no image of a family. And with an image of the space between the ship and a helicopter, I fought to refill my lungs. "Are you saying the helicopter will be hovering above the ship while I dangle by ropes in midair?"

The doctor nodded. "The medevac staff are professionals, very experienced. You'll be in the air for less than two minutes. It's quite safe, I assure you."

It seemed I was being given special treatment, and I knew I should be grateful. At least I would not have to endure another moment on the water-damaged ship, but still ... *Breathe in, breathe out, breathe in, breathe out,* I commanded.

"I'm sorry, Dr. Pearson. I appreciate you looking out for me. I just wish I'd stayed asleep a little longer."

"If you'd like, I can give you something—"

I shook my head, sending a shooting pain through my skull. "No. I don't want to be any more disoriented than I am." Doing my best to quiet my nerves and not think about having no ground beneath my feet, I tried to concentrate on my blessings.

I now had a name. *But who is Marnie Taylor?*

I now had a twin sister. *But are we identical, and do we even like each other?*

Then an even stranger thought popped into my head: *I don't even know what I look like.*

I wanted to know, but if I asked to see a mirror now, the doctor would send me straight to Bellevue. *Bellevue. How do I know about that?* Why were these random bits of information popping into my head? Why was this so-called amnesia retaining such trivia while blocking the most important aspects of me as a person?

Suddenly, hanging in midair by two glorified threads didn't seem like such a big price to pay.

Whatever it takes, I am getting off this ship and getting some answers.

Voices filled the air, coming from every direction—some were calling my name. The instant the door onto the deck opened, I could see the sun was low on the horizon. The early morning air bit into my cheeks. A loud clanging of metal on metal filled the air. I willed myself to concentrate, to identify the sound. Slowly, the uneven whirring of a motor captured my attention. *The helicopter?*

I glanced up. Dr. Pearson and the teacher stood on either side of the stretcher—watching over me. Though wrapped tight as a mummy, I began to shiver. "Dr. Pearson. What's that loud banging noise?"

He cleared his throat. "Heavy chains. They are securing four sets of ropes between the ship and the helicopter." He paused. "Remember, I told you the helicopter was not able to land on the ship's deck. The ropes from the railing to the helicopter keep it from drifting, assuring your safe transfer from the ship's deck."

Straight ahead, I could see the yellow basket the doctor had told me about swaying precariously back and forth. My stomach clenched. Again, trying not to think about what lay ahead and keeping my voice low, I asked, "Why are there so many people out here?"

Professor Gaspar leaned over to answer. "In addition to the crew members and medevac staff, I'm afraid you also have a lot of concerned classmates. And perhaps a few looky-loos."

I forced a smile. All I could think of was that yellow basket. Soon I'd be in midair—dangling by the thick ropes and swinging to and fro. I squeezed my eyes tight, wishing I was already an hour older.

Chapter

7

Friday, May 15, 12:30 a.m.—Greenwich, Connecticut

Ignoring the fear that gripped her heart, Ashleigh did her best to detach. No news of Callie—it made no sense. Were the ship's staff so distracted by Marnie's accident that they overlooked reporting Callie was unharmed? *If only I could reach Allison . . .*

When David pulled up in front of their home, Conrad said, "I've got it." He jumped out of the limo, paused to hold the door open for Ashleigh, then sprinted up the steps. Quickly unlocking the door, he headed straight to the phone in the library.

Ashleigh followed a few steps behind, the heels of her stilettos resonating off the marble tiles. With their youngest daughter, Juliana, spending her first week of summer at her friend Kaitlyn's house in the Hamptons, and with Elizabeth now back in Long Beach, their home seemed cavernous and empty. Even so, she dreaded calling Juliana with the uncertain news of her sisters.

Conrad checked the caller ID, then let his gaze drop to the paper beside the phone. "It's the same emergency number that's here on our orientation packet," he said while punching it in. With a scowl he failed to hide, he continued, "It's one of those damned recordings, thanking me for the patience I don't possess." He hit SPEAKER.

". . . we will be with you as soon as possible. Due to the high volume of calls . . ."

Although Ashleigh had expected communication with the *Rising Star* to be difficult, the weight of not knowing the severity of Marnie's injury or anything at all about Callie's well-being sent her stomach plummeting.

Doing her best to stay positive, she said, "The safety team's priority is most likely to report the condition of the injured before they share news of those who are unharmed."

"You're right. It just seems that by now, there's been sufficient time to communicate about all of the passengers . . ." Conrad began thumbing through the packet of papers they'd received at the semester-at-sea orientation, but he was unable to conceal his impatience from Ashleigh. After all, they'd been married more than twenty-five years.

As the irritating recording looped, Ashleigh said a silent prayer for her two girls.

1:00 a.m.—Queens, New York

Pocino's jaw clenched as the inflexible robot at the car rental counter said, "The supervisor won't be back for another twenty minutes."

"I'll take the Civic," Pocino reluctantly agreed. Grumbling, he signed the forms and took the keys. *Could have been worse,* he consoled himself. *At least I've got wheels.*

Moments later, throwing open the car door, he tossed his carry-on onto the passenger seat. Then he squeezed his ample girth beneath the steering wheel and shoved the rental agreement into the console. Extracting the Bluetooth device from the side pocket of the upright duffel bag, he then pulled down the visor and clamped it on.

When he hit the JFK Expressway, he pressed the Bluetooth button and barked, "Landes Investigations Agency." With no illusions of anyone being in the office at this hour, he left a brief message before it could slip his mind. "Something's come up. Had to cancel my return trip to L.A. Need someone to pick up my suitcase at LAX first thing in the morning before it grows legs and takes off for parts unknown." He'd call his boss again when he had a better idea of his plan of action.

Next, Pocino placed a call to Conrad Taylor's home line. It went directly to the answering machine. Wasting no time, he punched in Taylor's cell. It rang three times, then went to voice mail.

He decided that at this odd hour, he would just head toward Brooklyn

PD's 76th precinct, not far from the ship's terminal. If the Taylors didn't have any updates on Callie, he could get his old friend to help him plow through the inevitable bureaucratic BS. *Hell, I can crash in a nearby motel when I run out of steam.*

Even if all was right in the end, he might as well stick around for the inevitable backlash. Especially amid the media frenzy these days, there was one thing he knew for sure: The Taylors, being high-profile, were bound to be hounded by reporters.

6:45 a.m.—*Greenwich, Connecticut*

Ashleigh's iPhone vibrated against the glass on the coffee table. Though tempted to power it off until their call to the ship's communication center was answered, she glanced down at the screen. Her heart skipped a beat. Laying her hand on her husband's arm before pressing TALK, she said, "It's Juliana."

"Mom," Juliana keened into the phone, "We just woke up, and Kaitlyn's mom told us about the *Rising Star*. She said a ginormous wave hit the ship. Are Callie and Marnie okay? Have you heard from them? Are they still going to—"

"Whoa, Juliana. Slow down."

Juliana's silence was amplified by the background noise of the television at Kaitlyn's beach house, reporting on the disaster at sea.

"Darling, we got home late last night. There was a call from the ship's emergency communication center. We were told that Marnie had fallen and hit her head. Nothing too serious," she added, praying it was true. Until they knew more, there was no point in worrying Juliana about Marnie's amnesia. "She is being flown home—"

"Seriously?" But instead of delving into what happened to Marnie, Juliana asked, "What about Callie? Did she get hurt too?"

Ashleigh forced a tone of calm into her voice. "We've been up all night, unable to get through to the communication center. But don't worry, darling. If Callie was badly hurt, I'm sure we would have heard by now." She knew her statement was no more satisfying for Juliana than it was for her. But what more could she say? "Juliana, honey, we'll call you as soon as we get news that Callie is safe."

As she ended the call, the doorbell began to chime. Ashleigh's eyes locked with Conrad's. It was barely an hour past dawn.

Chapter

8

Friday, May 15, 7:00 a.m.—Greenwich, Connecticut

Still on hold, Conrad hit the SPEAKER button. Ashleigh shot to her feet, and he followed her to the entry, the portable phone clenched in his hand.

As Ashleigh swung open the door, he saw her body stiffen another degree.

"Mr. and Mrs. Taylor?" asked a skinny young man in pristine uniform.

At their nods, the boy introduced himself and said, "I am here on official business for the *Rising Star*." His voice shook. His eyes failed to meet theirs.

Taking in the sober expression on the young man's narrow face, and the way his eyes dropped to the envelope clutched in his shaking hands, Conrad felt a pounding in his eardrums. Unbidden, a memory resurfaced of that devastating Thanksgiving dinner more than twenty years earlier, forever etched in his mind. Moments after his mother had served their pumpkin pie with mountains of whipped cream, a noncommissioned U.S. Army officer had rung their bell to inform the family that his brother had been killed in action while serving in Desert Storm.

But Callie and Marnie had not gone off to fight a war. They had simply embarked on a fantastic educational adventure . . .

"It is with great sorrow," the young man continued, "that I must inform you. Your daughter was swept overboard yesterday evening and was lost at sea."

Conrad heard a horrible wailing breath as Ashleigh's hands flew to her lips. He pulled her close, ignoring the hammering of his heart. A tsunami of fear threatened to drown his calm. The words *your daughter* drifted through his head. *Which daughter? Was it Callie? Or had something happened to Marnie during the airlift between ship and helicopter?* The floor beneath his feet seemed to tip and roll.

Unable to conceal his unease, the smooth-faced young man in the ship's uniform went on. "Every inch of the ship was meticulously combed by the safety team. Not once, but three times. Unfortunately, when the rogue wave hit, your daughter must have been on deck." His voice quivered, and he drew in a breath before saying, "I must inform you that the student reported as missing and washed overboard was Callie Taylor."

"No," Ashleigh cried out. "That's impossible."

"Under normal circumstances, no one could accidentally fall overboard," responded the young man, his voice still shaky. "However, a seven-story wave has the power to lift someone off their feet and, regrettably, wash them overboard. Your daughter is one of two fatalities attributed to the disaster."

No, No, No, Ashleigh wanted to scream.

Conrad stood stoically beside her, his arm wrapped around her shoulder. Surely that couldn't be the end of her wonderful, beautiful daughter. *If she has fallen overboard, isn't there still a chance she can be rescued?*

Even as she perceived the thought, Ashleigh realized the futility of sending rescue boats out now. Nearly twelve hours had passed. It had taken too long to discover their daughter was missing.

And yet she couldn't accept that Callie was gone. Ashleigh had no superpowers, of course, but she had never been wrong about her girls' well-being. Even after the abduction of their newborn daughter from beside her hospital bed, over time Ashleigh had sensed that no real harm had come to her baby. She had always known somehow that whoever had taken Cassie loved the child deeply and would care for her until Ashleigh and Conrad could find her. And she hadn't been wrong. Erica Christonelli loved their Cassie, whom she'd renamed Marnie, with every beat of her heart.

Willing herself to be strong, Ashleigh sent a silent prayer. And by way of an answer, a very plausible scenario presented itself. Callie, as she often did, had simply lost track of time. She must have failed to make it back to the ship. As the thought crystallized, Ashleigh became even more certain she was right: Callie had never even left Southampton.

Chapter
9

Friday, May 15, 1:00 p.m.—New York–Presbyterian Hospital

Ashleigh's breath quickened as she stepped back into the lobby of the emergency room. Conrad was nowhere in sight.

He'd excused himself from the cramped hospital office a few minutes before she'd finished signing her name beside his on the mountain of paperwork presented by the admitting nurse. She hoped he had stepped out to call Pocino rather than to wage war once more against hospital protocol.

While no less anxious to see Marnie than her husband was, Ashleigh realized they must stay clear of the helipad. She knew Conrad would not risk getting in the way of the hospital's medical staff and the medevac team, but she also knew he was unaccustomed to the role of a bystander. Conrad was usually the one in charge.

But where is he now?

The buzz and rapid chatter, which had filled the room when they'd arrived, had dulled. The only sounds filtering through her grief-stricken haze were the air-conditioning, the droning voice of the admitting nurse, and the softer one of a young mother with an infant held close to her chest. The mother's eyes were hollow and pleading. Ashleigh knew that look all too well.

About to see if she could be of any assistance, Ashleigh heard, "Mr. and Mrs. Conrad Taylor." Her gaze darted across the nearly deserted waiting area to the double glass doors, where a heavyset nurse, clad in blue scrubs, held open the door leading to the ER.

Bolting through the entrance, Conrad spotted Ashleigh. She gave him an understanding yet questioning smile. He took hold of her hand, and together they headed toward the nurse standing in the open doorway.

He had much to share with his wife, who as usual managed to look confident and in control—the façade she managed to project in the wake of any storm. *How does she do it?* he wondered for the umpteenth time. He feared, this time, her false hopes could topple her.

Conrad knew he'd give anything to believe Callie had escaped this horrific tragedy, but he was a realist. Accepting the worst now was their only option. His heart had been ripped out. Going along with Ashleigh's optimism would only prolong the pain. Their daughter was lost to them. The only way through the darkness was to focus on helping the daughters who remained.

Following the nurse down the corridor, they passed several cubicles until finally she gestured them into yet another small office. "Dr. Harvey will be with you shortly," she said, gesturing to the metal desk and two chairs before quickly vanishing out of sight.

Conrad turned to his wife to share what he knew of the situation. "Sweetheart, I pulled a few strings to get a little information, but hospital protocol is totally inflexible. I'm told the airlift from the ship went well despite some heavy winds. The transfer from the medevac nurses and crew to the hospital staff also went without incident. Marnie was taken directly to radiology. Dr. Harvey has gone over the preliminary X-rays and has ordered more tests—he's the staff neurologist. Now that they have a bed for her in the ER, he's arranged for us to see her before she goes for further evaluation." He reached out to caress his wife's shoulder. "We'll only be able to see Marnie for a few moments."

"Oh Conrad. You know how sensitive she is," whispered Ashleigh. Twisting her wedding ring, she wondered aloud, "How is she taking all of this?"

To distract Ashleigh, Conrad filled her in on other encouraging news. "Ross says he's been connected with the Charleston Police Department through a buddy of his in the Brooklyn PD. He and a local detective will be allowed to board the *Rising Star* after it's properly docked, and the passengers disembark."

"Mr. and Mrs. Taylor?" A tall man with gold-rimmed glasses, an impressive stride, and ramrod posture stepped into the office, X-rays in one hand and Styrofoam cup in the other. As they exchanged introductions, Conrad couldn't help but notice Dr. Harvey's eyes failed to meet theirs.

Chapter

10

Friday, May 15, 1:25 p.m.—New York–Presbyterian Hospital

With his back to Ashleigh and Conrad, perched at the edge of their folding chairs in front of the generic desk, Dr. Harvey slid the first X-ray into the ominous display box on the wall behind his desk. The small, cramped hospital office took on a foreboding aura. Though Ashleigh was able to handle almost anything concrete, the unknown terrified her.

"While far from conclusive," began Dr. Harvey, "the X-rays show only a slight swelling behind the frontal lobe—"

"Excuse me," Conrad interrupted. "Have you seen our daughter? Had a chance to talk with her?"

Dr. Harvey set the remaining X-rays on the desk and lowered himself into a well-worn desk chair. "I understand your anxiety, Mr. Taylor. The mention of any condition affecting the brain is unsettling, so I'll get right to the point." He paused and took a sip of whatever was in the Styrofoam cup he held in his well-manicured hand. "Yes, I have seen your daughter, briefly. But I was unable to make a concrete assessment. She was quite . . . disoriented."

Before Ashleigh could ask for clarification, the neurologist raised his hand, palm out. "Marnie was given a mild sedative before being airlifted from the ship—an experience that in itself would produce disorientation. Sedation is a protocol for all medevac rescues at sea, to help alleviate anxiety or panic in the patient. Consequently, my preliminary evaluation is based mainly on these X-rays and the notes from the ship's doctor," he said, glancing at the open file on his desk.

Ashleigh readjusted her position in the uncomfortable chair, doing her best to follow along as the doctor's index finger moved across the dark spots on the X-rays, pinpointing the areas of Marnie's brain affected by the blow.

"These initial X-rays were taken to rule out any significant swelling or bleeding in the brain. Further evaluation is needed. Until Marnie is fully conscious—"

Ashleigh flinched.

Dr. Harvey sighed sympathetically. "That is not to say your daughter is unconscious exactly, Mrs. Taylor. Only groggy from the sedation."

A fraction of the tautness lifted from Ashleigh's shoulders.

"Dr. Pearson noted that your daughter experienced some memory loss. For example, she did not know her name. However, she did remember everything that occurred after she was found in her cabin and brought to the medical center. So until we have a better handle on your daughter's condition—"

Conrad folded his arms in front of him. "Can we see her now?" he asked, his leg bobbing up and down.

"Very soon." Removing his glasses, the doctor appeared to be searching for the right words. "Let me begin again, Mr. Taylor. As you're no doubt aware, there are many complexities of the brain. For Marnie, recovering all her memories may take a relatively long period of time. Or they may be fairly well intact when she awakens."

Ashleigh noticed she was fidgeting. She wanted to understand all about amnesia and what Marnie might be facing, yet she could hardly wait to be with her injured child—no matter how briefly.

"To put it simply, amnesia indicates a person has lost memories they once had," Dr. Harvey continued. "There are two types: retrograde and anterior grade. The latter occurs when the chemical balance in the brain is upset. The brain injury causes events following the accident to disappear from memory. When the brain chemistry later stabilizes, the brain and memory also start to work again. But as Dr. Pearson's notes indicate, your daughter is not suffering from anterior grade amnesia."

Ashleigh said a silent *thank-you* for this small blessing.

"Retrograde amnesia, on the other hand, covers memories of events that occurred before the injury. Rarely is a person's complete history wiped out. For some, however, a short period of time preceding or following the traumatic event is forever erased. Marnie may someday recall seeing the enormous rogue wave coming right at her, for instance, but might not recall the impact." The doctor rested his elbows on the desk. "It appears Marnie's retrograde amnesia—everything prior to being taken to the ship's hospital—is blocking her past. For example, Dr. Pearson reported she did not remember why she was on the ship. Nor did she recall that she has a twin sister."

Neither Ashleigh nor Conrad spoke.

Dr. Harvey leaned toward them. "Please try not to be alarmed, Mr. and Mrs. Taylor. Some patients lose hours or days, but in time, most memories return."

"I've heard of these scenarios happening in sports," Conrad said. "But how likely is it that Marnie will have long-term memory loss?"

The doctor leaned back in his chair, taking in the ceiling tiles.

Waiting for Dr. Harvey's next words, Ashleigh's stomach did a slow flip.

Finally, he replied, "I wish I could tell you. It's rare that retrograde amnesia is permanent, but . . . We'll know a great deal more after a CAT scan." Seeing the Taylors' agitation, Dr. Harvey rose and said, "Before we do any further evaluation, let's get you to your daughter, shall we?"

Ordinarily, Ashleigh would have asked about the significance of the CAT scan and a million other questions. But for now, she was placing everything else—everything other than seeing Marnie—on hold.

Chapter
11

Friday, May 15, 1:55 p.m.—New York–Presbyterian Hospital

"Stop. Please stop." Erica Christonelli wasn't sure how long she could hold back the tears welling in her eyes. *One more piece of advice and this dam is going to burst.* Her fiancé, Nelson, and her brother-in-law, Mike, had traveled here with her from Chicago for support. But the decisions were hers alone to make.

Maybe she shouldn't even be here in the emergency department. Maybe they all should have stayed in Chicago and waited for a call from the Taylors. And yet she and Mike had been the ones who had cared for Marnie during her formative years. They say a child's personality and values are set by the age of five. Erica had been Marnie's only mother until she was eight. She'd sat up with her night after night when the little girl was sick or scared. She'd bandaged Marnie's scrapes and cuts and taught her right from wrong. *Maybe there's nothing I can do here, but there's still no way I could have stayed away.*

"I'm sorry, really," she told the two men. "I know you are trying to help. But please let me handle this my way. I may be one hundred percent wrong, but—"

Nelson closed the distance between them. With his index finger, he tilted Erica's chin until her eyes met his. "Darling, there's no need to apologize. We have no business telling you how to handle this situation. We were trying to help, but we're out of our depth. You must do what you think is best for Marnie."

Mike nodded, his eyes cast down.

Erica kissed Nelson on the cheek and stepped up to the reception desk. The square-jawed nurse with the granny-style glasses nodded, not batting an eye as Erica explained that she needed an update on Marnie's condition, needed to talk with the doctor attending her. Erica's brief description of her unusual relationship with Marnie had not caused the nurse to raise a brow. Apparently, she'd heard it all.

But with no proof of her relationship to Marnie, Erica was told she would need the approval of the patient's biological parents—who were with the staff neurologist at present—before the hospital could release any information. Marnie's being of age did not seem to enter the equation. The rational part of Erica's mind accepted the hospital guidelines.

The emotional part of her wanted to cry at the injustice.

Conrad wrapped his arm across Ashleigh's shoulder, keeping pace with Dr. Harvey en route to see Marnie. When they arrived at last, the doctor pulled back the curtain and gestured for them to step inside.

Lying motionless on a narrow hospital bed, her face as pale as the stark white sheets beneath her, their daughter appeared far younger than her twenty-three years—and as vulnerable as she'd been as a child.

Marnie's eyes were closed, but Ashleigh found the steady rise and fall of her breathing comforting.

Dr. Harvey leaned down and, in a soothing voice, said, "Marnie, your parents are here."

Her head turned slightly, but her eyes remained closed. The doctor raised the head of the bed and tried again. Still no response.

Ashleigh wanted to wrap her arms around her child, but she held back.

Leaning further over the bed, the doctor pried one of Marnie's eyes open. She blinked once, then blinked again, before both eyes opened wide. Big and brown—and heart-achingly identical to her sister's eyes—they rested on her parents.

Ashleigh saw no sign of recognition.

"Marnie," Ashleigh and Conrad said in chorus, moving closer to the bed. Lack of recognition was what they had prepared for. But then Marnie's eyes misted in fear.

"My . . . parents?" she repeated, eyes wide and full of panic.

And Ashleigh's world shattered.

Chapter
12

Friday, May 15, 2:10 p.m.—New York–Presbyterian Hospital

With the doctor's words swimming through my aching head, I willed my eyes open. At my bedside stood two strangers—a dark-haired man with handsome features and a stunning woman with shoulder-length blond hair. Their hands were intertwined. Worried expressions marred their attractive faces.

My parents? Squinting, I tried to bring the two figures into focus. My stomach sank to my toes. Not a single memory bobbed to the surface. The sight of them rang no bells.

Panic flooded my veins. I attempted to focus beyond my blurry vision and commanded my breathing to slow down. Balling my hands into tight fists, I ran through my limited memory bank. Both doctors, the one from the ship and Dr. Harvey, had warned me not to panic. They said the amnesia was temporary. Yet I'd hoped with all my heart that the sight of my parents would trigger my memories.

But these strangers *are my parents. And they look too young . . .*

I took in what I could see of my own body, reassuring myself I was an adult—not a child. Then, before taking time to process, I blurted out, "How old am I?"

The pretty woman blinked but recovered in a fraction of a second. She stepped even closer to the bed and rested a cool hand on mine, carefully avoiding the IV. "Marnie," she said softly. "You'll be twenty-three in August."

"Sweetheart," cut in the man, who resembled 007, "we've been told temporary amnesia is common after a blow to the head . . ."

What the heck is going on inside my brain? Closing my eyes, I was baffled when a clear picture of the movie version of James Bond sprang to mind. Meanwhile, my parents of nearly twenty-three years, who were standing here in front of me, were virtual strangers.

"I'm . . . sorry. So, so sorry," I said, "but I don't recognize you. Maybe later when my brain unscrambles, and I've had some sleep—"

"Don't fret. Don't trouble yourself," Dr. Harvey interrupted. "What you're experiencing is natural under these circumstances. And now, Mr. and Mrs. Taylor," he continued, "Marnie is scheduled to have a CAT scan."

A sense of relief trickled through my body. I was too tired to focus, and I had no idea what to say to these strangers who were my parents.

Outside Marnie's cubicle, a young woman in blue scrubs, her hair pulled back in a sloppy bun, approached them. "Are you Mr. and Mrs. Taylor?" she asked.

"Yes," Ashleigh and Conrad said in unison.

"A woman is in the lobby. She says she needs to speak with you. The name was . . ." The young nurse paused. "Christonelli?"

Chapter

13

Friday, May 15, 2:55 p.m.—New York–Presbyterian Hospital

As she uncapped the water bottle, Erica looked once more at the ER wall clock and the second-hand circling at glacial speed. Her dry mouth craved something stronger. Swallowing hard, she recapped the bottle and slipped it back into her oversized handbag, willing the voices of temptation to vanish.

Although Conrad had confirmed on the phone that Marnie was safe, the ominous word *amnesia* overwhelmed her. Image after image of caring for Marnie—as a chubby baby, a playful toddler, a happy schoolgirl—flooded Erica's mind and brought tears to her eyes.

What if the amnesia has erased me from Marnie's memory? What if it has erased Nelson, and Uncle Mike and his partner, too? The very thought left her boneless, unable to form a rational sentence, much less an actionable plan.

Erica needed to talk with Marnie's doctors before deciding her next step. The Taylors could be right—being confronted with two families could prove overwhelming. *I want to see her as soon as possible. But I must remain strong. This is no time to buckle under.*

It had been ages since she'd craved a single glass of wine so desperately. Pushing away false illusions, she reminded herself there was no such thing as just one drink. *Once an alcoholic, forever an alcoholic.* And yet she felt so out of her depth—so utterly powerless. She couldn't just sit back and do nothing. But no matter what she did, she was bound to be wrong in one way or another.

Being on the outside was pure hell.

"Erica."

At the sound of the familiar baritone, she looked up to see Conrad and Ashleigh Taylor rapidly closing the space between them.

Waiting for them to speak, she glanced over her shoulder and made piercing eye contact with Nelson first and then Mike, pleading with them to remain nearby and yet silent. *This is something I must handle myself.*

"We've just spoken to Dr. Harvey, the staff neurologist who was called in this morning to evaluate Marnie's condition," Conrad began. "While his evaluation is only a preliminary—"

"Did you see Marnie?" Erica couldn't help firing her next question before Conrad had a chance to respond. "Did she recognize you?"

Glancing first at her husband, Ashleigh spoke up. "Yes, we were able to see Marnie for a few moments before she went for a CAT scan. But she did not recognize us."

Erica noticed that Ashleigh's voice quivered slightly.

"Dr. Harvey informed us she had been heavily sedated before being airlifted to the helicopter."

"How bad is it?"

"Physically, she has only a slight laceration at the hairline. But the doctor said it could take a long time for her to emerge from the amnesia fully. Or she may wake up tomorrow with her memory intact." Ashleigh shifted her gaze to her vibrating iPhone. "It's Juliana."

"Take the call," Conrad insisted.

Ashleigh headed for the lobby door.

Conrad's eyes drifted momentarily to the ceiling. "Our little worrywart," he said, his lips curling in a smile. He then continued as if there'd been no interruption. "We've been assured Marnie's laceration will leave no scar. As for the amnesia, only time will tell. But the prognosis is positive."

Conrad paused to give Erica time to process the news. "We notified the hospital that they should give you and Mike updates on Marnie's condition. We have no intention of interfering with your long-term relationship. But Erica, as I told you on the phone, until we have a better handle on the amnesia and how Marnie is coping, it's best that you do not contact her directly."

Erica felt the air being sucked out of the room. "Hold on, Conrad. Are you saying I can't see Marnie at all?"

"Surely you can understand that introducing a second mother figure . . . given her current state of disorientation . . . Erica, we must do what is best for Marnie during this difficult period."

Erica opened her mouth to object.

Conrad raised a hand. "No. We must expose Marnie to as little emotion as possible. We need to limit her confusion. We are seeking the advice of professionals, of course."

Erica sighed deeply.

Conrad lowered his voice, but that didn't soften the blow of his words. "We must put our personal desires aside for now, Marnie's recovery must be the number one priority."

Chapter
14

Friday, May 15, 9:00 p.m.—Brooklyn, New York

Ever since news of the rogue wave disaster hit the media, extra staff were required to report to the main offices of the Star Educational Cruise Line. Around-the-clock communications were now in place. Pocino had connected with the heavyweights at Brooklyn PD and pulled a few strings, managing to bypass much of the drama and pandemonium, with the help of Tom Holt, now with NYPD. Together, they had spoken directly to a spokesman for the *Rising Star*.

The news of Callie being swept overboard had ripped Pocino's heart to shreds. Anticipating his call to the Taylors, his gut wrenched. They were damned nice people who'd had more than their share of upheaval, angst, and grief. *And now this unthinkable tragedy.* His call to the Taylor home was picked up on the second ring. His insides back-flipped at the sound of Ashleigh's voice filtering through his earpiece. Gripping his cell, he sucked in his breath. No way could he tell her the devastating news—not over the phone.

"Ross? Conrad is on the other line with the *Rising Star*," Ashleigh said. "We've been told the rogue wave washed Callie overboard."

Pocino's breath whooshed out in a rush. In sharing the news of her daughter's death, how had her voice not wavered? But then again, this was Ashleigh, and it was far from the first time she'd rocked him on his heels.

"Please listen, Ross. I don't believe Callie went overboard." She reminded him of Callie's tendency to get caught up in the moment. "Something must have happened in England, causing her not to make it back to the ship in Southampton. I'm not delusional," she insisted. "I just know."

Your Spidey senses, Pocino was tempted to say. For once, he didn't blurt it out, taking time to process instead. He was quite familiar with Ashleigh's long history of uncanny hunches, although they weren't exactly on the same page about it.

"I know you don't give credence to intuition. But you've got to admit, Ross, it's served me well over the years," she continued in a rapid cadence. "So, hear me out. Conrad disagrees, but I feel there's a good chance Callie never boarded the *Rising Star.*"

"Based on . . .?" He feared the lady had moved from wishful thinking into a full-blown state of denial. For now, Pocino didn't challenge her optimism. But allowing her to get her hopes up might be worse in the end, when reality swooped in and smashed her hopes to smithereens. And he would be powerless to prevent it.

Not waiting for his agreement or rebuttal, Ashleigh went on. "As far as we know, all of Marnie's things—and Callie's—remain on the ship." She explained that personal property wasn't a priority in a medevac operation. "Could you go to Charleston on Sunday morning when the ship comes in?"

"That's the plan." He explained about getting help from Holt. "You might remember, he was a patrolman in Chicago when—"

"Yes, I remember," she interrupted. "Also, see if you can talk to Allison Dee or get her contact information? I've tried her cell, but there's no answer."

"The girls' dance teacher?"

"Yes, that's right. If you connect with her, please ask whether Callie"—her voice faltered, and Pocino heard her intake of breath—"attended any of her dance classes on the final leg of the trip. And ask her to call as soon as possible."

Pocino steeled himself to answer. The chance Callie had not boarded in Southampton were a million to one, but there was no point contradicting Ashleigh. Reality would sink in soon enough.

Switching to solid ground, he said, "Holt lined up a contact for me with the Charleston PD. Booked a red-eye for tomorrow night. Gonna catch a few winks now, but Holt and I will return to the shipping headquarters tomorrow before I fly out. Holt initiated a warrant with the Brooklyn PD, so we can tap into the passenger boarding and reboarding manifests. Then—"

"That sounds great, Ross," Ashleigh interjected. "But please make getting in touch with Allison a priority. There's poor cellular service at sea, and the number I have may be out of date anyway."

"Will do."

"We'd also like you to retrieve Callie's handbag. Her iPad and cell phone should be in there. Oh, and Marnie's laptop computer. It's an HP."

Okay, she wants to cut to the chase. If Callie's cell were on the ship, there would be little doubt she'd been on it as well. Charleston PD had ordered an immediate lockdown of their cabin, and he would be right alongside the local detective when she went in to investigate. "Sure thing. How about I grab their clothes while I'm at it?"

"Not a priority. Their cabin was flooded, so the clothes may have been sitting in seawater and not worth salvaging. Use your judgment."

"Got it." He hesitated. "How about Marnie's cell?"

"It was in her handbag."

After they said their goodbyes, Pocino's spirits sunk once again. Ashleigh was a damn savvy lady, and there was nothing he'd like better than to be proven wrong. Like everyone else among the Taylors' family and friends, he would be praying for a miracle. But the possibility that Callie had stayed behind in England—and had simply failed to inform her parents—was no more likely than the possibility of finding that special big-eyed needle in a stack of needles.

Another dagger of pain sliced through Pocino's heart. He hadn't felt so helpless since the murder of his four-year-old son, more than twenty years before, which had toppled his faltering marriage and ended his career with the LAPD. *Can't think about that now.* But the image of little Rocky Pocino and his infectious smile came anyway, as it always did when tragedy struck.

CHAPTER
15

Sunday, May 17, 7:30 a.m.—Charleston, South Carolina

Upon landing at Charleston International Airport, Pocino bolted from the 747 and headed directly to the Hertz counter. Moments later he signed the papers for the Dodge Durango he'd reserved.

He set the GPS on his BlackBerry for his motel before engaging his portable Bluetooth. En route, he placed a call to Holt's contact at the Charleston PD. "Ross Pocino here. I appreciate you helping me out on such short notice."

"Glad to help, Mr. Pocino," came a woman's deep southern drawl. Detective Calhoun would be accompanying him to the *Rising Star* when it docked around noon. "Gotta tell y'all right away that the ship is scheduled to dock at eleven thirty. I canvassed the area yesterday, talked with some of the staff at the terminal. Friends and families of passengers have been pouring in since last night. I plan to arrive shipside by eleven."

"No worries. Checking into the Days Inn shortly. I understand it's not far from the port." Braking at a stop sign, Pocino asked, "Where should I meet you?"

"Well, parking will be a bitch. Pardon my French, but it will be impossible. I'll pick you up in the squad car, Mr. Pocino. Say, ten forty-five? The blue-and-white will get us up close to the arrival ramp."

"Thanks a lot, Detective Calhoun. And by the way, just call me Ross. Only my dad answers to *Mister* Pocino."

"Sure thang, Ross, and you feel free to call me Dovey."

Dovey? Pocino was pretty sure he would stick with *Calhoun*, or maybe just *detective*.

He turned in to the Days Inn parking lot, hoping for a couple of hours' shut-eye. Skipping an equally longed-for shower, he set up a wake-up call, stripped down to his boxers, and hit the sheets. As soon as his head hit the pillow, it was lights out.

Moments later, it seemed, the damned room phone jarred him awake. Pocino rolled out of bed, took a quick shower, and pulled on his clothes. He was dying for a shot of strong black coffee, but a quick glance at the coffee machine announced he'd forgotten to plug it in.

Idiot, he grumbled inwardly, reaching for the plug and pressing the ON lever.

A horn honked outside his window. He checked his watch. 10:40. The Charleston detective's unwelcome early arrival left no time to wait for the coffee to drip into the cup. Not wanting to get off on the wrong foot with Calhoun, he headed out the door.

Their greetings were brief but cheerful. Pocino slid into the seat beside his new partner and explained his mission. Already the caffeine withdrawal was about to split his head wide open.

No time to dwell on it.

"The ship's in sight," Detective Calhoun said with a flip of her auburn ponytail. "May dock even earlier than predicted. Captain Cottle will speak with us after we've checked out the girls' cabin. Dean Nyquist and a couple of the master class students have agreed to speak with you too. They're also booked into the Days Inn, expecting our call." She paused. "Unfortunately, Miss Dee had a dance convention in Manhattan and couldn't wait. She left her schedule and contact numbers with the dean. He'll make himself available after all his students are in good hands. He has contact information for the teachers and other students who know the girls."

"Holy Toledo, you've really got things organized," Pocino said. "My priority is checking the twins' cabin before any of their property is touched. Since we'll get contact info, the interviews can wait. These folks want to get home and get this catastrophe behind them." He couldn't help but admit that if the worst-case scenario were confirmed, interviews would prove unnecessary. Despite praying for the miracle that the Taylor family needed, he wasn't much of a believer.

As predicted, the ship's terminal was jam-packed with vehicles and pedestrians. The overcast day, with its dark, threatening clouds, seemed to have no impact on the bustling crowd. Parked alongside cars of every make, size, and color was an alphabet soup of TV vans—CBS, ABC, FOX, NBC, CNN—their logos glinting in shiny metallic paints. Reporters zigzagged through the crowd, holding mics up to interview family members of those who had been on board the ill-fated *Rising Star*.

Calhoun drove the squad car expertly, weaving slowly through the concerned throng of parents, friends, and curious onlookers. Pocino perceived the anxiety running rampant throughout the crowd. The fact that Callie would not be among the students making their way down the gangway twisted him up in knots. Worse yet, he would be the one who would have to deliver the devastating news to Ashleigh—the outcome Conrad was already ninety percent certain of: Callie was, beyond a reasonable doubt, truly gone.

Calhoun maneuvered through the police barricade, parked a few yards from the first security checkpoint, and cut the engine.

Pocino put his game face on, ready to meet whatever the day ahead might hold.

Chapter 16

Sunday, May 17, 10:45 a.m.—New York–Presbyterian Hospital

"Dr. Prouse will be right with you," chirped the bubbly young receptionist, ushering the Taylors into the doctor's office.

Before easing herself into an armchair in front of the clinical psychologist's desk, Ashleigh let her eyes sweep over the large room. Lowering himself into the chair beside hers, Conrad appeared uncharacteristically ill at ease. Ashleigh knew he had felt more comfortable with Dr. Harvey, whose neurological findings, while not conclusive, were based on physical, tangible facts. Still, she was grateful Conrad had agreed to leave no avenue unexplored when it came to helping their daughter.

Blotting out the swirl of scenarios circling nonstop through her mind, she reminded herself: *Tackle one challenge at a time.*

Dr. Prouse, a tall, physically fit man in his late fifties, strode in, shutting the office door behind him. He folded himself into his desk chair and regarded them with compassion.

Following the brief introductions, Conrad rested his hand on Ashleigh's arm and began, "Thank you for taking the time to see us, Dr. Prouse. We spoke with Dr. Harvey shortly after Marnie arrived at the hospital Friday morning—before her CAT scan and other tests."

The psychologist leaned back in his chair. "When Dr. Harvey shared your daughter's test results, I was pleased to learn there was no significant swelling in Marnie's brain. Considering Marnie's 'unique background,' as you put it, we will begin by addressing the major psychological concerns."

Unique background. Ashleigh had used those words when making the appointment. While it was certainly true in this case, coming from

Dr. Prouse's lips the phrase sounded overly dramatic and a bit pompous. *As if each person's background were not unique,* she thought.

Feeling the light pressure of Conrad's hand on her arm, she turned in his direction. He was ready to take the lead and did so. As succinctly as possible, he filled the doctor in on Marnie's kidnapping at birth and how they were not reunited until she was eight. He also explained that the kidnapper had died before revealing to his wife, Erica, that the child she was raising was his and Ashleigh's abducted twin.

"That's incredible," the doctor conceded. "How did Marnie adjust?"

"I'd like to describe this part of the story, if I may," interjected Ashleigh. "We did not think it in Marnie's best interest to take away from her the only mother she had known for the first eight years of her life. So we made Erica a part of our extended family. Marnie and her twin, Callie, spent time with Erica and her brother-in-law . . ." She hesitated. Just speaking Callie's name sent an unbearable ache to her heart. "We all spent holidays together as a family. It worked pretty well—until the rebellious teenage years. But we got through them."

Ashleigh sank back in the chair. Her gaze locked with her husband's. "Is there anything else you'd want to add?"

"Volumes," Conrad said with a sad smile. "But I think you boiled it down to the need-to-know highlights for now."

Dr. Prouse nodded. "That's quite a story. And I certainly understand your concerns over not traumatizing Marnie any further as she struggles to remember who she is."

Ashleigh uncrossed her legs and leaned forward. "Exactly. Dr. Prouse, now that you understand our complicated situation, we need your guidance. How much of Marnie's background should we share with her *before* she regains her memory?"

Chapter

17

Sunday, May 17, 11:10 a.m.—New York–Presbyterian Hospital

Ashleigh sat alone in Marnie's room on the fifth floor, awaiting her return from a session with the clinical psychologist, staring out the window yet registering little of the outside world. Her mind circled from Marnie to Callie and back again. She willed herself to focus on where she might make a difference.

Things seemed a bit better today. Marnie was coherent and complained only of a dull headache. She would be released from the hospital tomorrow afternoon. But first she would meet with Dr. Prouse, who would administer a battery of tests to assess her psychological and emotional health.

Not a single memory from her past had returned, which made conversation with a daughter who viewed her as a stranger strained at best. Marnie remained polite but distant. Not at all herself. None of her sarcasm, wit, or over-the-top dramatics had resurfaced. And yet Ashleigh admired that Marnie was coping with her new reality better than she'd expected.

Conrad had stepped out to make some business calls while Marnie was in PT. *So many decisions to make—so little time.*

Although they had talked endlessly about their girls, neither of them had surfaced a single question regarding Conrad's unalterable schedule for the closing of one hundred Jordon's department stores. By hiring the best and most savvy merchants available, he'd built a dynamic team. But for the magnitude of what lay ahead, there simply were not enough hours in the day—even for a CEO as capable as he was.

With their entire family in crisis, today was all about them. But as Ashleigh well knew, the retail world wouldn't simply halt everything for one family's tragedy.

Before the disaster on the *Rising Star*, with all those Jordon's locations closing in the Midwest, Conrad was having a devil of a time scheduling the Taylors' trip to Southern California. But when it came to any milestones in their girls' lives, he had always cleared his calendar to be with them.

At the sound of heavy footfalls, Ashleigh turned from the window to face her husband. "I'm just been thinking, love. With so much on your plate, we need to figure out a workable schedule for the upcoming weeks. One that allows you to handle your professional obligations with the least amount of stress. Think that's doable?"

Despite Ashleigh's attempt to lighten the mood, a silence fell between them. Heaving a sigh, Conrad finally answered, "Under the circumstances, I simply won't be on hand for all the Jordon's closings." He shook his head. "I've considered every possible scenario, but there's no way to delay any of them."

His expression melted her heart. Under Conrad's ambitious and perceptive leadership, the company had opened its doors in Plaza Las Américas in San Juan, Puerto Rico—the first Jordon's department store outside of the continental United States. For the foreseeable future, however, Conrad had curtailed expansion outside the States and decided to tackle a "digital first" approach, based on the rising strength of mobile and Internet shopping.

Although online sales were indeed booming, eighty-five percent of total sales in categories carried by Jordon's and their competitors occurred in brick-and-mortar stores. Following thirteen years of phenomenal growth, however, Jordon's and its competitors had hit major headwinds in sales of fashion apparel. The warmest winter in a hundred years hadn't helped things, nor had lackluster tourist spending due to the strengthened American dollar. Last quarter's figures showed that same-store sales had a drop of 4.3 percent, which called for immediate action. Several cities in the Midwest had suffered the greatest losses in market share.

"Some of these closings will have to go ahead without me," Conrad explained. "With the number of people involved, any delay would create a scheduling nightmare." He had agonized over the ripple effect of all the lost jobs the closings would create. The damage extended far beyond individual job loss. It affects entire communities. Those left unemployed would no longer have money to spend, and their communities would no longer have the generous support Jordon's provided every year to their charities.

Before Ashleigh could protest, Conrad raised his palm. "Our family crisis is my priority. My team will take over."

"But—"

"I spent some time on the phone with Mark this morning. Knowing the importance of the initial meetings within the individual stores, he agreed to clear his schedule and accompany Spinelli to Pittsburgh next week."

Ashleigh couldn't be more thankful for Mark Toddman, Conrad's mentor and closest friend, and one of the most respected men in the world of retailing. And she was equally grateful that Conrad had been grooming the wonderful Paul Spinelli for the past three years to fill his shoes as CEO of Jordon's.

"Toddman and Spinelli are up for handling the job with transparency and humanity. Besides, I'll be only a phone call away. My team—"

Ashleigh tried once more to protest. "But I know how important this initial trip is to—"

"You and the girls come first. Always have. Always will." Conrad took both of her hands into his. "The world will not stop spinning because I'm not at the helm. It's only my ego elbowing its way forward that sometimes makes me feel my presence is so darn important."

Nevertheless, Ashleigh's heart sank at the thought of Conrad not going to Pittsburgh the following week. She was speechless.

"Look at it this way. If I'd been run down and killed in the streets of Manhattan, the plans for Jordon's store closings would not come to a screeching halt."

She managed a wan smile. "I understand. But I know how much this means to you and how hard you've worked on taking the sting out of these massive job losses. I won't be able to help the personnel directors with the outplacement for a while, but it would be utterly selfish for me to ask you to be here—"

"You're not asking. I told you, it's my place to be with you and the girls."

"I love that, darling. But just think. You can be on a plane and beside us in a matter of—" She broke off, staring deep into his troubled eyes. "Love, if there were a single thing you could do right now to cure Marnie's amnesia or solve Callie's disappearance, I'd be begging to have Mark and your team take your place."

Conrad stared into her eyes. "You really *want* me to go to Pittsburgh?"

Throwing her arms around her husband's neck, she said softly, "What I want is for you to go forward with your plans. There's really nothing you can do here. And you'll only be a phone call away."

With a rare look of uncertainty, he asked, "Are you sure?"

She nodded. "I'm just sorry I can't be with you."

"So am I."

His sincere offer to stay with her and the girls had touched her deeply. As much as she'd looked forward to accompanying him and assisting the store personnel directors with outplacement during the heartbreaking closures, it was out of the question.

Life must go on. What choice do either of us have? Not for the first time in their busy lives, Ashleigh wished she could be in more than one place at a given time. No doubt Conrad felt the same.

She could almost see the thoughts pinging through his head as he said, "Thank you, darling, for your support. And for bringing me to my senses. Even with Mark's generous offer to accompany my team—"

"I know, love. This is truly *your* responsibility. You need to be there, encouraging the loyal workers at Jordon's."

A dark cloud seemed to have lifted, only to be replaced by an expression of profound loss in his eyes. He sucked in a deep breath. "There is nothing I can physically do for Marnie right now. But darling, I won't leave until you accept this unthinkable tragedy. I must hear you say the words. Our Callie is gone."

Although his words were heartbreaking, it was his tone that crashed over her like the treacherous wave that had pummeled the *Rising Star*. But Ashleigh refused to let her optimism be swept overboard.

Chapter
18

Sunday, May 17, 11:20 a.m.—New York–Presbyterian Hospital

A swarm of ineffective words buzzed through Ashleigh's head. She would do most anything to avoid adding more stress to her husband's life. But she could not utter an outright lie.

She shook her head.

Conrad took a step back, his body stiffening. "There's nothing I'd like more than to believe Callie was somehow left behind in Southampton. But Ashleigh, it defies all the concrete facts." His voice softened. "I love your optimism. But this time, it scares the living hell out of me. Once that last thread of hope is gone, I must be here to—"

"To pick up the pieces?" Ashleigh shot back. "Please, Conrad, I am not oblivious to the facts. Yes, the ship's protocol fails to support my intuition. But I know what I feel, and I can't pretend to be without hope. Not even for you." Her eyes brimmed with tears. "If the worst-case scenario becomes a reality, I will deal with it. Darling, I'd like to think you trust me by now."

He reached for her hands and enclosed them in his. "I do trust you, love. You are amazing."

"I wasn't after kudos. I just wanted to remind you I can take care of myself and our girls in your absence."

Conrad's face fell, and she could see the regret in his eyes. But she knew he was only voicing his desire to prevent her from facing the devastation of Callie's loss on her own. "I know you are strong," he rushed on, "but I want to be here to cushion the pain of loss for you and the girls."

Ashleigh smiled. For more than twenty-five years, Conrad's desire to protect her had never diminished. Oh, how she loved him for always wanting to be there for his family. "Okay, so my Pollyanna spirit is not in sync with your down-to-earth realism," she said, trying her best to lighten the mood. "*Vivé la difference.*"

"We still have a week before you need to be in Pittsburgh," she continued. "Dr. Harvey said Wednesday might not be too soon for Marnie to travel to L.A. I think it's best we make plans." She sighed, then added, "In pencil."

Conrad let out a small chuckle. "My brain is in overdrive. It's a good thing we scheduled the Southern California trip before all this."

Ashleigh wasn't surprised. Of course Conrad would want to stay on track as much as possible with his planned visits to the profitable Jordon's stores. "My thought is that if you begin with the stores in and around L.A. on Wednesday, we can spend Tuesday with Marnie here at home before our flight the next morning."

"I can do better than that, love. I'll reschedule South Coast for Friday." He struggled to get the words out, and she knew he was thinking of Callie's graduation ceremony—the one they would no longer be attending.

Ashleigh squeezed her husband's hand. "I know your presence at the memorial service will mean a lot to Caroline and Elizabeth, love."

Before tragedy struck, they had planned to spend a couple of weeks in Long Beach for Conrad's store visits and the twins' graduations. Then Caroline Stuart, the daughter of Ashleigh's beloved grandfather figure, had a tragedy of her own. Her husband had unexpectedly died, and Ashleigh had offered to join Elizabeth in planning a memorial for him. In addition, Callie was to have shown Juliana and her friend Kaitlyn around the Long Beach State University campus, where they would be roommates in the fall.

But now everything had changed.

Refusing to dwell on what she had no power to control, Ashleigh blocked those thoughts as best she could. What was important now was going to Southern California for the memorial service—and helping Marnie figure out whether she wanted to take time off or begin her graduate program as planned at the University of California, Irvine. Unless her memory returned soon, starting grad school in the fall seemed unlikely. Even her chances of participating in her UCI graduation ceremony in June were uncertain.

Snapping back to the here and now, Ashleigh said, "Since we've already leased the condo, I might stay a bit longer if Marnie decides to begin her graduate program." And with Conrad in the Midwest, she wouldn't feel torn between staying a while longer near her girls and leaving her husband on his own in Greenwich.

As the words slipped from her lips, a plan began to take shape—a plan she would need to form and revise one day at a time.

CHAPTER 19

Sunday, May 17, 11:35 a.m.—New York–Presbyterian Hospital

As Conrad prepared to head to Jordon's headquarters for a brief meeting, he reminded Ashleigh that the hired limousine would be dropping Juliana off to join him there. Although he and Ashleigh had assured their youngest daughter there was no need to change her plans, Juliana could not be talked out of aborting her week in the Hamptons with Kaitlyn. "David will bring us back here to the hospital at about two o'clock."

Conrad took hold of both Ashleigh's hands and led her to the side of Marnie's hospital bed. Instead of giving her a quick kiss and being on his way, he lowered himself to the edge of the bed and pulled her down beside him.

Ashleigh's breath caught in her throat, but she managed to say, "You're worried about what I plan to share with Juliana." It wasn't a question.

"Love, your instincts are amazing, but . . ."

"Darling, please stop tiptoeing around. It's no secret you don't share my optimism."

Conrad could not ignore the cold, hard facts, and yet when tragedy struck, no matter how devastating, Ashleigh's optimism seldom wavered. Nor had she ever failed, in times of great need, to give her all to those around her. During every waking hour since the disaster at sea, they had discussed all the possibilities regarding what had happened to Callie. Conrad simply couldn't hide his frustration over their conflicting views.

Shaking his head now, he lamented, "I truly wish I could."

Ashleigh's back stiffened. "I'm sorry, love," she said. "I know my instincts defy logic, and I know you are trying to protect me from the backlash of false hopes. But I can't give up on Callie. My heart tells me Callie is alive, and we must find her."

Ashleigh's eyes glided past her husband's worried expression. She never spoke of mother's intuition, and yet she could not ignore her feelings. Deep inside she truly did not accept that her daughter had gone overboard. She would not even entertain that possibility unless she received confirmation of Callie's presence aboard ship on the trip from Southampton.

Ashleigh looked into Conrad's troubled, deep blue eyes. "I'm hoping for more information before Juliana arrives, but I promise not to plant false hopes. I just pray Pocino will call in soon and report." She didn't know which would be more unsettling for the eighteen-year-old: not knowing the fate of her sister, or thinking the worst had happened?

How can I tell Juliana we received word that Callie was swept overboard?

In response to the endless rounds of questions Juliana had fired at them over the phone, Ashleigh and Conrad had found they could not lie. They had told Juliana that Callie was the student whom the media reported missing. However, they had not shared the report of Callie's unthinkable fate, delivered by the young man from the cruise line.

It had been no more than a lie of omission, and yet it didn't sit right with Ashleigh. A strong bond of trust was the hallmark of the Taylor family. That trust, she knew, must not be broken—no matter how valid the reason. Omitting details was one thing, but Ashleigh would not shatter Juliana's trust with an outright lie.

Juliana had always loved both of her sisters with all her heart. Their bonds were strong—based on mutual trust and support. But when Marnie had returned to their family, Juliana had been four years old. She'd always been a bit closer to Callie, whom she'd known all her life. She shared Callie's easygoing personality, not Marnie's more volatile one. And yet it was Juliana who could read Marnie's moods and deftly step around them.

Conrad rose, kissed Ashleigh on the top of her head, and patted the pocket where he'd slipped in the BlackBerry. "We'll figure it out. Text me the instant you get any news. I'll do the same."

11:35 a.m.—Charleston, South Carolina

Pocino squirmed on the sticky vinyl seat. The squad car's AC was no match for the sultry heat wave passing through Charleston. Detective Calhoun turned to him, noticing his discomfort. She seemed to take mercy on him, pointing to the wide, green awning just inside the fenced area. It looked to Pocino like a good choice, despite being located a few yards from the frenzy of reporters, their microphones at the ready.

"Why don't we wait over there, Ross?" Calhoun drawled.

Pocino grunted his approval.

The *Rising Star's* gangway was finally in place, and passengers began to pour out from the ship. The ramp, a good fifty yards to his and Calhoun's right, was not close enough for conversation with the passengers, but that wasn't their intention.

The two detectives had a clear view of the herd descending the ramp, most carrying duffel bags or wheeling suitcases behind them. Some appeared grumpy and bedraggled; others were dazed or stoic. For the most part, Pocino was surprised to find, these young students looked as if they'd enjoyed a thrilling adventure—and couldn't wait to tell their friends and family all about it.

Pocino's gaze followed the departing passengers to beyond the fenced area, where hordes of reporters stepped deftly into their paths. He hadn't spotted Allison yet. He understood why Ashleigh had impressed on him the importance of finding the dance teacher and talking to her. But Pocino had no desire to delay boarding the ship. There was important information, and it could only be gathered by going aboard immediately.

CHAPTER
20

Sunday, May 17, 11:45 a.m.—New York–Presbyterian Hospital

Alone again in Marnie's hospital room, Ashleigh sent a silent prayer for strength and wisdom. She glanced at her watch, anxious for noon to arrive. Waiting for news of the ship docking in Charleston was draining her spirit—and her patience. She wanted the facts, and she wanted them now. Instinct and hope prevented her from considering a worst-case scenario, and yet now she felt as if she were the one adrift at sea.

No member of their extended family or close friends had remained untouched by the tragedy that struck the *Rising Star*. Her dearest friend had even thought to brighten the generic room with a huge bouquet of colorful flowers in a lovely ceramic vase, positioned on the bedside table where Marnie could enjoy their bright influence. Blinking back a tear, Ashleigh didn't need to look at the attached card. She felt Paige Toddman's presence. Knowing yellow was Marnie's favorite color, Paige would have been the one who chose yellow tulips and daffodils, accented by the dramatic orange and blue of a bird of paradise.

Paige and Mark were such a treasured part of their extended family that the Taylor girls had even adopted them as aunt and uncle. Paige's message on their home phone said it all: *Our hearts and prayers are with you both. We are here for you. Please call if there is anything we can do.* Ashleigh planned to call her this very evening—after she and Conrad heard from Pocino.

Rechecking the wall clock, Ashleigh saw that noon had come and gone. The *Rising Star* should be docking any time now. Spotting the remote control on the bedside tray, she picked it up and aimed it at the small TV mounted high on the opposite wall. Media coverage of the disaster, she knew, would be on multiple channels.

The TV blared, the screen filling with black-and-white static. No picture. Quickly locating the volume control, she turned it down and eventually found a news channel with live coverage. Members of the Charleston police force had formed a human wall between the ship's ramp and the throngs of onlookers. The ship had obviously arrived earlier than announced. The gangway, a good twenty yards beyond the wall of law enforcement officers, was empty. No passengers were in view.

Instead, the face of a local Charleston news anchor filled the small screen.

CHAPTER
21

Sunday, May 17, 12:15 p.m.—New York–Presbyterian Hospital

The headline—in big, bold letters on the upper left-hand side of the screen—read:

ROGUE WAVE TURNS SEMESTER-AT-SEA INTO PURE HORROR ON BOARD RISING STAR

"In the high drama on the high seas, more than eight hundred passengers on board the *Rising Star* are anxiously awaiting their return to New York," came the news anchor's voice. She glanced down, then raised her chin again and looked straight into the camera. "For days after the seven-story rogue wave pounded their ship, many student passengers were left without a suitable cabin—and in fear for their lives."

Nothing could have prepared Ashleigh for the clip that came next: a video taken on board the ship, recording each horrible second as Marnie and Callie had lived it. She watched, mouth agape, as the sea came crashing in, leaving half a foot of water sloshing from side to side between the beds in a small cabin. The breathtaking video picked up the sounds of rushing water as it poured into the cabin. Ashleigh knew this clip would be played and replayed many times over, transmitted virally to millions of viewers.

The anchor turned things over to a reporter on the scene, whose smooth, steady voice played as the screen flashed to one passenger after another, deboarding the ship. "Though a day late and in an unexpected port, the *Rising Star* has docked here in Charleston for necessary repairs after steaming back under its own power," said the voice. "It unloaded eight hundred and thirty-six passengers . . . with memories they won't soon forget."

The next clip showed a mass of dockside reporters scrambling to speak with the young passengers, many of who seemed eager to be interviewed. "It was like we were on the set of *The Perfect Storm*," chimed in one young man wearing a navy T-shirt emblazoned with the gold Star Educational Cruise Line logo. "Wednesday night, the weather turned wicked. We were rocked by forty-foot swells, gale force winds. It was sort of fun. We joked about needing seatbelts for our beds. Thought for sure our Thursday classes would be called off." He shrugged.

Sort of fun? thought Ashleigh.

"But no such luck," the student continued. "By sunrise, the ocean calmed, and our classes continued as usual. After class, I headed for the pool bar. I'd just ordered a smoothie when, from out of nowhere, this ginormous wave plowed into us. Slammed into us so hard, it busted windows, furniture, even knocked out ceiling tiles. Our cabin was flooded. Left us homeless." He grinned. "I got knocked right off my Nikes. Lost my smoothie."

Ashleigh knew she had better flick the TV off before Marnie returned, but she stopped herself when another phone video flashed on the small screen, again accompanied by the reporter's voice in the background. The camera panned in on passengers sleeping in hallways, wrapped in blankets, stretched out or leaning against the reception counter and walls of muster stations. "Six people are reported injured . . ."

Ashleigh's heart leaped to her throat. All her attention was riveted on the reporter's next words. But when no names were mentioned regarding the two missing passengers, she let out the breath she'd been holding. Her gaze remained glued to the TV.

". . . and more than seven hundred weary passengers leaving the ship will either drive or fly the final stretch to New York City, where the ship was originally scheduled to dock or just proceed directly to their final destinations. And the Star Educational Cruise Line has just announced a compensation arrangement for all passengers who took this historic yet traumatic journey."

Ashleigh found it hard to reconcile the horror she felt with the calm amusement the interviewees expressed. Many departing passengers were praising the way the staff and crew handled the crisis.

When a microphone was thrust toward a pleasant-looking woman with rumpled hair, the reporter asked how she felt about her treatment in the aftermath of the crisis. "The crew really went out of their way. They were marvelous," the disheveled woman said. "My cabin was on the starboard side, so I escaped the flooding. But I've been put up in a hotel, because those of us who are returning across the Great Pond have no place to stay until the repairs are completed."

"Are there any more cruises in your future?" the reporter asked.

"Already booked," she announced proudly. "When we get to New York, my fourteen-year-old granddaughter will join me. And when she gets to college, I'll make sure she has the opportunity to spend a semester at sea, just as I did. I've been a lifelong learner ever since!"

The next interviewee was a staff member. "And the *Rising Star* is scheduled to leave for New York and pick up more passengers—in just two days?" His voice rose with incredulity.

"Sure thing. We sail Tuesday evening. The damaged cabins and other areas will be good as new—some even better, with brand-new paint, wallpapering, carpeting, and furniture."

Ashleigh had heard enough. She pointed the remote at the TV. Somehow Callie's name had not been leaked to the media. At least that was a relief, she supposed. The *Rising Star*'s communication team had been true to their word of withholding the details about both Callie and the young Filipino waiter who was also believed to have been washed overboard.

But her relief was short-lived. Before the TV flicked off, out of the corner of her eye, Ashleigh spotted Marnie in the doorway, her dark eyes wide and brimming with tears.

Chapter

22

Sunday, May 17, 12:35 p.m.—Charleston, South Carolina

A sleep-deprived, totally pissed-off Ross Pocino followed Detective Calhoun up the gangplank for the last damn security check-in. Despite the heat, he craved a hot cup of java, bemoaning the lack of a single opportunity all morning to grab one.

Two men in crisp white shirts and navy uniform trousers stood beside a dented white podium. Calhoun flashed her Charleston PD badge before introducing herself and Pocino and stating their business.

The younger of the two cruise line employees looked down at a list of names on his clipboard. "You've been cleared to come aboard. I'll just need to scan your boarding cards."

As though we could have flown below the radar since the first security pricks scanned our cards? Pocino battled his inner child, got his temper under wraps, and sealed his lips.

"Eduardo will show you to the Taylor girls' cabin on Deck 4." He nodded to indicate the older, stockier security man beside him.

"Just point us in the right direction, and we'll take it from there," Calhoun said.

"I'm sorry, Detective. As a safety precaution, until total damage has been assessed, all visitors . . . um, including law enforcement, must be escorted while on board. Eduardo will take you to cabin 417." After a slight hesitation, he added, "We were told that a cleanup crew began last night. Since early morning, they've been clearing the cabins. Personal belongings left behind have been removed, so you might want to check with—"

"Thanks," Calhoun interrupted. "Cabin 417 was to be left untouched until our arrival."

"In that case, Eduardo will take you straight up."

Eduardo nodded and stepped forward. "Follow me, and please watch your step. Not all of the debris has been cleared."

As they traipsed down the hallway, Pocino hung back until Eduardo was far enough ahead to be out of earshot. He could no longer play the role of a silent observer. "I'm getting damn sick of all this bureaucratic BS. Aren't you?"

Calhoun grinned. "They're just doing their jobs, Ross."

Pocino shrugged. "Guess they gotta do what they gotta do. But in my book, taking our photos twice while boarding a ship that's going nowhere anytime soon . . . It's over the top. Nutso."

He took in the lobby as they dodged among wooden moving pallets stacked high with plush sofas and chairs and rolled-up carpeting. Things didn't look all that bad. The marble floors were clean and sparkling. A faint scent of cleaning materials and paint hung in the air.

"Expected to see a lot more damage," he said.

At the elevator, Eduardo punched the button for Deck 4. "Portside got the worst of it. But gallons of water rolled down the corridors and into the elevator lobbies, so starboard didn't completely escape damage. Most of the cabins did. The worst hits were on the lower decks. Maybe shipbuilders should think about moving the sick bay up a couple of decks."

"Yeah. I get your point," Pocino agreed. His mind turned to Marnie. She must have been scared out of her skull, and Callie . . . He shook his head as if that could dispel the image of a monster wave washing her over the railing.

"I'm surprised," Calhoun said. "It's been less than seventy-two hours since the rogue wave crushed the ship, yet you couldn't tell it from looking at these tidy areas."

"This area was not badly damaged," Eduardo explained. "And maintenance and cleaning duty on a ship are 24/7 jobs. Even after that humongous wave knocked us for a loop, cleanup began as soon as all passengers were accounted for and taken care of by the medical crew."

Not all the passengers were accounted for. Pocino ran the back of his hand over his sweaty brow.

Eduardo apologized. "Sorry about the temperature. The air-conditioning had to be turned off temporarily. It should be back up soon."

Pocino followed Calhoun and Eduardo to the port corridor on the fourth deck.

At the threshold of cabin 417 Eduardo ripped down the yellow tape crisscrossing the door, then fumbled in his pocket and removed a master key card. "Take your time," he said, unlocking the door. "I'll be close by."

Stepping through the door and onto a soggy carpet, Pocino blew out the breath he'd just taken. "Holy shit."

A strong odor of seawater assaulted his nostrils as he stepped far enough inside the cabin to make room for Calhoun. His gaze darted to the shattered glass door leading to a small balcony. Swallowing past an enormous lump in his throat, he pictured the Taylor twins making this their home for the past three months . . .

Don't go there, he warned himself.

Calhoun pulled a small notepad from her service belt.

"Hey. This room don't exactly appear to be untouched." Pocino gestured toward the sea-stained carpet beside the balcony door. "Broken window, but no broken glass. Dollars to donuts the water has been sucked out of this carpet, the furniture set upright . . ." *But has anything been removed?*

With a quick nod, Calhoun took in the scene. "Damage control and cleanup must've begun before word reached them to seal the cabin."

On the stripped twin beds, now covered in plastic, lay shoes, odd bits of clothing piled in neat stacks, and miscellaneous paraphernalia. A large designer-type rolling suitcase sat on the bed closest to the door, wedged up against a backpack and a lightweight duffel bag.

Pocino inspected the tops of the two built-in desks. One held books, all of them spread open—in an attempt to dry them, he supposed. The other held several sheets of paper that had dried out stiff as parchment. *Hope they weren't important,* he thought, *'cause they're history.*

"Here's the iPad," Calhoun called out, rummaging through the closet, "but no computer or handbag." She opened the narrow door to the bathroom.

Pocino cursed aloud. He'd been told the iPad would be Callie's—not exactly ironclad evidence that she had indeed been on the *Rising Star*, but a pretty good indication. Even though he had little confidence in a happy ending, he had hoped desperately that Ashleigh was onto something with her motherly intuition.

They still needed to find Callie's cell phone and handbag as well as Marnie's computer. He checked the outlets for a cell phone, opened every drawer, and even looked in the small refrigerator. Nothing of interest.

"Found a cell phone," Calhoun hollered. "Plugged into an outlet just beside the medicine cabinet."

Pocino scrubbed his pudgy fingers through his thinning hair, looking up to see the white cord Calhoun held in her hand. That would be Callie's phone. *The second nail in the poor kid's coffin.*

He resumed his search for Marnie's laptop, combing through the main cabin inch by goddamned inch. His caffeine-deprived head spun. *Maybe she left it in a classmate's cabin.*

More puzzling was the luggage: one large suitcase, one duffel bag, one backpack. *Odd.* It was possible the twins used a single large suitcase to conserve space in the small cabin. But a single backpack? *That don't compute.*

With a loud, unexpected rap on the cabin door, Eduardo stepped inside with an apologetic look on his face. "Captain Cottle has visitors from headquarters who are due shortly. If you wish to talk with him, it will have to be now. Afterward, of course, I'll bring you straight back here," he added.

A frowning Pocino glanced at Calhoun, who nodded curtly. They would have to go along to get what they needed. On this one, the captain was quite literally in the driver's seat.

Chapter
23

Sunday, May 17, 12:35 p.m.—New York–Presbyterian Hospital

Mesmerized by the surreally familiar sight and sound of water flooding a small ship's cabin, I did not speak or move forward. For what seemed an eternity, I stood statue still, my eyes glued to the tiny TV screen mounted high in the corner of my hospital room. *That has to be the ship I was on.* But if that much seawater had flowed through my cabin, wouldn't I have been soaked to the skin? Instead it was more as if I had been caught in the rain. Or a victim of waterboarding.

The thought was a strange one. *Where did that come from?*

The scene on the TV shifted to a lobby where students huddled, some looking frightened, others excited. I too might have been huddling there, if not for my precarious helicopter ride.

But where is my sister? I scanned the crowd. Was there another safe area where the students were hanging out? If I saw her, would I recognize her? Would I recognize anyone? Another weird thought crept into my muddled brain: If I was an identical twin, wouldn't picking out Callie, even from such a crowd, be like looking in the mirror?

My gaze shifted to the stranger who sat in the armchair next to my bed, her head tilted toward the TV. My mother. That's who they told me she was, and yet I felt no connection. What I felt instead was uneasiness and awkwardness. *Should I call her Mom? Mother?*

I willed her to turn toward me. My talk with Dr. Prouse had left me rattled. I had a boatload of questions, and craved answers.

She flicked off the TV, turning suddenly in my direction, "Marnie," she cried out, and jumped up from the chair.

"Sorry. Didn't mean to startle you." I was no doubt the cause of the hollow look in my mother's eyes, and the dark shadows under them. I commanded myself to stop thinking only of me. *Consider how lucky you are to have such caring parents.* Yet it was impossible to stop obsessing over my uncertain future. "I don't . . . I'm not sure . . . What should I call—"

The blond woman's smile filled with warmth and sadness. "You don't know how to address me," she said in a matter-of-fact tone. It wasn't a question. She totally got it. "Today I'm a stranger, Marnie, but that won't last forever."

I shrugged and stepped forward, not knowing what to say. But when she shortened the space between us and pulled me into a hug, I felt boneless. Her love was palpable, and at that moment, I had no desire to resist.

When we stepped apart, I forced myself not to divert my gaze. "What did I call you and—"

"Your father," she filled in. "You always called Conrad Dad." She hesitated. "And you called me Mom. Usually."

I wondered at her hesitation, but other questions seemed more important. "Okay. Mom it is." It didn't feel quite right, but I guess I'd get used to it. At least, I hoped I would. "I've had a ton of questions since I first woke up on the soggy floor of that boat, not remembering who I was or why I was there. It was scary." Of course, she already knew that. After all, she'd talked to both the neurologist and the shrink.

Has she already figured out what frightens me most?

Chapter
24

Sunday, May 17, 1:25 p.m.—Charleston, South Carolina

Captain Scott Cottle did not hold back. Sitting on the corner of his office desk, he took them step by painstaking step through the events before and after the accident. Yet Pocino couldn't help shifting in his seat, his right leg bobbing up and down. There was little in Cottle's tale of onboard drama that hadn't been covered already by the media. Nothing shed light on Callie's fate.

". . . couldn't be prouder of my staff and crew," Cottle continued. "They stepped up and made sure all the passengers were as comfortable as possible. For the most part, our passengers were understanding and cooperative." Cottle cleared his throat. "We did have one isolated criticism, however. Apparently one steward's handling of an elderly couple with a flooded . . ."

Pocino snuck a peek at Calhoun, who appeared to be taking in every word, encouraging the captain to blather on. A polite Southern belle, born and bred, Pocino guessed. *If only she'd cut the inane questions.* He didn't give a rat's ass about anything other than Callie Taylor.

Of course, without the detective, he'd be out in the cold while Charleston PD handled everything. So he gave her the benefit of the doubt, figuring she was obligated to show interest while representing the city and the department. *Gotta avoid ruffling feathers.*

When Captain Cottle asked if they had any further questions, Pocino seized his moment. "Captain, we've talked with your security staff about your procedures. Boarding, departure, reboarding . . ."

Cottle nodded.

"I need to be sure I've got it straight, so bear with me." He cleared his throat. "For initial boarding, passengers must show their room key, which I assume is their onboard ID."

Cottle nodded again.

"Security runs the key through a scanning machine and takes a photo." His gaze flickered to Calhoun, who seemed to have no objections to his line of questioning.

"Right," Cottle confirmed.

"On subsequent departures and reboarding, the cards are again scanned and the photos are compared with the person holding the card?"

"Precisely," Cottle said. "We do that for all passengers, the lifelong learners and their families as well as the students. To make sure no one is left behind. It's a fairly standard cruise ship procedure."

"So, you take a roll call, so to speak, at each port," Calhoun cut in. "Then, before the ship leaves the dock, you check to make certain all passengers have come aboard?"

"Right again."

"So, what happens if one or more passengers fail to return before your departure time?" Pocino couldn't imagine the ship waiting for latecomers.

"That's extremely rare, but it has happened. We have a record of all cell phones and make every attempt to reach any missing passenger." His eyes closed in concentration. "However, not everyone has cell phone coverage abroad. In that case, we contact the families. The passengers are advised of the protocol before the first boarding. It's reinforced during orientation and before each subsequent port. We never delay our departures for more than half an hour."

Calhoun broke in. "But—"

Cottle raised his hand to stop her. "If we must leave a passenger behind, every attempt is made to reach that individual. If we fail to make contact, we leave word at the terminal. Every passenger has been instructed to go to the terminal in such an emergency."

Pocino said, "Hold on, sir. I understand your security and protocols are tight, but a couple of things are nagging at me. Detective Calhoun and I have searched every inch of the girls' cabin. There's a missing laptop computer, and—"

"As I understand, the Taylor twins were enrolled in separate programs," Cottle explained. "One in dance and the other in creative writing. It's not unusual for students to study together. They often take their tablets or laptops with them. A computer could have been left in another student's cabin or elsewhere on the ship."

"That's what I was thinking," Pocino said.

"In the event we can't locate the computer, we'll have it replaced."

"Well, Captain, but there's another thing that has me scratching my head."

Cottle leaned forward.

"Have you ever had someone slip past the screening upon departure?"

"Never," Cottle said with a shake of his head. "You went through our boarding security today. You will soon experience our departure protocol. With five hundred and fifty students in our care, our security is rock solid." His eyes narrowed. "I see where your questions are leading, Mr. Pocino. But as you can see, there is no way Callie Taylor could have left the ship in Southampton a second time without us knowing."

Pocino frowned. "A second time?"

"Yes. A number of students, Miss Taylor among them, disembarked at the Southampton terminal for a field trip to London by bus. While en route, however, Miss Taylor became ill and was unable to go on." Captain Cottle explained that the bus had stopped to await transportation for Callie, who had returned to the ship and immediately reported to the ship's medical center. "Dr. Pearson, our staff physician, saw her straightaway. She had an extremely high temperature—103 or 104 degrees, I believe. Pearson prescribed medication, bed rest, and plenty of fluids. So you understand, she was simply too sick."

Pocino agreed that it seemed unlikely. Sick or no, Callie would've had her card scanned and compared to her photo, as was the procedure for everyone boarding and deboarding the *Rising Star*. But there was no record of Callie leaving the ship a second time in Southampton.

"Furthermore," the captain continued, "Miss Taylor's dance instructor informs us that Miss Taylor emailed her while aboard the ship. She explained that she had contracted a nasty flu and was unable to attend class. I was told that her sister . . ."—he glanced down at an open notebook on his desk—"Marnie also came down with the same bug and emailed the same excuse to her creative writing instructor." Cottle held out both hands and shrugged. "As much as I would like to, I simply cannot believe Callie Taylor remained in Southampton."

One thing still troubled Pocino: the lack of enough luggage for both girls. But he saw no point in mentioning it now. Captain Cottle was right—Callie had been lost at sea. It was the only realistic explanation. Wasn't it?

Chapter

25

Sunday, May 17, 1:45 p.m.—Charleston, South Carolina

Deep in thought, Pocino fell in behind Calhoun as Eduardo led them back to cabin 417. As they dodged carpenters, painters, and various workmen, not to mention their ladders and supplies, his brain kicked in. The captain had proved his point. There was no chance Callie could have been left behind in Southampton accidentally—not without setting off the proverbial alarms.

As for his concern about the luggage, there could be any number of explanations. One of the girls could have moved her things into the room of another student, perhaps someone in her master's program. He could no longer procrastinate on calling the Taylors. He would have to be the one to snip their last thread of hope, and the thought of it shredded his insides.

As if reading his mind, Detective Calhoun said, "Go ahead and make your phone call, Ross. I'll keep scouring the cabin, small as it is. No point in us bumping into each other."

Pocino was about to protest, but instead let the words die on his lips. There was no way around it.

Gotta get this behind me.

1:55 p.m.—Manhattan, New York

The vibration of his BlackBerry stopped Conrad midstride just as he reached the elevator. Heart thudding, he slipped it out of his jacket pocket and glanced at the screen. Lifting the phone to his ear, he took in a deep breath. "Yes?"

Through the phone came the sound of Pocino clearing his throat. "Afraid, I've got bad news, Conrad," came Pocino's voice, one word tripping over the next. "The ship protocol you outlined for me was on the money. Records show Callie was on the ship when it set sail from Southampton." Filling him in on the captain's conversation, Pocino spoke in a rapid cadence.

Conrad tried his best to tune in.

". . . and the twins' cabin is being searched for the . . ."

He thought he'd prepared himself for the news. Hadn't he been expecting it? But as Pocino filled him in on Captain Cottle's conversation in a rapid cadence, the words stabbed a part of his heart he never knew existed.

". . . shouldn't take long, since . . ."

To be honest, retrieving the girls' belongings couldn't have been lower on Conrad's priority list. His firstborn daughter was gone. He would never again see her smiling face, her dancing eyes. He would never again experience her zest for life.

Inevitably, his thoughts turned to Ashleigh, and then to Juliana, who would be waiting for him in the limo downstairs. *What should I tell them? How can I tell them?*

An image of Callie at her last dance solo flashed in his mind, her beauty glowing from within. Taking several deep breaths, he lifted his chin. Somehow, they would get through this tragedy—the most devastating tragedy imaginable. But how? Parents were not meant to outlive a daughter.

Ashleigh must be told first. Together, they would figure out their next move.

2:00 p.m.—Charleston, South Carolina

After his gloomy conversation with Conrad, Pocino rejoined Eduardo and Detective Calhoun in cabin 417. He'd been mulling something over ever since the Charleston detective had uncovered the cell phone during their first pass through the cabin. Turning to the ship's employee, he decided to cut right to the chase.

"There must be some sort of protocol for retrieving personal belongings left behind, right?"

"Of course, Mr. Pocino," Eduardo replied. "Immediately following the passengers vacating their rooms and disembarking, a room-by-room inspection is completed by a team of porters."

"And it looks like staff did a quick sweep of this cabin before Detective Calhoun and I arrived, because they didn't get the memo about the Taylor girls. Agreed?"

Eduardo nodded.

"So, where would the ship's staff store any items that had been left behind?"

"We have a Lost and Found department, where everything is logged in by cabin number. But I thought you already—"

"What we're looking for wasn't here," Pocino cut in. "Do you think I could check—"

"Well, sir, to get ready for our next voyage, we really must clear the ship now of all nonemployees. But if you tell me what you're looking for and leave me your number, I'll have someone check and get back to you."

"How soon?" Pocino asked.

Calhoun handed the security man her card. "Excuse our Yankee friend's manners, Eduardo, but we're sure you realize every minute counts. We think Miss Taylor's laptop, and perhaps other pieces of luggage, may have been left behind in this cabin, or possibly the cabin of one of her friends."

Eduardo nodded and slipped the card into his shirt pocket. "I'll give you a call as soon as I know anything. Would tomorrow morning be okay?"

Pocino thanked him, "I know your plate's been full the past few days. But I don't like leaving open ends."

It was more than that, though. Despite their meeting with the captain, and the firsthand experience with the ship's tight security protocol, Pocino wondered if Ashleigh might be right after all. Maybe there was a chance that Callie Taylor was not a casualty of the catastrophic wave, that she was still alive in Southampton. And if so, he was determined to prove it.

Chapter 26

Sunday, May 17, 1:55 p.m.—Manhattan, New York

Juliana greeted David as she climbed into the limo and buckled her seatbelt. Her well-planned universe had been flipped on its head. Callie was missing. Marnie's memory was wiped clean. *How could that be?*

Not much ruffled Juliana, and little was beyond her comprehension, but this was too much. None of her AP classes had prepared her for anything like this. She loved both of her sisters. They had always been there for her, even when they were far away at school.

Her dad stood outside the limo, a few feet away, talking with the general manager of Jordon's. Closing her eyes, Juliana silently voiced her frustrations. *Why did this have to happen now? Why did it have to happen at all?* She didn't want to believe it. Marnie might not know her. And Callie . . .

Please, God, just let my sisters be safe.

Juliana simply wouldn't think about something bad happening to Callie. It was a whole lot easier to look back to when her heart had danced with delight over Callie's decision to remain at CSULB for graduate school. It was the final step for Callie before going for her dance certification with Millennium—the world's premier commercial dance studio. It was all so cool. Even though Juliana had also been accepted to the undergrad programs at USC and UCLA, Callie's decision had tipped the scales. Nothing would've been better than the two of them in the same university, with Marnie only a half hour away.

But what will happen now?

She heaved a drawn-out sigh and turned to her dad as he slid into the seat beside her. "I don't get it," she said, skipping *hello* as though her father had heard the conversation she'd been having in her own mind. "How am I even supposed to talk to Marnie?"

He gave her arm a reassuring squeeze. "It won't be easy, but you'll figure it out as you go along—just like your mom and I are doing."

"One day at a time, right?" She was trying to lighten the mood, but her words fell flat. How could she joke when she didn't know whether Callie was safe? Usually curious, she didn't want to ask. She was too afraid of the answer, and she couldn't bear the thought of never seeing Callie again.

At the thought, a chill ricocheted through her body. *If Dad had good news, he would have told me.*

Just a few days earlier, she had hardly been able to wait for her sisters to get home. Their whole family had planned a trip to Southern California to celebrate with Callie and Marnie as each sister received her Bachelor of Arts. There was the sad event in memory of Aunt Caroline's husband, but Juliana had barely known him. She was also eager to show Callie her new ideas for their trio—in particular, the routine they'd begun choreographing before the twins began their semester at sea. They would be dancing to *Respect* by Aretha Franklin for the upcoming competition at the Tremaine Dance Convention.

I shouldn't even be thinking about that now. Nothing was as important as Callie coming home, and Marnie . . . becoming Marnie again.

"That's right, Juliana," her dad replied. "One day at a time. But sweetheart, so far, the news about Callie has not been encouraging. She has not been found on the ship."

"Maybe she never got on the boat." Juliana's voice cracked. "Maybe she never left Southampton."

"You have your mother's optimistic spirit. Never let that go." He leaned over and kissed the top of her head. "Mr. Pocino is in South Carolina with a detective from the Charleston PD. They're inspecting your sisters' cabin and talking with the captain, the dean, and other students who were with Callie and Marnie this past semester. We're not giving up hope. But Juliana, you must also know that sometimes bad things happen to good people."

She lifted her chin, hoping to keep the tears from trickling down her cheeks. "How about Miss Allison? If something had happened to Callie, wouldn't Miss Allison have called?"

"We're trying to track her down. I'm sure she'll get in touch as soon as she can." Conrad pulled his daughter close. "But right now, it's Marnie who needs us. She's facing some frightening days ahead, and she needs us to be strong."

Perceptive as ever, Juliana realized her father was trying to be positive. With that thought, she lost her battle. Welled-up tears spilled over, running freely down her cheeks.

He thinks Callie drowned when the monster wave hit.

Chapter
27

Sunday, May 17, 2:00 p.m.—New York–Presbyterian Hospital

Sinking down on the edge of my bed, I swallowed hard and gestured for my mother to sit beside me. Like a tightrope walker seeking balance, I tried to push fear aside and take that first step.

Before I had a chance to test my resolve, my mother spoke, seeming to weigh each word. "Your dad will be bringing your younger sister here shortly. Juliana. She insisted on seeing you right away."

Another stranger. I rubbed both arms to ward off an unexpected chill. *What if my memory never comes back? Will I forever feel like the new kid in school—like I don't belong?* Cutting off the negative thoughts, I told myself to stop obsessing and start getting answers. "How old is Juliana?" I asked. I had to start filling in some blanks. "Were we . . . close?"

With a nod, Mom said, "She's just graduated from high school. Despite the four-year age gap, you've always maintained a wonderful relationship with your little sister. Even after you and Callie went off to college in California." She shook her head, then shifted her position and reached for my hand. "For now—until you regain your memory—you can't help but view me as a stranger. But I need you to understand that you are no stranger to me, nor to any of your family and friends. I am your mother, and I love you."

I looked down at the floor. This was just plain awkward. Then again, talking like polite strangers wasn't working either.

"I've been trying to avoid saying anything that might make you uncomfortable," she continued. "But tiptoeing around is exhausting, and it's limiting our progress. In this strange scenario, saying the wrong thing occasionally is inevitable."

She's right about that.

"We must take a leap of faith and share what's on our minds. So, I suggest—"

"You suggest we take the gloves off?" I cut in. *Where did that come from?*

She smiled. "Yes. Marnie, you are a member of a strong family. We will get through this."

What about my twin? I wanted to ask.

Her eyes held mine for an awkward second, but she didn't offer anything further.

"What have the doctors told you about my condition?" I hoped she had a better understanding or any insight that would make the future less frightening. "Do you know I might never regain my memory?"

She nodded, her dark eyes reassuring. "But we were also told it is very likely to return. Let me share with you what knowledge your father and I have gained about the various types of amnesia."

"Gloves off," I reminded her.

A hint of a twinkle showed in her dark eyes. "I see your tendency to cut to the chase is still intact." She smiled, and strain eased from her brow. "Dr. Harvey feels there is only a small possibility you will not regain your long-term memory."

The horrible chill spread through me, numbing my body. "But Dr. Prouse talked about global amnesia."

"He covered that with your father and me as well." She reached for the pitcher on my rolling tray and poured two glasses of water. "Global amnesia is the most common type of memory loss, when the individual does not know her identity or recognize parents, family, or friends. The person may forget various skill sets and even words."

I picked up a glass and took a sip. My hand trembled as I waited for my mother to get on with facts that could help me unravel the mystery of my mind.

"As I understand it, global amnesia is a kind of umbrella that also includes autobiographical amnesia. A person with this type of amnesia may remember a great many things—a foreign language, the name of the president, how to drive, terms in business—but is unable to recall things about herself."

"Bingo. That's it." That explained what I'd been trying to figure out. So, it wasn't totally nuts that I remembered the words to a song, designer names, and other useless information, yet I didn't recognize my own family. "It's weird how I remember a lot of random, low-priority stuff but—"

"But not what seems most important," she finished for me, nodding. "I understand. Those gaps in memory are expected in any type of amnesia."

"But this seems like the worst kind." My voice rose into a question, betraying the fears in my head. "It's . . . paralyzing."

"I understand," my mother repeated. "The unknown is something I find most difficult to deal with." She took a sip from her glass and set it back on the tray. "Your father and I have been reading as much as we can about amnesia since . . . since you hit your head. But we are far from having all the answers. We must stay positive and figure it out together as we go along. And I'm sure we'll all have more questions for Dr. Harvey *and* Dr. Prouse."

"So, what do I do about it?" My eyes locked with hers. When she did not respond immediately, I realized I must sound like a frantic, ungrateful loser. I took a sip of water, hoping it would have a calming effect. *After all, I have a lot to be thankful for, I guess.*

"Your father and I came across a book that explained the human memory in terms we could grasp. And we were elated to find out that the author, a Dr. David Martin, is a prominent neurologist in Southern California. If your memory hasn't recovered in the next few days, we can arrange for you to see him when we—"

She slipped into the chair across from my bed so that her eyes met mine. "I don't want us to get ahead of ourselves. Just keep in mind that the inability to recognize family and friends is common in the initial stages of any type of amnesia. And all signs point to the fact that your anterograde memory is functioning."

"My *what*?"

"Sorry. I meant to avoid the technical jargon. That just means you appear to have no trouble remembering everything that has happened since the trauma. Anterograde memories are composed of new information. It's your retrograde or long-term memory that appears to be impaired right now. Only the memories of your past."

"Only? Like *only* my whole past life rolled out to sea?" As soon as I said it, I wished I could take it back. She was trying so hard. I had no right to put her on the defensive. "Sorry. I'm just so frustrated."

"Please, no more apologies. I know you are," she replied with a warm smile. "Darling, it's only been three days."

"It seems like forever," I said.

"Well, in some ways, it has been forever—from your brain's perspective, at least. We learned from Dr. Martin's book that the brain contains different memory banks, like filing cabinets that store different kinds of information. Autobiographical memory records include what we have experienced personally, and when and where it happened. Long-term semantic memories are stored in another area of the brain, the general information such as state capitals, how to solve equations, professional knowledge. Then we have short-term memory, which is stored in the frontal lobe. That's where we keep a phone number for just a few seconds after looking it up and dialing . . ."

As she spoke, I tried to unscramble the past few days. My stomach felt queasy as I realized all I had lost. And yet saddest of all was that I couldn't even remember what I'd lost. I willed my mind to stop turning inward, to focus instead on gathering as much information as I could.

". . . amazing psychological phenomenon, when an individual experiences the loss of the contents of one filing cabinet while other cabinets remain intact," my mother continued. "So a person with autobiographical amnesia might possess the same skills as she had before the loss."

"What skills did I have?"

"Oh, so many skills. But your great love is creative writing. When you found that Graham Bradford would be teaching a course—"

My heart leaped into my throat. I knew that name. "Graham Bradford? I know that name."

Chapter 28

Sunday, May 17, 2:10 p.m.—New York–Presbyterian Hospital

Ashleigh's heart lifted at the sight of Marnie's eyes glistening with recognition. *Maybe, just maybe, the fog is beginning to lift.* "What do you know about Graham Bradford?

"He's a famous author," Marnie replied eagerly. "Writes thrillers. He's won tons of international awards. An Englishman, I think."

Ashleigh nodded, then ventured, "Do you recall that he taught the first half of the creative writers' program on board the *Rising Star*?"

Marnie stared back, her expression blank.

Ashleigh silently reproached herself for pushing. *What did I expect?* Marnie's name recognition was intact, stored in the long-term memory—but her fall had affected the area of the brain that might have recalled a personal experience with that famous name.

Marnie squeezed her eyes shut for a couple of long seconds. "All I know is, I was on that ship for a semester-at-sea program, and my sister was there too, in another program. But I only know that because Dr. Pearson told me."

"Sweetheart, these first few days of adjusting to your temporary memory loss are bound to be the most difficult and frustrating. You and I must do our best to be patient with one another, even as we make missteps. We'll figure out how to make this journey more bearable. And as you begin to remember who you are, you must try to accept yourself."

Marnie rose, her eyes brimming with unshed tears. "I'll do my best. I need to learn who I was and who I wanted to be." She blinked back the tears and gave a tentative smile. "I'll try to stop dwelling on the negative. Was I always a 'glass half empty' sort of person?"

Ashleigh couldn't help but smile. "Not always." A cautious relief filled her heart. She'd always harbored the concern that Marnie might forever lean toward pessimism. Could the fallout from her accident have some positive aspects?

Fine lines crossed the smooth skin of Marnie's forehead as she gazed beyond Ashleigh, her eyes unfocused.

"You were known to withdraw at times, but as you got older those occasions became more rare. They usually surfaced when you thought your writing was not going well. We learned to give you space. You're also a very giving person. We noticed it especially with Juliana. She seems to have a magical way of charming you out of any extended funk."

Silence followed, and Ashleigh resisted the urge to fill it.

Finally, Marnie's eyes rested on hers. "So I majored in creative writing? And I'm supposed to return to UCI in a couple of months for my master's degree?"

"That was your plan."

"What was I writing about? Was I any good?"

"You're very good, on track to graduate with honors. With your application to the graduate program at UCI, you submitted the novel you completed as an undergraduate." She paused to give Marnie a moment. "Being selected to fill one of the eight open slots was a wonderful accomplishment."

"I was writing a book? About what?"

"You wrote a novel for middle-schoolers, called *The Terrible Big Bear Twins*, for which you received an A in your Introduction to Novel Writing class. But you still weren't satisfied it was any good."

Leaning closer, her expression tense, Marnie asked, "Did you read it?"

Ashleigh shook her head. "When I asked to read it, you said . . ." She hesitated. "Well, a fairly accurate quote would be, 'It sucks.' You wanted to fix a huge hole in the plot before you let me read it."

"But didn't you say I got an A?"

Ashleigh nodded and gave her a reassuring smile. "I'm afraid that kind of insecurity is part of a writer's DNA—no matter how good they are or how many awards they've won. For creative people like you, that insecurity may never entirely disappear." She decided to mention the name of Marnie's mentor once more. "When you heard Graham Bradford would be the instructor for the semester-at-sea program, that tipped the scale for you. You applied for the program, and you switched genres. You told us thrillers were more your style, and your novel was already written somewhat in the style of a thriller. You convinced us it was a good move."

"Well, I guess I'd rather read a thriller than a book for tweens." She paused, a frown crinkling her forehead. "Did I do a lot of reading?"

"You sure did. You told me you couldn't write if you didn't read a lot, and complained you never had enough time to read as much as you should. You listened to audiobooks whenever you had downtime. Getting dressed, driving to school, et cetera."

Marnie shrugged. "That makes sense."

"Try not to worry, love." Ashleigh lifted a reassuring hand toward her daughter's arm, but caught herself and withdrew it. "Although you can't remember what you were writing, your skill in putting words together in a meaningful way is lodged in your long-term memory."

"Maybe." Marnie sighed. "But right now I couldn't sit down and write an interesting story if my life depended on it."

Ashleigh saw the crestfallen look on her daughter's face. "From what I'm learning about the brain, it's not like opening a cupboard door and seeing everything spread out in front of us. It's more like a library classification system. You have to know what you're looking for. In your case, the good news is, there is no brain damage. Give yourself time to heal. You might even consider taking a semester off."

"And do what?" she snapped.

CHAPTER 29

Sunday, May 17, 2:20 p.m.—New York–Presbyterian Hospital

Juliana stopped abruptly in the doorway of Marnie's hospital room. Her mom sat at her sister's bedside, where the two were deep in conversation. She didn't want to step over the threshold. But the thud of her father's footfalls interrupted them anyway, and they stopped talking and looked toward the doorway.

When Marnie smiled at her, a lump formed in Juliana's throat. She couldn't force a single word through her constricted throat. Other than the patch of white gauze on the side of Marnie's head, she looked totally normal. *But if she were really okay, wouldn't she dash over to hug me? Wouldn't she call me Midget?*

The two sisters looked at each other for a drawn-out second or two before Marnie said, "Hi, Juliana. I guess you heard that my memory has been wiped away. So for a while, we'll—"

"You don't remember me?" Juliana blurted out. "Not any of us?"

Marnie shook her head slowly.

"I'm sorry," Juliana said, taking a step toward the hospital bed. "This is seriously weird. I don't know what to say." She gave a shy shrug, "So, I guess . . . Hi, Marnie. I'm your sister, Juliana." *That was lame.* "Sorry. Can I erase those dumb words?"

Marnie laughed. "We can make it up as we go along. I like the way you say what you think. You feel like family." *Maybe this won't be so bad.*

"I might even be able to help you remember," Juliana suggested, hoping it was true.

"Seriously?" Marnie gave her another smile—but her eyes lacked their usual sparkle. "Well, I'm willing to give most anything a try."

"Hmm," their parents said, almost at the same time.

Juliana frowned. Sometimes she loved when her parents were on the same page about something they've thought of or noticed. *And sometimes it's just one of those annoying Mom-and-Dad things.*

"We'll all figure this out together," Conrad continued.

Marnie looks okay, thought Juliana. *She doesn't sound all vague and disoriented like in the movies. I wonder if she remembers how to dance? Does amnesia affect muscle memory?*

Juliana immediately felt ashamed of herself for thinking about the dance competition when Marnie couldn't even remember her family. And when Callie was still missing . . . or worse.

CHAPTER 30

Sunday, May 17, 2:30 p.m.—Charleston, South Carolina

Moments after clearing the last security post, Pocino and Calhoun headed for the squad car in silence. As Calhoun opened her door, she offered her condolences. "Sorry, Ross. I guess the miracle we were praying for didn't materialize."

Pocino nodded. "Times like this, our job just sucks."

He climbed into the sweltering car and stared out the window, sweat dripping from his forehead. Ashleigh Taylor believes Callie got caught up in something and accidentally missed the ship's departure. But Ross was sure no such a thing could've happened accidentally.

The twins are identical, and they're damned smart. Is it possible . . . ?

"In spite of all the evidence, Calhoun, something's just not right," he blurted. "I need to talk with the Taylors about the twins' luggage. That light at the end of the tunnel may be improbable, but it hasn't entirely blinked out." He ran his stubby fingers through his damp hair. "In the meantime, could you follow up with Eduardo about tracking down the missing laptop and any other luggage? Maybe a stray backpack?"

Calhoun laid her hand on his forearm. "Sure thang, Ross. Eduardo has my card, but I'll keep hounding them. Sounds like you're not fully convinced the other Taylor twin went overboard?"

"I'm not sure what I'm thinking. Maybe it's just my stubborn mind refusing to face the facts. But the scenario that keeps thundering through my brain includes two irrefutable facts. Number one," he said, raising his index finger, "Callie reboarded the ship in Southampton, as verified by the ship's doctor. Number two," he said, lifting a second finger, "no one has confirmed actually *seeing* either of the twins on the ship prior to getting smashed by the rogue wave."

Pocino paused, peering directly at Calhoun. "The fact is, all reported communication with the Taylor girls was by email or phone—not face-to-face."

She stared back at him expectantly.

"Though the possibility may be remote, let's consider this: While the average Joe or Jill couldn't slip through the ship's tight security, an identical twin might—and perhaps did."

Calhoun shrugged. "That's a long shot, but not as improbable as seeing pigs fly."

"If Callie did slip away, she had to have planned it carefully—and in cahoots with her twin." *Could they have befuddled security and turned the impossible into the possible?*

Frown lines played across Calhoun's forehead. "I see what you're getting at."

"It's a quantum leap, but one I've got to take." He massaged his scalp with his knuckles. "Right now I need to meet with the dean and some of the twins' classmates. Then I'll place another call to the Taylors."

"Do you need me to join you, Ross?"

Panning the parking area, he noted it was still crawling with cops, some directing traffic while others were answering questions for the crowd of people who remained. The Charleston PD obviously had their hands full. Pocino realized he'd been damned lucky that Detective Calhoun was assigned to help with his investigation. Plowing through the red tape to board the *Rising Star* as a private investigator would have been a nightmare. Without her aid perhaps a total no-go.

He turned to the detective. "Thanks, Calhoun. I'm good to go it alone for now. But hey, without your help—"

She held up her hand. "Glad to, Ross. The logical side of my brain isn't quite buying your unlikely scenario, but I'll still be praying that it pans out. Keep me updated."

"And you do the same."

As they set off for the Days Inn, Pocino felt a little better about where things stood. And when Calhoun stopped along the way, so he could buy the biggest cuppa joe the Stop-N-Go had to offer, he felt a whole lot better.

Chapter

31

Sunday, May 17, 3:00 p.m.—Charleston, South Carolina

At precisely the appointed time, a distinguished gentleman with thick white hair, an open-neck blue dress shirt, and khaki trousers walked into the lobby of the Days Inn. Two young women accompanied him.

Pocino rose from the sofa where he had been waiting for them and extended his hand. "Dean Nyquist?"

The man nodded.

"Ross Pocino. With the Landes Agency."

John Nyquist began his introductions. "Most of the students either were picked up here in Charleston by their parents or are being sent home by various means of transportation. These two young ladies are traveling back to New York on the ship. Monica Lang was in Callie Taylor's dance program," he said, gesturing to the tall, dark-haired girl with a worried expression. "And this is Solange Richie, who was in the creative writing program with Marnie Taylor." He pointed to the student with a platinum pixie haircut. "I've explained to them, Mr. Pocino, that you're a private investigator whom the twins' parents hired in the aftermath of the accident."

Pocino nodded. "Thanks for your time, ladies. The hotel manager has arranged for us to meet in the employees' lounge, where we'll be more comfortable. If you'll just follow me." He led the small party down the hallway and into the lounge, where each of the four took a seat around the circular table.

Visibly nervous, Solange spoke first. "We were shocked to hear about Marnie's injury. She's so talented. Will she be okay?"

"Well, at least she didn't get washed over the railings," Monica said, her tone cutting.

Solange blushed. "Of course, that's a lot worse. I only mentioned Marnie because we became close friends since our first day on board. I didn't get to know Callie."

"Yes, many lives have been turned on their heads," Pocino added. "But no family could be more profoundly devastated than Marnie and Callie Taylor's parents and younger sister. You probably know that Marnie was airlifted from the ship. What you may not know is, she's experiencing temporary amnesia."

"Oh my God!" Solange exclaimed.

"Marnie remembers nothing about her past," Pocino continued, "not even her name. So I'm gathering as many facts as possible about what took place after boarding in Southampton, and on your return trip. *Before* the rogue wave."

"If I may?" Nyquist started. "In Southampton, first Callie and then Marnie came down with some sort of bug, or the flu. Callie was forced to abandon her London field trip and spent some time in the onboard clinic. Neither twin was well enough to attend classes after our departure from Southampton, but both informed their teachers. As I understand, neither twin felt well enough even to leave their cabin. Food was delivered to their room. They didn't want the bug to spread."

Pocino leaned forward on his elbows, his hands pressed together. "What about in the weeks before this final leg of the trip. Is anyone aware of either of the twins studying or spending time in the rooms of other students?"

"I don't know about Callie," Solange offered, "but Marnie never worked anywhere but in her own cabin. When we had free time, we always hung out on the pool deck or in the cafeteria. But that all changed after Professor Bradford's assistant fell in New York and had to be flown back to London."

Pocino's head snapped to attention.

"Professor Bradford chose Marnie to type up the draft for his next novel," Solange continued. "She was the only one who could decipher his chicken scratch. 'After that, she was always alone in her cabin, working on either her novel or his. We spent hardly any time together after that."

Caught off guard by this puzzling new detail, Pocino tucked it away to pursue later.

Monica spoke up next. "It was different for us. In the dance program, we would meet in the gym or theater to choreograph. I didn't see Callie after Southampton, but we texted each other. Every time she thought she might be okay, she'd stand up and the whole cabin would go into a spin. So she decided just to stay in bed. She was afraid she was contagious and asked me to take notes for her in class. I emailed them to her, but she was really sick. I don't know if she even read them."

"Your email was working at sea?" Pocino asked.

"Most of the time," Monica said. "A lot of us have hot spots."

"How about Marnie? Did you communicate with her in the past week?"

"No. I didn't know too many students except for the ones in our program. When we had any free time, we usually just hung out at the pool or the gym."

"Got it," Pocino said.

"Then on Thursday, just before the huge wave hit, Callie texted that she didn't feel like the walking dead anymore and was dying for a slice of pizza. We were supposed to meet on the upper deck."

"Upper deck?"

"Yeah. That's where they served pizza, day and night."

"Did you meet her?"

Monica shook her head. "I was leaving my cabin when we were hit. It felt like a massive earthquake. I was in the hallway and fell real hard against the wall. I ended up on the floor, super dizzy. People were running all over the place. There was a lot of shouting, but I couldn't make much sense out of it."

"Port or starboard side?"

"Starboard. It took a minute or two to figure out what was going on. Water began to flow into our hallway. My cabin wasn't flooded like a lot of the others, but it definitely smelled of seawater."

"Did you see Callie later?"

Monica sucked in her bottom lip as a tear slipped from the corner of her eye. "No. Everything was so confusing. We were told not to go out onto the deck. I thought I saw her on a stretcher, heading to the ship's clinic. But when I called her name, she didn't answer. I thought it must be her sister. Miss Dee was the only one who could tell them apart. Anyway, so then I called out Marnie's name. She still didn't answer." She paused. "But if she has amnesia, I guess she didn't even know her own name."

Turning his attention to Solange, Pocino asked, "And what about you? Did you see or talk with Marnie after you left Southampton?"

"I'm not sure."

"You're not sure?"

"Well, I called her room once, and I thought I recognized her voice, but she said it was Callie. I thought maybe it was Marnie, and she was still pissed at me and just didn't want to talk."

"Pissed with you?"

Solange nodded. "We had a blowup over a critique we wrote together, about *Wuthering Heights*. But maybe it *was* Callie and not Marnie who answered the phone. Maybe her voice sounded funny because she was feeling lousy with the flu."

"Even their parents can't tell their voices apart over the phone," Pocino acknowledged. "Did you exchange emails or text messages with Marnie after leaving Southampton?"

Solange shook her head. "No. Marnie and I never exchanged emails. Professor Bradford said anyone who was a serious writer had to avoid the Internet while attending his session."

"Avoid the Internet?"

"Yeah. Says it's too distracting. Leads to unoriginal ideas. He's really against it, and you know, it kind of makes sense now."

"I don't even know Marnie's email address."

Pocino scratched behind his left ear. "I've got a problem." *Things aren't adding up.* "It's pretty clear that the twins didn't spend much time in other students' cabins. But several items are missing from *their* cabin."

"Such as?" Nyquist asked.

"Marnie's HP computer, for one."

"Marnie never took her laptop to class," Solange said. "When we worked on our *Wuthering Heights* project in the library, she always brought her tablet. She was paranoid about her laptop."

Pocino leaned back in his seat. The missing computer was bound to turn up sooner or later. He decided to tackle the more perplexing issue: the missing luggage. "When you began your semester-at-sea, were you given a list of what you should have in the way of luggage?"

Dean Nyquist fielded the question. "During enrollment, we issue guidelines to each student regarding suggested clothing, digital devices, and so forth. Students are limited to one large suitcase, a carry-on or duffel bag, and a backpack for the various field trips."

"So every student has a backpack?" Pocino asked.

"I believe so."

Monica and Solange nodded in agreement.

Pocino sat forward. Switching gears somewhat abruptly, he asked Monica, "Did Callie ever express any desire to remain in Southampton?"

Three pairs of eyes opened wide with alarm.

Monica frowned. "Mr. Pocino, are you saying that you don't believe Callie was washed overboard?"

Chapter
32

Sunday, May 17, 3:30 p.m.—New York–Presbyterian Hospital

Ashleigh felt Conrad's arm wrap around her shoulder as they listened to their daughters' awkward attempts at conversation. Though tempted to jump in, she had no magic to offer. Being understanding and patient with others was something she'd been determined to instill in her girls from birth. Even as young children, they'd demonstrated consideration for others. She was pleased to see that they continued to do so now.

But the waiting game was not one of Ashleigh's strengths, and each of her daughters tended to mirror that impatience in her own way. Yet it could take a considerable period of time for Marnie to recover her memory—or learn to cope with the loss. There was little Ashleigh could do in the meantime but pray for strength for her entire family.

"Hey, I just thought of a cool idea," Juliana was saying.

"Okay. Spit it out," Marnie replied with a shrug.

Ashleigh waited for her youngest daughter's next words, wondering if Juliana might have found the key to help both girls relax and move forward with their relationship.

"Well, I read your novel . . ."

Puzzled at Juliana's confession, I glanced at my mother and then turned back to my younger sister. "You read my novel? But Mom said I wouldn't let anyone read it."

"Only me." A cocky smile spread across Juliana's face, and her eyes danced. "I'm special."

I couldn't help but smile. "Was it any good?" I asked. My life was little more than a blur, and this so-called novel didn't seem like much of a priority. But Juliana seemed so excited, and she had given up time with her best friend to come here and help unscramble my brain. I didn't have the heart to burst her bubble.

"It was last summer, when I should have been working on my AP English project. I was in procrastination mode. Read the whole book in one night. Didn't get a wink of sleep." She glanced at Mom. "Each chapter ended with a cliffhanger, so I kept reading. I only meant to read three or four more pages, to find out what else could go wrong for the terrible Big Bear twins. But I could never seem to put it down. It was a fun story."

"I wrote a story about bears?"

"No. The twins were from Big Bear. You know, in the mountains of Southern California." Juliana exchanged a glance with Mom.

Big Bear? It rang no bells.

"I asked if I could share the book with Kaitlyn, but you told me no. You wanted to fix it before anyone else realized it sucked."

Juliana's words echoed our mother's. My eyes shifted to meet hers. "Maybe it wasn't any good."

"Hold on," Juliana cut in. "You don't earn A's in college if you're not any good. Unless you're sleeping with the professor."

That got a reaction from both our parents. "Juliana!"

"Only kidding," Juliana said with a twinkle in her dark eyes. "So anyway, let me tell you the story. Maybe it will come back to you."

Dad pulled his cell phone from a jacket pocket, glanced down at the screen, and whispered something into Mom's ear. "You girls alright for a minute?" he asked. "We'll be right back." Then he and Mom stepped out into the corridor.

Juliana rattle on, but try as I might, I couldn't concentrate on a story written by the girl I once was—and might never be again.

Juliana's eyes sparkled with satisfaction as she leaned forward. "What do you think? It's total fiction, but to me it seems like those terrible Big Bear twins are a lot like you and Callie, only exaggerated."

"It's okay," I said, but I wasn't in the mood for a story. I wanted to learn about me—who I was and what the future held for me—not some fiction I'd written. "I'm sorry, little sister. I just—"

"Hey, watch it. 'Little sister' *totally* doesn't cut it. Midget's okay, but since I'm practically a college girl, how about Jules? Or just plain Juliana?"

I tried to smile. "You got it, Jules. I'm afraid I wasn't a very good listener. Later I'll read that story myself. It might jog my fuzzy brain. I might be in a better mood once I get my laptop back."

"Oh yeah. Where *is* your computer?"

"Still on the ship. But our mother . . . Mom says she sent an investigator to get it."

"Ross." Juliana nodded. "Well, how about your tablet?"

My eyes wandered over to the large Michael Kors tote handbag at my bedside. There was a Galaxy tablet sticking out of the top. "Do you think I have my book on there?" I asked.

"Well, that's where I read it. But when you were getting ready for your semester at sea, I remember you emailed most of your stuff from the tablet to your laptop. To free up space for class notes."

I noticed Juliana had a cute habit of puckering her bottom lip while she tried to concentrate. Then she made a helpful suggestion.

"But I'm pretty sure you also saved it in at least two other places. You were, like, freaked out about losing any of your writing. You saved every chapter of your novel to the computer or tablet, to a flash drive, and also to the cloud."

"Sounds like I was kind of paranoid."

"Yeah. You lost a couple of chapters one time, so I think it was pretty smart. Wish I'd saved my English AP essay in more than one place before my computer crashed last semester."

Pretty smart? I wasn't so sure. If my computer was never found, the flash drive would most likely also be lost. And to access the cloud, I'd need a password.

Besides, how could I pursue dreams I didn't even know I had?

Chapter
33

Sunday, May 17, 4:00 p.m.—Charleston, South Carolina

Pocino peeled down to his boxers, poured himself a bourbon on the rocks, and flopped onto the bed. His interview with Dean Nyquist and the students had left him with more questions and uncertainty than he'd had going in.

Reluctantly, he plucked up his phone and hit the connection for Conrad Taylor's cell phone. Subtlety had never been a part of his skill set, so he'd continue winging it. Besides, there was no point in pussyfooting around.

The phone rang once, twice, three times. Unwilling to leave a message, he disconnected. As he'd expected, less than two minutes passed before his phone rang.

Skipping the usual greeting, Conrad asked, "Are you in Charleston?"

Pocino cleared his throat. "Yes," he said, then cut straight to the facts. "Number one. No way could Callie have accidentally been left behind in Southampton. The security is airtight."

"That's what—"

"Hold on. There's more. Things aren't exactly adding up."

"Explain," Conrad said, his voice commanding yet skeptical.

Pocino couldn't blame him. Hell, he could hardly believe the convoluted scenario himself. Steeling himself, he asked, "Are you alone?"

"Ashleigh's here too. You're on speaker. We just stepped out of Marnie's hospital room."

Pocino swore under his breath, and his stomach roiled. He should have known he hadn't a prayer of bypassing Ashleigh—not even briefly. There was no way of keeping her out of the loop. With a mental shrug, he began, "Bear with me. My next couple of questions will seem off-the-wall, but I've gotta ask."

Conrad gave him the go-ahead.

"Do you know what type of luggage the girls took aboard the ship?"

"Luggage?" Ashleigh repeated. "Although there was limited space, each of the girls was allowed to take a large suitcase, a duffel bag, and a backpack."

Each. That was the key word.

The Taylors had weathered many traumatic situations with Pocino on their side. While Ashleigh wasted no time asking why, he had no choice but to share his suspicions. But not all of them.

"I don't want to give false hope. As I said, ship's protocol seems to ensure no passenger could accidentally be left behind. The system has built-in red flags, and the family would have been notified immediately."

"And?" Conrad's voice was tense.

"Well, there's no way a lone student could slip through the *Rising Star*'s security. But there's also no way I can explain three pieces of luggage going astray."

Pocino heard two hollow gasps on the other end of the line.

"Only one of the girls' luggage was on the ship?" Conrad barked.

"You got it," Pocino said. "So Ashleigh's intuition no longer sounds so far-fetched."

"Did you notice the brand on the large suitcase?" Ashleigh asked.

Strange question. Pocino wondered if Ashleigh's mind was traveling the same path as his. He pictured the large suitcase he'd seen in the cabin, but he was damned if he knew one designer from another. "Afraid that's not part of my skill set," he quipped.

Ashleigh's voice remained steady. "But you said ship's protocol would've made it impossible for a student to get left behind."

"That's right. To fool security, and the ship's staff, and the teachers on board the ship, the girls would have to work their twin magic. Marnie would have had to cover for Callie."

"*Twin magic?*" Conrad growled. "Pocino, are you saying what I think you're saying?"

"I can tell you one thing for sure." Pocino's body tensed. "No one *accidentally* missed the boarding."

Chapter

34

Sunday, May 17, 5:00 p.m.—Greenwich, Connecticut

Ashleigh looked out the limousine window and contemplated Pocino's theory. She simply could not buy into the deceitful scenario he'd laid out—and yet she wished she could. Anything was better than the thought of Callie being washed overboard. *It isn't like either of the twins to pull a stunt like this, and yet . . .*

Ashleigh shuddered. Lightheaded following Pocino's bombshell, she reined in her emotions. *There's no way Callie would have intentionally left the ship in Southampton. Is there?*

Sitting next to her on the smooth leather seat, Conrad had taken over explaining to Juliana how the next day would play out with Marnie's release from the hospital. The news that Callie might be safe in Southampton had given Juliana new hopes and a boost of positive energy after a difficult afternoon with her amnesia-ridden sister.

Ashleigh felt it best to take Marnie straight home to Greenwich tomorrow, where she hoped the familiar surroundings would unlock some memories. Although the family often spent time in their Manhattan penthouse overlooking Central Park, it wasn't truly home.

As father and daughter brainstormed further plans for the coming week and their trip to Southern California, Ashleigh tried to implant Pocino's theory in her brain. It failed to take root. Yes, the twins' well-honed switching skills could have thrown off security at the checkpoints, but working as Allison's assistant in the dance program had been Callie's dream come true. *What possible reason could she have for abandoning the program, or Allison? Or us?*

It made no sense. Callie and Marnie were mature young women now.

They were passionate about their chosen careers. Both knew what they wanted and went after it, heart and soul. What possible reason could there be for planning something like this? With Callie's graduation ceremony scheduled for only a week away—why would she have done something so reckless, so self-centered? And certainly Marnie would not have supported such a plan by covering it up.

I must talk to Allison.

Allison Dee, who had been forced to rush for her plane in South Carolina, had planned to call the Taylors as soon as she landed in New York—or so Dean Nyquist had informed Pocino. That could be anytime now. Ashleigh expected another avalanche of messages on their home phone. Hopefully one of them would be from Allison.

The moment David pulled up in front of the house, Ashleigh jumped out of the car, not waiting for her door to be opened. She dashed up the steps, keys in hand, and unlocked the door. Flinging it open, she glanced back over her shoulder before stepping inside. Conrad and Juliana remained in the limo, still deep in conversation.

Stepping into the foyer, Ashleigh scarcely noticed the pile of cards on the entry table, or the flower arrangements and plants lined up on the floor beside it. Instead she kicked off her shoes and ran across the plush carpet to the red blinking light of the answering machine. The number 17 glowed on the display panel.

Bypassing the first few well-wishers, she finally found Allison's message and pressed PLAY.

Hi. This is Allison, came the young woman's broken voice. *There are no words to express how horrible . . . I'm so—so very sorry. My heart is broken. I need to talk with you as soon as possible. As much as I want to be with you right now, I couldn't manage to get a substitute on such short notice. I must teach two dance workshops this afternoon. I don't have your cell numbers. I'll call again later this evening.*

There were a few seconds of silence as Allison attempted to speak through her tears.

If we miss each other, please call me anytime. Night or day.

She ended the voice mail by reciting her cell phone number.

The front door banged shut. Conrad's heavy footsteps and the faint whisper of Juliana's soft-soled shoes stopped at the entry table before continuing in her direction. When they stepped into the living room, Conrad held the thick stack of cards, and they both looked at her expectantly.

"Did Allison call?" Juliana asked, twisting a strand of her long hair around her finger.

"Yes, I just listened to her message. I'm calling her back now." She sank down on the sofa and patted the seat beside her.

Juliana plunked down and emitted a sigh.

When Allison picked up on the first ring, Ashleigh pressed the SPEAKER button.

"Oh Ashleigh, I'm so sorry for your loss . . . I don't know what to say," wailed the dance teacher. "Conrad and Juliana, you too. If only I hadn't—"

Ashleigh heard the young woman stifle a sob. "Allison, that rogue wave is no one's fault. Certainly not yours. We do have a few questions for you, though. Because we're not at all certain Callie was washed overboard after all."

Silence hung between them.

"Ross Pocino went aboard the *Rising Star* earlier today, to search the twins' cabin and talk with staff and students who knew them," Ashleigh went on. "He found—didn't find, actually—some things indicating Callie may not have been on board on the ship's return to New York."

The news seemed to sink in quickly for Allison, who went on to tell them at length about Callie becoming ill on the bus ride into London. "She wasn't feeling well even before we left the ship, but she didn't want to miss our three days in London. We were scheduled to see five musicals and stay at the Dorchester for two nights. Callie was particularly keen on seeing *Billy Elliott* at the Victoria Palace Theatre."

But as Allison explained, the bus wasn't more than a half hour from the ship when Callie became too sick to go on. Her forehead was burning up, and she seemed ready to pass out. Unsure what to do, Allison called the ship's doctor.

"He told me to get her away from the others and into a taxi, to send her back to the ship so he could tend to her there. I wanted to go with her but couldn't leave the other dance students. I had the bus wait until she was safely inside the taxi before we resumed our trip."

"Is that the last time you saw Callie?"

"Yes, but I talked with Dr. Pearson before our bus reached London. He said she'd returned safely to the ship." She paused. "I never saw her after leaving Southampton, but we communicated every day by text or email, right up until . . . the rogue wave . . ."

"Not by phone?" Ashleigh asked.

"I didn't call for fear of waking her."

"Allison, do you know if Marnie was on that field trip?"

"Yes, all the classes were going to London on the same day. But Marnie wasn't on our bus because the writers' agenda included touring the British Library and the Sherlock Holmes Museum, seeing a play at the Old Vic, and stopping in at the Fitzroy Tavern, where famous writers of the Bloomsbury Group used to hang out."

"So you never actually saw Marnie on the field trip." Ashleigh felt Juliana beside her, readjusting her position on the couch, and glanced up to see a frown crinkle Conrad's brow.

"I did, actually. All the master class students went to two of the musicals—the two evening performances—and we all went to the Harry Potter Shop."

Ashleigh swallowed hard. "Allison, do you think it's possible that Callie could have left the ship before it departed Southampton—and had Marnie cover for her?"

The line went silent for what seemed forever. Finally, Allison responded firmly, "I don't believe Callie would ever do something like that. She was very sick, I'm sure of it . . . She was not faking it. Besides, she absolutely *loved* the dance program and was looking forward to—"

"I know, Allison," Ashleigh interrupted. "I can't imagine either of the girls cooking up any such plan. Nor can I wrap my mind around Callie being swept overboard." Something just felt wrong about the whole thing. Especially now that Pocino had discovered that half of the girls' luggage was missing and unaccounted for.

Chapter
35

Monday, May 18, 9:45 a.m.—Greenwich, Connecticut

"David has the car out front, Mom," Juliana called out as she dashed down the hallway. She stopped abruptly in the doorway to Marnie's room.

"Be right there, darling," Ashleigh said, turning toward the door. "Just taking one last look around."

She and Juliana had spent more than an hour the previous night in Marnie's uncluttered, neatly arranged room—Elizabeth said Marnie's neatness was like a breath of springtime, but her sisters teased her about being OCD.

They had talked about the challenges ahead and brainstormed ideas for helping Marnie remember her past. Neither was certain about placing family photos on Marnie's nightstands and dresser. In the end, however, they agreed it might help jog her memory. When she came home, Marnie could decide if she wanted to keep them there or not.

"Do you think Marnie will forget she's a total neat freak?" Juliana asked, taking in her sister's bedroom once more.

Ashleigh smiled. "Once her memory returns, I imagine she'll be pretty much the same as she's always been, darling." Speculation over nature versus nurture had long been an ongoing theme in the Taylor household. Was Marnie's obsession for order innate, for example, or had she learned it in those precious first eight years with the Christonellis?

"We'll talk more on the way to the hospital," Ashleigh said, unconsciously straightening the rows of perfectly straight books on Marnie's étagère. When she turned, she saw Juliana's eyes had filled with tears.

That was nearly Ashleigh's undoing. Neither of them had spoken of

Callie or her whereabouts—or what possible reason she would have had to leave the ship instead of coming home. Today they would need to concentrate on Marnie. But avoiding all mention of her twin wasn't helping either of them.

"Try not to worry, sweet one," she said gently. "I can't explain it, but in my heart, I know Callie is safe."

9:45 a.m.—*Manhattan, New York*

Glaring sunlight lasered through the slit in the drapes, driving Pocino from bed. After pulling another all-nighter, he'd headed straight to the condo the Landes Agency maintained in Manhattan rather than rent a room at another two-bit motel. But he had no luck sleeping in.

The enthusiasm he'd felt over the missing luggage had dried up. He feared that Ashleigh's cockeyed optimism had rubbed off on him. What had he been thinking? He'd known the Taylor family too long to believe any of their girls would fail to inform their parents of such an important change in plans—and would fail to get in touch after inevitably hearing about the disaster at sea.

Pocino had returned from Charleston early Sunday evening to meet with Allison Dee at the Grand Hyatt in Manhattan. While she was finishing her last class and her conversation with a lingering student, he'd found a quiet corner and begun calling the East Coast numbers he'd obtained for the students in Callie's dance program. Male and female students alike were all on the same page when it came to describing Callie's enthusiasm for the dance program. No one believed Callie would abandon the program—neither the other dance students nor Miss Dee.

Miss Dee had insisted to him, just as she had insisted to Ashleigh Taylor, that Callie would not have lied to everyone or left the ship. Callie's aborted trip to London and Dr. Pearson's diagnosis of flulike symptoms added to the evidence. Callie surely had not left the ship in Southampton.

Another potential scenario began working its way into Pocino's thick skull. It was vague and utterly far-fetched. And yet . . .

A huge lump formed in his throat. There was not a thread of evidence indicating that Callie had any desire to stay behind in England. It was clear that Callie had been aboard the *Rising Star* when it departed.

I've come to the end of the line.

That thought lingered only a fraction of a second before another shot through his muddled brain. Although he no longer saw a perfect ending, he realized there was indeed something more he could do. Something, in fact, he must do.

Reaching for his notepad, he scanned down the pages until the name came into focus: Solange Richie. *Bingo.* With adrenaline surging through every cell of his bulky frame, Pocino poked in the number. The phone rang three times and then kicked into voice mail.

His gut tightened at the thought of his myopic focus on the dance department. *If only I'd spent more time with the Richie girl and the others in Marnie's writing class instead.* He felt like punching his fist through the wall.

Following the young woman's perky recorded greeting, he said, "Solange. This is Ross Pocino. We spoke in Charleston, at the Days Inn. I have a few more questions. Whenever you get this message, please call me. Even in the middle of the night. It's urgent. I must speak to you."

He left his cell number and hung up, cursing inwardly. *There are enough loose ends in this investigation to knit a goddamned sweater.*

CHAPTER
36

Monday, May 18, 11:00 a.m.—New York–Presbyterian Hospital

Ashleigh and Juliana rode the hospital elevator in silence, their eyes focused on the numbers of each floor as they flashed overhead. On the fifth floor, they stepped out and immediately saw Dr. Harvey standing at the high counter surrounding the nurses' station.

When Ashleigh reached the neurologist, she thanked him for meeting them and introduced Juliana. "Conrad is sorry he couldn't be here. With his full schedule, he felt it best to conclude his business now, so he can leave early to spend time with Marnie in our home."

The doctor nodded. "Hopefully the familiar surroundings will stimulate some memories. But Mrs. Taylor, don't be disappointed if that fails to occur. Though it must seem like a lifetime, it has been less than four full days since Marnie's accident."

"I understand. And if there is no significant improvement in this coming week—"

"You would be wise to get that second opinion."

"Yes. We've been reading Dr. David Martin's book on memory and understand he's a highly regarded neurologist."

"One of the best," Dr. Harvey agreed. "However, his practice is in Southern California."

"That's no problem. Marnie hopes to continue her graduate work at the University of California in Irvine. As a matter of fact, we have family commitments in the Long Beach area later this week. So as soon as Marnie is cleared to travel . . ."

Dr. Harvey's eyes narrowed. "The results of this morning's EEG confirm there is no longer even the slightest swelling of the brain. Therefore, I see no *physical* reason why Marnie should be restricted from travel."

Hearing the doctor's emphasis on *physical*, Ashleigh's insides did a slow roll.

"If returning to her childhood home does not stimulate Marnie's memory," the doctor continued, "perhaps other familiar surroundings, such as with your family in Long Beach, will do the trick."

Ashleigh let out the breath she'd been holding.

"And for a second opinion, I agree you could do no better than Dr. Martin. I would be more than happy to reach out to him to make sure Marnie gets an appointment . . ."

"I would appreciate that. Marnie's father and I would like to leave no questions unanswered. Her graduate program at UCI begins in August, and I am at a loss as to how to counsel her. When I suggested she might take a semester off, her temper flared. It was the first time since the accident."

"That's not alarming. She's bound to be upset and confused over her loss. And as you surmise, she will need your help. She is currently unable to make a rational decision." Dr. Harvey's smile was sympathetic. "Let me know when you would like to see Dr. Martin. I will give him a call and request an appointment for his earliest time slot. I will also suggest he refer you to a neuropsychologist."

Ashleigh saw the questioning look on Juliana's face, but explanations could wait. Only one thing was on her mind now.

"Is Marnie ready to leave the hospital?"

CHAPTER
37

Monday, May 18, 11:30 a.m.—New York–Presbyterian Hospital

I'd just finished pulling on my shoes when an unfamiliar nurse pushed a wheelchair into my room. "My mother and sister should be here any minute. I don't need a wheelchair," I said.

Wearing my jeans, a long-sleeved T-shirt, and a royal blue sweatshirt with the letters UCI emblazoned on the back, I felt more human. I had been a needy, helpless patient in a nightgown and robe for long enough, and I couldn't have stood another moment of it.

I wanted my life back.

But I couldn't just wait for my memory to reappear miraculously. The first steps were to step up, take control, and figure out who I was and what I wanted out of life.

The nurse smiled apologetically. "I can see you're getting around just fine, but I'd be in a heap of trouble if I let you walk out of the hospital on your own."

"It's hospital protocol," called a voice from the door.

Mom.

"Copy that," I replied, wondering what movie or TV show the phrase came from. I had gathered my courage and would much rather have walked out on my own two feet, but I didn't want to get the nurse in trouble.

As Mom folded my robe and nightgown and placed them in my overnight suitcase, I picked up the book on memory she'd given me. "I started reading this last night. You were right. Dr. Martin's explanation of the brain was understandable. None of that doctorese. I think I'm beginning to understand. Vaguely."

Mom smiled. "Good."

"Hey," Juliana said, reaching for the book, "I want to learn all about the brain and memory."

I looked at her and was reminded of the Energizer Bunny. "Sure, Jules, but it's not an easy read."

"The brain is totally cool. That's why I'm gonna be a psychiatrist." Juliana tilted her head to read the spine, and within seconds she was typing something on her iPhone. "Found it on Amazon. Okay if I download it? The Kindle version is only twelve bucks."

Mom nodded her approval.

Juliana looked over at me. "I'll download it onto my e-reader when I get home, but I want to start reading now on my iPhone." She paused, making direct eye contact. "I want our old Marnie back."

My stomach dropped to the floor of the stark hospital room. I didn't know who the old Marnie was. And I didn't know how to be her.

"Ready to go?" the nurse asked.

"Yes," Juliana and I said in unison.

We exchanged a smile, and the cloud lifted, at least a little. I felt surrounded by love. My mom and Juliana were no longer strangers. They cared about me. They felt like family.

"Hold on," Mom said. "We won't be leaving through the lobby doors. We'll be taking one of the corridors that lead to a side exit. To avoid the swarm of reporters."

"Reporters?" I repeated.

"Yeah," Juliana said. "There's a ton of them out there, and more at home. Even a few waiting for Dad yesterday when he left Jordon's."

Stories of the seven-story wave slamming into the *Rising Star* had dominated the news for a couple of days, but by the end of the weekend, coverage had all but dried up. Mom explained, however, that a

TV journalist had mentioned me by name and reported my having been airlifted to New York–Presbyterian Hospital. I was horrified.

But at least the report hadn't announced the nature of my injury.

Although we had taken a back staircase down to the ground floor, my heart raced as if I'd just charged upstairs instead. Was it because of our cinematic "escape" from the paparazzi, or simply because I was unable to picture my home? Now I was sitting in a limousine, and the bravado I'd felt earlier was gone. I didn't know what to expect. I couldn't conjure up an image of a single room.

Oh, dear God, please let the memories come flooding in.

I breathed deeply and looked around the elegant interior of the Lincoln Town Car. *Did I used to ride to school in this luxury automobile?* Gesturing to the driver, whom Mom had called David, I asked, "Should I know him?"

Mom placed her hand on my arm. "David has been with our family since you were in middle school." Her smile was sad but so beautiful.

I let out a sigh. "Well, I guess this is my life . . . for now. My past has been erased. I'll have to get used to it." I couldn't panic each time I met someone I used to know.

"Until you recover your full memory, it will be challenging. Just hold on to the fact that you're surrounded by people who love and care about you." She was so incredibly calm that I relaxed a little, settling back against the plush leather seat.

Looking out the window, I hoped for any glimmer of familiarity. "Are we almost there?" I asked, like a little kid on summer vacation.

"Greenwich is only about twenty-four miles from the city," Juliana explained, "but at this time of day, the traffic is gross."

I'd run out of questions to ask. Nothing about my life before the accident was coming back to me. No one—not even the doctors—knew what to tell me.

Closing my eyes, I tried to think about all the specialists and nurses I'd talked with in the past few days. I remembered each one, but what they had told me was a blur, just a lot of supposition. Every one of them gave me encouraging news. But no one could tell me how long it would take to regain my memory. Worse yet, no one could even assure me that my memory really would return in time. That seemed to be beyond the range of their test results and statistics.

The idea of my entire past being permanently deleted scared me senseless.

Stop! Don't think about that now.

One thing was clear to me. If I continued to obsess about my past, I would turn into a dreadful bore. I would sabotage my own future. No one would want to be around me—not even my own family.

Clinching my hands into tight fists, I made a promise. *I will stop obsessing about myself. I will learn as much as I can about my family and other people around me, and about this life.*

When I opened my eyes again, I saw scenery that seemed to be light-years away from the bumper-to-bumper traffic we'd left behind. We traveled past mansions with beautifully manicured lawns, and when David turned at last, the iron entrance gates parted to reveal what appeared to be a magnificent, sprawling estate.

David drove up a winding drive and parked in a semicircular area in front of an impressive white mansion, reminiscent of Tara from *Gone with the Wind*. I blinked. This must be my home, but it brought not a single personal memory to mind—only another movie reference. How could I remember nothing about living in this grand home?

Mom and Juliana were both looking at me, and I knew they were expecting a flood of memories.

I have none.

Tears filled my eyes. I didn't want to disappoint them.

Then unexpectedly, all my good intentions flew out the window. I felt angry and resentful, and another thought appeared in my head like an ominous cloud.

I can't—I won't—pretend just to make you happy.

Chapter
38

Monday, May 18, 1:00 p.m.—Greenwich, Connecticut

Mom gently took hold of my elbow. Somehow, she seemed to know I was barely holding it together. Like a robot, I allowed her to guide me through the tall, white doors of the stately home.

A time-traveler dropped into a strange new world couldn't have felt more out of place.

As if reading my mind, Mom said, "Darling, remember. It's only been four days."

"Since everything I was or ever wanted to be just up and vanished," I shot back before immediately recoiling. It wasn't her fault I'd become an empty bundle of nothing.

Juliana stamped her foot. "Hey, cut it out."

I stopped dead in my tracks.

"Juliana!" Mom said, shifting her attention to my younger sister.

"I'm sorry, but that's loser talk." Her eyes flashed to me. "Until your memory returns, Marnie, it's all about attitude." She turned back to Mom. "Isn't that what you and Dad always say?"

Mom's voice was quiet. "Everything is unfamiliar to Marnie right now, even our home."

"Right, but that's why I said—"

"You're right, Jules." The poor-me syndrome was rearing its ugly head again. Even though this house had failed to ignite the memories we'd all hoped for, I had to move on. "You hit it on the head. It's all about attitude. I've got to deal with the present." I paused, making eye contact with my mother and sister. "But I'll need your help."

Juliana grinned. "Right. First the attitude adjustment, then we start figuring things out." A sheepish, impish grin lit up her face. "And then we can talk about the dance convention."

Ashleigh half-frowned, half-smiled, knowing she should've expected Juliana to bring up the dance convention. "Oh, Juliana, this is Marnie's first day home. It's much too soon for that."

"I know you told me to wait a few days, Mom, but since Marnie—"

"Wait. What's going on?" Marnie cut in. Alarm was written all over her face.

Ashleigh gave Marnie's arm a slight squeeze and gave Juliana a meaningful look. "I believe it's a bit too soon for you to begin making such decisions, Marnie, but I told your sister we'd see how you felt about performing a jazz trio with her and her friend Kaitlyn. When you feel up to it, of course."

"A trio? But I thought Callie was the dancer."

Ashleigh felt a wave of emptiness spread through her. "Yes, dance is Callie's chosen career. But all three of you girls are excellent dancers. You began lessons in preschool . . ." She trailed off, recalling that she'd missed Marnie's preschool dance lessons because in those early years, she had been the one missing.

Taking a restorative breath, she willed herself to detach from all but the present. "Before the rogue wave turned our world topsy-turvy, Callie had talked you and Juliana into attending the Tremaine Dance Convention with her in Los Angeles. It's the weekend after next. She persuaded you to be part of a trio she choreographed."

"I've been working on the choreography ever since Callie said it was okay to make our trio into a foursome so Kaitlyn—"

"Juliana," Ashleigh cut in. "We need to table this discussion for now."

"Hold on, Mom. Maybe we can try. It might give me something to think about instead of . . ." Marnie looked to Ashleigh for guidance. "But what if I can't dance?"

Juliana seemed to think my so-called muscle memory would be different from the damaged memories in my brain. I wasn't so sure.

By the time she and Mom finished showing me around the house, my head was swimming. I just wanted to lie down and make the world go away. Luckily, they seemed to understand completely.

Now, alone in my unfamiliar bedroom, I slipped off my shoes, pulled down the bedcovers, and slid inside. Thirty minutes later I was unable to shut off neither the unanswered questions swirling through my damaged brain nor the emptiness inside. Rest eluded me.

There was no point just lying here, tossing and turning, so I gave in. There had to be a better use of my time.

I sat up and reached for the Michael Kors handbag, emptying the contents onto the bed. I set the Galaxy tablet on the bedside table and began looking through my Kate Spade wallet: some foreign currency, twenty-six American dollars, a Starbucks card, two credit cards, a couple of blank checks, some rewards cards. Nothing unexpected. At the bottom of the heap, I saw my passport. And a Samsung smartphone.

The phone showed thirty-two missed calls and a whole bunch of text messages. I began scrolling through them. The most recent one, from someone named April Clark, was followed by a whole string of equally unfamiliar names. The messages were somewhat boilerplate: OMG, How horrible, What can I do to help . . . Trying to decipher them made my head ache.

Instead of weeding through the rest of the texts, I opened the laptop carrying case Juliana had brought from Callie's room—also Kate Spade—and slipped the Mac Air onto my bed. Mom said my sisters, not me, were the Apple fans. Apparently, I preferred the Android operating system. But she said until my computer was returned or I got a new one, I could use Callie's Mac. I found an empty socket and plugged in my new lifeline.

Mom never spoke of Callie in the past. I hoped she was right. While I had no recollection of having a twin, every time her name surfaced, my heart began to race. Could it be twin telepathy?

On the other hand, if this raw, hollow emptiness was a kind of extrasensory perception, I would know whether Callie were alive or dead.

Wouldn't I? And the only things I knew about my twin were whatever I'd been told, mainly that we were identical in appearance but had very different personalities. How could I unconsciously feel the loss of a sister—a sister I couldn't even remember?

It was frustrating to be in the dark about so many things. *Is this what it's like to have dementia?* I pushed that negative thought away. Everyone kept telling me I had to be patient, but it felt like a lifetime since I'd woken up not knowing where I was, why I was there, or who I was.

Juliana had been the brightest light in my life since I woke up on the cabin floor in the *Rising Star*, but her friend Kaitlyn would be spending the next couple of days with us, so I doubted I'd see much of her. I looked forward to seeing friends my own age, but I knew I wasn't ready. I had to learn more about myself and the people who'd been part of my life before this disaster. The thought of trying to socialize sent my heart racing again. How could I make conversation? I wouldn't know what to say.

Before I could consider any social events, I decided to tap in to Callie's computer and look at our Facebook profiles. At least I'd get some ideas about what I'd been like and who my friends were.

I booted up the computer and crossed my fingers it was not password protected.

Chapter
39

Monday, May 18, 2:10 p.m.—Greenwich, Connecticut

As I watched the blue line creep across the Mac Air screen at glacial speed, every muscle in my body tensed. When the computer finally flashed to life, and the desktop appeared, I let out an audible sigh. No dreaded rectangular box in the middle of the screen. I was in luck. No password was required.

Next, I clicked on Safari, hoping Callie had not set up roadblocks. On the home page, there was an icon for Facebook. A bit of tension melted. This icon should lead straight to my twin's profile. If not, I'd be locked out of not only my twin's profile but my own as well. I had no recollection of passwords. They had vanished with the rest of my important memories.

My breath caught in my throat when Callie's profile opened, and my eyes drifted to the ceiling. *Thank you, thank you, thank you.*

The template captured my twin in a royal blue dance costume, leaping into a spectacular jeté—both legs perfectly extended, and toes pointed. The photo was set against an amazing night sky.

In the box in the lower left-hand corner was a photo of the two of us. Even though we did not dress alike, and had chosen different schools and career paths, it appeared we must have been close. Otherwise, why would Callie have posted a photo of the two of us on her timeline?

A weird feeling drifted over me. We didn't look exactly identical, but if our hair had been done in the same style—either down straight or up in a ponytail—I guess we would have. Because I was living completely in the dark, every detail was unsettling. I knew the dancer in the photo had to be Callie, but in the square inset photo, I didn't know which one was me.

I scanned Callie's timeline. I recognized the name of her dance instructor, Allison Dee. She had posted the last photos on my sister's site. They were all taken in London. In one photo, beside a group of about a dozen girls was a sign that read SADLER'S WELLS: LONDON'S DANCE HOUSE. Callie wasn't in any of the photos, of course. She had never made it to London.

I typed my name into the search bar, and my own Facebook page appeared. My template had a library in the background, and the same photo of Callie and I was in the square box in the left-hand corner.

From the looks of things, I wasn't much of a social media person. My last post was almost three months ago—in February. The text was about the upcoming semester-at-sea and what an honor it was to be selected for Graham Bradford's master class. There was also a video I'd posted of a panel of authors in the States. It featured the famous Brit along with James Patterson, Michael Connelly, Harlan Coben, Andrew Gross, Janet Evanovich, and Lisa Scottoline. I clicked on the link. They were discussing character development, and although I wasn't really in the mood, I laughed when Janet said, "If one of my characters tries to take over, I just shoot the bastard."

I closed my eyes. The authors in the video were somewhat familiar. They all wrote crime novels, mysteries, or thrillers. Had I wanted to follow in their footsteps? Did I still want to? I was nearly twenty-three years old and at a loss as to how to move forward. Maybe my passion for writing would return. But if it didn't, what was I going to do? How could anyone with an empty file cabinet of memories write a novel or do anything worthwhile?

Attitude, attitude, I reminded myself.

The more I scrolled down my timeline, the more disoriented I felt. Up through the first half of February, I had posted almost every day—at least four or five times a week. I even had a biweekly blog on the challenges of the writing life. I shared insights into some of my characters and short scenes from my works in progress—none of it the least bit familiar to me now. Then, in mid-February, I just disappeared.

It seemed reasonable that I might slow down while studying with the *Rising Star* program. But to just drop out without so much as a heads-up to my friends? That felt wrong.

Maybe it was hard to get a Wi-Fi connection at sea. But Callie . . .

I hit the back button so I could take another look at her wall. Being at sea hadn't stopped her from posting. *Seriously? That makes no sense.*

Callie was just as busy in the dance program, and yet she'd posted several times a week. I was a writer, and I had vanished from the social media scene altogether.

Chapter 40

Monday, May 18, 11:00 p.m.—Manhattan, New York

Pocino had spent the entire day chasing his tail. Every time he thought he got a grip on the fate of the missing twin, it slipped through his fingers.

He strode across the kitchen of the Landes Agency condo to the built-in desk, opened its long drawer, and ripped out a sheet of paper from a spiral notebook. Then he eased himself down onto a kitchen counter stool. He seldom committed his thoughts to paper, but this case had blown him off kilter. He had to clear his head, or he wouldn't get a wink of sleep.

His suspicions about the identity of the twin who was airlifted from the *Rising Star* had, at first, brought him to a screeching halt. Unsure if he was dealing with wishful contemplation or actual possibilities, Pocino began jotting down the facts. Aligned in clean, neat columns, maybe they would fit together like pieces of a puzzle.

People

- **Callie:** Gung-ho about the semester-at-sea from the beginning.
- **Marnie:** Not interested until it was announced Graham Bradford would teach the first half.
- **Callie:** Close to her dance instructor and classmates.
- **Marnie:** In awe of instructor. (Bradford was a loaner; he remained in London when *Rising Star* left port.)

Things—Missing

- Marnie's computer
- Callie's handbag
- Unidentified: One set of luggage—large suitcase, backpack, duffel bag

Things—Not missing

- Two cell phones
- Callie's iPad
- Callie's Mac (she didn't take it with her)

Drumming his pencil on the desktop, Pocino did his best to sort through fact versus supposition. As the facts piled up, his theory took firmer shape. The missing set of luggage gave credence to the belief that one of the twins had stayed behind on purpose. Accidentally missing the boat never added up. But a carefully planned departure would account for the missing luggage . . .

If so, this Graham Bradford had a lot of explaining to do. Because it would mean the missing young woman was not who everyone thought she was. It would mean Pocino's suspicion was correct: The twin in New York was not Marnie—but Callie.

An hour later, when Pocino's cell phone blared, he punched the TALK button at lightning speed. "Pocino."

"Ah, Mr. Pocino? This is Solange Richie. Sorry, it's late, but I just got in, and your message said—"

"No worries, Solange. Much appreciated," he broke in. "Since I met you in Charleston, I've thought of a few more questions I think you can help me with."

"Okay. Like what?" In the next beat she asked, "Hasn't Marnie's memory come back?"

"Not yet. So I need your help in painting a clear picture of what Professor Bradford was like and how he interacted with Marnie. I'll get straight to the point. Did Marnie develop a personal relationship with the professor?"

On the other end of the line, Solange hesitated. "Well, we were all wowed by him. He has an imposing demeanor, you know, and he's *so* good-looking. Marnie and I joked that his British accent was to die for, that it must have been what made the maidens swoon in Jane Austen's novels. But if you mean, did Marnie have a romantic relationship with him? No way. He's *forty-three!* And even though he's super famous, he's never really been photographed with a date."

Pocino frowned. "You think he's gay?"

"Not really. But he's not married. Out of earshot, we called him Professor Higgins. You know, like in *My Fair Lady*."

"So you think that's how Marnie thought of him?"

"Well, she never really said. As I told you in Charleston, she got off to a shaky start with him the first day of class when she brought up Internet research. But whenever anyone said anything the least bit negative about him, she was the first to come to his defense."

Pocino's ears perked up. "Negative? Like what?"

"Like that he was out of touch with technology," replied Solange. "His novels are great. They're best sellers and all, but geez, it's the twenty-first century, and he doesn't even use a computer. He writes all his manuscripts in pencil and does his research in libraries." She chuckled. "He said if it was good enough for Hemingway, it was good enough for any serious writer. He told us there's too much misinformation on the Web and writers waste way too much time messing around online instead of writing. But, I mean, to be totally off the Internet would be like slipping back into the Dark Ages."

"So Marnie converted to his way of thinking about social media and all that. And then she became like his assistant, helping type up the novel he was writing." Pocino paused. "Bradford's workshop is in England, right?"

"Right," came the reply. "The Sloane Square workshop. It's eight weeks long, and the students live in Sloane Hall—a large group of flats in London."

"When was the start date?"

"Soon after the ship reached Southampton. I don't know the exact dates."

"Do you think Marnie had any desire to remain in England with the professor?" Pocino said, trying for nonchalance.

"Well, I don't think she'd entirely given up on winning the last slot in Bradford's summer workshop. But it would've meant missing her graduation ceremony in California. She worried about how her family would feel about that. Anyway, he takes only five students each year, and there was a ton of competition, not just from our master class but from writers all over England. Marnie knew it was a long shot. Bradford had chosen the other four students, and each of them already had a master's degree in writing or literature. If Marnie beat those odds, I'm sure she would have told me. She would have told *all of us*."

Solange paused. "Hope I don't sound catty, Mr. Pocino, but although Marnie was a gifted writer, I really don't think she qualified for his superstar spot. Besides, if there'd been a winner from our class, Bradford would have announced it."

"OK, Solange." Pocino pressed forward. "But Marnie wasn't too crazy about having a different professor on the final leg of the voyage, right?"

The girl's response held a hint of defensiveness. "I think I got to know her well enough that she wouldn't have stayed in England without telling me—or at least someone . . ."

"So, she *might* have disliked the change enough to leave the ship in Southampton?"

There was a prolonged silence while Solange pondered the question. "Not really. The last time I saw Marnie was on the bus after our London field trip. If she hadn't reboarded, all hell would have broken loose. Besides Professor Gaspar told us Marnie had come down with the flu, and it was highly contagious, so he warned us not to have any personal contact with her."

"Did Marnie complain about not feeling well on the field trip?"

"Yes. On our last night, when we got back from seeing *Mamma Mia*, she complained about not feeling good. She hoped she wasn't catching her sister's flu. She went straight to bed."

"And the next day?"

"I don't know. She didn't eat breakfast, but I didn't think much about that since she hardly ever did."

"And on the bus back to the ship, did Marnie sit beside Professor Bradford?"

"Um . . . yeah. But if you think it was a budding romance, that's way off base. She'd become his stand-in assistant. Like I said, even though he's nice eye candy, he has an untouchable aura about him. What Marnie wanted from him was his secrets on how to write a best seller and grow a huge fan base."

Pocino wasn't exactly buying Solange's picture of the platonic relationship. If Marnie had bailed, there had to be a compelling lure—and a bachelor professor who looked and sounded like Hugh Grant's younger brother sure fit that bill.

Chapter
41

Tuesday, May 19, 3:05 a.m.—Greenwich, Connecticut

When I'd slipped into the unfamiliar bed the night before, I was unable to keep my eyes open. Now I was too wired to close them.

The room was as dark as the night sky. I raised my head and squinted at the clock on my bedside table. It read 3:05, but I wasn't tired. The only sound was a faint whisper of wind against the window. Through the half-open door, a dim slice of light shone from the nightlight in the hallway. I turned on the bedside lamp and swung my feet to the floor. I couldn't just wait until morning for Mom and Dad to tell me about our family and myself.

There are things I can find out on my own.

Before we were to have our "big talk" about my childhood later this morning, I wanted to at least Google my dad's name. *Since he's such a bigwig, there must be a lot of information about him online.* Maybe I would even learn something about the rest of our family. Every minute, it seemed, I was realizing there was *so much* I didn't know . . .

Yesterday afternoon, Juliana and Kaitlyn had brought my "favorite" from Starbucks—a double espresso. I'd *hated* it. Juliana was blown away, saying I used to be addicted to them and drank two, sometimes three a day. Even brushing my teeth couldn't get rid of that gross, bitter taste. I must have been deranged to love such high-test coffee. Or had the bump on my head altered my taste buds? Either way, Kaitlyn's cinnamon dolce latte had tasted way better.

"What's going on?" Juliana had raised her eyebrows into a comical arch. "You don't like whipped cream any more than I do."

So when I couldn't get back to sleep, I retrieved Callie's Mac Air and headed for the bed, where I propped up the pillows to make a backrest. Then I pulled up the comforter and sat cross-legged on top of it. I opened the laptop and activated it. Out of nowhere, the phrase *dona nobis pacem* came to mind. The translation, "grant us peace," whirred in my faulty brain. Did I take Latin in high school? Or was this something I'd learned at church?

At the moment, it didn't seem to matter. While I wasn't so sure I even believed in God, I didn't think He'd mind if I asked for help. I needed all the help I could get.

Searching online for information about Conrad Taylor, I found a ton of stuff, which came as no surprise. As seemed to be the case for the current and past American presidents, people either loved and admired him—or hated him with a passion.

My dad's great "sin" seemed to be replacing the department store named John Stewart's with Jordon's and changing the awnings from green to red on the iconic Chicago store. Why that was such a big deal, I couldn't imagine.

After a few hours of surfing the web, I'd learned more about my dad and his accomplishments than I ever needed to know. I'd also seen a heap of background about my mom. As far as everyone was concerned, she was awesome.

There was a ton of links to articles about my family—every one of us. Even Juliana, who had just graduated from high school with honors, was featured on several sites. We were famous, and it seemed too surreal. My brain ached with information overload. I could barely wrap my mind around it.

But when I unexpectedly came across several Google listings of my name—more than I ever could've imagined a twenty-two-year-old would gather—my desire to find out about anything other than my own past evaporated like a breath on a foggy night. Disconnected thoughts buzzed through my head as I repeatedly came across the same words.

Abducted.
Kidnapped.
Infant twins.
Long Beach Memorial Hospital.
And then I saw a photo of a baby named Cassie.

CHAPTER 42

Tuesday, May 19, 9:15 a.m.—Manhattan, New York

Pocino threw back the covers and padded into the kitchen. No point in more tossing and turning in bed. With his brain on instant replay, he had managed less than four hours of horizontal time. Only thing to do now was fortify himself with some strong black coffee.

After his late-night conversation with Solange, one scenario after another had bubbled up. Envisioning the twins deceiving both teachers and classmates while on board the *Rising Star* took no stretch of his imagination. Both young women were bright and clever. When orchestrated properly, their communication by email, text message, or even phone would've set off no warning bells. No one would've been the wiser.

But if one of the girls had remained in England, there had to be a credit card trail to follow. And he'd bet his own measly bank account that the missing twin out banging the plastic was *not* Callie.

Ignoring the three-hour time difference on the West Coast before slipping into bed early this morning, Pocino had called his boss with a request to make tracing the twins' credit card activity a priority. He might be grasping at straws even now, but he'd be damned if he would leave any possibility unexplored. Hopefully, Landes would get back to him posthaste with the information.

Pocino grabbed a one-cup pod of French Roast and popped it into the Keurig machine. Watching the coffee drip into his mug, he mulled over the call he would have to make to the Taylors later this morning. Logically, a student slipping through the ship's security seemed damn near impossible, but the missing luggage sent a different message. One of the girls had left the ship, and that girl had to be Marnie. Though it was still beyond his comprehension how such a thing could happen in the Taylor clan, it was a hell of a lot better than Callie being swept overboard. If Marnie's credit card placed her in England, then the next step would be tracing the whereabouts of her mentor—a piece of cake.

Pocino's ringtone chimed, in the tune of "That's What I Like." His grin widened when the name *Dick Landes* winked up at him. He hit the green button. "Ciao, boss."

"We hit pay dirt," came Landes's voice. "We've got activity on a MasterCard *after* the *Rising Star's* departure from Southampton."

"Bingo!" At this terrific news, Pocino felt some of the pressure fall away. *Thank God, we can tell the Taylors that reports of Callie being lost at sea are false.* But then another, not-so-terrific thought surfaced. "Could her card have been stolen?"

"First thing we checked," Landes replied. "So far, only one purchase has surfaced. On Wednesday, May thirteenth, a Callie Taylor with verifying photo ID charged the equivalent of over six hundred dollars on her MasterCard. That's three days after the ship set sail."

Pocino's stomach plummeted. "Whoa, hold on. Did you say *Callie's* card?" His thoughts volleyed. *Why would Callie stay behind in England? This doesn't compute.*

There was a beat of silence. "Strange question," Landes said. "Have you got another theory?"

"I did," Pocino grunted. "There's not a shred of evidence that Callie had any motivation for deserting her master class. And there's a heap of it that leads me to think . . ." He relayed the facts that had led him to believe the missing twin was in fact Marnie—a theory that was pretty much shot down by the news of activity on Callie's credit card. "It's not likely one twin would give the other her credit card, is it?"

Landes sighed. "Ross. What's going on? Surely Conrad and Ashleigh wouldn't fail to recognize which twin they've got here in New York."

Pocino didn't know what to think, but one thing was for sure—there was no innocent Taylor twin in this situation. "What boggles my mind is how any student could covertly leave the ship. Unless she never actually reboarded, and her twin managed to go through twice . . ." His voice trailed off.

Was that even possible? His rational mind said *no way*. Everything he'd learned pointed to Callie being too sick to pull that off. And anyway, Callie had no reason to leave the ship even if she could have. "Sorry, Dick. I'm thinking out loud and firing nothing but blanks. None of this makes complete sense yet."

"You told me Callie's handbag was the one missing, right?"

"Right. Callie's handbag and Marnie's computer are both . . . Wait a minute! What if the girls switched handbags?" *Maybe Marnie is the one who jumped ship, and she has Callie's handbag—ergo her credit cards.* The dots were beginning to connect.

Landes didn't seem convinced. "Ross, the Taylors have raised responsible young women. I can't believe the missing twin would fail to contact her parents, particularly since that rogue wave was a hell of a lot more than local news, unless she was prevented from doing so."

But if there had been foul play, Pocino reasoned, the twin's absence would have been discovered before the *Rising Star* left port. "The remaining twin would have been alarmed if her sister didn't make it back to their cabin. But I agree, the lack of contact is baffling. Unless Callie . . . or Marnie . . . was to have delivered the news when she arrived stateside."

"With the intel you've gathered on the girls, I would have reached the same conclusions," Landes allowed. "But would Marnie's hero worship really lead her so far astray? And would Bradford be willingly part of such a scheme? It all seems so—"

"Unlikely," Pocino cut in. "I agree. But look at this from Bradford's perspective. He's facing a nonnegotiable deadline, and his usual assistant has been disabled indefinitely. Marnie is the only one able to interpret his handwriting. Retaining her for a while in London could have been awfully tempting . . ."

"But the purchases on Callie's card were not made in England," Landes insisted. "They were made in a computer shop in Paris."

Chapter 43

Tuesday, May 19, 6:50 a.m.—Los Angeles, California

Dick Landes dropped the handset into its cradle and hit the INTERCOM key, considering Pocino's premise that a kidnapping or some other type of foul play would have ignited a missing student alarm. The theory had somewhat eased the small knot of tension that had been building in Landes's neck throughout their phone conversation. No, he decided now, foul play was not a strong likelihood. At least, he hoped not.

The fact that neither of the twins had gone overboard was good news. But that didn't mean all was well in the Taylor family. If Pocino's hunch was valid, the revelation that Marnie was the missing twin would rock the Taylors' world yet again.

Although Landes trusted the instincts of his longtime friend and most reliable investigator, he wasn't sure what to think right now. One moment Pocino was dead certain one of the twins had gone overboard and Ashleigh Taylor's instincts were nothing more than wishful thinking. The next moment he'd decided that somehow the twins had switched identities and Marnie had managed to leave with Graham Bradford while Callie covered for her. But the MasterCard showing up in Paris—with a Taylor twin attached to it—had thrown both detectives for a loop.

Maybe Graham Bradford had nothing to do with it at all.

How had one of the girls ended up in the City of Light? It seemed unlikely that Callie and Marnie would have intentionally switched IDs and credit cards—and no more likely than one of them would abandon her master class and fail to notify her family. Yet both master class teachers reported receiving communication from the twins aboard the *Rising Star*, which pointed to one twin covering for the other. But why?

Sandra picked up on the first buzz. "Yes, Mr. Landes."

"Has Kirkbride arrived?"

"He's just come in, sir. Would you like me to send him to your office?"

"Straightaway."

Landes leaned back in his desk chair. *What could possibly motivate either Callie or Marnie to abandon her semester-at-sea program?* The twins he had known since their childhood would never do such a thing without notifying their parents.

Light taps on his half-open door alerted him to the arrival of his new agent, Jack Kirkbride. The broad-shouldered, six-foot-four young man filled the doorway. He wore gray gabardine pants and a navy blazer with a light blue dress shirt. A blue geometric-patterned tie completed the ensemble. Kirkbride wore it well.

"Have a seat." Landes gestured to the chair in front of his desk. He took several minutes to bring Jack up to speed on the Taylor family's newest drama and Ross Pocino's newest theory.

"To be clear, then," Jack began, "you want me to follow up on all the purchases made in Paris. And to include information about the brand of each product."

"Right." Pocino had asked Landes for more details about what was purchased at the computer store in Paris. "The brands might lead us to the identity of the missing girl. Callie buys Apple products. Marnie prefers Androids. We need the intel ASAP." If the charges were for Apple products, the theory about Marnie sneaking off for a rendezvous with Bradford was unlikely. They would be back to square one.

"So the *identity* of the missing young woman is now in question?"

"Pocino's findings can't be ignored," Landes pointed out. The two detectives had agreed that they needed that information before phoning the Taylors. "Although we will inform the Taylors that we are certain Callie did not go overboard, we will not raise the possibility of the missing twin being Marnie instead of Callie. Not yet."

"I realize the girls are twins," Jack protested, "but wouldn't Mr. and Mrs. Taylor know—"

"Which is which? My thought exactly," Landes agreed. "But the Taylors and Toddmans have an annual Christmas celebration, and last year Conrad and Ashleigh admitted to Pocino that they could no longer tell the girls apart with absolute certainty. With one twin suffering from amnesia, I'm not sure the Taylors can rely on expressions and personality to know with absolute certainty which daughter returned home."

"It is complicated." Jack had been introduced to both high-profile couples recently, at the opening of the second Landes Agency office in downtown Long Beach, next to the old Walker Building.

Landes nodded. "And until we are one hundred percent certain of the identity of the missing twin, I don't want to throw them into any further complications." He instructed the new agent to get on the case right away. "While you're monitoring the credit cards, I'll reach out to Alexa in Paris. We've got to start a search for the missing girl."

"So, no trip to Paris in my near future?" Jack teased.

"Afraid not this time, Jack. We'll use our boots already on the ground in Paris. However, once we locate the girl . . ." Waving away his last words, Landes said, "Just hop on the intel. If Pocino's right, our clients have a whole new set of challenges lying in wait."

Chapter

44

Tuesday, May 19, 10:10 a.m.—Greenwich, Connecticut

Ashleigh hurried into the kitchen. "Sorry, love. As soon as I got off the phone with Erica, Elizabeth called."

Conrad looked up from his morning paper. "Any problems?" he asked.

"Not really." It wasn't entirely true. Ashleigh suspected Elizabeth had downplayed Caroline's inexplicable anger issues, but she didn't want to be sidetracked by such thoughts now. "Elizabeth has things under control. I'll tell you all about it after we talk with Marnie."

"Speaking of which," Conrad said, "it's nearly quarter after ten. Marnie seemed so eager to be filled in about her life before the accident. I expected her to have come down for breakfast by now."

Ashleigh smiled. "I'll see what's keeping her. She was in the shower around nine o'clock when Juliana and Kaitlyn went to say goodbye. You remember the girls went into the city for some last-minute shopping, right?"

Conrad nodded, but Ashleigh perceived that his mind was elsewhere. "I'm still not comfortable about Erica and Mike Christonelli meeting Marnie just yet," he said. "Are you sure that's the right thing to do?"

"No, not at all." There was a whole lot Ashleigh was unsure about when it came to Marnie's best interests. "But I don't believe there will ever be the right time to introduce Marnie to her second mother . . ."

"That's for sure," Conrad agreed.

Ashleigh reached for the pitcher of orange juice in the refrigerator and a plate of fresh croissants. "On second thought, let's talk with Marnie in her room, where she'll be most comfortable." She arranged the croissants, along with plates, glasses, cups, and napkins, on a white wicker tray. "I'll pour the coffee into the thermal decanter."

At the trill of the kitchen phone, Conrad said, "Go ahead. I'll take care of this call and be right up with the tray."

Ashleigh threw him an air kiss and headed for the stairs. A moment later, she stopped in front of Marnie's door and knocked softly. There was no sound from inside. Before she could knock again and call out her daughter's name, however, the door flew open.

Marnie, clad in a light T-shirt and jean shorts, had her hair back in a ponytail and her gaze fixed on Ashleigh.

As Conrad made his way down the hallway, Ashleigh barely registered the rattle of the breakfast tray. Marnie's hollow, dark eyes had captured her full attention. The pupils were dilated and shiny.

"Sorry," Marnie said. "I lost track of time . . ."

I'd lied about losing track of time. The truth was, I felt as though I'd been snooping into my own family and spying on my forgotten past, and I feared what I was about to discover.

My mother looked so worried. "I went right to sleep last night, but woke about three and couldn't go back to sleep," I confessed. "So I went online."

Dad set the white wicker tray down on my desk. "Unless you'd like to go down for breakfast, we thought it would be more comfortable for us to talk up here," Mom said, as if I hadn't spoken.

"Good idea," I replied. "Those croissants look delicious." I wasn't sure what else to say, especially now that I had a whole lot more questions to ask.

"How about some orange juice?" Mom asked as Dad pulled out the desk chair. She poured the juice into a glass and handed it to me. Then she poured coffee into the mugs, setting one on the desk beside Dad and the other two on my bedside table. Finally, she set the plate of croissants next to me before sinking into the upholstered chair beside it.

All eyes were on me as I sat down on my bed, then scooted back next to the headboard and folded my legs. "I'm not sure where to begin, really. I found out a whole lot about our family on the Internet. And about my life, too. A lot of it sounds like it must be fiction. Some of it must be true, but most of it I just don't understand."

My father rose from the straight-backed chair and crossed the room to my bed, where he sat down beside me. "Sweetheart," he began, "since you're a step ahead of what your mom and I planned to discuss, perhaps you should tell us what you've read and what questions it's raised."

"Yes, you're bound to have a lot of questions," Mom agreed, "and we'll do our best to answer all of them."

Although they were trying to hide it, it was obvious my parents were taken aback. My discoveries had derailed their well-planned introduction to my missing memories.

"Be prepared, though, Marnie," my mother continued. "While you can't believe everything you read on the web, I'm afraid you'll find that truth *is* often stranger than fiction."

Chapter

45

Tuesday, May 19, 7:10 a.m.—Naples, California

Elizabeth lowered the phone to the cradle. Her heart ached at the thought of the drama unfolding in the Taylor household. She wished she could be in Greenwich to help Ashleigh and her family, but she knew that was impossible. The fragile, newly widowed Caroline had no one but her for support.

Dabbing her eyes with the tissue balled in her fist, Elizabeth replayed in her head the image of Caroline's tear-stained face as she'd bolted up the stairs moments before. The death of Caroline's husband had catapulted her into a relapse of the paranoid schizophrenia she had been diagnosed with decades earlier. After spending some time hospitalized for her illness, Caroline had been doing well in recent years, and her talent in the world of art had helped with her healing. Yet, Elizabeth knew, even the renowned mathematician John Nash had experienced relapses and waged daily battles to avoid slipping back into paranoia.

It didn't help that Caroline's father, Charles Stuart, had been taken more than twenty years before from all who loved and revered him. Still, his spirit was ever-present within the walls of this Naples home and beyond. Elizabeth never missed him more than now.

As a highly regarded registered nurse, Elizabeth had been thrilled when chosen to interview with the iconic Charles Stuart, whose legendary intelligence, creativity, and foresight had created Bentley's, the landmark specialty department store known as a cathedral of merchandising. Charles's kindness, good humor, and character had quickly eased her nervousness and captivated her friendship. While theirs had not been a romantic love, Charles had captured her heart within moments of their first meeting. Despite a thirty-year age difference, there was no one to whom she'd felt closer—and no one whom she had admired more.

Comfortable nostalgia enveloped her, easing the rigidity between her shoulder blades. As if Charles had reached down and taken her hand, Elizabeth turned from the staircase and headed to the kitchen.

Elizabeth poured herself a hot cup of tea and slipped out the side door to the patio to sort through her options and organize her priorities before looking in on Caroline. Here on the patio of Charles's impressive home, located at the end of the Naples Plaza cul-de-sac, was where she and Charles had often wordlessly enjoyed their tea, gazing out at the glorious and ever-changing views of the vast Pacific Ocean. Here was where time had slowed and often disappeared.

Here, as they'd enjoyed the calming Naples scenery with sailboats and flocks of seagulls gliding by, Charles would share his concerns and ideas regarding family issues. As an only child and a childless widow at an early age, Elizabeth treasured Charles Stuart's family, and they became hers.

Ashleigh is so like Charles, she thought now. After all, he had been her surrogate grandfather. He, along with Ashleigh's saintly grandmother, had raised her from the age of two after the loss of her parents in a car accident. Elizabeth's heart raced with that unrelenting ache. *Why do bad things keep happening to such good people?*

That morning, in the haze of her manic suspicions, Caroline had surprised Elizabeth in the living room, on the call she had placed to the Greenwich home. "Is that Ashleigh?" she'd cried out, pointing to the phone at Elizabeth's ear. This outburst was followed quickly by accusation, as Caroline shouted, "She's plotting to send me back to New Beginnings! She wants you to stay with them, in Greenwich." Then she had flown from the room.

Aware of all that the Taylor family was dealing with, Elizabeth had instantly covered the receiver, not wanting to share her concerns over Caroline's instability. Yet she feared Ashleigh had heard Caroline's outburst.

"And how is Caroline coping?" Ashleigh had asked, the concern evident in her voice.

Elizabeth had averted Ashleigh's direct question, but she found she could not lie. Saying as little as possible, and with words in contrast to her fears, Elizabeth had assured her there was no need for concern.

Chapter

46

Tuesday, May 19, 10:20 a.m.—Greenwich, Connecticut

Ashleigh caught resignation darkening the blue of Conrad's eyes. The risk of Marnie learning the truth of those early years in the care of the Christonellis, without a buffer, had been a hot-button issue—one that had ignited several sleepless nights for both her parents.

Worried that Marnie's well-publicized past might surface and catch her unaware, the Taylors were equally reluctant to burden her so soon with her two-family upbringing. After consulting with all the doctors, however, they had agreed they must fill her in on her history as soon as possible.

Hindsight was twenty-twenty, of course, and Ashleigh regretted they hadn't sat down with Marnie the night before. Had they realized their daughter would get up in the middle of the night to ferret out information on her own, they would have done so.

Conrad was the first to speak. "As your mother said, real life often follows a twisted path. While many of the facts you may have found through Google are true, they are not the full truth. We hoped to be with you when you learned of—"

Marnie leaned forward, her eyes flashing at each of her parents in turn. Resting her elbows on her knees, she asked, "Was I kidnapped from the hospital on the day I was born?"

"That's right," Ashleigh said, as Conrad spoke those very words simultaneously.

Marnie did not immediately follow up. Winding the end of her ponytail around her finger, she gave a deep, dramatic sigh. "Finding *that* out was a lot more than I ever would have expected."

"And I'm sure that information was terribly unnerving," Ashleigh sympathized.

"Totally." Marnie tossed back the last of her orange juice and set the glass on the bedside table. "But rather than start at the beginning, what I'd like to know more than anything is why you didn't have Erica and Mike Christonelli arrested and thrown in jail."

Shock registered on my parents' faces as if they'd been hit by a bucket of ice water. Neither responded for an uncomfortable minute.

Maybe it was the wrong question to begin our talk, but I had to ask. I needed answers to help me control the incomprehensible facts that swirled through my head. Erica Christonelli had run away from New York and taken me to a place in California called Big Bear. She was an alcoholic who cleaned other people's houses. Weren't my parents upset that she'd taken me to California to live in a trailer park? Why had they done nothing about it? One of the articles even said the Christonellis later became a part of our extended family!

My parents exchanged a meaningful glance. Then my mother broke the heavy silence. "Darling, I'm not sure just what you read. The media coverage was extensive at the time of your abduction and periodically throughout the eight years before we were reunited. Some of the information you read is accurate, but not all of it is. And none of it reveals the whole story."

"Is it true that Erica Christonelli was a drunk?" I couldn't keep the accusatory tone from my voice. It was incredible to think they'd even let that woman near me after what she'd done.

"Whoa," Dad said. "I think we need to take a step back."

"Was she?" I asked, ignoring the warning tone in his voice. "I have a right to know."

"It is true that Erica developed an alcohol problem," Mom said. "I believe it surfaced after she found out you were our kidnapped daughter and moved the two of you out to Big Bear."

I had read something about her not knowing until I turned four that I was kidnapped, but I didn't get it. "If she didn't give birth to me, where did she think I came from?" None of the articles had explained that.

"Erica's husband told her you were the baby of an unwed mother who wanted a better life for her child."

"That was Mario. Right?" Not waiting for confirmation, I continued, "And he died before—"

"Hold on," Dad said. "For you to fully understand, I believe we need to start at the beginning."

Mom reached across and laid her hand on Dad's arm. They exchanged another one of their special silent communications.

"Your father's correct. You should know as much as we came to know about who Mario and Erica Christonelli were—before your birth."

I sighed, shaking my head in disbelief. *Are they going to defend my kidnapper?*

Chapter
47

Tuesday, May 19, 10:45 a.m.—Greenwich, Connecticut

Once again, Ashleigh found herself preparing to defend Erica, the woman responsible for turning their world upside down for four of those eight heartbreaking years. "This won't be easy, but we'll do our best to give you an overview of what took place in the lives of the Christonellis. As far as we were told, that is."

"I get it, Mom," Marnie said, nodding. "The articles and opinions I read on the web are confusing enough. Especially since I can't remember anything. Not now. Maybe not ever." She uncrossed her legs and leaned back against the pillows propped up on the headboard, resting her head in the cradle of her crossed hands.

Unable to make empty assurances about her daughter's future prognosis, Ashleigh ignored her daughter's negative attitude. The challenge soon disappeared from Marnie's posture, and she appeared ready to listen. Ashleigh—knowing her daughter's patience was typically thin at best, organized her thoughts and filled Marnie in on her history as quickly and succinctly as possible.

When she finished, Conrad pushed himself to his feet. "Sweetheart, we know this is a lot to take in. Your mother and I can't pretend to understand the motivation of a man who died before we even knew his identity. We know only what we have been told."

"And we will answer as many questions as we can," Ashleigh added.

Sitting up a bit straighter, Marnie said, "It's like the script for a bad soap opera, isn't it?" Bitterness seeped from Marnie's every word.

Ashleigh reached for her daughter's arm. "I don't have all the answers, darling. Your dad and I can't explain what we don't fully understand ourselves."

"Then why are you defending those people?" Marnie shot back. Then she waved her hand back and forth as if to erase her outburst. "Sorry . . . I really am sorry. But I have a boatload of questions."

Ashleigh took a sip of her coffee and quickly set it back down. "I understand how you must feel," she said quietly. She, too, preferred not to talk about the man who had taken Marnie from her bedside. "What Mario did was immoral and indefensible. However, Erica was innocent. She believed she was raising the child of an unwed mother—"

"Who wanted a better life for her child," Marnie finished, her words dripping with sarcasm. She sat up straight once more, her posture stiff. "Unless everything I read was a lie, Erica Christonelli was no innocent victim when I was four years old."

Chapter
48

Tuesday, May 19, 11:00 a.m.—Greenwich, Connecticut

The room fell silent. My parents exchanged a private look—a habit to which I was growing accustomed.

"Sweetheart," Dad said at last, "you are absolutely right. What Erica did was wrong. But throwing her in jail did not seem fair."

"May I?" Mom asked, gently squeezing Dad's arm.

He nodded.

Mom rose from her chair to sit beside me on the bed. "Not all things are black and white. As Dad says, what Erica did was wrong. And yet knowing the circumstances, I felt empathy."

"So it was okay that she took off with me? That she had me living in a trailer?"

"It was a mobile home," Mom said, "and nothing to be ashamed of."

"But no, that was not okay," Dad cut in. "Your mother had more empathy for Erica than I did. By the time we met her, she'd put us through hell for eight long years."

Ashleigh sighed. "As a mother, I could relate. Had I learned Callie or Juliana was a kidnapped child, after four years or even four days of mothering them . . ." She left the sentence unfinished. "The bond between a mother and child forms in seconds, Marnie. And Erica mothered you for eight years."

In my eyes, it made no sense. "But Erica did not give birth to me."

"No. But your bond with her was just as strong as if she had. In many ways, Marnie, biological birth is overrated."

What does she mean by that? I wondered.

"Please don't misunderstand. I loved all three of you girls even before the day of your birth." Mom slipped her arm around my shoulder. "Erica and her brother-in-law, Mike, are—"

"My babysitter, right?" I had read about Mike Christonelli. "While Erica worked at some fancy boutique? Before she went into hiding with me?"

Mom glanced at Dad, who was still pacing, and then said, "What I was going to say was this: Mike and Erica Christonelli are coming over this afternoon."

My mouth dropped open. My throat constricted. I wanted to scream.

Mom was still talking. "They may be able to answer some of your questions."

"I don't want to see them," I interrupted. "Not now. Probably not ever."

It was Conrad's turn to sigh. "No one is going to force you to see the Christonellis until you're ready," he assured her.

"What if I'm *never* ready?" Marnie replied. Ashleigh reached out and took both of her daughter's hands. Before she had a chance to speak, Marnie continued, "After what she did, I don't understand why you let Erica be part of our family. Why did you have to be so nice to her?"

"Oh, Marnie," Ashleigh said, "the decisions we made had nothing to do with being nice to Erica. Our focus was on what was best for you."

Marnie frowned. "I don't get how being nice to her was best for me."

Conrad's gaze shot to Ashleigh and then back to their daughter. "I must admit, it took me some time to get on board with the idea of the Christonellis becoming a part of our extended family. But it wasn't just the right thing to do for you. It was the only thing."

"You may not be ready to hear this," Ashleigh continued, "but I'd like you to try to understand. As much as we wanted you all to ourselves, you needed time to adjust. She was the only mother you'd known for the first eight years of your life. We couldn't just take her from you."

Ashleigh continued to explain what it must have been like for Marnie to adjust to a new life with her biological family. Conrad added his recollections to the mix.

"I guess I sort of understand," Marnie conceded. "But it feels weird." She took a few seconds as though to absorb it all. "And did I adjust?"

Ashleigh nodded. "I believe so. Though there were a few bumps along the road . . ."

Chapter 49

Tuesday, May 19, 2:45 p.m.—Queens, New York

Despite the 86-degree sunlight, Erica shivered. She was frightened, and reluctant to leave the security of Nelson's embrace, yet she could hardly wait to see Marnie. "I wish you could come with us today."

Nelson placed his finger under her chin and lifted it. "I understand. But there's no need to confront Marnie with *three* strangers. There will be plenty of time for us to all be together."

A tear slid down Erica's cheek. "Not anytime soon. Ashleigh's taking Marnie to Southern California this week. She might remain there all summer, until she begins her master's degree program."

"Are you sure?" Nelson asked. His expression changed to one of incredulity. "But how do they expect her to jump back into—"

"No, it's not for sure," Erica replied. "There are a lot of unknowns when it comes to amnesia. Ashleigh doesn't believe Marnie should enroll . . ." But that wasn't all that had Erica worried. "Ashleigh said Marnie didn't want to see us. She's only agreed because it might help her recover her memory."

Nelson wiped the tears from Erica's cheek. "We have no control over what the Taylors tell Marnie. We don't know what they've explained about the role you and Mike played in bringing her up. But I'm confident the love you've shared is bound to resurface."

Erica was grateful for the encouragement, but it would do no good. "I'm afraid the amnesia has erased our bond," she whispered. "Plus, Ashleigh said that Marnie got online early this morning, where she found—"

"A shitload of misinformation," Mike said. "Excuse the language, but why in the hell would they allow her to get into all that crap?"

"Mike, please. Remember, we must tread lightly. And Marnie is a young adult, in control of her own decisions."

"With Marnie getting most of her information online," Mike continued, as if Erica hadn't spoken, "she'll have a jaded perception of what took place and why. That would suit the Taylors perfectly."

"Stop it, Mike. This is getting us nowhere" insisted Erica. "Ashleigh and Conrad are not, and have never been, the monsters you make them out to be. Sure, they wish we'd never entered their life. But neither of them would do anything to harm or confuse Marnie. Particularly now."

"Well, even if they haven't turned her against us, we need to let her know—"

"Hold on, Mike. Marnie changed her mind about refusing to see us, but she's still looking to challenge our story." As much as Erica loved Marnie, there was no denying how confrontational she might be. "What we *need* to do is let her get her questions out. We can't react defensively."

"All of us—*including* her biological parents—have Marnie's best interests at heart," Nelson added. "Marnie is no longer dependent on parental consent, so we'll just need to take it one day at a time."

One day at a time . . .

At Nelson's words, thoughts of AA came crashing through Erica's mind. With all the stress in her life, she really should get to a meeting. A quiet panic came to rest on her shoulders as she looked at the two men in her life. Although neither Nelson nor Mike knew it, the previous night Erica had broken from nearly twenty years of sobriety.

4:00 p.m.—Greenwich, Connecticut

While Dad was upstairs handling last-minute details for his trip to the West Coast, Mom and I carried refreshments out to the gazebo, on a grassy knoll not far from the main house—about the distance of a city block. The Christonellis would be arriving any minute, and I was giving a second thought to my wish for privacy. I didn't know these people, and I didn't much like what I'd read about them. But since Mom was trying so hard to put a positive spin on this meeting, I put a lid on my negativity.

Moments after we set the trays down on the glass tabletop, a black Camry came into view. Mom hurried down to greet the two people who emerged. I sank into one of the chairs with the white-and-teal patterned cushions, glad she'd suggested meeting Erica and Mike here in the gazebo. The light spray from the cooling system had turned this rather hot day into a pleasant one. Well, nothing would make the next hour exactly pleasant, but at least the heat presented no problem.

I took a sip of my lemonade and tried to look relaxed while Mom made her way back with the two strangers—people who had totally messed up. Erica was a petite woman who looked a little heavier than in her photos online, but her curly, light-colored hair was the same—style as well as color. The man with her was her brother-in-law, Mike, though I barely recognized him. His online photos showed a man with wavy, black hair and a hunky body. His hair was now salt and pepper—more salt than pepper—and his body could only be described as stocky.

My knees began to bob up and down, and my hands shook unsteadily. I set my glass on the table beside the lacquered tray with the pitchers of lemonade and iced tea. All my questions vanished in the breeze of the fans.

What am I going to say to these strangers?

"Marnie," Mom began, looking a bit uneasy. I guess she was also having difficulty figuring out the right thing to say.

Then, before my mother could speak another word, Mike Christonelli bounded up the three steps into the gazebo, calling my name. "Marnie! We're so thankful that you're alright," he gushed. Then the awkward situation grew a thousand times worse, when he leaned over and attempted to hug me.

My body became brittle as toffee, about to snap in two. Erica's mouth dropped open, and I'm not sure what my mother's reaction was. But no one could've missed my shrinking away from Mike.

Should I introduce them, or let them find their own way?

Ashleigh was momentarily speechless, taken aback by Mike's bold action. Why was he invading Marnie's personal space? She looked like an animal caught in the headlights of an oncoming car. Ashleigh thought he had understood the need to take this first meeting slowly.

"I'm so sorry, Marnie," Mike said, taking a step back. "I didn't mean to frighten you. We were just so thankful you weren't hurt."

Marnie shot up from her chair and backed away, staring at him as if he'd grown a second head. "Not hurt?" she said with an undisguised note of disdain.

Erica stepped up into the gazebo but kept her distance from Marnie. Ashleigh saw that she was on the verge of tears, but she managed to keep them at bay. "We know this meeting must be unsettling. But I want you to know how much we love you. We want to help in any way we can."

Although Ashleigh was aware that her presence might be making Erica uncomfortable, she never wavered from her number one concern—Marnie. Taking in her daughter's rigid posture and wide-eyed stare, she lingered on the top step, near the entrance to the gazebo, waiting for a signal. The time did not seem right for her to leave. In fact, she had begun to second-guess the wisdom of this meeting.

Marnie spoke up. "Well. This is super awkward, but I guess you'd better be seated." She gestured to the empty chairs. "Iced tea or lemonade?"

After pouring two glasses of iced tea for her guests, Marnie looked up and gave her mother a nod, which Ashleigh assumed was a sign that she was okay on her own. She made a polite exit and was descending the steps when she overheard Marnie say, "I have a million and one questions. Mom tried to explain why your husband kidnapped me, Erica, but I'd like to hear your side of the story."

Chapter

50

Tuesday, May 19, 5:35 p.m.—Los Angeles, California

Jack Kirkbride bolted into Dick Landes's office without so much as a tap on the open door.

"Sorry to burst in like this, boss, but I knew you'd want to know ASAP. Pocino's hunch is right on the money." Jack had made an interesting discovery about the purchases on the MasterCard. "A Samsung Galaxy tablet and a refurbished BlackBerry phone. Not an Apple product in sight."

Landes leaned back in his desk chair, clasping his fingers behind his head. "So, as Pocino might say, those purchases sure do *compute*."

Jack winced at the pun. But Landes was right about Pocino and about the missing twin—Marnie, not Callie. "And with Marnie the one who stayed behind, the mystery of her missing computer is solved." After a slight hesitation, Jack went on, "So, are we ready to take action? To report to the Taylors that the twin living under their roof isn't Marnie, but Callie?"

"Ninety percent ready, I'd say."

"More like ninety-nine percent." Jack was unable to suppress a grin. When Alexa—their agent in Paris—had showed the salesperson a photo of Marnie, the man had remembered waiting on the very same "attractive American girl," as he had put it.

"He didn't recall a middle-aged author accompanying her, I suppose?"

Jack shook his head. "Said he spent time explaining how it was impossible to assign her the same phone number as the one she had in the States."

"You sent Marnie's photo?"

Jack scratched his head. "Well, it came from Mrs. Taylor, and she probably sent Callie's photo since she's the one believed to be missing . . . Does it make a difference?"

Landes shook his head. "Don't think so. And I don't suppose Alexa got an address?"

"Not one that opens any doors. The girl used her parents' Greenwich address and signed her name as Callie Taylor. If it is Marnie—and all evidence points in that direction—she also used her sister's passport when she went through customs into France."

The landline on Landes's desk rang twice, followed by a buzz on the intercom.

"Mr. Pocino is on line one," came Sandra's voice.

Landes hit the SPEAKER button. "Hello, Ross. Jack Kirkbride is here with me. He's hit what you'd call pay dirt."

Jack lowered himself into one of the chairs facing Landes's desk as his boss brought Pocino up-to-date on the latest intel from Paris.

"Kudos, Jack," Pocino's voice rumbled. "That squares with my theory and what we know so far. I'll circle back and thank Detective Calhoun for the legwork in South Carolina." He paused. "Maybe the girls had lookalike purses. Doesn't seem likely Marnie would take off with Callie's IDs and credit cards on purpose. Are you ready for me to phone Conrad and Ashleigh with this news?"

"Not quite." Landes sat forward and thumped a hand on his desk. "I'd like to get one hundred percent proof of identification before throwing this twist at the Taylors."

"Come on, Dick," Pocino scoffed. "We both know Marnie is the one who's missing. What's the chance the facts won't add up?"

Landes ignored him. "Get in touch with the Taylors immediately following this call. Tell them Callie's credit card and passport were used. Also tell them a salesperson in Paris identified the purchaser as the girl in the photo Ashleigh sent. Assure them she was not lost at sea. And ask them not to cancel the card. They'll understand it could be helpful in tracking her."

"Whoa!" Pocino fired back. "Dick, one of their girls willfully left the ship without telling them and has gone on for days allowing them to think she was washed overboard. That news is bad enough. But not telling the Taylors the extent of our—"

"I don't like this any more than you do," Landes interrupted. "However, before we reveal our suspicion—"

"It's a hell of a lot more than suspicion."

"Ross," Landes continued in a sterner voice, "our priority is to inform Conrad and Ashleigh what we know for certain—that Callie was not washed overboard—not to add the uncertainty of which twin is missing."

Jack listened intently as Pocino doubled down.

"Sorry, Dick, no can do. Our evidence that Marnie is in Europe is too damn compelling, and the Taylors aren't ones to tolerate being kept out of the loop. Callie is the one suffering from amnesia, and the family needs to know. They would resent the hell out of our withholding any information . . ."

Jack found it more and more difficult to remain silent. While he did not know the Taylors as the other Landes agents did, he felt Pocino's gut instincts were valid. Allowing the Taylor family to continue believing Marnie had returned home instead of Callie would only do more damage to the family—and would add to the confusion of the poor girl with amnesia.

"Ross, I'm every bit as uncomfortable as you are over withholding intel from clients. Particularly Conrad and Ashleigh," Landes countered. "But until we locate the missing twin, I don't want to further upset them. For one of these twins to have covered for the other's hare-brained scheme is not only out of character—"

"This whole damn drama is out of character!" Pocino's voice boomed over the speaker.

"And it's complicated by Callie's amnesia," Landes went on. "Bottom line: Share our confidence in the Landes Paris agents finding their daughter. But do not, under any circumstances, share our discovery about the mix-up with the twins' identity. Not yet, anyway."

Heaving a sigh, Pocino replied, "Got it, boss." He was off the line after one final *ciao*.

Jack felt out of the loop. "What can I do to help, boss?"

Landes took his time answering, and seemed to be eyeing Jack carefully. "The Taylors are friends as well as clients. So, although it's not exactly what you signed on for . . ."

Jack tried to connect the dots, but he had no clue where Landes was going with this.

Landes's expression was an odd one. "Pocino is following up on loose threads in Paris and London. Meanwhile, Jack, I have a unique assignment for you."

PART TWO

May 10–19

Chapter
51

Sunday, May 10, 3:30 p.m.—Southampton, England

Marnie's rapid heartbeat echoed in her ears as she slipped behind the uniformed security guard, willing Professor Bradford to distract him long enough for her to round the corner and travel the full length of the ramp, unseen. Dock Gate 4 was a good twenty yards behind her when she dared to steal a glance over her shoulder. No one was looking down at her from the side rails. The breath trapped inside her chest hissed through her lips at last.

She wanted to run full-out for the shuttle bus stop, leaving the *Rising Star* far behind, but knew it was a potentially disastrous move. Forcing herself to place one booted foot in front of the other, she maintained a steady clip. She couldn't risk attracting attention.

Marnie's cloud of apprehension began to dissipate at the sight of the big black arrow pointing toward the Meet and Greet parking area Bradford had described. The lot was laid out in sections with numbered rows, and she was certain she'd have no trouble locating his black Aston Martin hardtop convertible. As she spotted the empty, open-air shuttle bus pull up, the echoing in her ears slowed.

I've done it. I've done it.

Marnie felt triumphant. She could hardly wait for the reluctant professor to be clear of the ship.

Clad in a pair of dark-blue skinny jeans with a matching denim jacket, her hair tucked up into a royal blue beanie, she held nothing more than the keys to Bradford's car in her hand. Without her handbag, her tablet, or her cell phone, Marnie felt unbalanced. Everything she'd packed for the next two months was stuffed in her large suitcase, which Bradford was retrieving from the ship. She had taken it to his cabin before her stealthy departure. His own luggage had been deposited in the boot of his car following the London field trip, before he'd dashed back to the ship for hers.

Swinging one leg and then the other onto the dimpled steel floor of the shuttle bus, she looked back toward the ship. And froze.

Although the buses from the London trip should have returned more than an hour before, a late bus was entering through the Cunard Road entrance. Marnie chose the nearest seat and ducked down low in it, twisting her body toward the seat back and burying her head in the crook of her elbow. The bus passed at glacial speed.

It took a few more beats for her to begin to breathe. "Thank you," she whispered aloud, gazing skyward. The students on the passing bus were most likely in their own world, chatting, texting, or dozing on their way back from London—not checking out the lone passenger on a shuttle.

Being the only passenger on the shuttle felt weird, but Marnie guessed she'd better get used to weird.

Callie's angry words hammered in her head: self-centered, stupid. Marnie hated that Callie had been too sick to really discuss the situation. She hated not having more time to explain. Callie just had to understand: These two months with Graham Bradford were an opportunity no writer in her right mind would turn down. She would have been a fool to miss it.

Callie had said she would not cover for Marnie aboard the ship, but Marnie knew she could count on her sister. No matter how angry she was.

Marnie only prayed her parents would not flip when Callie handed them her letter. She had spent days wording and rewording her explanation: how important this opportunity was for her future, how walking in her undergraduate ceremony paled in comparison.

"Section C, row 23," the shuttle driver called out.

Marnie stood up and thanked the driver. "I'm so sorry. I don't have my wallet."

The uniformed man grinned, shaking his head. "Not a problem.

Never understand why you Yanks tip us for doing the jobs we're already paid for."

Pulling off her beanie and jumping down to the ground, Marnie pressed the button on the key fob. She heard a beep and pulled open the convertible's door, then immediately shut it. *You're in England*, she reminded herself, and walked around to the passenger door, on the left side.

She knew she'd been blessed with this opportunity, but she had more than the right-hand driver's side to get used to. She was on her own. It was up to her to learn as much as she could during the next two months—and to get along somehow with the volatile Graham Bradford.

The scent of the Aston Martin's pristine, dove-white leather seats reminded Marnie of her new boss's status, and what a bad start they'd had. She shifted her weight and uncrossed her legs, hoping he wouldn't take much longer. Was he having a problem with security? It seemed liked a lifetime since she'd slipped down the gangplank.

Initially, Bradford had been unmovable, adamant in his protests over her plan. "Subterfuge," he'd called it, refusing to accept her decision not to discuss the change of plans on a transatlantic call to her parents. Her rationalization—that it would be easier to ask for forgiveness than to ask for permission—had fallen flat.

Actually, it had caused him to explode. "If you intend to become an author worthy of a readership, you will have to grow up sometime. Get out into the world. Experience your own life," he'd bellowed. "A twenty-two-year-old woman hardly requires permission."

Their rage had volleyed back and forth for what seemed a very long time until, unable to endure another round, she had cast all caution aside. "Then you can just find someone else to type your bloody scrawls," she'd shouted before storming off. Immediately, she'd regretted throwing his own rude language back at him and wished she could take back her angry words. Allowing her temper to get the best of her wasn't smart.

Bradford expected perfection. His longtime assistant had been injured the day before the *Rising Star* departed New York, and Marnie had found a way to make herself invaluable to his writing process. But replacing Cathy Morgan on a full-time basis would be a challenge. In fact, it would be downright frightening.

And yet standing up to him had empowered Marnie. With Bradford's deadline rapidly approaching, and no one else who could decipher his writing and produce his typed pages the following day, Marnie was essential to the completion of his upcoming novel. She would no longer behave as an awestruck teenager. Kowtowing to the arrogant, cantankerous author for two whole months was something she was not willing to do.

I must gain his respect.

Sliding across the leather seat, Marnie recrossed her legs and wished again that Bradford would hurry. With all the windows rolled up and the hazy sun beating through the windshield, the interior of the car had become unbearable, but she dared not start the engine on his beloved car.

Instead, she threw open the passenger door—at exactly the wrong moment.

Chapter 52

Sunday, May 10, 4:05 p.m.—Southampton, England

"Bloody hell," Graham Bradford hollered as the passenger door of his black Aston Martin slammed into his midsection.

A look of horror unfolded on the Taylor girl's face, peeking out from the passenger seat. "Sorry, sorry, sorry."

That routine might work on others, but useless apologies didn't cut it with him. Bradford was no pushover. His ego had prevented him from agreeing to Marnie's plan right away. He had set strict ground rules. To assist her with leaving the ship, with no one other than her sister the wiser, he clarified exactly what he expected within the two months. She would type the previous night's work each morning, proofread it, and print the pages for him before noon. She would accompany him to his Paris and London commitments. She would be well paid and would receive his feedback on her own work. But most of his time, when not conducting the London workshop, would be spent on his own manuscript.

"Since my premier workshop focuses on independent work and feedback," he'd explained, "you will have time to work on your novel. And you may attend the afternoon wrap-up sessions with the four advanced writers selected for my novel cram workshop."

Sliding behind the wheel of the Aston Martin to wait for the van from the inn, he wondered again just how the next two months would play out. If this arrangement with Marnie Taylor failed, the repercussions were unthinkable.

She handed him the keys and asked if he'd had any problem leaving the ship.

"Awkward, to say the least," he replied. "I sent the security guard to fetch the suitcase you left in my cabin, but it took him far longer than anticipated. I was forced to make small talk." He scowled. "Definitely not my forté."

The Twin Oaks van pulled up a short while later, about three yards from the Aston Martin. With limited parking at the guesthouse, Bradford would have to leave his car in long-term parking until they returned from the Paris writers' conference. He punched the button on his key fob to open the boot so the Twin Oaks driver could load his luggage into the van.

Bradford climbed into the van, with Marnie following behind him. "Do you mind if I get my handbag out of the suitcase?" she asked, slipping into the seat across the aisle from his. "I feel a bit . . . undressed without it."

He sighed, second-guessing his decision all over again. "Wait until we get to the guesthouse."

He didn't have time to play games, and it ticked him off that his hand had been forced. His publishing deadline was cast in stone. If he had a single alternative, he would have abandoned her insane plan. The young woman sent mixed messages. Smart, strong-willed, capable—yet unable to stand up to her parents. And now it seemed she was unwilling to spend even ten minutes without her handbag and cell phone. It revealed a side of her he hadn't expected to find. Marnie Taylor and her unpredictable ways could end up spelling big trouble.

Her questions over the sleeping arrangements had caught him off guard too. Hadn't he made it crystal clear? Their arrangement was strictly business—nothing more. He'd given no hints of romance. Besides, even if he were so inclined, Marnie was more than twenty years younger— at an age when that kind of difference was huge. And no matter how attractive or engaging, he'd made a rule to avoid getting involved with any of his students. Aside from Hillary Spearpoint, he'd made a pact with himself not to ever get close to anyone again.

What had drawn Graham Bradford to Marnie, and caused him to take this risk, had nothing to do with romance.

Chapter
53

Sunday, May 10, 4:35 p.m.—Southampton, England

On the silent journey to the Twin Oaks Guesthouse, it took no genius to pick up on Bradford's dark mood. Bradford had given her the cold shoulder, taking out his ubiquitous pencil and yellow, legal-size notepad. As he began scrawling, Marnie was aware that he felt manipulated, so she racked her brain over how to move past it and find a way to regain his respect.

She reflected on the roller-coaster ride of highs and lows she'd experienced since stepping aboard the *Rising Star* and coming face to face with her idol. While her confidence hadn't soared, a layer of insecurity did fall away in class when Professor Bradford had shared one of her suspense-filled scenes as a good example of how to create tension. Yet the very next day, Bradford pointed out the lack of emotional conflict in another scene, and she'd tumbled back into insecurity, questioning for the gazillionth time whether she had what it took to become a successful author.

After jogging a couple of laps around the upper deck, she'd consoled herself by recalling the sixty-nine rejection letters Margaret Mitchell received before *Gone with the Wind* was picked up by a publisher. *I was accepted into the UCI graduate program, wasn't I?* Marnie thought. She had a lot to learn, but she was not totally without talent. And she was willing to give it her all.

Come hell or high water!

Marnie smiled as she recalled all the times she'd heard Uncle Mike use that expression.

She looked across the aisle at Bradford, still scrawling on his yellow pad. Occasionally he looked up and stared out the window, searching, as if he could pluck the words from thin air. Perhaps it was working. Each time his head dropped again, his pencil began moving deliberately across the page.

Marnie could barely believe she had the privilege of watching Graham Bradford work his magic right before her very eyes. Having him as her mentor was a dream come true. *I can handle his mood swings, she thought. If not . . .* Well, she had her passport and credit cards. *I won't be anyone's prisoner.*

She supposed his prickly mood shifts now and then mirrored her own. For the next couple of months, she would have to swallow her tendency toward rebellion and go with the flow. She'd make sure this remarkable time with Bradford ran as smoothly as possible. This opportunity was so much more than she might gain inside the four walls of a classroom. It was beyond any unpublished writer's wildest dreams.

A street sign announced the New Forest, and soon the van turned onto a narrow tree-lined road—Southampton Road, according to the signpost. When it pulled off to one side beneath a large tree, gravel crunching beneath the tires and pinging against the metal, Bradford tucked his yellow pad and pencil into his briefcase. Stepping out of the van, he turned and held out his hand.

Somewhat taken aback and being empty-handed other than the beanie clutched in one fist, Marnie took it.

"I'd like to get settled as soon as possible," he said curtly, guiding her from the van. "Our luggage will be brought to our rooms."

Marnie struggled to keep up with the long strides of the man who held the keys to her future. Beyond the van was a paved walking path that led to a large Tudor-style home. The dormer windows reminded her of the window seat in her very own room in Greenwich, which had seemed like an impossible dream when she was first reunited with her biological family. She closed her eyes now, waving away memories of herself as that eight-year-old girl.

Marnie's boots crunched through the loose gravel toward the impressive, hundred-year-old guesthouse. The moment Bradford stepped onto the single flat step, the front door flew open. A plump woman in a blue, puffy-sleeved dress and a white apron grinned. "Welcome, Professor. It's lovely to see you." Then she glanced at Marnie, her brow crinkling into a map of fine lines.

"Hello, Mary. Pleased to be here. I'm afraid Cathy has taken a tumble. Splintered bones in her upper arm and right shoulder," Bradford explained. "Marnie will be filling in." His smiled broadened as he turned to Marnie. "Just wait until you taste her apple crumble."

Mary blushed, mottled red skin glowing from her neckline to her pleasant, round cheeks. "I'll show you to your rooms then, will I? Dinner will be served at seven o'clock. Do you plan to join us?"

Bradford shook his head. "On a tight schedule. If you don't mind, I'll eat in my room."

Marnie tried not to show her disappointment. Well aware this was no vacation for Bradford, she'd nevertheless hoped to explore the area beyond the cruise terminal this evening. To think that Sir Arthur Conan Doyle was buried so nearby, in the cemetery of the All Saints Church in Minstead. What a great story visiting it would be to share with other Sherlock Holmes fans . . .

But she kept her mouth shut about Doyle's grave. Her goal was to be viewed as an asset—not a troublesome means to an end. "If it's alright, I'd like to work tonight as well," Marnie said quickly. She had no desire to sit down to supper with strangers, nor to go out on her own. "May I also eat in my room?"

"Are you sure?" Bradford asked, a scowl on his handsome face.

She nodded, hoping her voice would not betray her disappointment. "I'd like to look over my last chapter."

"Understood," he said as they followed Mary to their rooms. "Don't stay up too late. And set your suitcase outside your door before five a.m."

Her room was a wonderful surprise. The guesthouse had obviously gone through many renovations in its century or more of existence, but not at the expense of a four-poster bed and a quaint Victorian fireplace. A vase of fresh flowers had been placed on the mantle, and the armoire and dressing table were straight out of Cathy's boudoir in *Wuthering Heights*. As a nod to modernity, a flat-screen television sat on the dresser.

First things first, thought Marnie, unzipping and kicking off her boots. Her suitcase sat on a padded bench at the end of her bed. She opened it to retrieve her Juicy Couture handbag and set out her clothes for the next day. She would also need her tablet, so she could get to work on reviewing her novel's final chapter. Picking up her handbag, however, she noticed it was lighter than usual.

Zipping open the oversized bag felt strange too, and Marnie realized that zipping it closed was something she seldom did. Dismissing her concerns, she searched for her tablet, carefully at first, then frantically, pulling out her laptop, bras, panties, jeans, tops.

Her tablet simply was not there.

Marnie sank down onto the bed. Squeezing her eyes tight, she tried to think. It all came rushing back.

Callie had borrowed her Juicy Couture handbag for the trip to London, and Marnie had transferred all her stuff into Callie's Michael Kors bag. With Callie sick, and Marnie distracted by evading the ship's security, they had never switched their stuff back.

So Marnie had snuck her Juicy bag off the ship in her suitcase—with all of Callie's stuff in it.

Chapter

54

Sunday, May 10, 5:45 p.m.—Southampton, England

A blade of icy apprehension pierced Marnie's abdomen. *How could I have been so stupid?*

She dumped the bag on the bed and rummaged through the contents. Lip gloss, blusher, and all sorts of things spilled onto the bed. A wallet. A passport. Callie's—not mine.

The sudden implication hit her like a sack of dried cement. Her passport was missing. The one she'd need to show tomorrow for the flight to Paris.

A dark mist of her own making enveloped her. It only got worse when the image of Callie's gold iPhone, plugged into the outlet beside the medicine cabinet in their cabin, flashed in her mind's eye. She didn't have her phone. She didn't even have Callie's phone. She had no phone at all.

Could she persuade Bradford to return to the ship? No. It was after five p.m. The *Rising Star* had already departed. It was too late.

Uncertainty flooded her. How could she share this catastrophic mess with Bradford? How could she not? Bradford was expecting to leave for the airport at 5:30 a.m. Their flight was scheduled to depart at 6:45 a.m. She had only a few hours to figure it out.

At least I have my laptop, Marnie confirmed, extracting the carrying case from her suitcase and dumping it onto her bed. Looking for an outlet, she remembered she would need her converter for the British socket.

Her mind spun. She had to contact Callie as soon as possible—before the *Rising Star* was too far out to sea. Would Callie, sick as she was, even open her computer today? *Not likely, Marnie thought, but at least it will land in her mailbox while we both have an Internet connection.*

In the cabin that afternoon, when Marnie had gone to retrieve her packed suitcase, Callie was unable to even sit up in bed without feeling nauseous. Marnie had tried to explain her reasoning, but the angry words that had tumbled back and forth between them had rattled her. She hadn't made a dent in Callie's self-righteous armor. Now was her chance to explain without interruption.

The computer sprang to life, and Marnie quickly signed on. On the silver tray, beside the tea paraphernalia, was a folded placard with the password for the guesthouse's free Wi-Fi—an unexpected perk for which she was desperately grateful. She began to type:

Dear Callie,

Hope you're feeling better. You were so sick earlier today, and the timing could not have been worse for me to explain my plans. I was frustrated over not getting the chance to talk in London, and I said a lot of things I didn't mean.

Please understand why I couldn't let this opportunity slip through my fingers. If you had this kind of one-in-a-lifetime chance in the dance world, you wouldn't think twice about grabbing it.

You were right about why I didn't tell Mom and Dad up front. No, I don't need their permission. But I didn't want to be that "ungrateful brat" you and Jules sometimes say I am. Plus, Mom and Dad are cool. They're totally going to understand. They wouldn't prevent me from taking my shot. It was just too awkward to discuss my plan and defend it over the phone. Dad would probably have wanted Pocino to check out Bradford, and there was no time for that.

I explained everything to them in the letter I gave you. I know they won't be happy about my missing the graduation ceremony. But after sitting through yours, I bet they'll be glad they don't have to sit through another one a couple of weeks later. Jules sure will.

Please, please, please, Callie, when you give my letter to Mom and Dad, don't be a black cloud. I didn't tell them about Bradford being such a chameleon, and I'd rather you didn't either. I'm dealing with his frustrating personality because to me, it's worth it. The International Writers' Conference begins tomorrow in Paris, and Bradford has opened the door for me to attend—an unbelievable opportunity.

Marnie felt better after putting her explanation down on the page for her sister. Now for the hard part.

I need to tell you about a major screw-up. When you borrowed my Juicy handbag for the London field trip, I switched everything to your Michael Kors bag. But then I left it behind in our cabin accidentally. So the only thing I took to London was my overnight bag. Luckily, since we were with the group, I didn't need my passport or credit cards, and I had some cash in my jeans pocket.

When I got back today and dashed into our cabin before the ship left Southampton, I forgot all about the exchange. I grabbed my Juicy bag, but all your stuff is in it. Passport. Wallet. Credit cards. Whatever. Plus, I have no phone and no tablet. You have it all with the rest of my stuff, in your Michael Kors bag.

The biggest problem is the passport. I can probably get away with yours—I hope. And go ahead and use my credit card, since I'll have to use yours. We'll settle it when I get home at the end of July.

Tell Mom and Dad I love them. I'll be back in plenty of time for our celebration in August, and to begin my master's degree program after that.

Love you. And I'm counting on you,
Marnie

Chapter

55

Monday, May 11, 5:25 a.m.—Southampton, England

Dawn had found Marnie lying in bed, staring at the ceiling, still not sure how to break the news of her colossal brain freeze. As much as she wanted to avoid setting Professor Bradford off, she had no choice. They were heading for the airport, and the only identification in her possession now identified her as Callie Taylor.

How could she keep Bradford from viewing her as more trouble than she was worth? Throughout the night, she'd run through one scenario after another, but no magical words leaped to mind. With each tick of the clock, her goal of gaining his respect was moving farther out of reach.

Slipping the straps of her handbag and computer case over her shoulder, she stepped outside the door to her room. Her suitcase had already been picked up and taken to the van. The click of Bradford's door down the corridor sent a nervous flow of waves through her bloodstream. She hadn't yet worked up the courage to tell him.

Marnie had felt better after sending the email to Callie, but it wouldn't do much good for the next few days at least. If Callie was as sick as the day before, there was no telling when she might open it. But at least she'd understand why Marnie had no choice but to use her credit cards. With Bradford's prohibition against using the Internet, she'd have to find an Internet café to pick up Callie's response and figure out what to do.

She joined the professor in the lobby, where he was bidding the proprietor goodbye. After she and Bradford had settled into the airport taxi, she knew it was time to tell him about the passport mix-up.

"Professor Bradford," she began, doing her best to stay the quiver in her voice.

"Graham," he reminded her. "I am, after all, an author ninety percent of the time. Students need only address me as 'Professor' during the master classes."

"Thank you, Graham. I won't forget," she said, though it still felt strange to call him by his first name. She had avoided addressing Ashleigh as "Mom" whenever she could for the first couple of years after being reunited with her birth family.

Marnie tried again to ease into her confession. "Did you have a productive night?"

"I did indeed. After you type last night's work, I'll go over the unexpected twist Derek threw my way."

"I'd love that." This wasn't the first time Bradford had referred to Detective Derek Duncan as having a life of his own. Having read his popular thriller series and having worked through so much with her own fictional characters, Marnie could relate. She loved typing Bradford's manuscript for the latest Derek Duncan thriller for that very reason. Reading the first draft and discussing his thought processes—what revisions were needed, and why—were golden nuggets for Marnie to mine.

At this moment, however, she could focus on nothing of the sort. All she could think of was how irresponsible he would think her to be. But she must inform him the name on the passport in her handbag was not hers.

"How did your writing go last night, Marnie?"

"Not very well," she admitted.

Before she could say more, Bradford continued, "We all have periods when the task seems daunting. Never get discouraged. Remember, even badly written prose is better than a blank page."

Marnie had taken that advice to heart throughout his master class aboard the *Rising Star*. As Bradford continually pointed out, the written word can always be improved or edited. If it was as bad as she feared, it could be thrown out. The time she spent working on various ideas or phrases was never wasted.

"Just get your story out," he said now. "Lay aside your doubts and step out of your own way."

Marnie swallowed hard. *Time to step out of my own way.* "I didn't spend much time writing that new chapter for my novel last night because when I unpacked, I discovered something."

"Yes?"

"I don't have my ID."

Bradford's face stiffened. "Please tell me you are not without a passport."

Feeling the heat rise from her collarbone, Marnie said, "Unfortunately, I left all of my own identification—"

"*Bloody hell!* I don't have time for this." Next to her on the seat of the taxi, he breathed in deeply. His eyes bored into her. "Bloody hell," he repeated. "Without your ID, you can't even board the plane. I'll have to take you to the American embassy." He shook his head angrily.

"But Profes—Graham," she protested, "I *have* a passport—"

A look of utter frustration colored his face, playing across his chiseled features. "Marnie, you just told me you left without it."

She wanted to shout but willed herself to remain calm. "My sister and I switched handbags for our trip into London. All my things are in Callie's handbag, and hers are in mine."

"Let me get this straight. You took your sister's handbag by mistake?"

Not exactly. "I have my own handbag, but it's filled with Callie's stuff . . ." She didn't bother to finish. The more she said, the more he'd think her a ditz. "The good news is, I don't have to go to the embassy for a passport. I can use Callie's."

Bradford stared at her, shaking his head once more. "What next?" He was quiet for a moment. When he spoke again, he appeared unhappy but resigned. "Marnie, at the conference this weekend, I expect you to be able to take care of yourself—without any more unexpected drama."

"I promise. I'm sorry about this," she said. "I'm thrilled about attending the conference and doing some sightseeing in Paris. Like you always say, I need to be open and take in what life has to offer."

She just hoped that in Paris, life wasn't planning to offer any more drama.

At the first-class check-in counter, Graham rested his hand on Marnie's elbow, hoping to calm his young charge. She swayed from one foot to the other, her sister's passport tightly clutched in her hand as if it might take flight.

"Relax," he whispered in her ear, stretching out his hand to take the passport.

Looking up to meet his eyes, Marnie appeared very young and uncharacteristically unsure of herself.

An attractive blond in an Air France uniform took the two passports and tickets from Bradford's hand, her slightly accented voice trembling slightly. "You're *the* Graham Bradford, aren't you?"

Graham gave her as warm a smile as he could manage. "What a pleasant surprise. Unlike movie stars, we authors are seldom recognized."

The ticket agent beamed. "I'm a big fan. In fact, when I was told you would be on board one of our flights today, I brought my copy of *No Second Chances*," she confessed, reaching for the book and placing it on the counter. "Do you think you might sign it for me?"

"With pleasure," he replied. "But first I need to make a name change on one of my tickets. My assistant was injured and is unable to make this Paris trip. Ms. Taylor will be taking her place."

"Certainly, sir." The agent checked his passport briefly, then studied the photo on the other passport. She flipped to a later page. "How long will you be in France?"

"We'll be returning Sunday," Graham said, feeling his pulse quicken. "Is there a problem?"

Chapter
56

Monday, May 11, 6:05 a.m.—Southampton Airport, England

Marnie's back stiffened. Her mouth went dry. *It's not going to work.*

But the Air France ticket agent was still smiling at Bradford. "No problem. I just noticed the expiration date on Ms. Taylor's passport." She turned to Marnie. "If you're not planning to return home before the first of June, you must be sure to renew your passport." She handed the passports back to Graham. Inside each booklet was a boarding pass.

"Merci," he said, and turned away from the counter.

Marnie let out her breath, amazed that the woman had been oblivious to her distress.

Bradford chuckled. "Well, we dodged that bullet, as your American cowboys might have said. "I made sure to sign an especially warm note in her copy of *No Second Chances*."

Marnie explained in a whisper that Callie's passport was an old one. "Mine is the same. We must have been thirteen. I never noticed that it expires at the end of this month."

Still holding her twin's passport, Bradford flipped it open. "You look so much . . . I mean, your sister looks a bit younger, but I wouldn't guess ten years younger." His voice sounded sad.

Marnie managed a smile. "We were just out of middle school. At that age it was important to look older and sophisticated—*especially* for our photos."

Having reached Gate 5, they took seats close to the boarding kiosk. The seating area was not crowded, so Marnie placed her computer and handbag in the seat next to her and twisted to face Bradford. Although she still felt uncomfortable using his first name, now was not the time to be shy.

"Graham, I'm sorry. It never occurred to me the passport was about to expire."

He seemed to have had one of his famous changes of attitude. "Don't worry about it. You can renew upon our return to London. The student complex in Sloane Square is within walking distance of the American embassy."

"That's not the problem." He had to understand why she must get her own passport. "I won't be able to renew Callie's passport."

"Why not? She'd probably appreciate . . ." He stopped midsentence as though the realization had hit him.

"If they handle passports the same in England as in the U.S., they'll—"

"Need your fingerprints," he said, answering his own question.

"Our fingerprints are the only thing about us that are not identical." She gave a tentative grin. "Well, and our personalities, of course."

Bradford returned her smile. "Let's not worry about that now. We'll cross that ocean when we come to it."

About to protest, Marnie thought better of it. *When is all this deception going to end?* she thought. The ocean she had to cross was creeping closer each day.

7:15 a.m.—En route to Paris

Soon after takeoff, to Marnie's delight, the professor stretched out his long legs, slipped a crescent-shaped pillow behind his neck, and drifted off to sleep. Judging by the number of yellow notepad sheets he had handed her this morning, he'd probably had as little sleep as she had.

She slipped her laptop from the carrying case and set it on the tray. The more she input now, the more time she'd have for herself in Paris—in between the sessions she wanted to attend at the elite writers' conference there.

She closed her eyes for a nanosecond, breathing in the fragrance of the Armani aftershave Bradford preferred, and then got to work. Setting aside all thoughts of what lay ahead, she concentrated on figuring out each word scrawled on the page and, bit by bit, typing the penciled draft of chapter fifty-seven. She had not been privy to the first forty chapters of this new Detective Duncan story—Bradford's assistant had typed them up before he came aboard the *Rising Star* at the Brooklyn Terminal back in February—but throughout the semester she had come to know his style and preferences.

By the time the flight attendant requested, in both English and French, that all electronic devices be turned off for landing, Marnie had input nearly half of Bradford's latest pages into a new MS Word document. She felt good about the morning's work. She had turned her undivided attention to Bradford's novel, and at last she would prove herself an asset.

On top of that, she had the better part of a week to explore on her own and breathe in the beauty of Gay Paree.

Chapter 57

Tuesday, May 12, 8:15 a.m.—Paris, France

As the typed pages of Bradford's manuscript spewed from the printer, Marnie flipped open her laptop and took a moment to scan her email. Nothing from Callie had surfaced in her mailbox. Only unwelcome spam.

In the wee hours of the morning, she had been wide awake when Bradford had slipped the folder of yellow sheets under her hotel room door. She had finished the last page about an hour ago, gotten into the shower, dressed, and made her way to the hotel's business center.

Marnie spent her first day in Paris on the fashionable Avenue Champs-Elysées, acclimating herself to her surroundings. "Welcome to your home for the next few days," Bradford said when the limo door opened, and he stepped out onto the sidewalk, gesturing toward an elegant façade. "Hotel La Maison Champs-Élysées. You should be comfortable here. The shopping is, as you Yanks like to say, 'to die for.'" Marnie had been beyond excited. The conference location was perfect—exactly how she'd imagined it.

While the driver unloaded their luggage from the boot, Bradford explained that the hotel was in the heart of the Triangle d'Or—the epicenter of the city. "Remember, you must spend a considerable amount of time on your own novel," he'd warned. "No less than you would have done aboard ship."

Marnie smiled, nodding her agreement. "Understood."

Stepping past a lush topiary planter, she turned her head side to side, taking in the two sets of double doors that seemed to provide entrance into two separate hotels. Stepping into the foyer, she scanned the grand hotel's broad, winding staircase and white marble floors accented with small black diamond shapes. "This is fabulous!" she exclaimed.

Bradford gave her an indulgent smile. "La Maison Champs-Élysées has a rich past. As you can see, it was rebuilt from a set of town houses from the Haussmann period."

Though of modest size, the boutique hotel offered every possible amenity, including Internet in each room. But using it meant the charge would turn up on the hotel bill.

Although avoiding the Internet sometimes seemed impossible, it was a promise she'd made to Bradford.

But the need became more urgent with each tick of the clock. *Come on, Callie. This is no time for games.* A wave of panic washed over her. Why hadn't her sister replied to her email? Was she still too sick to fire up her computer? That thought brought more stress. Though Callie could do nothing about returning her passport while still at sea, being unable even to contact her sister set Marnie's nerves on edge.

When Marnie's rational mind failed to silence her nerves, she slammed down the lid of her laptop and jammed it back into the carrying case. Then she heaved a massive sigh and did her best to let go of her frustrations. Not having her own passport was crazy-making. But she wasn't going to let it ruin the entire conference.

9:25 a.m.

At the Terrace Restaurant of the Hotel La Maison Champs-Élysées, Marnie smiled tentatively at the two writers who slid into their chairs at the table Bradford had chosen, nodding as he made the introductions.

The young woman had alabaster skin and pale blue eyes in stark contrast to her long black hair. Her ensemble shouted goth: tight jeans, studded collar and bracelet, black punk T-shirt decorated with a weird purple design. Marnie recalled that Charlize was the feminine version of the name Charles, which meant "free."

This English bird sure lives up to her name.

"Lovely to meet you," Charlize said, giving her a wink.

Marnie wasn't sure how to take it. Mischievous, or just friendly? While not drawn to the girl's stark look, Marnie loved the twinkle in her eyes and had a feeling she and Charlize would become close friends in the next couple of months.

The tall, rail-thin young man stretched out his hand. "Alexandre," he said in a heavy French accent. "Pleased to meet you." His light-brown hair was pulled back into a ponytail, and he was clad in a dark blue sweatshirt with faded gold letters across the front, spelling NOTRE DAME.

Marnie felt relieved. While neither the serious young man nor the quirky girl were what she had expected, at least she wouldn't be totally on her own for the next few days in Paris. She hoped they would help her not only to make the most out of the conference and Paris, but also the London workshop—and to learn more about Bradford himself.

Since leaving Southampton, Marnie had been a little less sure she'd made the right decision. To grab hold of this opportunity, she had failed to be up-front with her parents. And Bradford's attitude and behavior had changed many times since they'd departed the *Rising Star*. An unexpected flutter in her stomach reminded her how little she knew about what to expect over the next two months.

But now, mesmerized by this awesome group of writers, Marnie listened to every word the professor and his students exchanged. It was reassuring to observe how truly interested Bradford was in their novels. He seemed to know so much about their individual stories, characters, and plots. His insights into their entire process were thrilling.

Will he become that invested in my work during the summer workshop?

If so, she would have no doubt she'd made the right choice.

Chapter 58

Tuesday, May 12, 11:45 a.m.—Paris, France

Marnie tore down the corridor on the heels of her new friends. The deafening roar that drifted down the marble-floored hallway left no doubt they were headed in the direction of the conference.

At a long table beside the closed double doors to the conference area sat four casually dressed young women. In front of them were four alphabetically labeled boxes. Charlize headed to the box labeled with the letters A–F. Before the staffer could ask, she said, with a broad grin, "Just plain Charlize. With a C." She winked again at Marnie. "No need for extra baggage."

While her new colleagues checked in, Marnie looked around. Filling the reception area were people clumped in groups of all sizes, all engaged in animated conversation. There were also many loners, some seemingly in a hurry while others meandered from table to table. Though it felt much like writers' conferences she'd attended in the U.S., there was a subtle difference—one she couldn't put her finger on.

The girl behind the box labeled S–Z looked up as Marnie approached and gave her name. "You've sure traveled a long way."

Marnie raised a brow.

The girl broke into a broad smile. "Accent's a dead giveaway."

"Accent?" *But I don't have an accent*, Marnie wanted to say.

The girl laughed and handed her a registration packet. "Suppose you think I'm the one with the accent?"

She was right, of course. "Guess it's all a matter of what you're used to," Marnie replied, though she had no idea what an American accent sounded like. To her, it was just the normal way of speaking.

"Enjoy the conference." The girl pointed to the bulletin board. "Any changes in the schedule will be listed there. Be sure to check each morning and after lunch."

Drifting away from the table, Marnie pulled out the schedule and scanned the workshop sessions. One caught her eye: "Character Therapy—and You Are the Shrink." She continued to run an eye down the full schedule, stopping again at "Your First Five Pages." Turning to Charlize, she pointed to another: "Pitch Witches."

"How are you at marketing? You pitch your novel, and they tear it to pieces." The budding novelist chuckled. "Honestly, I stick to the craft sessions. No matter how great the pitch is, a bum novel isn't going to sell."

"Right you are," Marnie said, mimicking Bradford's British lingo.

Charlize grinned. "So, have you finished your novel?"

Marnie shook her head. It was true—she hadn't finished the thriller. And her middle school novel was not worth mentioning. "What do you know about Jean-Christophe Rufin?" she asked, pointing to where he was listed as the opening speaker.

"Not a whole lot, other than he's a best-selling French author with an impressive list of awards."

"He's a lot more than that," Alexandre cut in. "Doctor, diplomat, historian, globetrotter extraordinaire. Rufin has won the Prix Goncourt—several times." His classy French pronunciation made the awards sound even more impressive.

As they wound their way through the crowd toward the open double doors, Marnie clutched her schedule. The large room was set up theater style. Charlize and Alexandre slipped into a row near the back of the room. Marnie slid in beside them. "Will the authors be speaking in French?"

Shaking her head, Charlize pointed to the monitors on either side of the podium. "I doubt it. But there are translator screens."

"Don't worry, *mon chou*," Alexandre added. "English will be used by many of the main speakers. Can't guarantee that for every workshop, but there will be translator boards in each of the breakout rooms."

"Mon chou?" Marnie asked.

Alexandre shrugged. "Just a friendly term."

Charlize grinned. "It means 'my cabbage.'"

"Cabbage?" *Darn, I sound like an echo.* "The only French endearment I recall from my one semester of French is *ma chérie*."

Alexandre snickered. "Hollywood is a little too fond of that one."

A wash of unease spread through Marnie's bloodstream. She was an outsider. One with a lot of questions.

Before Marnie could ask any more, a sudden hush rippled through the room. But the Frenchman was nowhere in sight.

An old woman clad in a caftan, with ramrod posture, stepped to the podium. Her white hair hung to her waist in a single braid.

"Hillary Spearpoint," whispered Charlize.

The petite woman did not speak for several long seconds. Finally, she introduced herself. "Unfortunately, Monsieur Rufin is unable to be with us at the moment." At the sound of restless bodies shifting, Spearpoint held up her hand. "Now, don't fret. His presentation has been rescheduled for a later time."

Marnie hoped she would be able to catch it.

"A best-selling English author has agreed to fill in. He will be here momentarily. You may have heard of him." The woman seemed amused with her own joke. "Goes by the name of Graham Bradford."

Bet he's thrilled, Marnie thought.

She leaned toward Charlize and cupped her hand at the side of her mouth. "Is she an author?"

"She's a jewel," Charlize whispered back. "Don't let her appearance throw you. She's a conference workshop leader. Sort of like a house mother at Sloane Hall."

"Bradford's London workshop?"

Charlize nodded, making her straight black bangs dance up and down.

"How old is she?" Marnie couldn't resist asking.

Alexandre guffawed. "Not sure. But her first book was published when she was ninety, and that was three or four years ago. She claims these are her most productive years."

"So, she works for Bradford?"

"Not exactly," he replied. "We haven't quite figured out how they're connected, but she is every bit as in charge as Bradford. They're on equal footing for the workshop."

"It's Bradford's status that makes it so hard to win a coveted slot," Charlize added. "But she's incredible. Makes sure we keep on track with our writing. She taught a lit class at Oxford when I was an undergrad."

Alexandre nodded. "At last year's International Writers' Conference, I sat in on Hillary's workshops on voice."

"Hillary?" Marnie asked.

Charlize shrugged her narrow shoulders. "At the workshop it's just Graham and Hillary."

As if he'd been summoned, Bradford came gliding onto the stage, his rapid footfalls heavy enough to silence the room.

CHAPTER

59

Tuesday, May 12, 12:10 p.m.—Paris, France

Marnie sunk down in her chair, wishing she could disappear. She knew Bradford would not approve of them taking seats in the back. On board the *Rising Star*, she and Solange had always tried to sit as close to him as possible, as if his writing brilliance would rub off on them.

Don't look this way, she prayed. At the front of the room, Bradford had not gone directly to the lectern, but instead stopped to talk with the white-haired woman.

"Had we known Graham would be taking over," Marnie said, "we might have moved up front."

Charlize elbowed her. "Don't sweat the small stuff. It'll drive you bonkers."

Marnie knew she was right, but she couldn't help feeling out of her league. She was lucky to work with Bradford on a one-on-one basis, even if it was mainly centered on his novel, not hers. Her gaze swept to Charlize, then to Alexandre and back again.

How I got here is a total fluke.

Locking her eyes on Charlize, she confessed, "I just don't want to mess up."

Charlize scrunched up her nose and looked at the ceiling. "Bradford's bark is worse than his bite. He's pretty cool most of the time."

"But why do you call him a chameleon?"

"That label is reserved for his cantankerous days." Alexandre leaned over, his smile broadening. "But in his domain, the one thing that makes him really hit the roof is catching anyone sneaking off to use the Internet."

"And how does working with no Internet work for you two?" Marnie wondered if they thought it was as archaic as she did.

"Takes time, but you get used to it," Alexandre said without a great deal of conviction.

"Rubbish," Charlize said. "I nearly lost my blooming mind without it. You can always sneak off to the Internet café in Sloane Square."

"Is that what you do?" Marnie asked.

"Not worth it," Charlize and Alexandre said in unison.

Charlize wound her thick black hair around her finger. "To be honest, I've become a believer. That's why I'm back this year. Don't have the self-discipline at home."

Bradford's dislike of modern technology had come as a surprise to Marnie, who still couldn't believe he wrote his manuscripts in pencil. "But how about research? Going online is such a time saver."

Her companions laughed.

"That was our argument," Alexandre said.

"The Web is quicker than searching in the library, but it provides a barrelful of temptations, distractions, and misinformation." Charlize heaved a sigh. "You get the point."

Marnie shifted her attention from her companions to the front of the room as Bradford stepped up to the microphone.

Mesmerized once more by her mentor, she listened intently to every word.

When the session came to an end, the three went straight to Hillary Spearpoint's workshop. Afterward, Alexandre and Charlize introduced Marnie to the elderly writer. As promised, though under five feet tall, the woman was a dynamo. And her explanation of that *elusive quality of a writer's voice* was one Marnie could relate to. Although she was aware of the importance of *voice*, she'd found it impossible to pin down. It had encouraged her to hear Hillary say, "You can't define voice. You just know it when you hear it." It was not difficult to understand why Bradford had teamed up with her.

It might not be easy, but the old woman was someone whose respect Marnie must gain.

Chapter 60

Tuesday, May 12, 9:15 p.m.—Paris, France

Standing in front of Café George V, where they'd enjoyed a light dinner, Charlize turned to Marnie. "We're meeting some of Alexandre's mates on the Left Bank for a pint of beer. Care to come along?"

"Thanks," Marnie said, "but I'm absolutely lost without my tablet. I need to get one before the conference sessions tomorrow. Plus, I need a new cell phone." She turned to Alexandre. "Where would you suggest?"

Alexandre pointed up the street. "The ACI computer store is only a few blocks further up, on this side of the street."

Marnie did her best to smile, though she did not relish the idea of being on her own in an unknown city. "*Merci, mes amis,*" she said, practicing the new idioms she'd picked up. "*A bientôt.*"

She watched Charlize and Alexandre disappear down the stairway to the Metro, seeming so comfortable with one another. Charlize had just laughed when she'd asked whether theirs was a romantic relationship, saying, "We're as different as chalk and cheese."

A few minutes later, Marnie walked through the doors of the computer store. A man with thick salt-and-pepper hair, clad in a blue shirt with the letters ACI on the pocket, approached her. "*Bonjour, mademoiselle.*"

Marnie paused a moment to take in the layout of the store, a miniature of any Best Buy, sans the TVs and major appliances. The roomy aisles and identifiable displays were just like the ones at home. The text beside all items was written in French, English, and several other languages. Unlike at Best Buy, though, there were few customers in the store.

"How may I direct you?" the gentleman asked.

His words were comforting, although she wondered how, without hearing a word, he had identified her as English-speaking. Brushing that question aside, she said, "I'm looking for a tablet and a mobile phone. Do you have the Galaxy Pro 7?"

"Of course. We carry most brands you might be familiar with." He gestured to a display of mobile phones in the next aisle. "If you'll follow me, *mademoiselle?*"

As Marnie looked through the array of Android phones, she asked if it were possible to have her same U.S. number, but was told it was not. The salesman recommended a refurbished BlackBerry Torch. "Since you will be in Europe for such a short time," he explained, "I can have this set up for you as a prepaid phone with two hundred minutes, for about one hundred euros."

It wasn't what she'd had in mind, but he was right. The prices under each item were printed in euros, pounds, and U.S. dollars. Her Galaxy phone—the one she had left in Callie's handbag—had cost about five hundred U.S. dollars, and it was only three months old. She didn't see the need to purchase a new phone that she would only be using for a short while.

Reluctantly, she said, "Okay, but while you are setting that up, would you point me in the direction of the tablets?"

Chapter 61

Friday, May 15, 10:55 a.m.—Paris, France

Bradford stormed out of the TV studio, fuming over how things had turned out on the segment for *Bonjour Paris*. Not only had the morning been a colossal waste of precious time, it had been downright humiliating.

The American author James Patterson had bowed out at the last minute due to the flu. With only French novelist Marc Levy joining Bradford on the set, the interview had lacked the anticipated debate. Whereas Patterson wrote a fifty-page outline before committing the words of his riveting stories to paper, Bradford and Levy were intuitive writers who allowed their characters to take the lead. With similar philosophies and work habits, he'd failed to generate sparks for the viewers.

On top of that, the host spoke so rapidly that Bradford had to rely on the translation monitors. Levy had been the first to respond to nearly every question, leaving Bradford little opportunity to disagree or add anything of significance. While he was no novice to TV interviews, he'd found himself agreeing with or repeating everything rather than articulating a single original idea.

What in bloody hell had Cathy been thinking? She had booked him for this blooming French TV interview tight up against his speaking engagement on the final day of the International Writers' Conference. No wonder it had been a disaster from beginning to end.

Bradford hailed a taxi that took him to Café Paris, where he paid the driver and alighted from the rear seat. The café was busy, but he spotted a handful of empty tables.

Do I have time . . . ? *Yes,* he decided, and risked a side trip to the kiosk on the corner. After being out of the loop for the past few days, he wanted a quick update on the news of the world.

The storage bins for newspapers in English were empty. Catching sight of the front page of all three French newspapers, however, his heart skipped a beat. He hurried to drop several coins into the slot for *Le Monde.*

The bold headline read: CATASTROPHE EN MER.

Lifting the Lucite door, he yanked out a copy, wondering, *What sort of disaster at sea?* Under the headline were photos of the *Rising Star* and clusters of passengers, young and old, huddled under blankets in a muster station. Bradford half expected to spot Marnie's twin among the hundreds of students.

Bloody hell.

As his eyes skimmed the page, he made an instant mental calculation. Their Southampton departure had occurred five days earlier, on Sunday. The ship must have been midway across the Atlantic. The article included a drawing with the caption *Vague scélérate,* depicting a gigantic wave that rose high above the ship. Monstrous wave indeed!

Translating the French to English in his mind as quickly as possible, Bradford read more of the cover story. His pounding heart sank. Damn it all to *hell.* Relief swept over him as he read there'd been no need for a rescue at sea. The ship was continuing the journey under its own power. Marnie's twin was not in danger.

His next thoughts led to an internal debate: Should he, and could he, withhold this news from his young assistant? His conscience demanded he give her the news—before she found out on her own.

But Marnie's obligation is to herself and me, he argued. He needed her help to complete the novel on time. Furthermore, Marnie had sacrificed a great deal for this opportunity. *At this point, there's nothing she can do for her sister. Why should she give up her dream?*

Cathy's full recovery was still months away. His latest thriller was being fast-tracked to meet the October 5 release date. The prerelease publicity was in motion. Booksellers in England and abroad were anticipating advance copies in September. And before handing his manuscript over to his trusted editors, he needed this time to finish self-editing his most recent draft.

Plus, there was something about this young writer . . .

In the next heartbeat, Bradford made his decision. There was no need to rock the boat. There was only one way forward: Marnie simply *could not* abandon their agreement and fly back to America.

Bradford turned away from the kiosk and headed back toward Café Paris, still perusing the French newspaper.

Now there was the problem of how to keep her from seeing the news and overreacting. The disaster on the *Rising Star* had occurred just last night. The media would be covering the story for the next day or two. And though the frenzy would eventually fade from the front pages, there were bound to be segments on every radio and TV station for up to a week. The BBC and other media outlets would be filled with follow-up stories on the rogue wave.

Impossible to keep the news from Marnie, he thought. *Unless . . .*

If he could keep Marnie out of earshot of the devastating news until Sunday, they would be back in Southampton and then she could decide what to do. Her twin sister would soon be reunited with their parents, and they would have Marnie's letter in hand. Marnie would be more able to make a rational decision about whether or not to go home.

His mind reeling, Bradford tucked the newspaper under his arm. He selected a table as far from the newsstand as possible, taking care to choose a chair facing forward so Marnie would be sure to spot him.

In France, Marnie would not tune into the TV. Accounts of the disaster were unlikely to remain front-page news in the ensuing days. By Sunday, the coverage in England would also have died down. He could not keep Marnie in the dark indefinitely. The gigantic wave was certain to be the number one topic of conversation among the other students at Sloane Hall. He had to buy as much time as possible.

Searching for justification, he read on. What he found ratcheted his guilt down a notch. The damaged ship was rerouted to Charleston,

South Carolina, but was not due to arrive until noon on Sunday. Marnie's parents would not know Marnie was not on board the *Rising Star* for at least a couple of days.

Once Marnie's sister was safely home, Marnie would not feel obligated to fly home, even if her parents attempted to pressure her. *No, her obligation is to her future, and to me.* It was an obligation she had fought for—and had willingly taken on.

At the sight of Marnie stepping out of a taxi in front of the café, a folder full of his novel's pages in her hand, Bradford refolded the newspaper, making sure to conceal the sensational cover story.

Chapter
62

Friday, May 15, 11:25 a.m.—Paris, France

Marnie didn't have to search for Bradford at Café Paris. He sat in plain view, at a table under a bright yellow umbrella on the outer rim of the restaurant's patio. As she stepped from the taxi, he gave a quick wave and a dazzling smile.

"*Bonjour*," she said as she neared the table. "I tried to tune in to your interview. At first, I got nothing but static."

Bradford's posture stiffened. "You didn't miss much."

Privately noting his rare show of humility, she pulled out the seat directly across from him. "I finally caught the last few minutes. You looked terrific, but I couldn't keep up with the translations."

A waiter appeared, handed her a menu, and set an espresso in front of Bradford.

Marnie placed the manuscript folder on the table and scanned the menu. When the waiter reappeared, she caught his eye. "*Pain perdu et espresso français, s'il vous plaît*," she said, doing her best with the accent.

Bradford arched a thick brow, gave his order in perfect French, and then paid her a compliment. "It appears you've picked up some passable French."

She thanked him and said, "Alexandre has been a big help. But when there's no English menu, I'm sticking to French toast." She reached for the folder and, in the next instant, felt the warmth of Bradford's hand covering hers. Her head jerked up, and the front cover of the manuscript folder fell closed.

"Marnie, I'm glad you're enjoying Paris. An author cannot write in a limited world. You must take in all you can, everywhere you go. The sights, the sounds, the fragrances . . . And most important of all, the people. Their dialogue, their gestures . . ." He pulled his hand back and downed his espresso. "Your time here will help you see the world in a whole new light."

Marnie drank in her mentor's words as though they were the water of life.

"I'll arrange for you to go on a tour of the major literary locations of Paris." Bradford handed her an envelope. "Here are your earnings—half in euros, half in sterling." His eyes locked on hers. "So you no longer need to use your sister's credit card."

Marnie nodded. She had exchanged her British pounds for euros in the hotel the night they arrived and hadn't needed to spend much money except for some food and taxi fares. "I used it only once, when I bought a new tablet for working on my book."

Bradford leaned forward. "In the future, be sure to use cash. You'll avoid all the foreign exchange fees."

"No problem," she said, sitting back in her chair.

"Here in Paris, as you'll learn—" The ring of a phone cut him off midsentence. He fumbled with the pocket of his blazer and pulled out his flip phone. A frown distorted his handsome features.

Excusing himself from the table, Bradford scraped back his chair, rose, and took a few strides toward the street—leaving Marnie to wonder exactly what he thought she might learn in Paris.

Chapter 63

Friday, May 15, 11:35 a.m.—Paris, France

Bradford stepped onto the sidewalk to take the call, careful to keep his back to Marnie. Following a brief greeting, his usually cool-headed colleague launched into a blistering speech.

When she finally paused to take a breath, he cut in. "Hold on, Hillary. I understand your concern. I just learned of the ship's disaster in the past few moments. There's no need for panic. I'm handling it." He explained that he had considered telling Marnie about the incident right away. "However, that is not in her best interest."

Hillary broke in. "Not in her—"

"At this point, there is nothing she can do but worry. Besides, Marnie's parents do not yet know she is not on board the ship." Bradford enlightened her on Marnie's cockeyed rationale for informing her parents in writing rather than by phone. "News of Marnie's decision to remain in England should not come before her sister's safe arrival and Marnie's note of explanation." He was sure that's what she would want. "Since no fatalities have been reported, there's no need to upset Marnie or her parents now."

As he spoke, he realized it was true. He felt a bit less of a scoundrel.

"Graham, now it's your turn to listen." Hillary's voice boomed in his ear. "I understand about not alarming the parents with this news before the ship docks in Charleston. But you simply must inform Marnie. Before she finds out on her own."

Bradford sighed. "With Marnie's limited French, I can shelter her from this unactionable news, at least until we return to England."

Hillary was not to be silenced. "Unactionable?" she repeated. "Rubbish. The girl has a twin sister on that ship. You simply cannot keep her in ignorance until after the ship docks."

Bradford had to disagree.

Hillary Spearpoint was a person he respected more than anyone else he'd ever known. She had been his English teacher at the lowest ebb of his young life, helping him unlock his storytelling talent. She had been there for him when no one else was. He hated keeping secrets from her, but explaining about Marnie using Callie's passport would only complicate things. This time, he had to insist on doing things his way.

"Hillary. I'm doing what is best for all involved. Once Marnie's sister is safely home, I will bring Marnie up to date on the news."

"Graham, are you aware that Marnie Taylor is from a powerful family? If you withhold news of their daughter's—"

"Don't lay that burden on me, Hillary." He confessed to himself that he knew little about Marnie's family, although since she and her sister were taking advantage of the semester-at-sea program, he assumed her parents had money.

"I suppose you've heard of Jordon's department stores?"

"Of course." *Who hasn't heard of the largest group of department stores in the United States?*

"Her father is the CEO."

Bradford let the information sink in, then told himself it made no difference.

"There's bound to be a backlash," Hillary continued, "when the Taylors learn they were not informed that their daughter abandoned her semester-at-sea, and with the professor's knowledge . . ."

Bradford loosened his tie. "Marnie Taylor is an adult. As such, she did not need her parents' permission. However, it was her responsibility—not mine—to inform her parents of her decision to abandon ship."

He reminded Hillary that Marnie had been the one who offered to type his drafts following Cathy's accident. For that work, she was receiving compensation that was more than fair. "Though the value of the International Writers' Conference and our Sloane Square Workshop would be considered more than adequate compensation, ethically, I prefer not to accept a volunteer or enter an arrangement that could be interpreted as a quid pro quo."

He heard a sigh on the other end of the line.

"Graham. That may have been true when you entered this arrangement, but the situation has changed."

"I know it has. And I will handle it. Now, I really must get back to my breakfast," he said, followed by a hasty, "See you in Sloane Square in a few days." He flipped down the cover of the phone.

As Hillary had pointed out, the disaster at sea had changed everything. He would give Marnie the news as soon as they returned to Southampton—after her twin was safely stateside.

Chapter 64

Friday, May 15, 11:40 a.m.—Paris, France

Marnie sipped her espresso and noticed that Bradford continued to distance himself from their table. *The phone call must be important*, she thought.

Excited over the planned literary excursion in Paris on Monday, she began making a mental agenda—one that would allow her to work on her own writing today, as Bradford had suggested. She had made a breakthrough in her novel, and the words seemed to be flowing lately. Of course, she couldn't stop writing even if she wanted to. But mediocrity was not for her. If she couldn't write memorable, compelling stories, she would write only for herself.

Bradford's feedback always created an emotional roller-coaster—his praise lifting her to the sky, his criticism dropping her to the bottom of the sea. Back at the beginning of the master class on the *Rising Star*, his comments about the opening pages of her novel had knocked down her confidence. She had worked on those six pages for days, writing and rewriting a dozen times or more, until it was truly the best she could do. It had seemed perfect. Her classmates had given her the thumbs-up when she read aloud, despite the usual nitpicking over word choices.

But Bradford had neither praised nor criticized. Instead, he had asked a series of provocative questions, fired in rapid succession and leaving no space for her to respond. "What are the stakes? Will winning the competition make a profound difference in your protagonist's life? What will happen if she does not win?" His interrogation told her she hadn't dug deep enough. The stakes she'd laid out weren't high enough. Her writing wasn't good enough.

Bradford strode back to their table now, explaining that Hillary had returned to Sloane Hall and was ensuring everything was in order. Then, as if there had been no break in their conversation, he said, "You must immerse yourself in the total Parisian experience, Marnie. Our field trip introduced you to only a smattering of what Paris offers to the creative mind."

Marnie nodded eagerly.

"And yet to excel, you must avoid flying off day after day to gather new experiences—or worse, simply waiting for the muse to appear. You are a writer, and thus you must write." He slapped a hand on the table. "You must discipline yourself to write each day, even if only a couple of pages. By the end of the year, you will have written over seven hundred pages—and in those seven hundred pages, you are bound to find the makings of a story."

Over the course of the semester-at-sea program, Marnie had come to understand his perspective. As Professor Bradford had described, she often felt a disconnect after leaving her characters "on their own" for a few days. It was important to write every day, to remain connected. Otherwise, she soon found herself turning out a heap of "rubbish," as he called it. The goal was simply to keep writing.

"Tomorrow, aside from working on my pages, I'd like you to devote yourself totally to your own novel," Bradford continued, his steely eyes piercing hers. "We will meet for breakfast and then again for dinner. I recommend no outside contact with the world. Full concentration for the entire day is bound to be productive."

Marnie was grateful for the advice and could hardly wait to get started the following day. But there was one thing bothering her: Tomorrow evening, the *Rising Star* was due to dock in Brooklyn.

She had finally come to grips with the reality that there was no way to reach her sister until the ship was no longer at sea. Yet she felt an irresistible urge to talk with Callie, and not just to explain about the mix-up with their handbags. Marnie couldn't help but feel that something was wrong. She needed to reassure herself that her twin was okay.

The night before, shortly after her head hit the pillow, she'd jolted upright in bed, her thoughts on Callie. Her head had throbbed so badly, she'd climbed back out of bed and taken not two, but three Advil tablets.

What exactly was wrong, she couldn't say. Was she concerned about Callie's health after her bout with the flu? Was she worried about how they had left things? Not exactly. In her heart, she knew Callie would put their angry words behind her and do her best to smooth the waters with their parents.

Sitting across from Bradford now, at a café thousands of miles from her family, a sudden feeling of homesickness came knocking like an unwanted stranger. All at once, Marnie missed her sister more than she'd imagined she would. They'd been separated for the first eight years of their lives. They had gone to separate colleges for the past four years. But they had talked to each other two or three times a week and lived within just an hour's drive. As they'd left childhood and adolescence behind, they had formed a strong, unspoken bond. Was it due to the phenomenon of identical twins, written about in all the psychology books? Or was it just the closeness of sisters growing up together?

Marnie sat back in her chair, calculated the time difference between Paris and New York, and came to a decision: If Callie or her parents didn't call by Sunday morning, she would call home herself.

Chapter

65

Sunday, May 17, 4:45 a.m.—Paris, France

Marnie woke after another night of tossing and turning. She'd missed few of the illuminated digits on her bedside clock as they clicked by in slow motion. She hadn't had a full night's sleep all week, and she didn't even have jet lag to blame. Judging by the fit of her jeans, she'd lost weight, too. Then there were the unusual bouts of headaches over the past few days, which continually made her nauseous . . .

It was only 4:48 a.m. in Paris, six hours ahead of the time at her parents' home. The *Rising Star* must have arrived in Brooklyn by now. Callie would have shared the letter with their parents. Part of her wished she had added long-distance service to her smartphone, although even if she could call home, she wouldn't do so yet. As desperate as she was to hear Callie's voice, to know her twin had recovered from the flu and everything was okay, she must give her parents time to read and talk over her note. They would need time to absorb and come to terms with her decision. Mom would be the first to realize the value. Dad would take longer.

But if Marnie hadn't heard anything before this afternoon, she would have to act.

8:55 a.m.

Graham Bradford wasn't exactly broadsided by Marnie's announcement of her intention to call home. With the *Rising Star* originally scheduled to dock in Brooklyn the night before, he'd expected Marnie might be experiencing anxiety over her parents' reaction to her letter. He had prepared a monologue to explain that the ship had been involved in an accident, but had hoped to deliver it on their way to London—not here in the Maison Champs-Élysées restaurant, where they sat sipping their morning coffee.

Bradford started by reviewing his latest revisions over breakfast with Marnie, talking over the elements of the freshly printed pages of his book. He made a point of discussing his word choices and explaining exactly why he'd cut one of the scenes from the chapter Marnie had typed the day before.

"But I loved that scene," Marnie had protested.

"It was a good scene," he'd agreed, "and I'd spent quite some time on it. Yet while it contains some nice-to-know information, it does not move the story. In fact, it slows the pace."

As he'd explained further, Marnie's eyes lit up. "I get it," she'd said, nodding slowly. "And I can't wait to reread it. I understood about getting rid of all the unnecessary words, but your phrase 'less is more' didn't register before now." She'd clapped her hands together like a child and said, "Thank you, thank you, thank you."

"One thanks is sufficient." His lips had turned up in a smile. "I believe you will fit nicely into the workshop. You're *beginning* to demonstrate a grasp of many advanced aspects of the craft. Now you will have an opportunity to apply what you have learned during your semester at sea."

He'd made sure to emphasize the word *beginning*. She had to know there was a great deal more to learn.

"In the workshop, you will work on your own novel," he continued. "You will find the critiques from the other writers illuminating. By the end of the workshop, you will be ready to move on to your graduate degree program with confidence."

As his young companion finished her French toast, Bradford thought more about how familiar this whole scene seemed. It brought his grief back to the surface . . . And then she had made her request, letting him know the circumstances had changed.

He could see her unease as she explained that she had to contact home, to know that Callie was okay—and that her parents understood and accepted her decision.

"Of course. I understand," he said. "You need to call home. But Marnie, unfortunately I have some rather unsettling news I must share with you first."

Marnie set down her coffee cup, which was halfway to her mouth. "Something has happened to Callie." It wasn't a question.

"Your sister is fine," Bradford quickly asserted when he saw the color drain from Marnie's oval face. He hoped it was true. "First, I want you to know there is absolutely no need for concern."

"Tell me," she said, her voice hard.

"Trust me, Marnie, I've had your best interests at heart. My only concern was to save you needless worry. There was nothing you could do to help. Right or wrong, I saw no reason to give you the news of the mishap aboard the *Rising Star* earlier. When I saw the headlines—"

Marnie leaned forward, nearly toppling her glass of water. "What kind of mishap?" she demanded.

Reaching out, he laid his hand on her tightly clasped ones. "I've spent two sleepless nights since learning of it."

She gazed down at his hand, her eyes flashing a warning, and he instantly withdrew it.

"The *Rising Star* was broadsided by a rogue wave," he went on. "But no fatalities were reported, nor was there any reason to abandon the ship. Your sister is in no danger, and the ship is sailing under its own power. I felt it would be best to give you the news this evening when we returned to London, after the ship has docked and your sister is safely home."

"The ship was supposed to dock yesterday in New York," she said, her voice rising.

"Yes, and I've spent two sleepless nights since learning—"

"Two nights." Her voice rose, her expression one of having been betrayed. "You've known about this for two nights. And you decided to keep me in the dark?"

"Believe me, Marnie, I've wrestled with the timing of when to give you the news."

Marnie shot from her chair. "How about the minute you found out!"

"Sit down, Marnie." Bradford spoke through gritted teeth. His voice was low, and harsher than he'd intended. "The ship has been rerouted to Charleston, South Carolina. It is due to dock around noon today."

"I need to call my parents," was Marnie's only reply. "*Now*."

Chapter 66

Sunday, May 17, 9:10 a.m.—Paris, France

Despite Bradford's plea, Marnie refused to sit back down. She'd known something was wrong for the past few days, but she hadn't wanted to believe it.

"Graham, I'm not five years old. You trust me with your manuscript, but you don't respect me enough to treat me like an adult?" Before he had time to respond, she asked, "And just how do you know my sister is alright?"

Bradford's vice-like fingers gripped her arm. "Do not cause a scene," he said, sotto voce, his face screwed up in anger. "To be treated as an adult, you'd bloody well better start behaving like one."

Then his features softened, and he looked down at his hand as if surprised. Marnie looked down to, and he quickly released her arm, gesturing for her to be seated.

Reluctantly, she sank into her chair.

"Not informing your parents of your plans up front was a childish decision," Bradford continued calmly. "I regret going along with it. However, you put yourself in this situation, and you must deal with it. The last thing your parents need is for you to add more drama to their lives before your sister is safely home."

As much as she hated him for keeping the news from her, he was right. Calling home now was the worst thing she could do. Her parents were unaware that she had stayed behind. She must wait until Callie was safely home—until they had time to read her carefully worded letter and process her decision.

But she ached to talk with her sister. Every nerve in her body was on high alert.

"You're right, Graham. I messed up." She sighed. "I've painted myself into this corner. I'm the one responsible for isolating myself from my family. I should have found a way to tell my parents of my plans up front. My rationale no longer makes sense—even to me."

She was grateful when he didn't comment further.

"But you had no right to keep the news from me," she went on. "I don't need that kind of protection. Being left in the dark doesn't work for me. How can I trust you after this?"

"Of course you can trust me, Marnie." Bradford looked down at his wristwatch, then back up at Marnie. "I have a plan."

Bradford pushed his plate aside, folded his napkin, and leaned on the table. "After your parents read the letter this evening, they will know where you are. They will have no difficulty locating me or the Sloane Hall residence."

That thought made him more than a little uneasy. Now that he knew Marnie's parents were people of power and means, he feared they might go to any length to see their daughter returned home—immediately.

"So, there's nothing to worry about," he continued, putting aside his concerns over his novel's deadline. "I'm sure you will soon be in contact with your family. And at their initiative. Agreed?"

Marnie nodded her head slowly.

"Flying home, of course, is not an option you're considering?"

"Of course not," Marnie agreed, not meeting his eyes. "I have no intention of abandoning your manuscript before it's ready to be submitted to your editor."

"Well then, we'll both be glad to get to Sloane Square this evening—and get back to work." Bradford hoped his cheerful words hid his concern. He had noticed that while Marnie no longer wore the shattered expression of betrayal, she had failed to mention the workshop. *If she decides to go home early, I'll have to do my best to minimize the damage.*

He knew from experience that fate had a way of shattering agendas, no matter how well planned.

Chapter

67

Sunday, May 17, 4:15 p.m.—Paris, France

On the silent ride to Charles de Gaulle Airport, thoughts of her family dominated Marnie's mind. Bradford had said no one was badly injured, but the roiling beneath her ribs told her otherwise. Callie had not gone unscathed. Something was very wrong.

I need to be with her, and she needs me.

According to Bradford, the rogue wave hit the ship on Thursday night mid-Atlantic time. Calculating backward, she realized her parents must have known of the disaster for three days already and yet been unable to do anything but wait for their daughters' safe return. Knowing how action-oriented they were, she could only imagine how difficult this time must have been for them. Would they be glad Marnie had not been on board to face the danger? Or would reuniting with only one of the twins make things even worse?

Either way, one thing was certain: With Callie's return, life in the Taylor home would once again be thrown off balance, and Marnie was to blame. Her actions now seemed immature and self-centered, exactly as Callie had said. If only she could turn back the clock . . .

Just stop it, she told herself. She had been taught from an early age to deal with reality—not to waste precious time wishing she could change the past. *Yes, I went about it all wrong. But I made the right decision for my career as a writer.* Here she was, working alongside the man who was everything she hoped to be as a writer. No real harm had been done. Callie was safe, and so was she.

Even so, vague ideas had begun to swim in her head. Was there a way she might fulfill her end of the bargain with Bradford even if she were to go home early?

Compartmentalizing was a skill her mother had perfected, and more and more it seemed she had inherited it. Now, she shifted her thoughts from her sister back to her parents. She was a grown woman, but they still perceived her as their little girl. It wasn't hard to envision their reaction to her decision to go AWOL.

She suppressed a nervous giggle. *Going rogue*, her dad would've said. The irony of that particular phrase did not escape her.

As they approached the Air France terminal, Bradford pulled their tickets from inside his coat jacket. "You'll need your passport," he said.

She tried not to let his comment ignite more anxiety.

In a semi-trance, she slipped Callie's passport from an inside pocket of her handbag and gave it to him without a word. Her handbag had remained open, with the manila folder that housed his manuscript sticking out a few inches from the top. Her responses were staccato, limited to a word or two—not her typical vivacious style. Unlike on the trip from England, she didn't even feel concern over the fraudulent use of her sister's identification.

After getting boarding passes, they headed for the designated gate. Marnie remained unusually quiet, still reeling from the news and worried about her sister. She was beginning to regret her recent actions.

Once they boarded the plane and fastened their seatbelts, the nonstop flight gave her an hour and twenty minutes of uninterrupted time to think. Unable to ignore either her churning stomach or the recent bouts of blinding headaches, Marnie realized she needed a contingency plan— one that would allow her to fulfill her obligation to Graham Bradford from home if need be.

Chapter
68

Sunday, May 17, 10:45 p.m.—London, England

"Wake up, sleepyhead," came a man's voice to Marnie's right. "Look outside. Time to get acquainted with your home for the next couple of months."

Where am I? Marnie's eyes popped open. Her head throbbed. *How could I have fallen asleep?* Bradford had expected the drive from Southampton to take almost two hours. She hoped she hadn't snored or snoozed with her mouth gaping open. If she had, she didn't want to know.

Straightening her posture, she rubbed the crook of her neck and peered out the window of the Aston Martin. The ambient glow brightening the sky left no doubt that they were on the outskirts of the city. Old residential buildings filled the dim streets, each as identical as an unfrosted sugar cookie. They slowed at a roundabout and turned into a cul-de-sac, where she noticed a bookstore next door to a chemist's shop and several other brightly lit shops.

Bradford pulled into a metered parking place alongside a group of apartment buildings—or flats, as the English called them. "You'll find everything you need within walking distance," he explained, "as well as a number of designer boutiques." Charlize had told her she could even walk to Harrods, and neither Hyde Park nor Buckingham Palace was far away. She'd also mentioned a cybercafé, in case Marnie felt a compelling need to access the Internet.

And she did feel that need—every other moment that passed.

Marnie unbuckled her seatbelt as Bradford climbed out of the car and placed a parking permit in the window. Pushing open her door, she stepped into the cool evening.

Bradford had parked several car lengths from the building he'd pointed out. As he pulled their suitcases from the boot and set them on the sidewalk, Marnie glimpsed two young men at the top of the building's cement steps. The overhead light revealed Alexandre and a taller, well-built guy. At first it was difficult to make out his features, but when he stepped forward, the overhead light revealed him to be super attractive—some real eye candy.

Oh, stop, she warned herself. All she needed right now was to fall for someone on the opposite side of the globe. What she should be doing was figuring out how to get online and email her parents—or find a phone and call them.

Her straying mind was interrupted by a squeal from Charlize, who dashed down the steps to give her a welcoming hug. "Welcome to the land of eight-day workweeks, Marnie," she joked.

Alexandre followed behind, giving her a brotherly hug, before introducing her to Ian, who was tall, dark, and silent. "Let's haul your things up to your flat," Alexandre said as the two blokes took off with her bags and Bradford's.

Glad for the help, Marnie slung the strap of her handbag over her shoulder and reached for the handle of her smaller suitcase. As they disappeared up the steps and through the front door, she read the placard above the arch: SLOANE HALL.

The door swung open again, and Hillary Spearpoint appeared, flipping her long white braid over her shoulder. She looked from Bradford to Marnie and back again. She gave Marnie a careful smile and pulled her in for a brief hug.

"Welcome to Sloane Hall," she said, a gnarled hand gesturing to the staircase. "Your accommodations are on the third level. Charlize will show you the way." Then she turned to Bradford. "How about a nice pot of tea and some biscuits?"

Marnie was too surprised by the hug to notice the lines of worry spreading across the old woman's forehead.

Chapter
69

Sunday, May 17, 11:05 p.m.—London, England

The moment Marnie was out of earshot, Bradford turned to give Hillary an expectant look. "We need to talk," his dearest friend and colleague responded.

Bradford placed his hand on Hillary's skeletal arm and led her through the large open area on the first level, toward the communal kitchen. "You were right," he said, shaking his head. "I could not protect Marnie from the disturbing news about the *Rising Star*. She was planning to email home, so I told her everything I knew about the accident this morning over breakfast, before we left Paris."

As they reached the kitchen, Hillary removed her arm from Bradford's grasp and stood rooted in place. "So why are you having *all* of Marnie's luggage moved in?" she said.

"Why shouldn't it be?" he asked, although Hillary's thoughts were transparent. *She thinks that I'm being monstrously selfish—or that I'm overstepping my bounds as Marnie's mentor.* "Marnie needs to get settled in."

"The situation has changed, Graham," she replied. "The girl should be with her family, for her sake as well as theirs. The world will not come to an end if you are a week or so past your deadline."

Bradford shook his head. "Marnie's sister experienced a horrific few days aboard the *Rising Star,* but that is no reason for Marnie to be hightailing it home."

"Graham, we are not discussing some minor mishap. A seven-story wave broadsided that ship." Hillary shifted from one small foot to the other. "It was a catastrophic event."

"Please. Let's sit down and talk." An uncomfortable silence settled between them as Bradford filled the teapot, plugged it in, and placed two cups and saucers on the breakfast room table. He pulled out a chair and gestured toward it. "She can do nothing constructive at home, Hillary. And she would quickly become resentful about missing the workshop. You saw her in Paris. She's thrilled to be a part of it. From her perspective, this is the opportunity of a lifetime."

Hillary seemed reluctant but sank down onto the chair.

"She is certainly not being taken advantage of," Bradford reassured her. "I am giving as much as I am getting. As we discussed in Paris, this young woman has a great deal of potential. But she is far from a seasoned writer. I believe I can bring out the best in her—"

"Bloody hell, Graham." Hillary raised an eyebrow. "You're out of character here."

Hillary should know—she was the one person who knew his character best. She had known him as a thirteen-year-old student, and when she'd discovered he was on his own and living in his dad's car, she had taken immediate action. She had moved him into her guest room, encouraging his writing talent and inspiring him as she adapted to the role of surrogate mother. As an unmarried English teacher, she had been unable to afford going through the hoops to become Bradford's legal guardian. Still, Hillary's role had quickly become that of maternal compass and mentor—a position she still held.

Bradford sighed. "I know. But I honestly believe Marnie should stay the course, Hillary."

"But why? Why do you need her here so badly? You know damn well HarperCollins isn't about to forgo the revenue for the latest Derek Duncan thriller."

"Of course not." He hesitated, wondering how much to tell Hillary. "However, I have an obligation. My deadline has already been extended, and the promotion calendar is set. Would you risk the goodwill of your publisher by throwing their entire promotional calendar off track?"

Hillary squinted, adding still more wrinkles to her thin face. "What did the girl's parents have to say?" she asked.

"Marnie has not yet spoken with her parents."

Hillary's eyes widened. "Why, in heaven's name, would she not call her parents right away?"

Sidestepping her question, Bradford said, "You know me better than to think I would try to take advantage. I already have a Plan B for getting my manuscript in on time, and it does not require Marnie remaining here in London. But she owes it to herself to stay the course."

Chapter 70

Sunday, May 17, 11:15 p.m.—London, England

As she opened the door to her flat, Marnie's eyes widened. "Wow! Is this all mine?"

"Yeah. We each have our own flat," Charlize confirmed, going on to explain that each of the six individual flats—two on each upper level—featured restored hardwood floors, new paint, and area rugs, but otherwise remained relatively untouched. Not so, however, for the first level. Bradford's signature had barely dried on the sales documents a few years earlier when he had gutted it to form a large conference area, a kitchen, and two loos. "The internal renovations began right away, but no alterations were permitted to the outside of any of the buildings in this historical area of the city."

Marnie covered the space between the cozy living room and the open bedroom door in a few long strides and saw that her large suitcase was already on the bed. Exploring the rest of the flat as Charlize kicked off her boots, she discovered a small water closet and her own kitchenette. *Truly self-contained*, she thought. *Except for Wi-Fi.*

While these present accommodations were not luxurious, she'd never expected to have a full apartment to herself. Everything would be perfect—if only she could hear Callie's voice and know that nothing bad had happened to her. Only then could she settle down. As it was, she was not sure she should even unpack.

Like the rope in a tug-of-war, Marnie felt she was being pulled one way and then the other. She needed to talk to someone.

She checked the time on her tablet—after six p.m. on the East Coast.

Callie was probably heading back home to Greenwich with their parents and Juliana. Marnie wondered if they had read her letter. Were they worried about her? Had they been trying to contact her the entire afternoon?

"Hey," Charlize called out while rummaging through the cupboard, "I could use a spot of tea. You?"

"Perfect," Marnie said, a bit of tension evaporating. Hillary had stocked the kitchen with the essentials. Turning on the kettle, Marnie soon learned that Charlize's choices mirrored her own—English breakfast tea with cream, no sugar. She placed three tea bags in the pot, poured boiling water over them, and filled the small cream pitcher beside the sugar bowl.

"Let's take it into the living room," Charlize suggested. She placed all the paraphernalia on a tray and carried it to the low table in front of the sofa.

The familiar ritual reminded Marnie of Elizabeth.

"Now. What's going on?" Charlize demanded, though her smile was friendly as usual. "You look like Atlas, with the weight of the world on your shoulders."

"Busted," Marnie said with a sad grin. "I could use a good listener right about now."

Charlize plopped down on the sofa, tucking her slim legs beneath her. "I'm all yours. Time to reveal whatever it is that's got your knickers in a twist."

"Am I that transparent?" Marnie whispered.

"What kind of a writer would I be if I couldn't read between the lines?" Charlize grinned. "So how about you start at the beginning."

Marnie began by telling Charlize about the letter she wrote to her parents and her plan to elude security on the *Rising Star*—and Bradford's objection to what he labeled her "subterfuge."

"So you never rang your parents?"

Marnie shook her head. "Have you heard the expression 'It's easier to ask for forgiveness than for permission'?"

Charlize smiled. "Yeah. That one's made its way across the pond."

"I've been out of contact with my family for the past couple of weeks, and worst of all, I left my sister on her own to face the disaster at sea."

"And you gave the letter to your sister? She was on the same ship as you and Graham?"

Marnie nodded. "In the master class for creative dance."

"It's that ship that was tossed around by that mega-wave."

Marnie nodded again.

A look of alarm arose on Charlize's pale face. "It's been blanketing the news since Friday. Even in Paris, you couldn't turn on a TV channel without seeing it. Photos of flooded cabins. Students huddled in public areas."

"Yes, Graham told me."

"But they're reporting new information tonight, about—" She stopped abruptly and stared at Marnie. "Didn't you know?"

"Know what?" Marnie leaned forward, sensing that her devastated world had just gotten a whole lot worse.

"A student and a waiter have been reported missing. Washed overboard," Charlize said slowly. "The names haven't been released, but that student has to be . . . you."

Chapter
71

Monday, May 18, 12:15 a.m.—London, England

Marnie's mug nearly fell from her hand. The room tilted. "What do you mean 'washed overboard'?"

Charlize wrapped her arm around Marnie's shaking shoulders. "Oh, my God. I'm so bloody sorry. You can't have seen the news yet. You've been traveling all—"

"Tell me everything." Marnie could hardly breathe.

Charlize swallowed hard. "We heard it on TV earlier this evening, when we went to the pub for dinner."

"Heard *what*?" Marnie nearly shouted.

"The latest reports say two people are still unaccounted for. They were presumed to have been on deck after the monster wave hit, and . . ." Charlize's voice quivered. "Search and rescue teams went over every inch of the ship. The conclusion was that both had been lifted off their feet and washed overboard."

Marnie felt the icy grasp of her new reality. *My poor parents . . . If they haven't read my letter yet, they must think I'm lost at sea—or worse.*

She jumped to her feet and dashed toward the bedroom, where she pulled on her leather jacket and slung her handbag over her shoulder. Silently cursing Bradford and his antiquated rules, she barked, "Where's the nearest public phone?"

Charlize raised her brows and stood up from the sofa. "Sloane Square Hotel. Less than two blocks away. Come on. I'll go with you."

The two girls raced down the stairs and up the darkened street. As they neared the roundabout, Marnie spotted the neon sign of the hotel directly across the way. Paying no attention to the big white letters painted on the street, she glanced to her left and stepped off the curb.

The last words she heard were those of Charlize shouting, "Marnie, *look out!*"

Chapter
72

Monday, May 18, 12:25 a.m.—London, England

Charlize froze momentarily, then spun into action. She flew to Marnie's side and leaned in close. *So much blood.* But the steady rise and fall of Marnie's chest, while shallow, told Charlize her new friend was breathing.

A husky voice cut into the cool night air. "Bloody foreigners."

Charlize looked up through the dim light from the streetlamps into the haggard face of an elderly taxi driver.

"Ran right in front of me cab, she did. Wasn't me fault." He paused and hunkered down beside Charlize. "Is she breathing?"

Charlize nodded. "She needs an ambulance. Ring 999."

"I was just heading home. Minding me own business." He straightened up and pointed down at Marnie. "She didn't even look. Just flew straight in front of me cab. You saw her . . . Right?"

Charlize remained at Marnie's side as the driver shambled back to his cab and made the call.

The ambulance arrived on the deserted street at last, amid the blare of sirens and flashing lights. The nameless taxi driver headed straight for the two constables emerging from a police car.

A team of three uniformed medics stepped out of the yellow and black ambulance. The two with the stretcher went straight to Marnie while the other retrieved her handbag from the street. "Do you know the victim?" the third man asked Charlize.

"Yes. She's an American student. Do you think she's going to be okay?"

"We'll give her the best possible care," the medic assured Charlize. "We'll know more soon."

She watched as the other two medics wrapped a plastic brace around Marnie's neck, lifted her onto the stretcher, and then placed it in the ambulance. There was blood on the bonnet of the cab and in the street. Too much blood.

Fear seized Charlize. "Can I ride with her to the hospital?" she asked the medic.

"Are you family?"

Charlize shook her head. "She has no family here."

"I'm sorry, but you can't ride with us. You'll need to get to hospital on your own. We're taking her to Chelsea and Westminster, on Fulham Road. Check in with Emergency."

"But she's my roommate and—"

"Young lady," one of the constables cut in, "I understand you witnessed the accident."

Watching the retreating back of the medic as he sprinted to the ambulance, Charlize ignored the question. "Marnie's all alone," she persisted. "I *must* go with her."

"Don't worry, Miss. We'll see that you get to hospital. I am Constable Bristol. And you are?"

"Charlize Marshall," she said without hesitation as she looked into the round, friendly face of the constable. His tailored uniform was unrumpled, and he wore a crisp white shirt with a neatly knotted navy tie. Though he was of medium height, the tall helmet on his head made him appear taller.

The siren droned lower as the ambulance drove off.

"Well, Miss Marshall, first I need some information. I take it the girl is a friend of yours?"

She nodded briskly. "Can we go now? I'll tell you everything I know on the way . . . Please."

"Soon," Constable Bristol said, gesturing to the taxi driver. "While both of you witnesses are here, I have just a few questions."

Charlize took a deep breath and met the constable's eye.

"What is the victim's name?" he asked.

"Her name is Marnie . . . We just met this past week. I don't know her surname." She thought for a moment and added, "Her handbag is in the ambulance."

CHAPTER 73

Monday, May 18, 12:55 a.m.—Chelsea and Westminster Hospital

Charlize bolted from the police car the instant Constable Bristol's partner opened her door. Her heart pumping overtime, she moved swiftly toward the double glass doors under the Accident & Emergency sign. "She just can't be waking up to strangers," she called back over her shoulder to the two officers.

"Go ahead," Constable Bristol shouted after her. "I'll catch up."

He was right behind her as she burst through the doors and wove her way through other waiting patients to the reception counter, staffed by a harried nurse dressed in white and wearing an old-fashioned cap, slightly askew.

Charlize barged in front of the bearded man at the front of the queue. "Sorry," she said, "but I need to find my friend. She was hit by a taxi in Sloane Square and was brought here by ambulance in the past fifteen minutes or so."

The nurse looked past Charlize to the bearded man.

"I need to be with her," Charlize said breathlessly. "She's all alone, with no family in the UK."

The bearded man shrugged and said, "Carry on."

"Full name," the nurse asked.

"Charlize Marshall."

The nurse jabbed at the computer keyboard. "No one by that name has been admitted this evening."

Charlize frowned. "No, that's my name."

With a weary sigh, the nurse said, "The *patient's* name?"

"Marnie. I don't know her last name."

The nurse's scowl could have melted stone. "You don't know your friend's surname?"

"The medic from the ambulance has her handbag. She's an American, so she's bound to have a passport."

The nurse tapped some keys on the computer. Finally, she looked up and reported, "No one by that name has been admitted this evening."

Charlize opened her mouth, but no words came out. *How can that be?*

"The victim in the accident in Sloane Square is a young woman," Constable Bristol said over her shoulder. "In her twenties, I'd guess."

"Twenty-two," Charlize added.

"We do have a new entry matching that description," the nurse said, "but the name you gave me is not the name of the patient of record."

"How could that be?" Charlize argued. "Is she conscious? Has she given you her name?"

The nurse stared at her, then addressed the constable instead, gesturing to a nearby set of doors. "This way to Admissions, sir. They'll have the young woman's relevant information."

"May I come with you?" Charlize asked. "I only met Marnie last week, but she should see a familiar face."

Constable Bristol nodded and strode through the doors toward Admitting. Charlize trotted behind him, trying to keep up with his long strides.

"Good evening, Agnes," Bristol said to the young nurse at the Admissions desk.

"It's morning now, Constable Bristol," Agnes corrected. "Are you here for the American girl?"

"That's right. Miss Marshall was with her at the time of the accident."

"Is she alright?" Charlize asked.

"She is stable, but in critical condition. Come right this way." She led them into a small room that held merely a metal desk and two chairs and handed Charlize a form. "Please be seated."

When Charlize read the first line of the form, her mind went into freefall. The name on the form was not a familiar one.

Callie Taylor?

Chapter
74

Monday, May 18, 1:20 a.m.—Chelsea and Westminster Hospital

"That's not her name," Charlize said loudly.

"Pardon?" Agnes said. "That's the name on her passport and other identification in her handbag."

"May I see it?"

Agnes hesitated.

"It's alright," Constable Bristol said.

Agnes handed her the passport and American driver's license.

Charlize recognized Marnie in the photo on both documents. "On the passport, it looks like her, only younger. But her name is Marnie."

"Are you sure?" Bristol asked.

"Well, that's the name she's used while working with Graham Bradford."

Constable Bristol's brow puckered. "The author of the Derek Duncan thrillers?

Charlize nodded. "She and I are attending his summer workshop. He introduced her to us last week as Marnie."

"Did she use the same surname?"

Charlize shrugged. "Don't know. She may have. Maybe she was using her sister's name . . . But I don't have a clue why she would do that. It makes no sense."

Bristol sat down in the chair beside her. "You say you were introduced to this girl by Graham Bradford."

Again, she nodded. "I must call him."

"Better yet, I'll take you back to Sloane Square. Need to find out more about his role in all this," the constable said. "But first I'll need to take your statement."

"Take your time," Agnes said. "I must get back to the front desk. I'll leave you to discuss how you might get the contact information. We'll need to inform her next of kin."

"Inform her next of kin?" Charlize cried out. "Does that mean she's going to—"

"Oh, I'm terribly sorry," Agnes replied quickly. "That was a poor choice of words. What I meant is, we must notify the family that she is here. It's our policy for any patient entering our facility as a result of an accident or crime." She gave Charlize a sympathetic look. "Your friend is in critical condition, but stable. She did not sustain a fatal injury."

She left the room, and Charlize began to explain to Bristol why they had gone to Sloane Square. "No one on the ship except her sister knows Marnie stayed behind in Southampton. She wrote a letter to her parents that her sister was to deliver, but somehow everyone must think she was washed overboard. Marnie was desperate to let her family know she was safe . . ."

The second the words left her mouth, her heart sank. "Please, can we find out how badly she was hurt?" Charlize broke down in tears. "It's all my fault," she moaned. "Maybe if I hadn't shouted her name when I saw her about to charge out into the street—"

"This accident was not your fault," Constable Bristol said gently. "Can't tell you the number of accidents that occur in this very same way. Foreigners look left rather than right all the time when they step into the street." He paused. "Our priority now is to inform the family of Callie Taylor—or whatever her real name is—of the accident." He agreed to check on the girl's condition before taking her to Sloane Hall.

Charlize wiped away her tears, hoping Graham could shed some light on why her new friend was using a different name.

Chapter 75

Monday, May 18, 4:05 a.m.—London, England

When Constable Bristol pulled the patrol car up in front of Sloane Hall, Charlize pointed out Graham's convertible. There were no empty parking slots, so Bristol flipped on his hazard lights and double-parked beside the Aston Martin.

Charlize wasn't looking forward to being accompanied by two police constables while she discussed this complicated, sensitive issue. Being the bearer of this news would be hard enough in private. Was Marnie in some kind of trouble? Why was she using a different name from the one on her identification? If only Charlize could run everything by Marnie—what she should or should not share with Graham.

When she attempted to open the back door of the patrol car, however, she discovered it was locked. "Excuse me, Constable," she said, "would you please unlock my door? I'll just skip ahead and—"

"I'm afraid not, Miss Marshall. We'll be accompanying you to meet Mr. Bradford."

Charlize swallowed hard. No point arguing. She hadn't a prayer of persuading the constable to break protocol. She didn't want to make trouble, and yet Marnie's parents must be informed. But how would that conversation begin? *Your daughter wasn't washed overboard, Mr. and Mrs. Taylor, but she was hit by a taxi. And she's been living under an assumed name . . .*

Charlize felt tears forming. She blinked them away. Marnie had given no thought to the consequences—her only objective had been to reach her parents and set their minds at ease.

Heat flushed Charlize's cheeks. Marnie's irrational decision to keep her parents in the dark had backfired. Having to be the messenger was bad enough. Now Charlize would have an audience.

Climbing from the backseat, Charlize pulled out her key to Sloane Hall. Constable Bristol and his partner followed her up the concrete stairs, remaining a couple of steps behind her as she unlocked and threw open the door.

Sloane Hall was veiled in darkness, with only a nightlight in the kitchen and another on the wall, between the foot of the stairs and the old-fashioned elevator cage, to illuminate their way. *Everyone must be asleep,* Charlize thought, tiptoeing forward. She didn't relish the idea of awakening Graham in the middle of the night.

Graham Bradford yawned. He'd had a productive night at his desk, and he felt good about the latest revisions to his manuscript. But just as he was about to climb into bed, he heard the electric whir of the elevator. Distrusting his ears, he quickly checked the clock. A little after four.

There's no bloody reason for anyone to be up here at this hour.

He hurried to pull on his robe and push his feet into his well-worn slippers. Bolting across the living room, he threw open the door.

Emerging from the elevator was Charlize, with a police constable on either side of her.

What kind of trouble could she have gotten herself into?

One of the uniformed men introduced himself as Constable Bristol and his partner as Constable Thomas. "We're sorry to disturb you at this early hour, Mr. Bradford. However, one of your students has been in a serious accident."

"Marnie?" Bradford asked, directing his gaze at Charlize.

She nodded, then described in brief what had happened.

Bradford's heart raced. "Is she badly hurt?" he asked.

"She's in a coma," Charlize said, her voice trembling. "No one can see her right now."

"We were told it's a drug-induced coma, not one sustained in the accident," Constable Bristol clarified. "They'll know more later today."

Bradford barely gave a thought to why Marnie and Charlize were even heading to the roundabout at that hour. He must get to Marnie.

"Excuse me, Mr. Bradford," Bristol cut in, "but I need to ask you a few questions. We've run into a bit of a complication. The hospital administration needs to know the young woman's full name in order to contact her family."

"Of course," Bradford said, a monster of a headache shooting across his brow. "Her name is Marnie Taylor." *Surely, Charlize could have told them that much.* "I don't know her middle name, but—"

"It's imperative, sir, that we obtain her legal name."

"Her legal name?"

There was a rapid knocking at the door of his flat. It flung open, and in walked Hillary, clad in a blue chenille robe and fuzzy blue slippers, her white hair flowing down her back. "I heard the elevator, Graham. What is going on here?"

"Sorry to have awakened you, Miss . . .?" Bristol said.

"Hillary Spearpoint," she said firmly. "And you didn't wake me. At my age, I don't spend a whole lot of time sleeping."

Bristol introduced himself again and explained why they had come. "As I was just telling Mr. Bradford, the passport and driver's license found in the young woman's handbag identified her as Callie Taylor, not Marnie Taylor."

Hillary's expression remained tranquil, as if nearing a century old meant nothing could surprise her.

"Bloody hell," Bradford said for the umpteenth time since departing the *Rising Star*. *I'm forty-three bloody years old,* he thought. *How on earth did I become a part of this tangled web of deception? And how am I going to explain it now without looking like a damn fool?*

Avoiding his role in the ongoing drama, Bradford made his explanation of Marnie's use of her sister's ID brief, with only the need-to-know information. Apparently, his explanation was all that was needed to send the constables on their way.

The moment they left, he asked Charlize to fill him in on the shocking news of the two missing individuals who were presumed to be lost at sea—the news that had sent the two girls out in the middle of the night in search of a public phone. As his stomach roiled, his brain began to reel, and his thoughts traveled to Marnie's family and the anguish they must be suffering.

Why had he been so inflexible about contacting her family? He was responsible for her being in harm's way.

Then a far more devastating dilemma sprang to mind: Marnie had not been washed out to sea. Instead she was hit by a blooming taxi in the middle of the night.

Chapter 76

Monday, May 18, 4:40 a.m.—Chelsea and Westminster Hospital

Marnie's eyelids refused to open. They seemed glued shut. Through the paper-thin slits between her eyelashes, she saw only shadows on a background of bright light. She could lift her head no more than a fraction of an inch. Things were happening all around her: loud voices, clanging noises, shadowy images moving closer. It didn't take much of a leap to figure out that she was in a hospital.

The last thing she remembered was someone shouting her name. Then she'd been hurled off her feet, and everything had gone black. Now, her skull felt as fragile as a lightbulb about to burst. She tried to raise her hand to her head. She couldn't.

The memory of the accident slowly came back to her, along with the startling news about a student lost at sea. Her heart pounded wildly in her chest. She had to reach her parents.

Needles of pain pricked the back of her eyes as she tried to piece together what had happened. She had never reached the hotel in Sloane Square, where she had planned to phone her parents. She had been hit by something—a car, maybe?—and now she was in a hospital. But where was Charlize? Did she also get hurt?

Tears spilled down Marnie's cheeks—tears she could not wipe away.

She felt a gentle touch on her face, and then a deep voice said, "Callie, I'm Dr. Benson. You were in an accident early this morning, but . . ."

His voice faded in and out as his fingers moved gently over her face. She couldn't concentrate. *But what?* she wanted to shout.

"Next, Callie, we will be removing this breathing tube . . ."

I'm not Callie, she tried to say. Her mouth was dry, and her tongue felt as if it were embedded in quicksand. Exhausted by the effort, and unable to form a single word, she drifted off again.

4:55 a.m.—London, England

Bradford cursed himself for using the noisy elevator, whose whirring sound had alerted Hillary. He had shaved quickly, then pulled on a pair of snug jeans, a blue dress shirt, and a navy blazer, hoping to slip out before Hillary had a chance to dress.

"Wait up," she called out, closing the door of her flat behind her and hurrying toward the elevator cage on her short legs. She was dressed in a clean caftan and a comfortable-looking pair of dress shoes, with her ivory hair twisted haphazardly into one long braid.

Reluctantly he brought the elevator to a stop on the third level, still hoping to persuade Hillary to stay behind.

After learning the reason for Marnie's misidentification, Charlize had agreed to remain at Sloane Hall to inform the other students of Marnie's accident.

"Hillary," he said now, stepping out of the elevator, "I know you are concerned about Marnie, but there is no need to come to the hospital so early this morning. I'll only be taking care of paperwork."

"Graham, I know how you feel about the hospital, and I'm coming with you," Hillary replied. "End of discussion."

Bradford sighed and stepped back into the elevator. There was no use arguing.

Bradford closed the passenger door of his Aston Martin and dashed around the car, removing the parking pass. When he slipped behind the wheel, Hillary was fidgeting with the safety belt. With her arthritic hands, fastening the belt in place was never easy.

"Here, let me give you a hand," Bradford said, clicking the buckle.

As Bradford turned from Lower Sloane Street onto King's Road, Hillary asked, "What are your immediate plans?"

"My immediate plans are to take care of Marnie's admission papers," he said, avoiding her real question.

"Don't be obtuse, Graham," she said. "When do you plan to contact the child's parents?"

He hadn't quite decided how to approach that problem—not bothering to correct her about Marnie being no child. There was no justification for avoiding her parents, despite the inevitable repercussions—his past rationalizations now seemed irrational.

"As soon as we clarify Marnie's condition," he said, "I will get her parents' contact information and ring them."

He consoled himself with the fact that the Taylors now had Marnie's letter in hand. *At least they know she's in London—and she came to no harm aboard the ship.*

Chapter 77

Monday, May 18, 5:20 p.m.—London, England

Marnie continued to fade in and out of consciousness. She had no concept of time passing. How long had she been here? People were talking about her as if she were somewhere else. She had so many questions but couldn't manage to utter a single word. All she knew was, she was frightened. She kept hearing the word *coma*.

The doctor had said he would look in on her in the evening. Was it evening yet? She thought she'd heard someone say *Good afternoon*, but that seemed a very long time ago. If only the doctor would return soon . . . She tried to force herself to stay awake. When he'd talked about the accident, she had been unable to focus on what he was saying.

Bradford and Hillary had come in earlier. Or had that been just a dream? They had stayed for only a couple of moments, it seemed. Maybe she'd fallen asleep while they were there.

She desperately wanted to communicate. Her heart pumped faster—so at least that part of her body seemed to be working. Unable to move a single finger or open her eyes, she felt helpless. Floating in and out of consciousness, she didn't know if she'd nodded off for minutes, hours, or perhaps even days. One thing stuck in her mind: Bradford had promised to call her parents as soon as he knew more about her condition. He had told her not to worry, as if worry were something she could turn off like the tap in the kitchen sink. She hoped she had not dreamed it. Even now, she was drifting back to sleep.

And if this paralysis was more than temporary, she had no desire ever to wake.

When Bradford had first laid eyes on Marnie's bruised face and body that morning, any remaining urgency for meeting his publishing deadline had died an instant death. She looked so young—so vulnerable. He knew how quickly that vibrancy could be stolen from her. And he knew he must contact her parents as soon as possible.

Half a day has passed, and I haven't rung the girl's parents. He told himself he was waiting to learn the severity of her injuries and the prognosis for her recovery.

Bradford and Hillary remained at the hospital until early evening, when Dr. Benson entered the room at last, apologizing for the delay as he completed his rounds.

"So our patient is named Marnie. Not Callie?" The doctor led them to a private corner of the reception area, where they seated themselves on a sofa. "Currently, Miss Taylor is in a medical coma—one that is induced by drugs for her safety," he began, lowering himself into a chair.

"The nurse told us her condition was not as devastating as her appearance," Hillary blurted.

Dr. Benson nodded. "Miraculously, Miss Taylor seems to have broken no major bones. But she did fracture two ribs and bruise both the hip and the elbow. Her brain . . ." He did not finish the sentence.

"Dr. Norman Benson . . . Dr. Norman Benson," the loudspeaker blared.

The doctor bolted from the armchair. "I'm afraid I'm the only one on call in A&E this evening," he explained. "But there's no need to worry. Miss Taylor's injuries are not life-threatening."

"But—"

"I'm sorry, but I must be on my way." The doctor dashed across the reception area. "There is little you can do for her right now. Please come back tomorrow morning. We'll know more after the CAT scan."

Bradford rose from the sofa, utterly speechless. Hillary headed straight to the reception desk to demand an explanation.

"One moment please," the receptionist said as she lifted the phone receiver. "I understand . . . six o'clock a.m.," she repeated. She ended the call and turned to address Hillary. "The doctor will begin his rounds at six o'clock tomorrow morning. Now, if you would please leave the contact information for Miss Taylor's parents . . . ?"

Chapter 78

Tuesday, May 19, 6:15 a.m.—London, England

Marnie heard a woman's loud voice calling out, "I think I saw her eyes moving." Again she tried to open her eyes wide enough to see—and to be seen. Swallowing hard, she moved her thick-coated tongue around her mouth, attempting to generate moisture. "I'm awake," she tried to shout.

"It looks like she's trying to talk," the same loud voice said.

"Marnie." This time she heard a rich baritone and felt a hand on hers. *The doctor?*

"Good morning, Marnie. I am Dr. Benson. If you can hear me, please blink your eyes. Or try to move a finger if you can."

She forced all her energy to her fingers but didn't have the strength to move even one. She had to let the doctor and nurses know she was awake.

Her thoughts floated past. Hadn't she heard *good evening* not too long ago? Had another day passed? *What day is it?* Well, at least her parents would have her letter by now. They must know she had not reboarded the ship in Southampton. They would contact Bradford. They would find out the truth.

I wasn't washed overboard. I'm right here. I'm okay. Well, at least she hoped she would be okay soon.

The doctor lifted an eyelid and shone a nauseating light in her eye. "Good morning," he repeated.

Stop, Marnie wanted to shout. Her eyes snapped open, then closed once more. Again she tried to speak. Again she failed, and instead began floating back into a gray cloud.

"We're eager to know the extent of Marnie's injuries and her expected recovery, Doctor," Bradford said upon arriving at the door to Marnie's hospital room later that morning.

"Certainly," Dr. Benson said, stepping outside of the room and closing the door behind him. He explained that her semiconscious brain might be able to hear much of what went on around her. "I expect her to continue to emerge from the coma at short intervals throughout today."

"She's regaining consciousness?"

"Yes. She is a very lucky young lady," Benson continued. "Her CAT scan revealed a small spiral fracture at the base of her skull." Before they had a chance to ask, he explained. "In one so young, that is no cause for alarm. It will heal quickly. Fortunately, there were no hematomas."

"Blood clots?" Bradford asked.

"Yes," the doctor replied, explaining that a hematoma was a solid swelling of clotted blood within the tissues. "The impact broke no bones. But Miss Taylor did fracture two ribs, and both the right hip and an elbow were bruised. However, those injuries will heal quickly and completely. Her black eye and other bruises will disappear even more rapidly. I expect a full recovery."

The doctor glanced up at the wall clock.

"I understand her parents are in New York and have yet to be notified. If you can give us that information, we will have them contacted. They may wish to make travel arrangements."

"If you don't mind," Bradford said, "since Marnie has been under my care, I would like to be the one who breaks the news to her parents."

The doctor gave him a strange look but nodded, handing over his card. "Please have them call my office directly."

Bradford thanked him. Throughout the night, he'd rehearsed the speech he would deliver to Marnie's parents.

PART THREE

May 19–25

Chapter

79

Tuesday, May 19, 5:55 p.m.—Los Angeles, California

Jack's leg bobbed up and down. He wasn't sure what to think. This was decidedly not the type of assignment he'd envisioned when he signed on with Landes Investigations two months earlier.

"You begin tomorrow," Landes said. "The family has a full schedule. Ashleigh and Marnie arrive on JetBlue at Long Beach Airport, along with the younger sister and her friend."

"And I'm supposed to call the twin 'Marnie' instead of 'Callie'?" Jack asked. "You're discounting Pocino's intel?"

"You know I'm not. It's just until we have rock-solid proof," replied Landes. "Their flight arrives at eleven forty-five. Pick them up two hours later at the Taylors' leased house in Long Beach, on the peninsula."

"Not at the airport?"

Landes shook his head. "They'll be renting a vehicle. But you'll need to take Ashleigh to Fashion Island in Newport Beach that afternoon, and then take Marnie to Aliso Viejo. That should give you a chance to get acquainted."

"And the other girls? Will they be—"

Landes shook his head. "The younger sister and her friend will be visiting with family in Naples that evening." He explained about Elizabeth and her home at the former residence of the late Charles Stuart.

This is my new assignment—to be a babysitter? Jack thought impatiently. He didn't wait for Landes to explain. "Boss, I want to help solve this case, but I'm not sure how becoming the family chauffeur . . ."

"I have my reservations as well, Kirkbride, but what we have in mind goes way beyond that."

Jack was baffled. "We?"

"Yes. Ashleigh Taylor has asked for this specifically. You will take this opportunity to get to know Marnie. Since you are only a few years older than the twins—"

"Pardon me, Dick. Be it Marnie or—more likely—Callie, what do you expect me to learn from a girl who can't remember anything?"

Landes shrugged. "The doctors have said her memories could resurface at any time."

Jack was still doubtful. "Just how am I going to get to know this young woman from behind the wheel of a car?"

Landes chuckled. "You'll figure it out. First off, you'll be bringing her to see a prominent neurologist in Aliso Viejo." He explained that the Taylors had the necessary clout to get them squeezed into his tight schedule. "The first appointment is for Marnie, at five o'clock. The second is for her parents, two hours later. "Will I be transporting Mr. and Mrs. Taylor as well?"

"No. Conrad has meetings at Jordon's in Fashion Island and has his own rental, which is why Ashleigh will be meeting him there.

Jack had his marching orders, like them or not. Though he knew the Taylors were longtime clients and good friends of Dick Landes, he remained mystified by this assignment. *What does Landes hope I might learn from Marnie—or Callie?*

Chapter 80

Wednesday, May 20, 11:40 a.m.—Long Beach, California

Fidgeting with my seatbelt, I stared out the airplane window. Another unfamiliar scene flashed by as we taxied down the runway. The trip from JFK to Long Beach Airport had taken more than five hours, yet my Galaxy cell phone read 2:40 for an instant when I powered it back on, before adjusting from Eastern to Pacific time.

My throat was dry. I swallowed hard. Less than a week ago, I'd been knocked off my feet by a freak wave, banging my head hard enough to erase my past. I'd finally begun to adjust to the home in Greenwich . . . and now here I was, on the opposite side of the nation with a family I barely knew—and I had a twin sister who had jumped ship and was now hiding in Paris.

All I knew about my past life was what others had told me. Today I would be meeting Elizabeth, who Mom told me was like a surrogate grandmother, and my Aunt Caroline, who had a history of mental illness.

Although I'd been given the rundown on my extended family, not having a single memory of a family member was freaking me out. Keeping the lid on my rising panic took all my willpower. I was beginning to suspect patience had never been my high card.

Mom shifted in her seat as our plane pulled up to the ramp, an uneasy expression spreading across her smooth skin.

"Mom. Don't worry. I'm going to be okay."

"Marnie." She hesitated. "Don't feel pressured. If you feel it's too soon to participate in the Tremaine Dance Convention—"

From across the aisle, Juliana cut in. "Mom, we talked about this. You said—"

"I know what I said, sweetheart," my mother replied patiently.

I didn't want to be the cause of everyone's anxiety. "It's okay, really," I said. "If I liked to dance before the accident, the convention is probably a good idea. I want to get my life back." What I still wasn't sure about was the trio. It seemed all too possible that I would mess up.

Sucking on her bottom lip, Juliana rolled her eyes. "You'll be great. Remember what we talked about? Dance doesn't come from your head. It's all about—"

"Muscle memory." *I really like this kid.* "Okay, okay. This afternoon while Mom and I are getting my head examined again, you and Kaitlyn can work on choreographing the number. If I can catch on well enough not to embarrass us, I'll do it."

The FASTEN SEATBELT light blinked off, and I stood to retrieve my carry-on from the overhead bin, wondering if I should voice my concern. Finally I blurted out, "What I'm really worried about is whether to start the graduate program in August."

"We'll figure it out," Ashleigh said gently. It wasn't enough, but it was all she had. She hadn't fully regained her emotional balance since the disaster involving the ship. Never had she felt at such a loss as a mother. There was no one right move—no easy solutions. *I'll figure it out*, she repeated inwardly. She must, and so she would.

Following Marnie's return to their home in Greenwich, Ashleigh and Conrad had many sleepless nights discussing the pros and cons of having their daughter move back to Southern California to begin work on her graduate degree. *Would it be best to delay her first semester, or should she stick with the original plan?*

Marnie had spent the previous year obsessing over whether she'd be accepted into UCI's highly competitive graduate program for writers. With all the stress, she'd lost ten pounds. "I need more time," she'd told anyone within earshot. "This manuscript sucks. Maybe I wasn't cut out to be a writer."

Had Marnie been looking for approval? Or did she doubt her ability? Even now, Ashleigh wasn't sure, and neither was Conrad. Nor could they help her. It was something only Marnie could work out.

When her acceptance to the graduate program finally came through, and the head of the program, Professor Ben West, had called to welcome her, she'd been elated even as she confessed her misgivings. "Typical writer's insecurity," he had said. "Forever afraid our best isn't good enough. It's part of a writer's DNA, and something none of us ever fully overcome."

Ashleigh knew that if her daughter regained her memory in the next couple of months, she would be furious and depressed over a delay. Yet if it took longer, and she remained disconnected from what she called her "writer's voice," launching her into the program too soon could be even more devastating.

The hustle and bustle around her snapped Ashleigh out of her circular thought processes. Gathering their carry-ons, Marnie, Juliana, and Kaitlyn appeared to be engrossed in some heavy-duty conversation. Marnie's rapid bonding with her sister was a good sign—a big plus despite the uncertain days ahead. Ashleigh was grateful.

Nearing the baggage area, Ashleigh handed the JetBlue ticket envelope to Marnie, pointing to the stapled baggage stubs. "While you and the girls wait for our luggage," she said, "I'll check on the rental car."

Once the girls had collected the luggage, they met Ashleigh at the Avis counter and boarded the shuttle to pick up their car in the rental lot. Juliana began telling Marnie and Kaitlyn all about the peninsula area and the four-bedroom house the Taylors had leased. "It's right on the beach, and you can see the *Queen Mary* and the fancy oil islands with their palm trees and waterfalls . . ."

As Juliana continued, Ashleigh kept her eye on her other daughter, waiting for her to show a spark of recognition.

Chapter
81

Wednesday, May 20, 12:40 p.m.—Long Beach, California

When we turned onto Pacific Coast Highway, Mom began pointing out various sites along the way. None produced any flashes of recognition.

"This is the area in Long Beach known as Belmont Shore," she explained.

"It's cool, Marnie," Juliana said, pointing down the street. "Tons of small boutiques and terrific places to eat." Then she asked, "Can we go to Dominico's for lunch, then explore some of the shops in Belmont Shore?"

"Slow down, love," Mom said. "You'll have plenty of time to explore and show off all your hot spots, but first we'll get unpacked and see what Elizabeth has planned. With the memorial for Caroline's husband this Saturday, there might be some ways we can help her out."

"Sure thing," Juliana said.

Mom had told us this was a difficult time for Elizabeth. Fearing that the stress over her husband's death might send Aunt Caroline into another relapse, we would have to play it one day at a time.

"Aunt Caroline's the one I told you about, remember?" Juliana turned to Kaitlyn and discreetly moved her index figure in tight circles beside her temple.

Mom pointed out the body of water on both sides of the short bridge we crossed.

"This is Alamitos Bay," she said. "Our house—the one we've leased since you girls started college—is on the ocean side, about half a mile from here, on the peninsula between the bay and the ocean."

"Nice," I said, because I could think of nothing else to say. My heart sank. Apparently, I'd gone to college in this area for four years, but just as in Greenwich, not a single sight looked familiar.

Mom continued to direct my attention to the bay side of the street. Near the end of the peninsula, she turned down a very narrow street. "Sixty-third Place," she called out. A couple of car lengths before the end of the street, she turned into a very wide driveway that ran behind a huge beach house and continued to a second equally large house and a two-car garage.

Juliana and Kaitlyn scrambled out of the backseat. Mom raised the trunk of the white Mercedes and then rummaged through her handbag for the house keys as we unloaded our suitcases. Kaitlyn cupped her ear and cried out, "Is that the ocean I hear?"

"It is," Mom said. "The shoreline is less than fifty yards from the front of the house."

I took in the crisp, salty scent of the sea air, remembering absolutely nothing.

Chapter
82

Wednesday, May 20, 1:05 p.m.—Long Beach, California

As the girls disappeared into their bedrooms with their luggage, Ashleigh pulled hers into the master bedroom and picked up the phone on the bedside table. Before unpacking, she made a quick call to Elizabeth.

Phone in hand, she strode to the floor-to-ceiling window and gazed out onto the calming ocean view. The phone rang several times, then went to voice mail. "Hi, Elizabeth, just checking in," Ashleigh began. "Wanted to let you know we've arrived and to confirm the plans for this afternoon. Please give us a call when you have a chance. Otherwise, we'll be heading over shortly. Love you. Bye."

Heaving the larger suitcase onto the quilted bench at the foot of the bed, she flipped the lock and was about to begin unpacking when she heard the doorbell.

It has to be Elizabeth, she thought, and dashed down the stairs.

Throwing open the back door, she saw a tall, good-looking young man who reminded her of Conrad, in both eye and hair color. He introduced himself as Jack Kirkbride—the new investigator she and Landes had agreed might be of assistance to the family.

Before Ashleigh had a chance to properly introduce herself, the young man said, "I'm sorry to trouble you so soon after your arrival, but Miss Elizabeth asked me to stop by. She requests she be given the next hour for some alone time with Miss Caroline. Then she'd love for you and the girls to come to the house. She said there was nothing for you to worry about." He paused, a frown playing across his forehead. "It seems Miss Caroline took off in the Bentley earlier today with no driver's license. I was called in. Fortunately, she had not gone far and was found in the neighborhood." After sharing a few details, Jack said, "Miss Elizabeth is confident she has everything under control."

"I hope that's true," Ashleigh said, not wanting to go into detail. "Since her husband's death last week, Caroline seems to be slipping back into depression." That was all the young man needed to know.

Jack nodded. "I appreciate the opportunity to speak with you privately for a moment to clarify the role you'd like me to play regarding . . . your daughter."

Ashleigh noticed he didn't say *Marnie*.

"I'm also hoping you might add some insight," he continued. "Anything in particular you'd like me to know or do for you?"

"Certainly, Jack. And, since we'll be getting to know each other better very soon, please call me Ashleigh." She walked over to the kitchen counter and reached into her oversized handbag. "Now that you mention it, I would like you to do something for me."

She handed him a small paper bag embossed with the Carlingdon's logo. Inside, lying on a thick bed of tissue paper, was an eight-ounce glass in a Ziploc bag. "I would like you to have the fingerprints checked on this, please."

Ashleigh knew she was going on nothing other than maternal instinct—no real facts existed yet to support her perceptions. "I may be off base, but I'd like the results as soon as possible."

Jack didn't appear to be surprised. "Would you like to tell me what you suspect?" he asked.

Ashleigh hesitated for a fraction of a second. "Since my daughter returned home, she is not at all like herself. The injury she received on board the ship could account for it, but . . . We are hoping this evening's meeting with Dr. Martin will give us a better perspective."

Jack merely nodded.

"I may be off base, but I'd like the results as soon as possible," Ashleigh went on. "And Jack, this ID verification is just between us. If I'm wrong, I could be causing my daughter unconscionable damage."

"I understand," Jack said, then confirmed he'd be back to pick them up at three. They said their goodbyes. And yet, though he betrayed nothing with his mild expression, somehow Ashleigh felt she was not alone in her suspicions.

Chapter

83

Wednesday, May 20, 1:15 p.m.—Long Beach, California

Following Jack's departure, Ashleigh felt a need to leave right away for Naples but knew the girls must be ready for lunch.

Having given Avis the driver's license numbers for both Marnie and Juliana in case she needed either one to drive, she called out for Juliana, who instantly appeared in the kitchen doorway. Handing Juliana the keys to the rental car, she explained the new game plan. "Since you know the area, sweetheart, and you must all be hungry, I'd like you to drop me off in Naples and take the girls to lunch. I want to visit with Elizabeth and your Aunt Caroline before our appointment this afternoon."

"Cool," Juliana said. She went to tell the others and grab her handbag.

A short time later, Juliana pulled into the familiar driveway of the beautiful Stuart home. A wave of nostalgia blurred Ashleigh's vision. This home held scores of bittersweet memories.

"What time do you need us to come back and pick you up?" Juliana asked as Ashleigh slipped out of the car.

"Elizabeth said we could use the Bentley when in need of an additional car for the next couple of weeks. But please return Marnie to the beach house by three so we can leave for Aliso Viejo. That gives you plenty of time for lunch, and after you drop Marnie off, you can show Kaitlyn around Belmont Shore." Ashleigh waved goodbye.

Picturing her grandfather behind the wheel of the vintage Bentley, which was now parked in front of the open three-car garage, a flood of happy memories brought a lump to her throat. She headed for the house, recalling how blessed she'd been to have Charles Stuart as her guiding light throughout her childhood.

She hesitated momentarily before tapping lightly on the rim of the screen door. Despite being the legal owner of this home, she had never walked in without knocking.

When her knock went unanswered after nearly a full minute, however, she gently opened the door, stepped inside, and stopped to listen. Hearing nothing, she took a few soundless steps forward. Elizabeth's voice, low and tender, filtered into the empty kitchen before she reached the threshold to the living room. Though she could not make out Caroline's responses, the pleading tone brought her to a full stop.

Elizabeth sat on the sofa beside Caroline, her arm wrapped lightly around the trembling woman's shoulders.

Ashleigh was on the verge of retreating when Elizabeth spotted her in the doorway.

"Please, Ashleigh, come and join us," Elizabeth said.

"Hello, Ashleigh," Caroline said, her voice revealing little emotion.

Ashleigh returned the greetings and expressed her sympathy over Caroline's loss, hesitating to embrace her and upset Elizabeth's soothing influence.

Although Elizabeth and Caroline were about the same age, Caroline looked decades older. The mascara now running down her cheeks emphasized her deep wrinkles, and her eyes held a vacant look.

Caroline acknowledged Ashleigh's concern, sounding almost robotic. "Thank you. I was sorry to hear of the devastating accident at sea. I am looking forward to seeing all the girls."

Ashleigh struggled with her response, not knowing what to make of Caroline's demeanor. "Yes, Juliana has been looking forward to spending a bit of time here later today."

"And Marnie?" Caroline asked.

"Until her memory returns, I'm afraid we are all little more than strangers to her," Ashleigh replied uncertainly.

"I told Caroline all about the accident," Elizabeth reassured her. "She knows about Marnie's memory loss—and that Callie remained in England for the time being."

Ashleigh was momentarily startled, but she quickly caught on. Avoiding drama—as much as possible—seemed wise. At this difficult time in her life, Caroline certainly did not need to know Callie was missing.

"Caroline has been looking forward to having Juliana and her friend join us for dinner tonight," Elizabeth continued.

"That was our plan," said Ashleigh, "but if you'd rather not—"

A flame ignited in Caroline's eyes. "Are you afraid to leave your daughter in the home of a crazy person?" she lashed out.

Startled, Ashleigh considered her response.

Elizabeth dropped her arm from across Caroline's shoulders and shot to her feet. "There will be no self-deprecating talk," she said, as if speaking to a child in the throes of a tantrum. Her voice was calm but stern.

"Caroline," Ashleigh said in a soft tone, "all I meant was that with the loss of your husband, this might not be the best time for visitors."

"Sorry," Caroline said, her gaze shifting between Ashleigh and Elizabeth. "Since Don left me, I have been snapping at everyone. Even Elizabeth."

Ashleigh noted the odd way Caroline expressed the death of her husband.

"We'd love to have the girls this evening," Elizabeth said, turning to face Caroline. "I think their presence would do you good."

"You miss them, don't you?" Caroline accused.

Elizabeth stiffened. "Of course I do. I've missed being surrounded by their love. Much as I missed yours while I was on the East Coast. Now, let's avoid this middle school mentality. Loving them takes nothing away from our relationship."

Ashleigh admired the way Elizabeth faced conflicts with Caroline straight on—never soft-pedaling her response. No one could ask for a gentler or more understanding woman than Elizabeth, but when riled, she was an iron fist in a velvet glove. She would put up with no bad behavior—not even from Caroline at her worst.

"Yes, yes, I'd like them to come to dinner," Caroline said impatiently. "I understand you and Marnie will not be joining us?"

Although Ashleigh pitied the jealous, unstable woman, Caroline

Stuart did not lack intelligence. She wanted Elizabeth to remain with her in Naples, and she would do whatever she could to achieve that goal.

"There are some things we need to discuss, Ashleigh," Caroline whined.

"That's right," Ashleigh agreed.

Chapter
84

Wednesday, May 20, 9:20 p.m.—London, England

Graham Bradford slammed down the receiver of his landline at the precise moment Hillary charged into his living room. Beating her to the question she was bound to ask, he said, "So far, I've had no luck in reaching Marnie's parents. I've done everything possible to contact them . . . Nothing but roadblocks."

He braced himself. The look on Hillary's face told him she was about to reproach him, but there was nothing she could say that would make him feel any worse than he already did.

"The girl's father is an important CEO. He's bound to have staff who relay messages to him," Hillary rasped. Her expression was stern. "And surely you have tried the Taylors' home phone number?"

Bradford whisked his hand across the air as if to dismiss all those options. "When I said 'roadblocks,' I wasn't exaggerating. I know it's hard to believe, but I am unable to get in touch with any member of this high-profile family. I've run into one bloody wall after another. Conrad Taylor and his family seem to have vanished from the face of the earth."

He gestured for Hillary to sit down on the sofa as he lowered himself into his favorite armchair.

"When I called her father's office in New York, I was told he is out of town. His executive secretary is on vacation, and there was no one at the Jordon's headquarters authorized to give me his personal information."

Hillary sunk back into the cushions of the sofa, straightened her caftan, and crossed her bony hands in her lap. "Well, Graham, we must move forward. I presume you are making this your highest priority."

Bradford knew what she was thinking: The Sloane Square Workshop was scheduled to begin the next morning as planned. And there was still his novel to think of . . .

"Before we dash down the wrong road, Hillary, you should know that I no longer give a tinker's damn about my eroding deadline." He leaned forward. "That priority flew out the window with Marnie's accident."

"That easily?" the old woman asked, a skeptical expression on her wrinkled brow.

"That easily," he responded. "And you know bloody well why."

Aside from Bradford's personal reasons for prioritizing Marnie's well-being, letting go of his panic over the publisher's deadline wasn't as hard as he had imagined. It was just like before going on holiday, when time is running out and one must let go of many of those must-do tasks. Furthermore, Marnie's hard work in Paris had helped a great deal, and making his deadline wouldn't be as difficult as he'd first thought.

"Marnie's a quick study," he explained, "and she has produced a well-edited first draft, which has made my editing a lot easier. I'm also farther along than I—"

Bradford's cell phone buzzed. Slipping it out of his pocket, he glanced at the display. He didn't bother to finish his thought. Instead, he leaped up from his armchair.

"It's the hospital."

Chapter
85

Wednesday, May 20, 9:30 p.m.—Chelsea and Westchester Hospital

Marnie's eyes blinked open. While her lids no longer felt glued together, her skull felt like a leaden balloon. She was flat on her back and unable to raise it more than a couple of inches.

Swishing her tongue around the inside of her mouth, she found she craved water. "Is anyone there?" she ventured, sensing she was not alone.

"Her eyes are open," a familiar voice said. "I think she's awake. She's trying to say something."

But I was hollering. Wasn't I? She tried again to create some moisture in her dry mouth. "Water," she whispered.

"Did you say you wanted water?"

Marnie blinked a couple of times before Charlize came into focus.

"Yes," she croaked, grateful to see the pale face of her new, vivacious friend.

"Thank God, Marnie. I was afraid you might never wake up."

There was a sound of scurrying feet, and Marnie soon saw another shadowy figure. As it drew closer, she made out a nurse in blue scrubs. "No," the nurse said. "You can't give her that." A hand reached in and took the glass from Charlize. "Here, use this."

Marnie couldn't see what "this" was, but in the next moment, Charlize leaned down and said, "Open your mouth."

Ah, so cool and wet and refreshing. In her mouth was a tiny sponge soaked in water. "Thanks. More please," Marnie said. After a few refills of the saturated sponge, she asked Charlize, "Are you alright?"

"Me? Are you kidding? I'm fine. I wasn't the one who stepped in front of the blooming taxi."

A sharp pain splintered her skull at the thought of it. "Is that what happened?"

Before Charlize could respond, two more figures dashed into the room, both speaking at once: Graham Bradford and Hillary Spearpoint.

Marnie tried to sit up, but her head threatened to explode.

"Would you like me to raise the back of your bed?" the nurse asked.

Marnie made the mistake of nodding, which sent needles of pain to her eye sockets.

Every sound seemed magnified, and suddenly Marnie wanted everyone to go away. Before she could make that request, a flood of memories washed in. No, she couldn't just fall back asleep and make the world go away.

"Graham," she began, "my family. They *must* know I'm okay. You have to tell them I didn't get washed overboard . . ."

Bradford leaned forward, barely able to make out Marnie's words. Was she saying something about notifying her parents?

"Of course," he said, "I've been trying to reach your father, but I need your help."

But Marnie had closed her eyes.

Charlize stepped in closer to the bed, her eyes wide with alarm. "Has she fallen back into the coma?"

"No," the nurse said. "She is no longer in a coma. She's just fallen asleep—the result of her pain medication. Her reaction is stronger than most." She began ushering them out the door. "Now I'm afraid I must ask all of you to leave."

"But we just got here," Bradford protested.

"She needs her rest," the nurse said.

"The doctor said she seemed to be emerging from the coma," Charlize said. "I rang as soon as I knew."

"We're already well past visiting hours anyway." The nurse closed Marnie's door behind them. "You may come back first thing tomorrow morning."

Chapter 86

Wednesday, May 20, 2:35 p.m.—Naples, California

When Caroline excused herself at last to take an afternoon nap, Ashleigh slumped down on the sofa beside Elizabeth, mentally drained.

Elizabeth let out a sigh. "I'm so sorry. If I hadn't felt an overwhelming need to give my full attention to Caroline after her misadventure, I would not have had that handsome young Landes agent bring you the news." She paused, her brow creased in worry lines. "You shouldn't have to deal with this right now, and yet I couldn't have you walking in blindsided. Since Don's death, Caroline seems to be slipping back into depression."

Ashleigh grasped Elizabeth's hand. "Without your support, Caroline would completely fall apart."

"I know," Elizabeth said, "but I'm not sure it's enough. I will do everything in my power to keep her in this home, but if that is not possible . . ."

Ashleigh knew what the alternative was. "New Beginnings is a wonderful facility. It's not a death sentence, nor would it necessarily be forever. Caroline's mental health was restored in the past." She reminded Elizabeth of John Nash's story, as told in the movie *A Beautiful Mind*. "By once again focusing on her art, along with your support, she can regain control of her life."

"I plan to be here for her." Tears rolled freely down the smooth skin of Elizabeth's cheeks.

Wrapping her arm around Elizabeth, Ashleigh said, "I understand. I know she loves you. And I don't believe she would ever intentionally hurt you." Still, she was concerned about Elizabeth's well-being as well as Caroline's. "If flare-ups continue, like the one you described today, there may not be a choice."

"It's clear that Caroline continues to view you as a threat," Elizabeth said.

"That does not make her mentally ill," Ashleigh replied. "Being paranoid about my having the title to the Stuart home is understandable. While we know Charles placed his home in my name to protect her, it is to be Caroline's home. For as long as it is a suitable place for her."

Elizabeth dabbed her eyes with her ubiquitous white hankie. "I love her too, but I can't stand it when she challenges you about your intentions."

"She just lost her husband," Ashleigh said, "and she feels insecure."

"Oh, Ashleigh." Elizabeth squeezed her wrist. "How can you be so patient and compassionate? Especially with one daughter missing and another unsure of who she is . . ."

Ashleigh leaned into the loving woman, knowing that in fact she had learned much about patience and compassion from the very woman who had asked the question.

After parking the Bentley in the driveway of the beach house, Ashleigh found she had a few minutes to herself. In the master bedroom, she gazed out once more through the floor-to-ceiling windows, awed by the beauty of the ocean yet painfully aware of how life-threatening its power could be.

Just then her phone vibrated. She smiled when she saw her husband's photo on the screen. "Hi, love," she answered straightaway.

"I just stepped out of the GM's office and have only a couple of minutes," Conrad said. "Want to fill me in with a broad brush?"

Not on the phone, she thought. *And not with so little time.* "Nothing that can't wait until dinner this evening. But that appointment with Dr. Martin is not coming a moment too soon."

He asked about Elizabeth and Caroline, then signed off to return to his meeting.

Pressing the disconnect button, Ashleigh realized she could hardly wait to be with her husband and hear his thoughts.

Chapter
87

Wednesday, May 20, 3:15 p.m.—Long Beach, California

Standing in front of the mirror in another unfamiliar bathroom, I slipped the band off my ponytail. Brushing out my hair, I prayed the meeting with the famous Dr. Martin would give me hope. I didn't think I could take another "only time will tell" session.

While I could hardly wait to meet the impressive doctor whose book I was attempting to read cover to cover, I feared he might tell me my self-diagnosis was correct. If I had what he labeled autobiographical amnesia, there was no cure.

"Our ride's out front," Mom called out.

"Be right down." I snapped the band on my wrist to remind myself to drive away negative thoughts. Then I slipped it off, wrapped it around my ponytail, and dashed downstairs.

As I passed the living room, I saw that Juliana and Kaitlyn had moved the dining room table and chairs to make a dance floor for the practice of our upcoming trio.

"We'll have the choreography all worked out by the time you get home," Juliana said as she set the last of the chairs upside down on the table.

"I thought you were going to dinner with Elizabeth."

"We are," she said, "but not until five thirty. We should all be home around the same time to practice. We'll show you there's nothing for you to worry about."

"We'll see about that," I said as I headed out the back door. Earlier, when Juliana had played our song in the car, my body had begun to sway. I just hoped my feet would know what to do.

3:50 p.m.—Newport Beach, California

With Jack at the wheel, they made it from the peninsula to Fashion Island in just over thirty minutes. Conrad had called earlier and asked Ashleigh to meet him for an early dinner at the Cheesecake Factory instead of at Jordon's. When the Mercedes pulled up in front of the restaurant, she spotted him crossing the parking area.

She rolled down the window. "Hi, love." Her husband returned the greeting.

Jack jogged around the car, opened the rear door for Ashleigh, and turned to introduce himself to Conrad. They exchanged a greeting and shook hands.

"Great timing," Conrad said, helping Ashleigh from the car while Marnie scrambled out the other side.

"I suggested she ride in the front with Jack," Ashleigh said, noticing the look of puzzlement on Conrad's face.

"Okay," Conrad said, though his expression said the opposite. Addressing Jack, he said, "I appreciate you playing chauffeur tonight."

"Glad to help out," Jack said.

After getting a big bear hug from Conrad, Marnie slipped into the front seat.

The Mercedes pulled away from the parking lot, and suddenly Ashleigh and Conrad had a few hours to themselves.

She stepped in close, and he enfolded her in his arms right then and there. "Though we've been apart only twenty-four hours, I've never missed you more," she said.

Conrad chuckled. "Me too." He began to describe the meetings with the local GM. Then his face turned even more serious as he asked about Elizabeth and Caroline. "And I take it our daughter has experienced no lightning bolts of recognition."

Ashleigh shook her head. "Afraid not. This appointment with Dr. Martin is coming not a moment too soon." The words *our daughter* replayed in her head.

She began to wonder if Conrad's thoughts were traveling down the same bumpy road as hers regarding their daughter's true identity.

4:05 p.m.—Aliso Viejo, California

The girl sitting in the front seat of the Lincoln was drop-dead gorgeous, but she was not Marnie. In fact, Jack was certain she was Callie, even though the photograph did her no justice.

He felt uneasy about saying nothing regarding her identity, but he agreed it would be best to wait until the truth was confirmed. Knowing Ashleigh Taylor harbored the same suspicions made him feel a bit better. She had failed to call her daughter by name. Jack couldn't bring himself to call the girl *Marnie* either.

En route from Newport Beach, Jack had avoided personal questions. He mentioned the light traffic for this time of day, the nice cool weather, and other innocuous and boring topics. Glancing at the car clock now, he saw that they had nearly an hour to kill. "Are you into Starbucks?" he asked.

"Sure," she said, giving him a brilliant smile, one that lit up her eyes. She gave an exaggerated shrug. "I guess you know my long-term memory is only about a week old. But I know I like those cinnamon dolce lattes."

When he pulled into the parking area near Starbucks, he said, "We have plenty of time to sit inside. The doctor's office is just over there." He gestured to the low-rise stucco building across the way.

Once they'd gotten their orders and found an empty table, Jack remarked, "So, cinnamon dolce lattes had a strong hold on your memory bank."

She shook her head. "Afraid not. I learned quite by accident. Juliana ordered an espresso for me in Greenwich just a couple of days ago, telling me it was my favorite. But it left a bitter taste in my mouth. I couldn't believe such strong coffee had been my favorite. I hated it. But I loved the latte."

Holy shit, Jack thought. When he'd handed Ashleigh's glass over to forensics to run the tests on the fingerprints, he had tried to impress upon the lab technician just how urgent an answer was. He could hardly wait to get the results.

Chapter
88

Wednesday, May 20, 4:15 p.m.—Newport Beach, California

"This early dinner is perfect," Ashleigh said. With so much on their minds, they ordered quickly and began sharing their thoughts the moment the waiter left the table.

After confirming their minds were traveling down the same road, they agreed to listen to Dr. Martin's thoughts before bringing up their joint suspicions.

The din of dinners being served and tables cleared, and the high-pitched chatter surrounding them, faded when Ashleigh gazed into her husband's understanding blue eyes. She was blessed to have him as her forever partner. "So, you don't think I'm delusional?"

Conrad set down his glass of merlot. "Of course not." He reached across the table for her hand. "I'm sorry I wasn't on board earlier. I thought it was just your perpetual optimism."

She squeezed his hand. There was no need for a response.

"Having the fingerprints checked was a wise move." He took another sip of his wine. "The day I left for California, it occurred to me that Marnie was not at all like herself. She seemed more positive and calm than I imagined she could ever be, particularly under the circumstances." He explained that he, too, had noticed the unwashed dishes left in the sink and the clothes scattered on the floor, which was so unlike the old Marnie. "But I felt that it must be due to her head trauma."

Ashleigh nodded her agreement. "Dr. Martin might be able to shed some light on whether a blow to the head could cause such drastic changes in behavior."

4:50 p.m.—Aliso Viejo, California

"Hey. It's nearly five," Jack said.

Thrown off balance, I glanced at my cell phone, unable to believe the time had passed so quickly. I hadn't laughed so much or felt so relaxed since my accident. Jack was terrific. My embarrassment over his knowing I remembered nothing of my past had faded in moments. It was a relief to talk to someone with no expectations, no shared experiences, no disappointment over my lack of memory.

I liked Jack Kirkbride. I felt like he was a friend—my only friend. In less than an hour, he'd helped transform my attitude, and in a good way. Since learning about the Christonellis, I'd been resentful of being robbed of my early life with my family. But after Jack's candid account of his own childhood, which was far less than perfect, I realized how lucky I was. I had not one, but two families who loved and cared about me.

Meanwhile, Jack had grown up with none. Yet he'd sought neither sympathy nor praise when he shared his background with me. Adopted at birth, he had never met his biological parents. Outsiders probably thought he'd landed in the perfect family, wanting for nothing as a child. His adoptive father was an Illinois state senator and his mother a socialite from Chicago. Unlike most adopted children, who were wanted and adored, Jack had had a lonely childhood. Reading between the lines, I saw him as the token child of self-absorbed parents who were enmeshed in politics. They left his formative years in the hands of a nanny, who died just before Jack's fourteenth birthday. "She was the best," he'd said. "But when she died, I was old enough to take care of myself."

That statement had brought tears to my eyes . . . But before I could comment, he had reminded me of the time.

We raced out the door and across the parking lot.

At the doctor's office, he walked me to the door of Suite 104 but did not step inside. Instead, he said kindly, "When you're ready to leave, I'll be here."

I was surprised by how much his simple words encouraged me.

Chapter
89

Wednesday, May 20, 4:55 p.m.—Aliso Viejo, California

The receptionist was seated at a mahogany desk beside the doorway to the doctor's office. She called me by name just as I stepped over the threshold. After making some polite conversation, she handed me a clipboard. My heart thudded. I knew nothing about my own medical history.

I looked over the top sheet nervously, but to my great relief there were no questions I needed to answer—only a highlighted place requiring my signature for the release of medical information. As I handed the clipboard back to the receptionist, Dr. Martin appeared in the doorway to his office and ushered me in.

After we exchanged greetings, I took a seat at the end of the sofa beside his armchair. The doctor was a nice-looking man of medium height, with sandy hair and a warm, friendly smile. He began by asking me to tell him what I remembered of the accident.

"Well, I'm sure you read all about the rogue wave."

"Yes, Marnie, but my only interest is in you personally. Begin with your first memory following the accident."

I crossed and then uncrossed my legs. "Well, I woke up on the floor of the cabin I shared with my twin sister. I—"

He raised his hand to cut me off. "When you awoke, did you know that you were in a cabin you shared with your sister?"

"No."

"Let's stick with your own experiences. Describe things from your particular perspective."

"OK. Sorry. Well, I awoke fully dressed, lying on a wet carpet. I didn't know I was on a boat, but I felt a rocking motion. Besides not knowing my name, I didn't remember anything about the semester at sea or my twin sister."

"But you do remember being on the floor of the ship's cabin?" he asked.

"Yes. I remember being confused. My head hurt, and I heard voices and footsteps outside my door, but I didn't know where I was. I was totally disoriented."

"What is the next thing you remember?"

I thought for a brief moment. "I remember feeling dizzy. To keep from toppling over again, I had to hold on to the furniture and the wall."

For the next half hour, we went over everything I remembered in those moments, step by agonizing step.

"Thank you, Marnie," Dr. Martin said. "I believe it is safe to say that your anterograde memory—the memories you've formed since the accident—is fully intact."

"Dr. Martin, I've read most of your book on memory. I know retrograde are memories I had before the accident. Those are now gone." I couldn't hold back a deep sigh. "What I need to know is if . . ."

When I couldn't finish the question, the doctor gave me an understanding smile. "You want to know whether this amnesia is temporary or permanent."

Nodding, I felt tears welling in my eyes. I pushed them back.

"I sincerely hope your amnesia is temporary." His expression was warm and apologetic. "I am pleased you've taken the time to read my book. Your familiarity with the terminology is a significant help." He paused. "Your X-rays confirm that you have what we refer to as global amnesia."

I nodded. That was the umbrella term for all degrees of amnesia.

He went on to describe how memory works, using the same filing cabinet analogy my mother had used back in the hospital in New York. I knew I should listen and wait until he came to the end of his explanation, but I had to ask him something right away.

"Doctor, could I have autobiographical amnesia?" My voice shook. If he confirmed my suspicion, I didn't know what I'd do.

CHAPTER 90

Wednesday, May 20, 5:15 p.m.—Aliso Viejo, California

"Whoa," Dr. Martin said, his face clouding. "Let's not jump to conclusions, Marnie. We do not have enough information to say that is the type of amnesia you are experiencing—or to rule it out."

"But Dr. Martin—"

"Autobiographical memory records what we have experienced personally, including time and place. With this type of memory loss, we don't remember our family, the people we've known and been close to. Nor do we remember what happened, or when and where. However, much of our long-term memory is still there."

The idea of autobiographical amnesia was terrifying to me, because it seemed like what I was experiencing. "I remember all sorts of random trivia but none of my personal information," I confessed. As I spoke of my greatest fear, I felt nauseous. My head began to throb, and the tears I'd been holding back began to spill down my cheeks.

Dr. Martin rose from his armchair and came over to where I was sitting on the sofa. He sat down beside me and handed me the small box of Kleenex from the end table.

I dabbed my eyes.

"I need you to listen to me," he said. "A limited amount of knowledge can be a dangerous thing. Try to be patient, and pay attention to what I am attempting to explain . . . Can you do that?"

"Yes," I said in a squeaky voice I didn't recognize.

"You must understand that all the autobiographical amnesia symptoms we've discussed are also present in the early stages of global amnesia. With any type of amnesia, most of our retrograde memories vanish immediately following an injury. Most return at various stages and after various spans of time. However, some memories do not return. Memories of the brief time before an accident, or of the moment of the impact, may be entirely lost."

"So, I don't have autobiographical amnesia?"

He shook his head sadly. "We have found no cranial damage, but we don't yet have enough information to rule it out."

It was all getting way too complicated. "I'm sorry, Dr. Martin, but my parents told me patience has never been one of my virtues. I understand you can't tell me what you don't know. And since my time is almost up, I still have two important questions."

The doctor returned to his armchair and told me to go ahead.

"My graduate degree program in creative writing at UCI begins in August."

His head bobbed, but he said nothing.

"If I don't go back to school, I don't know what I'll do. But I don't remember what I was writing. And I have no idea how to begin writing something new. Do you think this is something I should pursue, or should I just give it up?"

Leaning forward, he said, "Don't be so hard on yourself. It has been less than seven days since your accident. You may not remember what you were writing, but you most likely still possess the skills of putting words together in a meaningful way. You have a couple of months to see whether ideas begin to gel. If not, maybe you can delay the start of your graduate program. Take a couple of writing classes, and perhaps do something else just for pure enjoyment."

My stomach churned. The idea of asking my second question frightened me. But uncertainty was worse, so I forced it out. "Worst-case scenario: Autobiographical amnesia is not reversible. Right?"

"That is correct. But let's not jump to that conclusion."

I shook my head. "I'm not. But I can't stick my head in the sand. What do people do when they have no memories of their past?"

Dr. Martin stretched out his legs and crossed his ankles. His warm, caring eyes looked directly into mine. "Are you sure you want to spend our last five minutes exploring the slim possibility that your amnesia may be more than temporary?"

"I do." There wasn't a doubt in my mind. Not knowing the worst was preventing me from thinking of anything else. Doom and gloom scenarios kept replaying in my head. "Once I know the worst, maybe . . . maybe I can begin to figure out how to deal with it." I hoped I sounded more confident than I felt.

"Alright," the doctor said. "Using my filing cabinet analogy, let's suppose the cabinet containing your personal memories has been damaged and that information cannot be retrieved. Your cognitive ability is intact. You also have many other cabinets of memory in other areas of your brain to draw upon."

I wasn't so sure.

"You mentioned that you remember various random bits of information, such as words to songs, names of famous people, and so on," Dr. Martin continued. "Therefore, many segments of your long-term systemic memory have not been affected by the blow to your head."

"But my cell phone is filled with text messages, emails, and voice messages from friends and extended family members," I explained, on the verge of losing it again. "I haven't returned any of those calls or messages. I don't remember who those people are or what we did together. I have nothing to say. I'm living in a world filled with strangers who know me!"

The doctor leaned forward again, steepling his fingers. "Since you insist on going down this road, the very worst-case scenario is this: The cabinet with your personal memories may be irreversibly damaged. However, since you have family and friends who care about you, with their aid, you can recreate your past."

Like how? I thought, my stomach tightening. He raised a finger, I settled back in my chair and said nothing.

"One, there is no shame in amnesia. You must be candid." Raising a second finger, he continued, "Two, before you plan to meet with a friend, have someone in your family go over photos and fill you in on the things you did together—"

"Enough," I said, holding out my hands. "You're right, doctor." There was no point in exploring unanswerable questions. I no longer wanted to travel down this dark, dreary road.

Straightening my posture, I lifted my chin and looked into the doctor's serious eyes. "My memory will come back. Until it does, I will remain positive." I must instill this mantra in my foggy brain, repeating it over and over to myself.

No point in dwelling on a dreary tomorrow that might never come.

Chapter
91

Wednesday, May 20, 6:00 p.m.—Aliso Viejo, California

When Dr. Martin walked me out of his office, Jack was waiting in the reception room. Though his presence was not unexpected, I felt weak in the knees at the sight of him. I was glad he was there. I didn't want to be alone.

After shaking hands with Jack, the doctor picked up some papers from his receptionist's desk and handed them to me. "If you need to change the appointment for your PET scan, the number is at the bottom of the page. Otherwise, we should have the results by the first of next week."

I thanked him and turned to leave.

"Remember to call Dr. Fieldson's office in the morning. They are expecting your call. He will fit you into his schedule for this week."

"Thank you, Dr. Martin," I said, even though I had no intention of talking to another shrink so soon. That was a battle for another day.

On the short walk to the car, Jack asked, "Are you hungry?"

I gave him a grateful look. "Starved."

"What are you in the mood for?"

I grinned. "Anything but raw fish sushi."

We settled on Domenico's. On the trip back to Long Beach, I continued to feel that connection with Jack and wondered if he felt the same way. *Maybe he's just being nice to his clients' daughter, the girl with amnesia . . .*

It took a while to find a parking place, and there was quite a crowd at the front of the restaurant. I feared he might be one of those guys who couldn't tolerate a long wait, but Jack appeared unbothered. He gave me a warm smile. "Be back in a flash."

He disappeared toward the back of the restaurant. Returning in moments, he introduced me to the manager, a friendly man with tousled hair and an engaging smile who seated us at a relatively quiet table for two.

So Jack is a guy with influence here in Long Beach . . .

As we waited for dinner to be served, he asked no questions about my appointment. Instead, he talked about Belmont Shore and all the terrific shops and restaurants I must put on my agenda. While it was a relief to have no questions I needed to answer, somehow that made me want to share my confused, conflicting thoughts even more. And I liked the idea of sharing them with Jack Kirkbride, who offered no judgment—and who wouldn't be disappointed over what should be a shared memory as my well-meaning family did.

After the waiter ground the fresh Parmesan onto our entrees and disappeared, Jack's eyes met mine. "I don't want to pry, but you looked upset when we left the doctor's office. Is there anything I can do to make you feel more comfortable in this strange new world?"

7:00 p.m.—Long Beach, California

When Callie—he had no doubt now about her identity—set her fork down, her dark brown eyes held his for a few long seconds. Then he picked up his beer and took a long pull. "Sorry. I—"

"It's alright," she cut in. "I was just taking a moment to consider. Other than restoring my memory, I don't think there's anything anyone can do. But it would be nice to have a sounding board."

Although he was still afraid to overstep his bounds, Jack swallowed his fear and hastened to add, "I'd love to be your sounding board. I have been told I'm a good listener. One of my classes in law school was on negotiating skills, but it was really all about listening. I aced the class." He grinned.

She took a sip of her water, then set down the glass. Her gaze was direct, yet cautious. "Where do I begin?"

He remained silent. *This is strictly business,* he reminded himself. He was on the job—*and* on the Landes Agency expense account. She was the daughter of a client. *But she looks so lost and so damn vulnerable* . . .

She told him of her experiences since waking up on board the *Rising Star* and being airlifted by helicopter.

"Hard to believe all that has happened to you just since last Thursday." *Callie,* he wanted to say. Using no name was awkward, but he'd be damned if he'd call her *Marnie.*

Better not slip up, he chided himself.

Looking across at her still nearly full plate, he said aloud, "But you've only taken a few bites of your dinner."

She looked down at her plate and took a small bite, a curtain of shiny blond hair covering one side of her face. "Sorry. I've been doing too much talking. You must be bored out of your mind."

"Not at all. Besides, as riveting as swinging in the breeze between the ship and helicopter is, I know there's a lot more. Waking up with amnesia had to be devastating."

Placing her fork on the edge of her plate, she leaned forward, her elbows on the edge of the table, her chin resting on her intertwined fingers. She took in a deep breath. "It was. It still is. And not knowing if my memory will ever return is even more frightening."

He wanted to reach out and touch her hand, but resisted. "I don't know a lot about amnesia, but don't most of those lost memories eventually return?"

"Usually, but not always," she explained, parroting Dr. Martin's analogies.

"Autobiographical amnesia?" Jack repeated. "Never heard of it."

"It's rare. And irreversible." She appeared to be holding back more than tears. "I'm trying to be positive, but I can't help thinking about my whole past being stolen from me." She paused. "Do you know about the Christonellis?"

Jack took a moment to consider his response. She was willing to open up to him, thinking that she had been the one kidnapped as a baby. As if waking up with amnesia were not traumatic enough, Callie was being asked to remember and take on an identity that was not her own. It didn't seem fair, but what could he say?

"Yes."

"Well, I met them yesterday. And I most likely hurt them very much." She sighed. "Mom tried to explain, but I don't understand why my parents allowed them to continue as a part of my life . . ."

Jack had read the Taylors' back history, yet he too was at a loss. As Callie continued to beat herself up about not being able to be warm and understanding when the Christonellis had come to see her, he felt like punching his fist through the wall.

One way or another, he had to put a stop to this charade before further damage was done.

Chapter
92

Wednesday, May 20, 7:00 p.m.—Aliso Viejo, California

Ashleigh and Conrad arrived right on time for their seven o'clock appointment to find no one sitting behind the receptionist desk, and the door to the doctor's office standing ajar. Rather than tap on the half-open door, they sat down in the attractively decorated waiting room.

In the next moment, the outer office door opened, and a sandy-haired man, dressed casually in a yellow polo shirt and gabardine pants, stepped into the reception area with a half-eaten sandwich in his hand. "Mr. and Mrs. Taylor?" he said.

Ashleigh and Conrad exchanged a glance. "It's a pleasure to meet you, Dr. Martin," Conrad said. "We greatly appreciate you making the time for us in your busy schedule. Please, finish your sandwich."

"The pleasure is mine," Dr. Martin replied, his gaze warm and friendly. "As you've discovered, my receptionist is gone for the day, but she made a fresh pot of coffee before she left. Would you care to join me?"

Ashleigh was about to turn down the offer but changed her mind when the words *join me* echoed in her head.

"Thank you," Conrad said, as the doctor set three mugs on a silver tray, quickly filled them, and invited the couple into his office.

Dr. Martin took a discreet bite of his sandwich and sank back into his armchair. "I found your daughter to be a bright, perceptive young woman. I was pleased to discover the active role she is taking in understanding her situation."

"Have you had an opportunity to look over the summary of Marnie's background we provided?" Conrad continued.

"Yes, certainly. Dr. Harvey sent an extensive report. We also spoke by phone. I agree with your decision to share Marnie's childhood background with her. In my opinion, it was your only option."

"Then you are aware that when Marnie was a teenager, she was diagnosed as borderline bipolar," Ashleigh said.

"Yes. I've also gone over the information sent by each of Marnie's doctors, before and after the accident."

"Although our daughter has shown some signs of frustration since the accident, she has been much more even-tempered than we expected," Ashleigh said. "Also, her obsessive neatness seems to have disappeared. And she's demonstrated little of her former mood swings. Just a great deal of frustration, which is completely understandable under the circumstances."

Conrad made direct eye contact with Ashleigh, and she gave him a nod. It was time to move forward. "What my wife and I are wondering, Dr. Martin, is whether you feel such major personality changes could be due to the head trauma."

The doctor picked up his coffee cup but set it down without taking another sip, considering the question. "Well, in short, yes. A change in personality is quite possible. To what extent depends on the severity of the injury." The doctor took a moment before he spoke again. "I cannot give you a definitive answer regarding those concerns. The changes you describe could be related to the head trauma, but I must admit such changes do seem extreme."

"So it is possible our daughter's amnesia has caused a significant personality change?" Ashleigh asked.

The doctor cocked a brow. "We do not yet have enough information about Marnie's case. She has been self-diagnosing, I am afraid, and fears she might have autobiographical amnesia."

Conrad slipped an arm around his wife's shoulder, as the doctor continued.

"It is far too early either to diagnose or to rule that out. A PET scan will give us more specific information. Since you are staying in Long Beach, my assistant scheduled one for Marnie tomorrow at Long Beach Memorial."

"We can make that work," Ashleigh said, remembering that Juliana and Kaitlyn would be visiting the dorms at that time. "But our daughter had a CAT scan at New York–Presbyterian Hospital."

Dr. Martin nodded. "I understand. A PET scan, or positron emission tomography scan, takes an image of the brain. It uses a radioactive substance called a tracer to look for disease or injury. It complements the CAT scan X-ray."

"Excuse me, Dr. Martin," Conrad cut in, "but our situation may be a bit more complicated than most. We need your advice on an extremely sensitive and life-altering issue for our family."

Chapter
93

Thursday, May 21, 7:45 a.m.—Chelsea and Westminster Hospital

Marnie awakened to sunlight filtering through a large-paned window to the right of her bed. She did not know that she had been moved from the brightly lit, noisy ICU the previous evening after her visitors departed. Now she was in a quiet hospital room for two. She could not see beyond the wall of curtains to the left of her bed, but a light snore, followed by a whistling noise, told her she was not alone.

Though she was thankful to be awake and alive, apparently with all her faculties, the urgency to call home pressed in on her. She searched around her bed for a call button but found none. If only there were someone to help her to her feet . . .

Pulling back her covers, she gingerly swung her legs in the direction of the window. The movement caused the room to spin.

After a few seconds, her world settled. Feeling a bit stronger, she grasped the bedrail, stretched out her foot, and felt for the floor. Though it was cold on her bare foot, she stretched out her other one. With both feet firmly planted on the floor, she didn't feel too bad—other than her throbbing head.

Her black-and-blue hip felt tender. So did her ribs. And judging from the bruises and the tenderness of her entire body, she knew she must look frightening. *What about my face?* Placing both hands on her cheeks, she pressed gently from jaw to hairline. On her right temple, she felt a gauze-like bandage. The left was smooth and unbandaged.

As she was making up her mind whether to check herself in the mirror, a young nurse entered her room, then let out a gasp. "Miss Taylor, you shouldn't be out of bed."

"Well, I am," Marnie replied matter-of-factly. "I need to call my parents. But first, I need a robe."

The nurse looked horrified. "Please, let me help you back into bed," she whispered, glancing toward the curtain. "I'll have a phone brought to you."

"Bloody hell. What do you think you are doing?" Graham Bradford's distinctive voice echoed off the walls. To Marnie's surprise, Hillary followed a few steps behind him.

"I need to call home." Marnie hated the miserable, whining tone of her voice.

"First get back into the blooming bed."

Bradford's piercing gaze sent spirals of heat up her neck. The hospital gown was just like the ones at home: completely open down the back. Even though her writing mentor could not see her from that angle, a jolt of embarrassment overtook her, and she backed up to the bed.

The nurse shushed the visitors and scurried across the room to help her.

Once Marnie was settled, Bradford made his report. "I've failed to reach your parents. No one answered your home number in Greenwich. I attempted to get in touch with your father yesterday at Jordon's and was told he was away on important business. Although I said the message was urgent, I was not given a phone number to reach him."

"Did you talk to his secretary, Ellen?"

"I was told she is on vacation. And when I finally managed to track down your home number, all I reached was an overloaded answer phone—not a living soul, and no way even to leave a message."

"What day is it?" Marnie's head reeled. "How long have I been here?"

"Today is Thursday."

"Thursday," she repeated. She and Charlize had left Sloane Hall late on Sunday night . . . more like early Monday morning. She ticked off the days in her head. "Oh, my God. Three days ago?"

"That's right," Hillary said softly. "You've been in a drug-induced coma."

"What do you mean? I've never fooled around with drugs. Not even weed."

Bradford seemed to be stifling a smile, although Marnie didn't see what was so funny. "No one is accusing you of drug use," he explained. "The doctors put you in what is known as a medically induced coma. When you stepped in the path of the taxi, you were hit hard enough to fracture a couple of ribs. You were given pain medication to get you through the first few nights and let your body heal."

"I understand," Marnie said. As interesting as it was to relive her accident, she had a more urgent priority. "So, my sister has been home for two days?"

"At least," Bradford replied. "The *Rising Star* docked in Charleston on Sunday night and moved on to Brooklyn on Tuesday. Either way, I assume your parents were there to meet her."

Marnie knew she should be breathing a sigh of relief. *By now everyone knows I was not lost at sea.* But she still felt the need to talk to her family—to know if Callie was okay. What if *she* was the unnamed student lost at sea?

After gathering her thoughts, Marnie said, "No one is home in Greenwich right now, and the housekeeper only works part-time." She paused, doing her best to remember the schedule. "You said it's Thursday? My whole family is probably in Long Beach by now." Callie's graduation was the next day. With her father's hectic schedule, he had planned store visits around Callie's graduation.

"Do you have contact information for them in Long Beach?"

She shook her head. Then her hands shot to her temples. She pressed gently on the bandaged right side and more firmly on the left, hoping to lessen the pain. *I must remember to keep my head still.* "All my contacts are on my phone . . . which is in Callie's handbag."

Bradford pulled a chair up beside her bed for Hillary.

The clock on the opposite wall said 7:55 a.m.—almost 3:00 a.m. in New York, and midnight in California. "Graham, would you please sign me out of here?"

"Are you out of your blooming mind?"

"I know I must look like holy . . . terrible, but I don't feel that bad.

I need my computer." Despite Bradford's edict prohibiting emails, this was no time to tiptoe around. "I may have an email from my sister and parents. Besides, all of my phone numbers are on my computer." She paused. "It's too late at night to place a call to either coast. And anyway, I don't want my parents to know about my accident yet." *Not until I test the family waters . . .*

"The time of day is unsuitable for a phone call to the U.S.," Hillary agreed, "but your parents must be told of your accident as soon as possible."

Marnie started to shake her head, but the pain shooting through her skull stopped her. "Not until I know how Callie is—and how they've reacted to my news."

Chapter
94

Thursday, May 21, 3:00 a.m.—Los Angeles, California

Pocino's phone jarred him awake. He'd set the sound on high so he'd be sure to hear any call coming in from Landes London.

Despite no specific evidence pointing directly to the involvement of Graham Bradford in Marnie's disappearance, the writing professor seemed like their best bet for finding her. Perhaps there had been a gap between the end of his master class on board the ship and the start of his London workshop—long enough for a trip to Paris with Marnie, for whatever goddamned reason.

Landes had given Pocino the go-ahead yesterday afternoon to contact Liam at Landes London. They should have their beat on Bradford by now.

"Liam here," came the Irish-accented voice. "We ran down the info on your author in a heartbeat. His whereabouts are well known. You were spot-on about his being in France."

Knew it, thought Pocino.

"He was a keynote speaker for some prestigious writers' conference. Didn't return to Sloane Square in London until late Sunday night." There was a pause. "Afraid I've got a bit of disturbing news about the Taylor girl."

"Is she alive?" Where that come from, he didn't know. *She has to be alive? I can't be the bearer of more bad news.*

Liam scoffed. "I said bad, not catastrophic. As I understand, like many of you Yanks, she looked left when she should have looked right."

"Huh?"

"Stepped out in front of a taxi."

Pocino swung his feet to the floor. "How bad?"

"Nothing broken other than a couple of ribs. More than a wee bit banged up, though, and plenty bruised. She's been in a coma for days."

"A coma!"

"Medically induced. She's out of it now. And that's not all."

Pocino huffed a sigh. *What next?*

"The young woman admitted to the hospital is not registered as Marnie Taylor. The one they've got is Callie."

Pocino cursed. He refused to believe it. "That identity has got to be wrong."

"Given what you laid out, I agree." The London agent explained that he had been unable to contact Graham Bradford by phone. "We have an address, so I'll hightail it over to hospital the first chance I get, to see for myself. Then I'll call on Bradford at that Sloane Square address. His workshop is due to start today."

Now wide awake, Pocino said, "You'll need to tread carefully. Don't speak to the girl yet."

"Why on earth . . . ?"

"Best not to confuse things. The clients—her parents—are questioning the identity of the twin here in California, the one everyone believed to be Marnie."

"The one with amnesia?"

"Right. The parents are no longer sure which is which, especially after the girls spent four years away at college. They look too much the same. The family can only identify them by their personalities."

Liam took a moment before responding. "Right you are. The bonk on the head adds a whole new dimension."

Pocino agreed. "But the connection with Bradford's workshop leaves no real doubt as to her identity."

"So you don't need us to dig further into which twin is which?"

"Nah. This case is gonna explode as soon as our lab gets the fingerprints of the twin with amnesia. Callie, no doubt."

Liam hesitated again. "You planning to make a jump across the pond to escort the wayward girl home?"

"Not a chance. If she's still in recovery, I suspect her mother will be the one to accompany her home. If not she's an adult, so she may return home on her own."

Chapter
95

Thursday, May 21, 6:15 a.m.—Long Beach, California

Jack was wide awake when his phone beeped, not having slept a wink. He grabbed it without missing a beat. "Kirkbride."

The lab tech's confirmation on the fingerprints was music to Jack's ears. "Sweet. I knew it. Thanks, Joe. I owe you." He disconnected, immediately hitting the number for Dick Landes's cell.

Jack had felt the strain of being forced to keep his lips sealed on Callie's identity from the moment he met her. As she'd revealed her inner struggle over entering the graduate program in creative writing, it was all he could do to keep quiet. Now she could be freed from the burden of trying to fit into an identity that was never hers. Surely Landes would agree.

A groggy voice answered. "Hello?"

"Sorry to wake you, boss. But this is urgent." The fingerprint results left Jack in no doubt. Pocino's inkling had been spot-on. "The amnesia victim is not Marnie. It's Callie."

Ignoring Landes's grumbling, Jack rushed on. "The Taylors need to be brought in right away."

"Jack. Stop. Listen." Landes's tone was insistent. "There's been an accident."

"What?"

As Landes described Pocino's early morning phone call and the situation in London, Jack struggled to take it all in. Marnie had been in a freak accident in London. The Taylors would need to be told—and not by telephone.

Jack's heart went out to Callie and her parents, who would have to take this bad news along with the good.
Is there no end to what fate has dumped on this family?

Ashleigh and Conrad arrived at the new Landes Agency offices in Long Beach at exactly seven. Entering the reception area, they wove a path around a tall ladder and the workmen engaged in finishing the installation of crown molding.

"Sorry for the mess," Landes called through the open doorway.

Stepping across the threshold into his private office, Ashleigh looked through the wall-high windows overlooking the peaceful Long Beach harbor. On the round conference table between Landes's desk and the wall of windows were four coffee cups, a large platter of Danish, a pitcher of water, and four glasses.

Landes asked Jack to close the office door. It muffled but did not completely block the noise of the construction in the reception area. "Had I known we'd be having this early morning meeting," he said, pouring out four coffees, "I would have rescheduled the workmen. I wanted to catch you before you hit the road."

"No problem," Conrad said as he and Ashleigh slipped into their chairs. "We appreciate you making allowances for our tight schedule."

Ashleigh heard something in the outer office crash to the floor, followed by raised voices.

Landes sat down in his desk chair, swearing under his breath. "Jack, please begin by filling the Taylors in on the lab report."

Jack nodded. "The fingerprint confirmation is solid. The twin who experienced the disaster on the *Rising Star* and who is now suffering from amnesia is . . . Callie." What we still don't know, however, is why Callie had her sister's identification."

Ashleigh exchanged a glance with her husband. She knew neither of them was surprised. "Thank you for the fast turnaround, Jack."

"After sharing our suspicions with each other last night," Conrad added, "we concluded it was surely Marnie, not Callie, who stayed behind in England. After all, she was the one who had a reason. She is in awe of Graham Bradford."

Ashleigh nodded. "What we could not come to terms with is how either of our girls would leave the ship without discussing their plans with us up front. If you knew the twins, you'd understand. It's out of character for either of them."

Jack nodded.

"Marnie has been known to be impulsive, but not irresponsible or uncaring. Not since her teen years—"Conrad cut in. "This is a blow to our family values. For Marnie to sneak off the ship undiscovered is mind-boggling. That she did so without so much as a phone call . . ." His eyes communicated how betrayed he felt.

Ashleigh squeezed his hand. "The girls often borrow each other's handbags and clothing, but never their IDs. That still makes no sense."

Jack spoke up. "I don't want to step out of line, but—"

Ashleigh jumped in. "Nothing is out of line that might help us understand Marnie's disappearance."

"It's not about Marnie. It's Callie."

"Callie?" Conrad repeated.

"When we stopped for dinner last night following her appointment, she opened up to me. Trying to fit into her sister's identity is tearing her apart." Jack looked directly at both Ashleigh and Conrad, his eyes pleading.

Ashleigh looked at the young man's anguished expression. He had taken his assignment to befriend their daughter to the next level. He truly cared. "Thank you, Jack. We are aware of the added trauma that can come from pushing an amnesia patient in the wrong direction. Until yesterday, we weren't sure whether her personality changes could be attributed to amnesia, and that prevented us from becoming suspicious immediately." She glanced at her husband. "We'll definitely inform Callie today."

Landes stood up from his chair and began striding back and forth across his office. "Now, I have some additional news. Pocino rang me at a little past three a.m." He stopped dead in his tracks. "We've heard from Liam, in our London office."

Ashleigh felt the tension knotting her neck. Her instincts told her the news was about Marnie—and she still couldn't shake the feeling that something was very, very wrong.

CHAPTER
96

Thursday, May 21, 7:15 a.m.—Long Beach, California

"Like a dog with a bone, Pocino followed his instincts," Landes continued, shaking his head. "The charges on Callie's MasterCard in Paris threw him off, but only for a micro-minute. When we discovered the purchase was an Android device and not Apple, we had evidence pointing toward what Pocino had suspected. Marnie was the one motivated to stay behind in Southampton."

Conrad's posture stiffened. "Just how long have you suspected?" Pushing back from the table, he glared at Landes and stood up. "And why in the hell would you withhold such vital information?"

Looking directly into Conrad's angry eyes, Landes held up a hand. "I made a bad call. This is on me, and me alone. Pocino and Jack both wanted to bring you and Ashleigh into the loop from the get-go, but I put the kibosh on any communication until the missing twin's identity and location were confirmed."

Ashleigh sprang forward in her chair. "You know where she is?"

Landes nodded. "In London, as you suspected."

"Did Marnie leaving the ship have something to do with this Graham Bradford?" Conrad growled.

"That's our premise," Landes said. "It has yet to be validated. The London office traced Bradford to a Sloane Square address. Pocino says that's where he holds his elite summer writing workshop. So far their calls and visits are going unanswered."

Consumed with anger, Conrad began to pace.

"You have every right to be angry." Landes poured a splash of water into a glass and took a quick sip. "I was wrong, but I had the best of intentions."

Lowering himself back into the chair nearest Ashleigh, Conrad reached for his coffee.

"I made a judgment call. You were dealing with so much already, and I didn't have an ounce of proof." Landes shrugged and took a swig of water. "I figured there was nothing to be gained by burdening you with a hunch. Keep in mind, until Tuesday evening—not even two days ago—all evidence pointed to Callie being on deck when the rogue wave broadsided the *Rising Star*."

Landes's point hit home. Conrad could hardly believe this nightmare had begun only one week earlier. Now was the time to focus not on how the investigation was handled, but on getting his daughter back.

"Dick," Ashleigh said, "while I understand your reservations, we never want to be left out of the loop. That said, let's move on. I'm glad Liam will eventually contact the professor, but has anyone spoken to Marnie?"

Landes closed his eyes. "No one has spoken to her yet. We hope to contact her through Bradford. In the meantime . . ." He shook his head. "What we do have is a bit more bad news."

Conrad gulped down the lukewarm coffee and set the cup back in its place. "Dick. *What the hell happened?*" he snarled.

Beside him, Ashleigh seemed frozen in place.

"First, I want you to know Marnie was not seriously injured." Landes rubbed his temples.

"Seriously injured by what?" The words exploded from Conrad's lips. In his peripheral view, he saw the alarm register on Ashleigh's lovely face.

"Marnie was in an accident. She stepped into the path of an oncoming vehicle. No serious injuries, but a couple of cracked ribs and plenty of bruises. She was placed in a medical coma for a couple of days for observation. She came out of it yesterday."

Conrad's heartbeat soared. He reached for Ashleigh's hand and grasped it.

Chapter
97

Thursday, May 21, 7:25 a.m.—Long Beach, California

"Marnie is registered at a hospital in Chelsea, but as *Callie* Taylor," Landes explained. "Liam was heading there this morning, to make a positive ID."

Ashleigh knew she couldn't wait that long. "Dick . . . I want to talk with her now," she said. "Surely an English hospital makes phones available for patients."

"Of course," Landes said, buzzing his secretary on the intercom. "Sandra, please get the number of the Chelsea and Westminster Hospital. Dr. Norman Benson is the staff doctor who's been treating Marnie."

A few moments later, Sandra stood in the doorway to Landes's office. "I have the number here," she said, handing a pink slip of paper to Ashleigh. "Would you like me to place the call now?"

"That would be great, thank you," Conrad said.

Sandra gestured for the Taylors to follow her toward the small conference room to her right. Several minutes later, she returned. "I'm so sorry, but Marnie has been released from the hospital."

"Her injuries must not be too serious," Conrad assured Ashleigh, who released the breath she'd been holding.

Knowing her husband had a point, Ashleigh tried to put everything into perspective, but the idea of an ocean between her and Marnie shredded her heart. She nodded. Her knees felt as though they were made of rubber.

"Give me a moment," she said, and picked up a pitcher from the round tray in the center of the conference room table and poured herself a glass of water. *If only I could wrap my arms around Marnie and tell her how much we all love her.*

"According to the hospital," continued Sandra, "She was accompanied by a Graham Bradford." With a raise of her brow, she asked, "The author?"

The nerve in Conrad's jaw twitched as he punched a fist into his open palm. "Had her typing up his manuscripts," he muttered. "Marnie may be an adult now, and responsible for her own actions, but Bradford had to be involved somehow with her slipping through ship's security. And what legitimate reason can there be for a famous forty-three-year-old author to sneak a student—"

"Darling," Ashleigh said, "Marnie is no silly schoolgirl. Nor is she known for doing something against her will. Her worship of Bradford may be starry-eyed, but it is not romantic. She admires his talent." Reaching across the table, she rested her hand on Conrad's forearm. "What Marnie was over the moon about was the opportunity to understand Bradford's writing process. Remember her telling us of the Sloane Square Workshop he holds each summer?"

"Vaguely," he replied. "She said she didn't have a chance of getting in."

"But she hadn't given up hope. I suggested it was something to look forward to after she completed grad school." Ashleigh had pointed out that Marnie had enough on her plate for the summer, with graduation as well as the job she'd lined up in display at Jordon's Westminster, in Orange County.

Conrad rubbed his jaw. "I didn't think it was a serious consideration. Did she ever mention it again?"

"No. I'd forgotten all about it, until this morning. But if she was selected for Bradford's elite workshop, I know she'd have wanted to take advantage of it."

"If that were the case—"

"We would have supported her," Ashleigh said, finishing her husband's sentence. "But she's so darn headstrong, she may have thought we would try to talk her into waiting. Maybe that's why she didn't tell us about her plans."

She could breathe a little deeper now. The pieces were falling into place.

First things first. Once the Landes London agent confirmed the details, they would call the Sloane Square complex. But before getting Marnie on the phone, Ashleigh wanted to speak with this Graham Bradford.

Conrad locked his eyes with hers. "Now, about Callie . . ."

With the Atlantic Ocean separating her two wounded chicks in need of nurturing, and with Callie's head trauma ruling out a trip to London, Ashleigh blotted her eyes and began to compartmentalize. Conrad was right. Callie would need her parents now more than ever.

"I think it's time to call Dr. Martin," he said. "We're in uncharted waters, and we can use all the guidance available."

"I'm sure he'll squeeze us in somehow." Ashleigh pulled the doctor's card from her handbag and dialed the number. She gave her name to the receptionist and explained their urgency. "We just need a few moments, at his earliest convenience."

"I'm sorry, Mrs. Taylor, but—"

There were voices in the background. Then the doctor's familiar, warm voice greeted Ashleigh. "This is Dr. Martin."

Ashleigh flicked on the speaker. "Our suspicions were confirmed, Doctor. You spoke with our Callie last night. Callie, not Marnie, is the twin with amnesia." She was pleased when the doctor seemed to see the news in a positive light.

"Discovering she never intended to become a writer should bring considerable relief," he explained. "I found Callie's coping skills to be quite remarkable under the circumstances. She mirrors her parents' positive attributes and comes across as someone who looks for opportunities rather than obstacles." While he refused to rule it out prior to her PET scan, he again pointed out that autobiographical amnesia was extremely rare. "She is fighting hard not to be negative or become depressed. And fortunately, you've discovered her identity before the start of the school year. It may not be as much of a problem as you might think."

"Excuse me, Doctor, but where do we begin?" Conrad asked. "How do we tell Callie she is not who she's been led to believe?"

"Just like that," the doctor said. "Dealing with missing memories is a life-altering experience. At least now, on top of that, she won't be attempting to fit into a foreign role. My bet is that this turn of events will be a boost to her self-confidence."

Ashleigh ended the call, and as she and Conrad made their way to their rental cars, she confessed her relief. Dr. Martin felt, as they did, that Callie would be relieved to know her true identity. "Callie has her PET scan at ten a.m. We'll need to talk to her before that."

"No time like the present," Conrad responded. "And once we hear from Landes London, we can catch up with Bradford and Marnie late tonight—or first thing in the morning, London time."

"Sounds like a good plan," Ashleigh agreed.

CHAPTER
98

Thursday, May 21, 7:25 a.m.—Long Beach, California

I awoke to the sound of pounding on the bedroom door. Sunlight streamed through the slats of the blinds. I squinted at the clock on the bedside table.

"Marnie," a duo of voices whispered, before the door eased open and Juliana and Kaitlyn appeared.

I sat up. "What's going on?"

"Mom said you have a ten o'clock appointment at the hospital, so we need to start rehearsing our trio."

"Are Mom and Dad up?"

"Up and out," Juliana said. "They were meeting Dick Landes at the Long Beach office. Then Dad will be hitting the stores. Mom said she'd be back in plenty of time for your appointment." Without taking a breath, it seemed, Juliana pressed on. "Kaitlyn and I worked out the kinks in the choreography last night, after we came back from dinner with Elizabeth and Aunt Caroline."

"How did that go?"

Juliana shrugged. "Aunt Caroline asks a lot of questions. She seemed okay at first, but when I said we didn't know why Callie was in Paris, she went bonkers." She looked at me, her head cocked. "You remember that they found out Callie was in Paris, right?"

I could almost laugh about it. "Jules, I'm not *totally* wacko."

"I know you're not." She paused, one hand on her hip. "Anyway, didn't you read our note?"

"What note?"

Juliana rolled her eyes. "*That* note." She pointed to a sheet of paper on the floor beside my bed.

"Sorry. Didn't see it." Reaching down to pick it up, I saw bold letters written with a blue Sharpie: TRIO PRACTICE AT 7:00. MEET US IN THE DINING ROOM. "Okay, I'm awake now." I grabbed my leotard and jazz shoes from my suitcase and then headed for the bathroom. "Meet you downstairs in ten."

Before the bathroom door clicked shut, Juliana called out, "You want a bagel?"

"Sweet. Thanks."

I flew downstairs, eager to get started despite my nerves. There were bagels, cream cheese, and OJ on the kitchen counter. I took a bite of bagel and a gulp of juice, and then joined the two girls in the spacious dining room.

The only furniture remaining in the room was a small table on which Juliana had set her iPhone and a pink Beats speaker. She turned on Aretha Franklin's "Respect" and began demonstrating the choreography for my part. The music was uplifting, and I felt my body begin to sway. I could hardly wait to try it out.

"Ready?" Juliana looked up at me. "Six, seven, eight . . ." Her hand extended in my direction, and the rehearsal began.

The choreography was well planned, and I felt the music in every pore of my body. Juliana mirrored my movements on the floor, counting out each beat. After two run-throughs, with us doing only my part, she said, "You are sooo ready."

Kaitlyn went to restart the music, saying, "Marnie's totally got it. Let's practice the whole trio."

My sister positioned the three of us on the hardwood floor of the dining room. The music came on full blast. In unison, we began. The beat of my heart fell into the rhythm. I wasn't scared. I was excited. I hadn't felt this good since . . . well, as long as I could remember. And Juliana was all smiles.

"I'm loving it," I shouted above the blare of *Just a little bit, just a little bit . . .*

My heart sang. This was so much fun, so easy. I followed the choreography to the letter, but on the third time through, I felt so comfortable that I just let loose. My body had a mind of its own, and I just kept spinning.

And then Juliana gasped, her eyes widening in surprise.

Chapter 99

Thursday, May 21, 8:05 a.m.—Long Beach, California

Conrad followed Ashleigh up the long driveway to the beach house, parking the BMW directly behind his wife's rented Mercedes. Switching off the ignition, he set the emergency brake. Good thing practically every vehicle had Bluetooth these days. He'd canceled his store visits the instant that his priorities had shifted once again.

Ashleigh switched off the engine too but remained behind the wheel.

Conrad walked forward and opened her car door, questioning her with a look.

Ashleigh looked up at her husband, her face calm. "I just needed a moment to wrap my mind around this latest twist in our universe."

Conrad forced a smile. "That, my love, will take a lot longer than a New York minute."

Ashleigh's calm expression turned to a look of surprise when Juliana came flying out of the house, calling their names as she ran down the driveway.

"Whoa. Slow down, pumpkin," Conrad said.

Ashleigh smiled at the old nickname that still slipped so easily from his lips. But their youngest daughter's expression appeared troubled. *What else could possibly go wrong?* Caroline and her unsteady state of grief immediately shot to mind.

"What is it, darling?" Ashleigh asked.

"Mom . . . Dad . . . You've got to listen to me, even though it might sound totally nuts."

"Welcome to our world," Conrad muttered in an attempt at levity.

"I'm serious, Dad. Listen, Marnie must be the one in Paris. It's *Callie* who has the amnesia."

Stunned, Conrad and Ashleigh exchanged a glance. Neither spoke, until at last Ashleigh asked, "How did you figure it out?"

"*You knew?*" Juliana stared at them, a steely glint in her dark eyes. "You knew, and you didn't tell me?"

"No, Juliana," Ashleigh replied quickly. "We just learned the truth this morning." She sighed. "After we brought your sister home from the hospital, I noticed a few things that seemed out of character for Marnie. But since we didn't know how a head trauma and amnesia might affect someone's personality—"

The color drained from Juliana's face. "But why didn't you tell me?"

"I'm so sorry, darling. If it makes you feel any better, I shared my suspicions with your father only last night. We thought it best to wait for confirmation." Juliana's indignation suddenly gave Ashleigh a deeper understanding of why Landes had kept his suspicions to himself. "But what makes *you* so certain?"

"The pirouettes."

"Pirouettes?" Conrad repeated.

Ashleigh understood. "You practiced the trio."

Juliana nodded. "After a few practice runs, she just started spinning like a top."

Ashleigh had to smile. Even back in high school, no one on the girls' dance team could manage those multiple pirouettes like Callie could. It's one reason she had won the dance scholarship in her senior year.

Ashleigh was sure their perceptive daughter would know better, but she had to ask. "You didn't say anything to her yet, did you?"

Juliana rolled her eyes. "Of course not, Mom. What would I say? She's confused enough already. But once she knows, I bet she'll be a lot happier."

"You think so?" Ashleigh and Conrad said simultaneously, exchanging a glance.

"Sure. She's really stressing over the writing. And you should see what a great time she's having with the dance."

"Darling, did she remember the original choreography for the dance?" Ashleigh asked.

"Maybe. But I showed her first, so I can't say for sure. Anyway, I think dance takes a different kind of memory. Her body was moving with the music. I don't know if she remembered it in her head from before." She stopped short. "But what about Marnie? Does that mean Mr. Pocino found her in Paris?"

"Marnie is safe, sweetheart," Ashleigh replied. "She's in London now, but there's a lot we don't yet know. As soon as we do, we will sit down as a family and figure out how to move forward."

"Hey, pumpkin, let's get into the house," Conrad said. "Where are the other girls?"

"They're in the dining room, still practicing. With Callie in our trio, we're sure to win a platinum. But when are you going to tell her? She needs to know who she really is."

"Hey, Jules, come on back," Callie called out from the backdoor. Even from that distance, Ashleigh could see the joy and excitement on her daughter's face.

Chapter
100

Thursday, May 21, 8:15 a.m.—Long Beach, California

As the two girls ducked back into the house, Ashleigh slipped out of the car and gave her husband a kiss on the cheek. "Setting aside everything in your topsy-turvy retail world means the world to me, love."

"Hey," Conrad said, "I'm here until this merry-go-round comes to a stop. We're in this together. I have no higher priority."

Tears pricked Ashleigh's eyes. Conrad was her rock. Together they would weather this storm.

"Love, I don't like being left in the dark any more than you," Ashleigh said. "But Dick's intentions were good—just as ours were when we didn't share our suspicions with Juliana."

"We're not eighteen-year-olds, nor are we inexperienced with life's challenges," Conrad shot back.

Ashleigh blinked.

"Sorry, love. I didn't mean to snap."

"I understand, love." She knew that with the pressure he was under at Jordon's as well as on the home front, it was a miracle he kept the lid on his emotions. "But would we have done anything differently with Juliana? I think Dick just needed to be sure his suspicions were correct before he rocked our world unnecessarily."

Conrad sighed as they began walking toward the house. "So, we'll have our talk with Callie now, while Juliana and her friend are visiting the dorms?"

Ashleigh nodded. She knew Juliana would want to be there, but she would understand. It would be rather awkward with Kaitlyn there.

But . . ." She paused, tears clouding her eyes as she thought about Juliana a few minutes ago, asking, *What about Marnie?*

Afraid it would create more questions than they could answer, they had not mentioned Marnie's accident.

With Juliana and her friend on their way to CSULB, I was the last to get dressed and dash downstairs. Mom and Dad were sitting at the kitchen table, talking in low voices over mugs of coffee.

"Do I have time to finish my bagel?" I asked. "After the workout Juliana put us through, I'm starved."

"Of course," my parents said in duet.

As I slipped into a chair across from my parents, I realized I missed Juliana. Despite our age difference, I liked having her around. Had I always felt so awkward about sitting down with my parents without my sisters around? I answered my own question: My discomfort stemmed from having no past, nothing to say.

"Darling," Mom said, "your dad and I have some news to share with you. It's going to be confusing, but we believe you'll find it to be a relief. There's no easy way to tell you this . . ." She took a sip of her water. "You are not Marnie, darling. You are Callie."

My whole world seemed to spin and then come to a sudden stop.

I am not Marnie. I am Callie.

I twisted my ponytail around my finger as that reality began to take shape. "You mean I never wanted to be a writer . . . I never dreamed of writing a blockbuster? I've always wanted a future in the world of dance?" *Could this be true?*

"That is right, Callie." Mom looked like she was on the brink of tears. She walked over to give me a hug.

Callie. That's me.

I felt numb.

"The ship identified you as Marnie," Dad cut in. "You didn't know who you were, and all the identification in your handbag . . ." His voice trailed off.

Mom picked up the conversation. "The thought of you leaving the ship in Southampton never made a lick of sense to us. You were in your element during the semester at sea. You were floating on air when Allison Dee asked you to be her assistant for the master dance class. You've known her since preschool."

And what about you? I wanted to scream. *Didn't you know your own daughter?*

"We all began to notice traits in you that were out of character for Marnie," Mom continued. "But because we didn't fully understand amnesia and the extent to which it could change someone's personality, we missed—or maybe misjudged—those signs."

I pushed my bagel aside—my appetite was gone. Even though a stream of relief filled a part of me, I felt a flush of anger rise from my neck to my face. "How long have you known?"

"We did not receive confirmation until early this morning." She shared giving Landes Agency a glass with my fingerprints on it, which had revealed my identity.

"But how long have you suspected?" I thought about last night's meeting in Aliso Viejo. "Did you suspect I wasn't Marnie when you sent me to Dr. Martin?"

"We suspected, yes, but we couldn't risk being wrong. We needed to consult an expert." Dad rose from the table and refilled his coffee mug. "Callie, we did our best to learn as much as we could—and as fast as we could."

Beads of perspiration broke out on my forehead. This was just too weird.

"Did you suspect I was Callie before you arranged for me to meet with Erica and Mike?"

"Absolutely not," Dad said. "Even though the Christonellis were pushing for a meeting, we would have preferred to avoid it—even though we believed you to be Marnie. We did not want to take a chance of you being blindsided by hearing the truth about your—her—childhood."

I sort of got why they would do that. But it didn't make this any easier.

"Callie, we are so, so sorry for what you've been going through,"

Mom said. "We hated to withhold the information, but the thought of having you ping-ponging from one identity to the next and then back again filled us with terror. We had to wait until we had physical proof of who you are."

And now there was proof. Everything had changed, and yet nothing had changed. Yes, my perception of who I'd been, and my goals in life, had been flipped upside down. But the amnesia was just as terrifying as before.

CHAPTER
101

Thursday, May 21, 5:30 p.m.—London, England

Emotionally drained, Graham Bradford found it impossible to slip back into the world of Detective Derek Duncan. For the next hour or so, his popular PI series was on hold. *Maybe a cup of tea could get the juices flowing,* he thought. Heaving himself from his favorite armchair, he heard the whir of the elevator and the clang of the cage opening on his floor.

He checked his Rolex. After a long day of intense one-on-one meetings with each of the workshop students, he wasn't expecting anyone else at this hour.

Without her usual warning knock, Hillary burst through his living room door, her face was red with agitation.

Now what?

Hillary was a sensible, caring woman with no flair for melodrama, other than on the written page. For the moment, Bradford chose to delay her inevitable censure. "I was just about to make a pot of tea. Care to join me?" he said, making his way into the kitchen.

She ignored his invitation but followed him, her wise, gray eyes boring into him as he filled the kettle. "I just went in to check on Marnie, and to my surprise—"

Bloody hell.

"Hillary," Bradford said, "before you condemn me, know that it wasn't my idea."

"It's unconscionable, Graham. Marnie was just released from hospital. She has been in this complex less than two hours, and already you—"

"Hillary, hear me out. I've made mistakes over the past week or so—outrageous mistakes. But I did not ask Marnie to do any work for me this evening. I turned down her offer to type manuscript pages—*twice*." He explained, "Marnie told me she was not yet ready to tackle her own novel, but she had insisted she'd go mad if she didn't have something productive to do, so I finally gave in. "I cautioned her not to overdo it."

Hillary continued to stare him down. "You know full well she won't stop until she's finished puzzling out the scribbling on your stack of draft pages. And what about contacting her family? That must be her top priority now."

Hillary would settle for nothing less than a solution—a solid plan of action. However, he had tried every possible avenue for reaching Marnie's family. It was now out of his hands.

Marnie adjusted the pillows behind her back and leaned against the double bed's headboard. The pounding in her head calmed to a dull hum. Still, the sea of words on Bradford's yellow sheets of paper began to blur. Her ability to concentrate had vanished, so she powered off her laptop.

If only it were that easy to shut off my brain.

Her mind continued to circle through what she knew and what she suspected. It was Thursday. Callie had been off the ship for four days, or at least two. Their parents had surely read Marnie's letter by now. She was unable to find a phone number for her parents in Long Beach.

Why hadn't her parents called Sloane Hall looking for her?

Pressing her face into her palms, she fought against an overwhelming sense of abandonment. Were her parents so angry with her decision to stay in England that they didn't even want to speak to her?

Unable either to be productive or to fall asleep, Marnie slid her feet to the floor and padded to the kitchen. Despite her aching hip, she did her best not to limp.

There was no coffee, so she filled the kettle and pulled out a couple of bags of PG Tips, England's No. 1 tea. Then she took out a slice of bread and popped it into the toaster. At the sight of her reflection on the shiny surface, she grimaced. The bruises on her face had faded slightly, but the ugly, yellow-shaded flesh surrounding them looked worse, and her left eye was still nearly swollen shut.

A rapid knock on the door cut through her thoughts. "Come in," she called out. "I'm in the kitchen."

"Holy hell," Charlize scolded her as she walked through the flat. "What if I'd been Jack the bloody Ripper?"

Marnie laughed. "Last I heard, he was bloody dead." Then, using her best English accent, she said, "Fancy a spot o' tea?"

Charlize whistled when she got a good look at Marnie's face. "Bloody, *blooming* hell. Still looks like you were on the losing end of a really bad spat."

Throwing her hands in the air, Marnie said with a grin, "Why can't the English teach their children how to drive on the right side of the *bloody* road?"

Charlize grinned back. "How do you feel?"

"Like I was hit by a ten-ton *lorry*." Marnie's grin faded. "Seriously, I feel a lot better than I look."

"And so you should, after your Sleeping Beauty routine—"

"Not of my choosing." Her toast popped up. "How about some toast and jam with your tea, instead of cookies? I mean, biscuits?"

"Just tea, please," Charlize replied. "I'll get the fire started while you finish up, and then we'll have what we Brits call 'a wee natter.'"

Déjà vu washed over Marnie as she set the white wicker tray on the coffee table and sank into the armchair. Tilting her head back against the soft leather, she stared up at the stippled ceiling. "I was just thinking—"

"You're a lucky lass?"

"Yes. Less than a week ago, I was on top of the universe, thinking I *was* the luckiest writer-in-training on planet Earth. I wasn't looking forward to my parents' reaction, but I could deal with it. But now, putting them through hell when they thought I had drowned . . . It's something I never imagined." She revealed her fears that her parents were too angry even to talk to her.

"Blimey. Don't beat yourself up, Marnie. No one saw that ginormous wave coming."

Unexpected tears spilled down Marnie's cheeks. "I totally screwed up, Charlize. If only I could do a rewrite of the past week and a half," she said without a trace of humor. "I should have called them. If I hadn't taken the chicken's way out—"

"Hey, don't get your knickers in a twist. No one tells their mums and dads all their plans. Mine are totally whacked out about my wanting to be a writer. 'We sent you to Oxford so you'd be qualified for a real job,'" Charlize mimicked. "I'm old enough to know what I want, and so are you. If they aren't on board, it's just too blooming bad."

Marnie's stomach was in knots. "After all that happened, I need to hear from my family. But no one has called."

"Marnie. Be reasonable. You lost your mobile."

"But why don't they call me here at Sloane Hall?" She couldn't push away the feeling that her family was punishing her for her covert actions. "Callie was pissed I was leaving the ship, but she never holds a grudge. She would have given our parents my letter, telling them I couldn't pass up the opportunity to work with Graham."

"Maybe they're waiting for you to call them," Charlize suggested. "Do they know you have no way to reach their unlisted cell phones or their house in California?"

Unlisted. A thought occurred to Marnie. What did her father do when he needed to find a number that was unlisted?

Call the Landes Agency. That would not be an unlisted number.

Suddenly Marnie had a fail-safe plan to reach her parents. She just had to decide when to put it into action.

Chapter
102

Thursday, May 21, 10:25 a.m.—Long Beach Memorial Hospital

When the lab technician called out, "Marnie Taylor," Conrad squeezed Ashleigh's hand. "We'll take care of correcting your records during your scan," she heard him whisper to Callie, seated on his other side.

They had already waited in the Radiology lobby for nearly half an hour. Now that Callie had been called in for the PET scan, the technician explained that they should plan on spending at least two additional hours at the imaging facility. The actual scan would take no more than thirty-five minutes, but preparation and resting periods were required before and after the image was taken.

When Callie disappeared with the lab tech, Ashleigh and Conrad walked down the long corridor to the Admitting office. Correcting Callie's medical records took considerably longer than they expected. "I understand, Mr. Taylor," the young woman behind the desk began, "but the authorization for the PET scan is for Marnie Taylor, not Callie."

The nerve in Conrad's jaw twitched. Reading her nameplate, he said, "Miss Greenburg—"

Ashleigh saw his exasperation and stepped in. "I understand you are following protocol. As my husband explained, Callie is an identical twin, and the amnesia caused confusion over her identity. Dr. Martin, the neurologist who ordered the PET scan, will confirm the scan should have been prescribed for Callie."

When they finally left the young woman's cubicle, Ashleigh slipped her arm through Conrad's. Like many personnel directors she'd worked with in the past, Miss Greenburg read the hospital protocol as hard-and-fast rules, not taking into consideration that no set of rules could be written to cover every contingency. All too often, Ashleigh knew, common sense and logic were in short supply.

"Let's go to the kiosk," she suggested. "I'd love to get a latte. And while you check in with the stores, I'll bring Elizabeth up to date on the Taylor merry-go-round and see how she's getting on with Caroline."

"I hope things are settling down there. We have enough on our plates without having to deal with more drama." Conrad spoke with a note of finality.

"I couldn't agree more, love, but if things continue to go south, we may have no choice but to get involved. Elizabeth may need our help. If Caroline's instability continues . . ."

Pulling her in close, he kissed the top of her head. "We'll do what we have to do." He heaved a sigh and said, with a chuckle, "Bringing things into prospective, the situation at Jordon's doesn't look so bad. It seems there's ongoing chaos on every front."

When Ashleigh leaned into him, she felt a weight being lifted from her soul. "At least now we know the agenda items, if not the order."

CHAPTER
103

Thursday, May 21, 1:30 p.m.—Long Beach, California

When we got back to the peninsula, I dashed upstairs to change into a pair of shorts, a T-shirt, and flip-flops. Making my way back downstairs, I planted a smile on my face, striving for upbeat and optimistic. Like Mom.

I was not nearly as strong or selfless as I needed to be. It was something I'd have to work on. Having at least a few moments to pull myself together before facing my parents again was a blessing.

With all the unsettling changes Dad was juggling in the world of retail, along with our ongoing family dramas, both my parents had enough to deal with—without my adding to their worries. I knew I had to keep my fears in check and focus on the future.

With the burden of a false identity lifted, I should be, quite literally, dancing in the street. Dance was so right, I felt it in my bones. And yet all I'd done upon learning was challenge my parents for not telling me sooner. I hated the idea of disappointing them. Although my memory was on the blink, the closeness in my family was apparent. The care and love and concern Mom, Dad, and Juliana showed to each other—and to me—was palpable.

Which only increased the mystery of Marnie's disappearance.

While lying on the table for my PET scan, something had occurred to me: I must have known why Marnie had not reboarded the ship in Southampton. With a family as close as ours, I couldn't imagine my sister just disappearing without an explanation. But any knowledge I'd had was washed out to sea following the blow to my head. The more I strained to surface those memories, the more frustrated I became—and the less positive I felt. The only tangible results of my efforts were blinding headaches.

I let out a tense breath of relief when I saw that Mom and Dad had not been waiting for me in the kitchen. They were already out front by the patio table, where a wicker tray was filled with colorful plastic glasses along with pitchers of iced tea, lemonade, and water. There was also a plate of sandwiches, which we'd picked up at the Vons deli counter.

It was a beautiful day with a gentle breeze, and the sun glinting off the ocean as waves lapped the shoreline in front of the beach house. "Didn't mean to keep you waiting," I said.

"You didn't," Mom said cheerfully.

I picked up half a sandwich but didn't take a bite. I had two important questions, and I needed answers.

"Did Jack know who I was last night?"

My parents exchanged a look.

"It's a long story," Mom said.

"Jack Kirkbride was privy to Pocino's investigation but was unable to share what he suspected," Dad explained. "Dick Landes only lifted his gag order in our meeting this morning."

"But they're supposed to be working for you."

"Callie," Dad said, "I'm afraid wanting to be in the know is in your genes. But while I don't like it any more than you do, your mother has convinced me that Dick's rationale was solid."

I supposed I would have to forgive Jack for acting under orders from his boss. And it did seem as though they were all looking out for my best interests. But I still had one other question.

"So, I guess what I'm really curious about now is, if I'm Callie—where in the world is Marnie?"

"The Landes Agency turned up evidence that the purchases on your MasterCard in Paris must have been made by Marnie," Conrad said, putting his sandwich down.

"On my card?" Callie asked.

Ashleigh nodded. "You had Marnie's handbag, so it stands to reason—"

"She has mine," Callie said.

Ashleigh nodded again. "Ross Pocino is working with a Landes agent in London. They have located your sister at a writer's workshop there, with Graham Bradford."

"Marnie's professor on board the ship." Callie sank back in her chair. "What did they tell you about Marnie? When is she coming home?"

Ashleigh and Conrad spent the next few moments telling Callie what they had learned about Marnie, including her accident, though they knew far too little about it themselves. They even expressed their disappointment over Marnie's covert behavior.

"I still can't understand why she didn't inform us of her intentions," Ashleigh said sadly.

"I bet she told me." Tears welled in Callie's eyes. "What's the first thing you plan to say to Marnie when you talk to her?"

"I don't know, darling," Ashleigh replied, glancing at Conrad. "But maybe you can help." She pushed an iPhone across the table. "I believe this is yours, Callie."

Callie looked at the screen blankly.

Ashleigh knew all the unanswered calls, texts, and emails—mostly from people with different names than those that were on Marnie's phone—must seem overwhelming.

"There are way too many to sort out," Callie said. "Besides, I'm not ready to start figuring out who they are and how I know them. I'm not returning any calls before my memory kicks in."

"That's fine, Callie," Ashleigh replied gently. She prayed once again that her daughter's memory would not take long to return. "But perhaps you could check for any communications from Marnie?"

"It might help us understand why your sister had such a monumental lapse in judgment," Conrad added.

Callie sat back in her chair and seemed to be mulling something over.

Perceptive as ever, Ashleigh noticed the tension suddenly vanish, as though the string had been untied from an overfilled balloon. "So . . . I'm . . . not a writer." She grinned as the realization hit her. "I'm a dancer. How cool is that?"

Chapter
104

Thursday, May 21, 3:00 p.m.—Long Beach, California

I stood at my bedroom window, looking out at the oil islands and doing my best to sort out my new reality. A future in dance was something I could wrap my mind around. I felt less uncertain over my immediate future. And yet I still had a ton of questions . . .

A light tap on my door brought my soul searching to a halt. "Come in," I called out.

"Glad I caught you," Juliana said as she entered the room. "Mom said you came up for a short nap."

I smiled. "As if I could sleep. I just wanted a little time on my own."

Looking crestfallen, Juliana asked, "Do you want me to leave?"

"No, Jules. I'm glad you're here. Where is Kaitlyn?"

"She went out to collect shells."

"Mom and Dad told me how you figured out I wasn't Marnie."

Juliana's face broke into a grin. "It's more like I figured out you were *you*. Nobody does those pirouettes like you. So . . . welcome home, Callie." She gave me a quick, bashful squeeze.

I laughed. "I'm trying to adjust, but it feels weird. I was Marnie this morning, and now I'm Callie. I don't only have a different name—I have different goals and a different personality. It's like auditioning for one part and then being cast for another."

"But . . . aren't you happy?"

I shrugged. "Sure. Happy about dance, anyway. My body seems to know what to do when the music comes on."

From the start, Juliana had perceived how disconnected and

in-over-my-head I'd felt over a career in creative writing. She had pushed me to try dancing, and I loved her eagerness as well as how hard she was trying to make me comfortable in my own skin. Neither of us had a clue as to the challenges that lay ahead if my memory did not return. But we'd spent quite a lot of time talking about my problem. That part didn't change simply because I was Callie instead of Marnie.

"Hey, I'll figure it out," I said. "So, how did your visit to CSULB go? Guess you'll be the one showing me around the campus this fall rather than the other way around."

"I wish you'd been with us when Sam showed us around today." She cocked her head. "I guess you don't remember Samantha."

I shook my head, which was empty of past experiences. I didn't know how I'd begin to get reacquainted with former friends. I just knew I had to do it, and boy, would it be awkward.

"Well, Samantha's your best friend and roommate," Juliana continued. "She's going for her master's degree in dance too. When she heard about the rogue wave, she made a jillion phone calls to our house phone and probably to your cell." She frowned and rolled her bottom lip. "Do you still have Marnie's cell?"

"No. Mom gave me my iPhone today."

"Well, I don't know all of your friends, but we've known Samantha forever—well, since before elementary school. You both started to dance when you were about four."

"Was she in the semester-at-sea program?"

"No, I don't think she could afford it. She's on a scholarship." Juliana explained that Samantha's parents were divorced, and she worked part-time during the school year and full-time for the summer, to help with living expenses. "I think she took your place working with the fashion director at Jordon's in Westminster. You used to work there on weekends during the school year. You modeled, helped the fashion director, or whatever."

With a flip of her wrist, she continued, "Anyway, when Sam was showing us around the campus, I told her about your amnesia. She really wants to see you. In fact, she asked if it would be okay if she came over after dinner tonight."

Heat crawled up the base of my neck as I gulped air into my lungs. Unbidden, a thought shot to mind: *This is the first day of the rest of your life.* I didn't want to become some recluse. Getting to know one person at a time seemed like the best way to begin.

I nodded. "Okay. I've got to get the first meeting behind me. It might as well be tonight."

Chapter 105

Friday, May 22, 7:15 a.m.—London, England

Graham Bradford had been restless ever since Marnie's accident. Now he had all but abandoned his novel, unable to form a single coherent sentence even for his author's note. Disgusted, he tossed his yellow pad on the end table, then headed to the kitchen to brew a pot of tea.

How prosaic, eh, Graham? What do we Brits do in a crisis but make a cuppa.

Sarcasm aside, he realized that the only way to clear away the thoughts about his inevitable conversation with Conrad Taylor was to write them down on a notepad. Until he freed his mind of all else, he'd be unable to give his full attention to his author's note—much less his protagonist.

He returned to the living room with his tea tray and settled down in his armchair with the notepad. After about half an hour he finally was back in the zone. The words flowed, and he was able to return to the novel. Derek's well-honed PI skills would soon bring about a resolution. If Bradford could keep up this pace, he'd finish the second draft before the weekend was over.

The ringing landline broke his concentration. *Might as well answer*, he thought. The sentence on the end of his pencil had evaporated anyway.

He picked up the receiver. "Good morning," he said. "Yes, this is he . . ."

Bloody hell.

It was Marnie's father. Bradford silently cursed himself for not being the one to initiate the call. *Not that I didn't try* . . . Now he wished he'd let the call go to voice mail.

Grabbing his notepad, he glanced at the words he'd scribbled. "I am relieved to hear from you, Mr. Taylor," he lied. Then he went on to describe the roadblocks he'd encountered in trying to get in touch.

"Mr. Bradford," Taylor cut in, "the first thing we want to know is whether Marnie is alright. We've learned little about the extent of her injuries."

"Dr. Benson says Marnie will soon be right as rain." Bradford described her injuries as best he could. "But the doctor said she must avoid air travel for the next few days. Would you like his office number?"

"We have the number, thank you. I plan to call the doctor after we speak with our daughter."

Bradford winced. "Mr. Taylor, I know you have a great many questions. But before you proceed, please accept my most sincere apology to you and your family. I was wrong to allow Marnie to abandon her semester at sea. While I believed our arrangement to be mutually beneficial—"

"Mr. Bradford," Taylor broke in. "My daughter, while legally considered an adult, is only twenty-two years of age. She had no intention of enrolling in the semester-at-sea until she learned you would be teaching the master class."

"I am flattered, Mr. Taylor," Bradford replied.

On the other end of the line, Taylor failed to respond.

Realizing his gaffe, Bradford quickly added, "But I assure you there has been *nothing* untoward in our arrangement. It has been strictly on the up and up." A thin line of sweat ran down his forehead. This was all wrong. He hadn't planned to start off on the defensive.

"Are you telling me you did not take advantage of her misguided hero worship?"

"I most certainly did not!" Bradford protested. As he spoke the words, however, Hillary's warnings came to mind—and he realized he'd done exactly that.

12:05 a.m.—Long Beach, California

Conrad took a restorative breath. He didn't trust this Bradford fellow. While he knew of the dangers of a blood clot following a head injury, he would trust medical advice only from the doctor.

Keeping his voice calm and measured, he began again. "Mr. Bradford. We've gotten off to a bad start. This will get us nowhere. Please, I would like you to explain exactly what led up to Marnie leaving the ship in Southampton."

"Please, call me Graham," came the voice at the other end of the line. "I believe you are aware that Marnie began typing my handwritten pages after my assistant's accident. And you may know that I am compensating her with a generous salary as well as participation in my advanced summer workshop at no cost."

Pompous man. Conrad reined in his urge to respond and listened with gritted teeth.

"Marnie avidly pursued the chance to work with me and to attend my advanced summer workshop," Bradford continued. "She expressed that the opportunity to gain insights from watching me craft my next novel were priceless . . ."

As Bradford prattled on, Conrad pulled Ashleigh close and whispered, "Anything you'd like to add?"

She nodded. "Excuse me, Mr. Bradford, this is Ashleigh Taylor, Marnie's mother. If you don't mind my changing the subject, what we'd like to know is why she traveled with you to Paris."

Conrad's hands clenched into tight fists as images flashed in his head of the debonair forty-three-year-old author in Paris with his daughter. After listening to the man's explanation of how Marnie had spent her time since leaving the ship, he could wait no longer.

"Mr. Bradford, just how did you manage to slip Marnie through the ship's security?"

Chapter 106

Friday, May 22, 8:10 a.m.—London, England

The weight of Taylor's words brought Graham Bradford to his knees. The question of his culpability in Marnie's leaving the ship undetected was his greatest shame.

Battling the undertow of his rationalizations, which no longer held a hint of logic, Bradford was temporarily speechless. He should have been more prepared for this inevitable question.

While Marnie's ability to decipher his handwritten pages into a manuscript was a godsend, he'd told himself he also was making it possible for her to achieve her goals. But that was not the whole truth. The truth was, his self-indulgence had done the Taylor family irreparable harm.

"Mr. Bradford?" Taylor said, following a prolonged silence.

A lump the size of a boulder formed in Bradford's throat. Come what may, he was through lying to himself.

"Mr. Taylor. You are correct in assuming your daughter could not have departed the ship without setting off alarm bells unless I assisted her. I was one hundred percent in the wrong in doing so." He hoped to placate Taylor by explaining that he did his best to persuade Marnie to inform her parents of the arrangement before she left the ship. "I would like to assure you, sir, that even though Marnie is a beautiful young woman, I have always viewed her through the eyes of a mentor. The arrangement between your daughter and me is strictly business. Nothing more."

"And that involved *covertly sneaking* my daughter through the ironclad security system, not to mention *transporting* her across an international border?" Sarcasm dripped from Taylor's every word.

Bradford quelled the urge to react defensively. He'd earned Taylor's scorn.

Clearing his throat, he repeated once more, "I deeply regret my lapse of judgment as well as the considerable angst I have caused you and your family. I should have followed my conscience and terminated our arrangement after Marnie insisted on informing you and her mother of her plans by letter, rather than by phone."

"By letter?" Taylor repeated. "We received no letter."

Taylor's wife spoke again. "Mr. Bradford, do you know when or how Marnie sent her letter?"

"She gave the letter to her sister to deliver upon her arrival in the U.S." Bradford paused. "From the tone of your question, I presume this letter was lost at some point. Perhaps when the rogue wave hit the *Rising Star*?"

"Apparently so," Taylor agreed.

Bradford took a sip of his cold tea, grimaced, and set it back in the saucer. His grimace deepened as he listened to Taylor's next accusation.

"Though I want to believe your apologies are sincere, Mr. Bradford, it appears you gave no thought to the effect that Marnie's failure to complete her semester at sea would have on—"

Bugger this bloody humble pie routine.

"Mr. Taylor, I am sincerely sorry. But it's unfair for you to make me your sole whipping boy. Marnie is a grown-up and headstrong young woman. Neither she nor I anticipated any such disaster at sea. And if not for that rogue wave, you would have learned of Marnie's decision. As I understand it, she only wished to take advantage of valuable opportunities for her future."

A rather long silence followed, which Taylor finally broke. "Thank you for your explanations, Mr. Bradford. While we do not agree on your handling of the situation, there's no point in running it into the ground. May we please speak to Marnie now?"

"Of course. She is anxious to hear from you and has also expressed great concern over her twin. Her flat is a level below mine. I will ask her to return your call from this landline right away." Bradford then added, "And you should know, she planned to call your investigation agency today at the crack of dawn in the States, in search of your contact information on the West Coast."

Hanging up and checking the clock, Bradford was surprised. Only twelve minutes had elapsed, yet he felt as if he'd been on the hot seat for hours.

Chapter
107

Friday, May 22, 8:25 a.m.—London, England

Jolted from a deep sleep by her "Sea of Love" ringtone, Marnie squinted, attempting to bring the world into focus. She couldn't call the U.S. for hours, so why was Graham waking her up so early? After all, he was the one who'd insisted she take the darn sleeping pill.

"Hello," she said, failing to keep the grogginess from her tone.

"Your parents just phoned," he said. "They would like you to return their call."

Relief and concern jousted in Marnie's sleepy mind. "But it's the middle of the night there." *He already knows that,* her sleepy mind informed her. "Were they ticked?" she asked, followed quickly by, "Is my sister okay?"

"You will need to get the specifics from your parents," he replied. "Obviously, they were not pleased about being kept in the dark. They received no letter."

In the next moment, she was limping into the bathroom and throwing cold water on her face. Now the problem was waking her fuzzy brain up and recalling her well-rehearsed words for her parents.

Bradford was standing in the doorway of his flat when Marnie stepped off the elevator. "I'm going down to talk with Hillary, so you can have the flat to yourself for a bit," he said. "Your parents' phone number is on the pad beside the phone. It includes a country code, so be sure to dial every digit."

Marnie tried to mentally resurrect the essence of her carefully worded letter. She didn't believe Callie had intentionally withheld it. She prayed her sister had painted a positive picture of her decision. Surely, she wouldn't allow them to think she'd been washed overboard.

Marnie spotted the notepad and began punching in the numbers: 001 0562 432 1280. Her hand shook. *How long did my family believe I was lost at sea?*

"Marnie," her parents said, one voice overlapping the other.

At the sound of her father's deep baritone and her mother's sweet greeting, she burst into tears, unable to eke out a single syllable. "I'm here. Just give me a second, please." Gulping back sobs, she could not recall a single sentence she'd planned to say. "I'm so, so sorry," was all she managed. "I should have called, but I never expected—"

"We'll discuss that later," her dad said.

"Yes," her mom agreed.

"I just found out the other day that Callie got hurt. Is she okay now?"

"Yes, love," said Ashleigh, then quickly asked, "How about *you?*"

How much should I tell them?

"Marnie," said Conrad, "we were told you stepped in front of a taxi and were in a medical coma for over twenty-four hours."

What did Graham say? But now that it was out in the open, she confirmed it. "That's right. I looked left when I should have looked right. Ended up with a bunch of ugly bruises." Wanting to change the subject, she went on, "I didn't know about the monster wave hitting the ship until Sunday."

She didn't want to tell them Bradford had kept it from her.

"You didn't hear about the disaster until *Sunday?*" Ashleigh said.

Conrad added, "But it was blasted across worldwide media."

"I was at a writers' conference in Paris and missed the news." Marnie figured at least it was a partial truth. "When I heard about it on Sunday morning, I wanted to call home, but I decided you were already worried about the ship, and I heard no one was badly hurt."

Marnie was now fully awake and able to explain.

"I thought you would find out when Callie got safely home. By then you would get my letter, and all would be explained. I took a long time composing it, explaining all the reasons why I couldn't turn down this opportunity . . ." Her voice and her resolve started to crumble. "I'm sorry, Dad, Mom. I totally messed up."

"Oh, honey, I understand," Ashleigh said. "Your dad and I love you very much. We just want you to be okay."

"On Sunday night, when I found out about the missing student, I knew I had to call you right away. And I was on my way to a public phone to call you when the taxi hit me . . . " Emotionally exhausted and out of breath, Marnie slumped back on the sofa and shut her eyes. "If Callie had only given you my letter like I asked her to . . ."

When the call ended, she felt more confused than ever. If only they'd told her about Callie's amnesia at the beginning of their conversation.

Chapter 108

Friday, May 22, 8:30 a.m.—London, England

Hillary heard the screech of the elevator and opened the door to her flat. Marnie's silhouette in the open elevator car announced she was on her way to the floor above. Hillary shuffled to her kitchen, where she set about cooking breakfast for two.

Soon afterward, she heard the metallic click of the door closing and called out, "In the kitchen."

Not bothering to ask if Bradford was hungry, she deftly cracked a couple more eggs and turned the rashers of bacon. "Have a seat. Breakfast is almost ready." As she flipped over the eggs, she gestured to the piping-hot pot of tea. "Pour yourself a cup."

Blotting the bacon on a paper towel and sliding the eggs onto a couple of plates, Hillary removed the apron she wore over her caftan and joined Bradford at the square table for two.

"Marnie's talking with her parents," he said, picking up a piece of the crisp bacon.

"I assume her parents initiated the call, since it's unlikely you'd call them in the middle of the blooming night."

"Right you are."

Knowing the encounter couldn't have been a pleasant one, she listened without interruption. Bradford took her through the challenging phone call, step by excruciating step. She felt pride in his owning up to his culpability. *He's a good man.* She was sure he had not realized the extent of his fixation on the girl. Even now he denied it to himself.

But Hillary knew better.

"You've done the right thing," she said.

"Bloody hell, Hillary, I should have done the right thing long ago. I should have nipped that ludicrous plan in the bud when Marnie asked me to be complicit in sneaking her off the *Rising Star*."

"You know what they say about *should haves*."

"Would have had to be deaf over the past thirty years to have missed your take on it." Bradford set down his fork and ran his hands down his thighs. Looking straight into her questioning eye, he said, "I deeply regret not heeding your advice."

Hillary smiled. "If hindsight were foresight, we'd all live perfect lives."

"Right again." He ran his index finger under the rim of his turtleneck, the green of his shirt reflected in his sad, hazel eyes. "For my role in this past week's devastation, I've earned an eternity in hell."

Flipping the braid over her shoulder, Hillary asked, "Have plans been made for Marnie's return to the States?" She knew he would agree now that Marnie must go home.

"Not yet," Bradford replied. "But that is where she belongs. Even if she were to remain here, it's unlikely she could be productive when her family has gone through hell and she's loaded with guilt."

Hillary readjusted herself in the chair. "How will Marnie feel about missing out on the workshop?"

"I've thought about that, and—"

"You aren't thinking of giving her credit she hasn't earned."

"Of course not," Bradford said. "That would be not only dishonest, but a disservice to Marnie. Fortunately, she already has more than enough credits to earn her bachelor's degree."

As Bradford spoke, Hillary saw that he seemed to have aged a decade in the past week. There were deep lines of his handsome face, and his eyes lacked their former clarity and sparkle.

"She can complete her writing project at home and send it to me," he said. "I will give her the credit, provided she earns it with the quality of her work."

"And who will type your manuscript?" Hillary asked.

Bradford gave her a rueful smile. "Again, you were right. Don't rub it in." He hesitated. "I'll give Cathy a call later this morning. With her injured arm, she still can't type. But there's nothing wrong with her eyes. When she's feeling up to it, she can interpret my scrawls for a hired typist."

So the problem turns out not to be as insurmountable as he once believed.

Hillary stared at him, chuckling. Sometimes she still saw that thirteen-year-old boy . . . "I won't ask why you didn't think of that before," she said.

Chapter

109

Friday, May 22, 9:05 a.m.—London, England

Marnie sat in stunned silence on the far end of Bradford's sofa for what seemed a very long time, and yet the long hand on the clock had moved forward no more than a couple of minutes. After speaking with her parents, she felt let down. Why did they have to say the decision was hers? Putting the ball in her court had somehow left her feeling empty. She wanted to be with Callie, but she had a lot of thinking to do before her parents' next call.

Sometimes, total independence really sucks.

Replaying the conversation with her parents, she felt foolish. At no time throughout this whole disaster had she acted like an adult. Even her apology was self-centered. And then to find out Callie couldn't even remember her family anymore, much less who she was . . .

Marnie was gripped by a wave of self-loathing. *How could I have been so stupid? If only I could take back all my petulant decisions of the past two weeks.*

It had been last Thursday night in Paris when a massive headache had jolted her from sleep. Now she was convinced Callie's head trauma was the cause—and probably also the cause of the reoccurring headaches she'd experienced even before her own accident here in London.

Closing her eyes, Marnie tried to move past regrets and focus on the way forward.

Her parents had not insisted she return home before the end of the workshop, yet she could no longer stay. Knowing her place was at home, she'd never be able to concentrate. On the other hand, she had an obligation to Graham Bradford—one she must fulfill.

The thought alarmed her. *What am I going to say when he returns to the flat?*

If she was going to call Erica and Mike, she had better hurry. Her mom had agreed she should and had given Marnie their phone numbers. It was very early in the morning in Chicago, but Marnie needed to hear their voices—to let them know she'd had no intention of causing them so much worry.

Even though Ashleigh had brought Erica up to date, Marnie was afraid her second mother had become unglued over her failure to get in touch. Erica must hear for herself that nothing catastrophic had happened.

The phone rang several times. She was about to hang up when she heard an out-of-breath *hello*.

"Hello, Nelson," she replied.

"Marnie. It's great to hear your voice. Your mom and Mike have been trying to track you down."

That sounds a bit ominous.

A moment later Erica was on the phone, with one sentence running over the next. "Darling. We've been so worried. Dick Landes called and told us about your accident. Are you okay?"

Marnie took a second to catch up. "I'm so sorry, Mom." *OMG. How many more times will I have to say that?* "I'm fine. Just a few bruises."

"I know, Ashleigh told us."

Damn, damn, damn. Why couldn't anyone keep things to themselves? She decided to keep quiet about the broken ribs—unless that too had reached the family rumor mill. She didn't want them to worry, nor did she want to discuss her gigantic screw-up over the phone anymore.

After a few more moments of discussion, she apologized again—this time for calling at such an ungodly hour—and prepared to sign off. "Give my love to Mike and Bill." Then, before her Mom could ask more questions, she said, "Love you all," and put the receiver back on the hook.

Chapter
110

Friday, May 22, 9:20 a.m.—London, England

Graham Bradford thrust open the door to his flat, his thoughts focused on the mechanics of how to get Marnie home where she belonged. Halting midstride, however, he saw her wedged into the corner of the sofa in a limp heap, her face buried in the crook of her elbow and her legs curled under her.

Obviously, the call to her parents had not gone well. The sight of the fiercely independent young woman stripped of her bravado melted his heart. He wanted to take her in his arms and comfort her. But that was not his role.

"I take it your parents—"

Her head jerked up, and she lifted her chin. "Sorry. I didn't hear you come in." She held a crumpled tissue in her fist and dabbed at her swollen eyes. "Did my parents tell you my sister has amnesia?"

"Yes. My heart goes out to her and to your family," he said. "I will help you in arranging the earliest flight—"

"But I agreed to help you finish your manuscript. Even though I can't stay for the workshop, I attended the conference and—"

"Marnie, under the circumstances, you are free of obligation."

She eyed him suspiciously. "Are you trying to get rid of me?"

He smiled. "No. You've been a good assistant and a talented writer, and if you continue to work hard, you have a promising future."

Her burning eyes held his.

"I've got everything worked out," he continued. "Are your parents arranging your return flight?"

"We didn't talk about that."

Taken aback, he said, "You didn't?"

She leaned forward, her elbows on her knees. "Graham, if Callie hadn't been hurt, I wouldn't think of going back home before the end of the workshop, or the completion of your manuscript. I would stay and finish my short-story project and make what progress I could on my novel."

"Your parents would be okay with that?" He could not conceal his tone of incredulity.

"I know they want me to come home, but they made no demands." She paused. "It would be so much easier if they did."

"To justify your opposition?"

She blinked. "Am I that transparent?"

He said nothing.

She explained that her parents had never been demanding—that both were experienced negotiators, and most of the time were more persuasive by letting the girls make the final decision. "I should have listened to you and Callie and told them about my plans."

Bradford thought of Hillary, and how a disappointed look was her greatest weapon.

"Forget about what you should have done," he insisted. "Deal with what is. *Should haves* are always too late." He was sure he sounded just like her parents. "It's clear that they were hurt, but they love and care about you. Now, you can't put Humpty Dumpty together again, so let's move on."

"Thank you. I need to be with Callie. But if it weren't for her amnesia, I'd remain regardless of my parents' opinion."

He tried to explain there was no need for guilt about leaving him in the lurch. "You are not. I have a plan that also frees you to return home as soon as possible—and still allows you to earn the credits for the semester at sea."

Marnie expressed her relief, but still did not commit to returning to the States. "I'm not obligated to do as my parents' demand, you know."

"Marnie. Are you telling me there is no plan for your return?"

Shaking her head, she said, "Not exactly."

"Well, once you have a plan, I'll help you book the flight, unless your parents prefer to do so." Unexpectedly, he thought of the upside. "At least with your early return, the problem of your sister's expiring passport is solved."

CHAPTER
111

Friday, May 22, 10:05 a.m.—London, England

Back in her own flat, Marnie sat very still on the sofa, in part to calm the aches and pains in her bruised body, but also for fear of breaking the spell. *Graham said I had talent.* Although he didn't downplay the work that lay ahead for her to hone her craft, his kind words made her feel like dancing around the room. Metaphorically, of course. That was all she could manage until her ribs healed.

Charlize flopped down on the sofa with an exaggerated sigh. "Your brain obviously isn't hitting all cylinders. You've got it made. One-on-one sessions with Graham Bradford. It's an opportunity of a lifetime. With parents who are letting you call the shots, why would you even think of hightailing it back to the States?"

"I told you, my sister—"

"Cut the crap, Marnie. You're not responsible for your sister's amnesia. There's not a blooming thing you can do for her. You can't make her memory reappear, and without her memory, she sure doesn't miss you."

Charlize gave a dramatic sigh.

"I'd give my soul to be in your place. This is the second year in Bradford's workshop for Alexandre and me, but we've never even been to his flat or had a peek at his drafts. We work our butts off ten months a year to afford this summer workshop. You've had it all handed to you on a platinum-gold platter, and you're willing to let it all go down the toilet."

"You're not listening, Charlize," Marnie said. "Although my parents said it was up to me whether I stayed or came home, the undercurrent was clear."

"So, you really don't have a choice? Your parents will withdraw their financial support if you stay?"

"No. Of course not. But—"

Marnie always found it hard to explain that the grass wasn't always greener on the other side. True, the stork had dropped her down an awesome chimney, but her family was not as ideal as it looked from the outside. The standards they set were almost impossible to live up to. And because they were always so calm and controlled, she appeared to be a drama queen. It would be a whole lot easier if they just gave her hell for her goof-ups. It was hard to let off steam when her parents—her mother especially—always reacted so *reasonably*.

"If the situation were reversed, Callie would be there for me," she told her new friend. And it wasn't just a twin thing, but a family thing. She would feel the same way if it were her younger sister or her parents. "The truth is, I messed up big time. I can no longer concentrate on my work. That won't change until I see for myself that Callie is okay."

And who knew? Maybe seeing her mirror image would trigger Callie's memory.

Charlize scrunched up her nose and shrugged. "Families, right? Well, I'd better get back to work," she said, heaving herself to her feet. She gave Marnie a decidedly unstuffy squeeze and headed for the door.

Marnie wished she could get back to writing too. That was the whole reason she had started this mess.

Chapter
112

Saturday, May 23, 10:45 a.m.—Long Beach, California

My trembling hands fumbled with the small clasp of my necklace. To my horror, tears of frustration sprang to my eyes.

"Need some help, Callie?" Juliana strode into my bedroom dressed in a short, sleeveless black dress with a matching lightweight sweater over her shoulders. Black patent four-inch heels replaced her usual thong sandals, and she wore her shiny dark hair down and draped over one shoulder.

"Wow! Where is my *little* sister?"

"Hey, I clean up pretty good," Juliana quipped, her dark eyes dancing.

Kaitlyn paused in the doorway. She wore a royal blue dress and stilettos, her straight brown hair flowing past her shoulders. Both she and Juliana looked so grown-up. What a transition from their usual shorts or jeans and their hair pulled back in ponytails.

Juliana walked up behind me, pulling my zipper the final inch to the top of my full-skirted dress. "Dad said we're going straight to the yacht club. Aunt Caroline and Elizabeth already had help in getting the stuff to the club."

I slipped into my heels and ran the brush through my hair once more.

Juliana looked at me, her arms akimbo. "It's going to be okay, sis. You aren't the only one who won't know or remember most of the people at the memorial. We'll be with Elizabeth and Mom and Dad. All we need to do is smile and say, 'Nice to see you.'"

Apparently, I wasn't doing a very good job concealing my fears.

"I'll have to pretend to remember the people I've met before and smile when they tell me how much I've grown, and how they can't believe I'll be starting college," she went on. "At least you have a good excuse for not remembering."

"Thanks, Jules. I'll be fine as long as I have a cape to make me invisible."

Juliana giggled. "Willing to share?"

"Is everyone ready?" Mom's voice rang out.

Dad was waiting at the bottom of the stairs. His mouth broadened into a smile. "What a gorgeous harem. May I have the privilege to escort you to the yacht club?"

Mom said something I didn't catch and kissed Dad on the cheek as she picked up her handbag from the credenza in the foyer.

Moments later, we were all in the Mercedes driving to the yacht club. We talked for a short while about the weirdness of me thinking I'd been my sister for the past week, and then Juliana and Kaitlyn began telling Mom and Dad about their time on campus. I tuned out, lost in my thoughts about my reunion with my roommate Samantha.

It had been as awkward as I'd feared. She'd been terrific and had tried to jog my memory bank—but it was empty and immune to jogging. Though she said she understood, I saw the disappointment in her soft blue eyes each time I failed to remember the occasion she'd just described.

Remarkably, when I told her I had no idea when I'd be ready to move back into the apartment we shared, she'd remained upbeat, doing her best to hide any letdown. I simply couldn't move from the peninsula house until Marnie returned.

I longed to come face-to-face with my twin. That might be exactly what I needed to begin chipping away at the cement wall between my present and my past. If not . . .

I don't want to go there.

Our parents had shared with Juliana and me their conversations with Marnie and the celebrity author in London. There still was no definite plan for Marnie to return home—and even if she did, I wouldn't know what to say to her.

Chapter

113

Saturday, May 23, 11:15 a.m.—Long Beach, California

As Ashleigh entered the familiar reception area of the yacht club, memories of Charles Stuart flooded her mind.

The last time she'd entered this club was for the celebration of her grandfather's exemplary life. His dream of excellence in retail shopping came to life in the "cathedral" he had built—the landmark Bentleys Royale. While Ashleigh thought about him a great deal and missed him very much, she was glad he had not lived to see the dismantling of his retail empire. And yet she was pleased that the landmark store Charles had poured his heart and soul into had survived. While no longer a department store, it was now a unique law library. Purchased for ten million dollars, it had been restored to its original glory at the cost of another ten million.

Visions played in her mind of the throngs of individuals from all walks of life who had come to honor Charles all those years ago. From this man and her grandmother, who had raised her after the accidental death of her parents, Ashleigh had developed her values, her work ethic, and her love of quality department stores.

At the age of ninety-four, Charles Stuart's personal motto had remained steadfast: *I must earn my day by creating something worthwhile.* Before he drew his last breath, he'd been working on his third book. He believed excellence equaled quality products, quality service, and creative, exciting presentation. His philosophy was something Conrad put into practice too: "People do not come to department stores to fill their needs. They come to fill their wants. Therefore, it is our job to create desire."

"Mom," Callie called out, pulling Ashleigh from the past.

Ashleigh looked up to see Pocino moving toward her with a huge floral arrangement held against his barrel chest. "Downstairs or up?" he asked.

Ashleigh gestured to the reception table. "How about here for now. I'll check with Elizabeth to see if she prefers to put it elsewhere."

Pocino carefully set the arrangement in the middle of the table, between the guest book and the framed photos of Caroline's late husband, Don Munz.

Ashleigh's stomach flipped. Had Ross spotted Callie, whom he'd known since she was an infant? Should Ashleigh introduce them? This was to be the first day of many awkward first days for Callie. Ashleigh couldn't afford to remain tongue-tied.

Why didn't I think this through?

While her mind spun in uncharacteristic indecision, Callie stepped closer to the table and said. "Hello, Mr. Pocino. I know you know me, but my memory is out of order, so I hope you won't be offended that I don't remember you."

Pocino grinned. "Not a bit. It's an honor to re-meet you, Callie."

"I know you are the one who figured out I wasn't my twin," she continued. "Thank you for giving me my life back."

"My pleasure," he said. "Now, how about helping me with the rest of the flowers? We'll start creating some new memories—maybe better ones."

"Sure," Callie said, returning his smile.

Ashleigh's eyes met Conrad's. *Who would have thought?* She didn't need to spell it out. Callie making the first move had come as a pleasant surprise, but Pocino's savvy response surprised her more.

Elizabeth had stopped at the bottom of the stairs, her eyes tearing as she observed the touching scene between Callie and the gruff teddy bear of an investigator.

Giving her a warm hug, Ashleigh said, "Perhaps this is a turning point for Callie. I believe Dr. Martin helped empower her, letting her know there was no shame in memory loss." She asked if Elizabeth needed help.

"So far, all is well," Elizabeth said. "But how about Marnie? Have you spoken to her? Is she well? When is she coming home?"

"We spoke to Marnie this morning. *Very early* this morning." Ashleigh wrapped her arm around Elizabeth's shoulder and relayed the doctor's report. "Considering her run-in with an English cab, our wayward little chick did not fare too badly."

Elizabeth raised a brow. "Physical wounds in one so young will heal quickly. I'm more worried about her emotional health."

"Our conversation was brief," Ashleigh continued, "but you know how hard she is on herself. She kept telling us how sorry she was. We let her know how much we all loved her, but I'm afraid by the time we hung up, she may have felt even worse."

A series of creases crossed Elizabeth's forehead as Ashleigh explained Marnie's frustration and concern for her sister. Elizabeth shook her head, understanding how helpless and sad Marnie would feel upon learning of Callie's amnesia, especially from so far away.

"On a brighter note, April called today." Ashleigh's heart had soared when April had called to offer her condolences—and reported that Mark and Paige would arrive at JFK the next day. Conrad was counting on Mark being on board for the upcoming store closings.

"That *is* good news, dear," Elizabeth said. "And perhaps once you return home, you and Paige will find some time to squeeze in a lovely heart-to-heart."

Chapter
114

Saturday, May 23, 3:40 p.m.—Long Beach, California

I changed into a pair of white denim shorts and a teal T-shirt. By the time I'd slipped into my sandals and headed downstairs, Juliana and Kaitlyn were waiting.

"How about going to Belmont Shore to check out more of the shops?" Juliana said.

"You two go ahead." I had made it through the memorial service, but having to explain my amnesia, and straining to pull up a memory of each new face I saw, had gotten tiresome.

"You don't want to go?" Juliana asked. "What better place to start relearning your way around than among all the cool boutiques?"

"It is a really cool place, and we couldn't have a better guide," Kaitlyn gestured to Juliana. "She knows all the hot spots."

"Not today. I'm feeling a little worn out."

Juliana gave me a quick hug. "Well, if you change your mind, just call my cell. You've got the number in your contacts, right?"

I nodded. My phone contained her number, Mom's and Dad's numbers, and the numbers of a boatload of strangers.

"Uh-oh. Do I hear the 'poor me' routine?"

I managed a smile. "You got me, Jules. I'll snap out of it. Just now, though, I've had enough for today. I don't think I'll change my mind."

I really was tired, but I was also anxious for them to be on their way. I wanted to call Jack. I was hoping he'd insist on showing me around Long Beach.

After the girls left, I dialed the number. On the fourth ring, I was about to hang up when Jack uttered a breathless, "Hey."

"Hi. This is . . . Callie Taylor."

"Was hoping you'd call."

"You sound out of breath."

"That's because I am. Just finished my daily run."

He didn't seem to be working—that removed one obstacle. The other was his sense of obligation. I hated the idea that he might feel like he had no choice. "You said I should feel free to call anytime. But it's a Saturday, and you don't owe us anything—"

"Callie, I *want* to show you girls around," he said.

He had used her name for the first time. She liked the way it sounded.

"Juliana and Kaitlyn went off on their own, and Mom and Dad went over to my Aunt Caroline's. They're staying there for dinner."

"How did the memorial go?"

"A few rough patches." Callie didn't mention how worried her parents were about Elizabeth. It had been plain to see that Caroline was far from stable following her husband's death. "But Mom said it went better than she expected."

"Fabulous. So it appears you're on your own. What would you think about checking out the Pirate Invasion?"

"Pirate Invasion?" I repeated.

"It's like a Renaissance fair, but with pirates. Sword fighting, cannons, a mock trial, even a hanging."

"*Really?*

"Don't get too excited," he chuckled. "The guy who gets hanged always walks away afterward. It's close to your place—on the beach near the Belmont Pier."

His enthusiasm made her smile. "Sure. I didn't feel like going shopping in Belmont Shore, but pirates sound like fun." She wanted to see him. Even more, she wanted to find out what he might know about her and her twin.

I jumped at the flash and loud boom from the first cannon. Covering my ears, I prepared for the next blast.

"Come on, matey," Jack teased. "Let's explore the pirates' bounty."

"Hang on," I said, slipping off my sandals before stepping onto the sand. "Have you attended one of these before?"

"No. I'm also a virgin." His face colored as the last word escaped through his lips, and he gave a sheepish smile. "What I meant to say is, I'm a first-timer. Like you."

I laughed, amused at his eagerness to correct his slip of the tongue.

The sun was shining. It wasn't too hot, it wasn't too cold, and best of all, Jack and I had no past experiences he expected me to recall. Once again, he made me feel relaxed—more so than since this whole nightmare began.

As we wove our way through the crowd of onlookers on the beach beside Belmont Pier, I noticed scores of people in pirate's costumes, but in my denim shorts and T-shirt, I fit right in with the majority. Kiosks covered the length of the pier and were scattered in a wide arch across the sand. The booths sold a variety of things: jewelry, pirate paraphernalia, handcrafted items. Pirate duels were taking place near the water's edge between two large cannons. Floating near the shoreline, three pirate boats engaged in reenactments.

We explored every kiosk, finding many interesting items. I admired a handmade necklace strung with stones in muted shades of aquamarine, ivory, and turquoise, and the next thing I knew, Jack had bought it for me.

"I can't accept this." I couldn't hide my embarrassment.

"Sure you can. I won it from my friend Jake." He gestured toward the third kiosk. "That's his place. He lost our bet on the sea battle. I accepted the necklace as payment. You liked it, and since he was unlikely to part with cash, it was a three-way win."

I slipped the necklace out of the bag and undid the clasp. "It's so unusual," I said. "I love it. Thank you very much."

"Here," he said, stretching out his hand. "Lift your hair."

I did, and he fastened the clasp.

It had been a fun afternoon so far, but we'd talked of nothing personal—and I still needed to find out what Jack knew about me and my twin. So I was glad when he offered to play chauffeur again, returning me to the beach house to get freshened up and then back out for a bite to eat, to a place called Tequila Jack's.

Deciding what to wear took more time than I'd imagined. I didn't want to appear as if I looked on this evening as more than it was. After all, this was just an assignment for Jack. And yet . . .

Chapter
115

Saturday, May 23, 6:45 p.m.—Long Beach, California

Jack turned up the long driveway to the beach house. Two windows darkened as a light blinked off, just before the back door swung open. As he pushed open his car door, Callie appeared.

The sight of her took his breath away. Her blond hair hung past her shoulders, shimmering in the early evening sunlight. She wore a royal blue maxi dress that swayed as she walked toward him.

Jack swung his long legs from beneath the steering wheel and dashed around the car to open the passenger door. Feeling like a middle school boy, he rubbed his damp palms on his khaki trousers.

Callie gave his Corvette the once-over. "I love the shade."

"Right you are, and it matches your dress perfectly." He returned her smile. "Since we're on our own tonight, I drove my ride instead of the company car."

When they reached Shoreline Village, Jack pulled a ticket from the meter box and parked near Tequila Jack's.

"I love this," Callie cried out with childlike delight, surveying their surroundings. "How cool to be surrounded by water on three sides. Can we walk around after dinner?"

"Of course," Jack said with a wistful smile. Having spent time in Long Beach since she was a child, including four years at university, she had to have been familiar with the area. He couldn't have had a better reminder of Callie's amnesia.

I held my questions as Jack and I were led through the trendy, dimly lit Mexican restaurant to be seated on the patio. Beyond the crowded boardwalk, the sun set behind a sea of bobbing boats.

I looked down at the menu, unsure of what to order. "What do you suggest?" I asked.

"My favorites are their baby back ribs and the chile rellenos."

"Ribs sound good, but I'm afraid I'd wear as much as I'd eat. I'd like the chiles rellenos."

After the waiter took our order for signature margaritas and entrées, I leaned across the table toward Jack. There was something I had to get out in the open.

"The other night, when we went to Domenico's, you knew I wasn't Marnie."

Her words slammed into him like a head-on collision. He should have seen it coming. Mesmerized by the vulnerable Callie Taylor, he was unprepared.

But before he could respond, she said, "I understand, Jack. I really do. Although I wish I'd known a lot sooner—like when I woke up on the ship."

He was surprised to see a twinkle in her eye.

"I know you would have told me if you could," she continued. "I guess no one wanted me to ping-pong from one identity to the next until they were sure."

"Yes, Callie," Jack said, reaching across the table and placing his hand on her wrist, "I knew. It drove me crazy, not being able to tell you. I was ninety-nine-point-nine percent sure. I didn't want to wait for one hundred percent proof." He paused, his gaze holding hers. "You probably didn't notice, but I never called you by name. I never called you Marnie."

Her beautiful chocolate eyes blinked, then held Jack's for a very long second or two. "I'm afraid I didn't notice. But I understand how awkward it is, trying to avoid calling someone by name. That's how I felt with my parents." She sighed and took a sip of her margarita. "This amnesia thing has seriously messed with my brain. It's really a bummer not remembering anyone's name or what we did together."

He sat back and listened intently as she went on to describe what else was making her crazy: her "missing" twin.

"Although I guess that was *me* who was supposedly washed overboard." Callie laughed.

Jack was impressed with her resilience despite the pain she was going through. What could have possessed Callie's twin to go rogue—and worse, to fail to get in touch the instant she learned about the ship's fate? He found the whole thing very frustrating, but he remained silent.

"I must have known she stayed behind, and why she did. Apparently, she sent a letter with me, though it got lost somewhere along the way." She looked down. "My not being able to remember those details caused my family so much pain."

Jack had been trying to wait and let Callie say all that she needed to say, but this was too much. "Callie, you can't possibly blame yourself."

"No. I know the blow to my head caused my amnesia. But it doesn't stop me from wishing I had—"

"None of this is your fault." He leaned toward her again. Callie had spent more than enough time trying to fit into Marnie's head, and he'd heard enough about her tonight. "I never met your sister. But I do know she's the one who has thrown your family into turmoil."

Chapter 116

Saturday, May 23, 9:05 p.m.—Long Beach, California

"Hope you've saved some room for frozen yogurt," said Jack as we left the restaurant. "There's a great little ice cream spot on the boardwalk." He must have seen the doubtful expression on my face. "First, we'll explore the village and work up an appetite, okay?"

As we strolled along the boardwalk, I focused on the lights twinkling off the water and the happy people walking by. Jack stopped midstride in front of a sign that read HARBOR CRUISES. A ramp led to one of the larger boats in the bay.

"How do you feel about spending the next half-hour cruising Long Beach harbor?"

"Sounds fun," I said, though I couldn't stifle a frown.

"Too soon?" he asked anxiously.

I smiled gratefully. "No, I think I'm okay. It's just . . ." I looked down at my sandals, not sure if they were allowed aboard the boat.

Jack seemed to be reading my mind. "No problem," he said. "I'm sure people come aboard in all sorts of strange foot gear. There are rubber mats installed in all the right places."

I looked at the glistening white boat with SPIRIT CRUISE written on the side of the upper cabin in red letters.

"You game?" Jack asked.

"Sure," I said, wondering if I had ever done this before.

Jack purchased two tickets for the last tour of the evening. Then he reached for my hand, and we took the narrow ramp leading to the ship.

"Let's go up on top," Jack said. "That's where we'll get the best view."

Two couples and a chatty group of four girls were already settled on the upper deck. There was no shortage of good seats, and Jack led me to one in the ship's bow. The ship cast off a few minutes later, and the guide began his spiel.

The scent of the salt water was stronger than I'd expected. I steeled myself, trying not to think about waking up to the smell of salt air aboard the *Rising Star*. But the laughter of the girls was a pleasant sound. They were already having a good time, and the adventure had barely begun.

Jack rested his arm on the back of the bench behind my shoulders, his clean fresh scent enveloping me.

As the boat left the pier, a heavy breeze began blowing my hair in my face. Maybe I should have told Jack I couldn't step on another boat. *No. I can't allow my fear to take root.* Rummaging in my handbag, I found a scrunchie and wrapped my flying hair strands into a ponytail.

I did my best to concentrate on the guide's voice over the loudspeaker giving a brief history of this area of Long Beach. But Jack's nearness was pleasantly distracting.

This is a magical place.

"Much has changed in the past several years," our guide said, pointing out the area called the Old Pike. He said it was the home of an indoor plunge pool, a huge roller coaster, and all sorts of wild rides. Once it had been the playground of boatloads of sailors. "This area is light years away from what it was before and during World War Two . . ."

As we passed the nearby loading docks with their cranes reaching far into the sky, the guide informed us that Long Beach was the home of one of the nation's largest harbors. He also directed our attention to the twinkling lights of Signal Hill, a mix of working oil wells and magnificent homes.

"Thank you so much, Jack," I said as we reached the open water. "This is fun. A perfect way to end a terrific evening."

"My pleasure," he said, with a dramatic bow and a boyish grin, "but our evening hasn't come to an end." He reminded me that we had yet to stop at Ice Cream on the Boardwalk as he'd promised.

How can it get any better than this?

Later, Jack took my hand as I stepped off the boat onto the ramp. "I may not remember anything about my past life," I told him, "but I won't forget this evening."

"Glad you enjoyed it." When he smiled, it wasn't his brilliant white teeth against his suntanned face that took my breath away. It was the warmth and glow in his eyes.

Lost in the blue of those eyes, I struggled to remind myself that my parents were clients and that Jack had been asked to show me around. "I did. But I hope I didn't take you away from something important tonight."

He frowned. "Callie. I thoroughly enjoyed the evening. I may have been asked to show you around the other day—"

"It's okay. I understand." I tried to make my voice sound cheerful.

"No. I don't believe you do."

Jack pulled up behind the beach house. Back at the harbor cruise, he had tried to tell Callie she meant far more to him than a work assignment, but he'd stopped before saying too much. He feared it would be crossing the line. But while Jack was no believer in love at first sight, Callie had haunted his every waking moment since they'd met.

This evening he hadn't been working. He'd brought his own ride and charged nothing to the Landes Agency. But it was clear that Callie was interested in nothing more than friendship.

He shook his head. He'd been a damn fool. There was a fistful of reasons why he shouldn't attempt to turn what had begun as an assignment into a date. Romance was the last thing she would be thinking about right now. Her priority was getting comfortable in her own skin.

And once that happened, she'd be out of his reach.

Chapter
117

Sunday, May 24, 9:15 a.m.—London, England

Marnie tapped lightly on Bradford's open door.

"Come in," he shouted from the kitchen, before walking in with two cups of espresso. He gestured to the sofa as he set the cups and saucers on an end table. He spoke before she had a chance. "As you know, your mother rang."

"What did she say?" Marnie blurted out, reaching for her espresso.

"Well, Dr. Benson told your parents that you should not fly until at least Saturday."

"My parents talked to Dr. Benson?" She hoped there was no mention of the hairline fracture at the base of her skull. It had freaked her out, even though the doctor assured her it was not serious and would mend itself.

Bradford nodded. "And your mother confirmed that she and your father have no objection to you remaining in Sloane Hall for the rest of the workshop. The decision as to when you return home is in your hands."

Marnie felt her pulse race through her fingertips as she set the small cup in the saucer. It rattled as she set it down. "See, I told you. I've messed up. My parents are so upset, they don't even want me to come home."

"After speaking with your mother, I can assure you she is very much looking forward to seeing you—and to speaking with you by phone later today. I understand your concerns about returning home."

Marnie picked up her espresso, took a sip, then set it down in the saucer. "I'm sorry, Graham, but without a family of your own, I don't think you understand."

He didn't respond for a long moment. But when he did, his voice was quiet. "I do understand, Marnie. And on the contrary, I did have a family once. A wife and a daughter . . . she was about your age . . ."

Marnie cocked her head. "You did? I don't recall you stating that in your author bio."

He blinked, then said, "Let's not get sidetracked. You have a decision to make."

Marnie swallowed hard. She wanted to hear more. What did he mean when he said *had a wife and a daughter*?

Bradford leaned back and placed his intertwined fingers behind his neck. "If you're concerned about our working arrangement, I told you I have it handled," he said, explaining his plan to get his manuscript to his editor on time, by getting his regular assistant back to work with the help of a typist.

"But you'd be paying two people to do my job," she protested. "And what about my sitting in on the talks about your latest revisions?" She'd given Bradford her word. Was he trying to get rid of her now?

"Nothing to concern yourself about. It's a small price to pay for a sensible resolution." He also reminded her that his regular assistant would be available, and that he didn't need much of a sounding board now that he was on his final draft.

To Marnie, his motive seemed clear. "You no longer need me or want me to be here."

Bradford leaned forward, elbows on his knees, chin resting on his interlaced fingers. "Is that what you think?"

"Doesn't that about sum it up?" Marnie asked.

When Bradford replied, it was in his Professor Higgins style. "If I didn't care about you reaching your potential, I wouldn't have given you so much of my limited time. You are a gifted writer, and I'd like nothing more than to help you mold that raw talent." He paused. "But Marnie, I need you to consider this key question: Are you able to fully immerse yourself in your writing right now?"

Marnie looked down at the folded hands in her lap. "Not really," she admitted. Her guilt had robbed her of motivation and concentration, and she feared her writing would appear amateurish, especially in front of the other students in the workshop.

He nodded. "So, let's stop seesawing. The decision is yours to make."

Silence thundered through the room. All the conflicting thoughts flittered through her head, until finally she knew what she must do. Taking in a lung full of air, she said, "Do you really have someone to type your manuscript?"

Bradford's mind had whirled after hanging up the phone with Ashleigh Taylor, his mood darkening with the weight of his culpability. Her brief call had left him more conflicted than ever.

Marnie's was a no-win situation. How could he advise and protect this vulnerable young woman? Marnie was bound to experience loss whether she remained in London or returned home the moment she was cleared to fly. There seemed no clear-cut solution. Reviewing the pros and cons ad nauseam, he'd felt impotent.

"You got it right when you said my head isn't in my work," she said. "And it won't be until I see my sister and the rest of my family. I haven't even spoken to Callie, and I'm not sure what to say when I do. But I know I can get back on track when I get home. I won't let you down."

Relief flowed through Bradford's veins. Marnie had made the right decision. Staying would do more to damage her future.

"I know you won't."

Marnie took a few deep breaths. "I hope you know how grateful I am for all the opportunities you've given me. Please let me know if there's anything I can do to help you before I head home."

He nodded. "It's time to call your parents today and tell them you'd like to return home at the end of the week."

"I guess I never had a choice," she whispered. He recalled her explanation two days earlier, about the need to see Callie, to know for herself that her twin was alright. "If possible, I'd like to return today or tomorrow."

Bradford frowned. "That is not an option. You will not have the doctor's release to fly before Saturday."

"That's ridiculous. I'm fine. There is no reason why I can't fly."

Pursing his lips, Bradford said, "Hmm. I don't recall you stating that you had a medical degree."

"Very funny," she said. "Seriously. I'm fine."

"You're fine here on the ground."

After Marnie left his flat a few minutes later, Bradford replayed the phone call with her mother. He could have given himself a swift kick. Much of this mess was his fault for remaining in limbo. He had to regain control of his life.

Indecisiveness had the potential to seriously damage his career.

Chapter
118

Sunday, May 24, 10:05 a.m.—London, England

"Marnie."

Unlatching the elevator cage on the third floor, Marnie took in Hillary's petite silhouette, backlit in the open doorway of her flat. "Good morning, Miss Hillary."

"Please, join me for a cup of tea. I'd love to have a chat before you return home." Hillary turned on her heel and disappeared into her flat.

Marnie saw that Hillary's swift gait was not that of an old woman. Though her shoulders were slightly rounded, she held her chin high and her eyes peered straight ahead.

"Sure," she said. She both admired and feared Hillary Spearpoint. The feisty author, though caring, never soft-pedaled her opinions. It was hard to believe she was in her nineties.

Marnie wondered what Hillary would think of her early departure.

Though this was the first time she'd stepped inside Hillary's flat, it was pretty much as she pictured. A typical English tea trolley had been set up. Hillary had obviously been waiting for her. The trolley held a blue-and-white patterned teapot, two matching cups and saucers, and a plate with half a dozen biscuits.

Marnie sank wordlessly onto the sofa, waiting for Hillary to begin. But the older woman said little while pouring tea into the two cups, other than inquiring how Marnie felt.

Looking her up and down with a look of concern, Hillary said, "I'm afraid you've lost nearly a stone since we met in Paris." She shook her head sadly. "It's a shame we didn't have the opportunity to get to know each other better. Bradford thinks a lot of you and tells me you have a great deal of potential."

Marnie looked down at her loose-fitting jeans. "A stone?"

"Approximately fourteen pounds—merely a point of reference." Hillary paused as if searching for words. "Forgive me, but I must voice my concern. I know this is not something most people think about but taking care of your body is extremely important for a functioning brain."

"Thank you for your concern," Marnie said, and she meant it. But she swiftly changed the subject. "I may be returning home on Saturday."

"Have the arrangements been made?"

"Not yet. Miss Hillary, had the disaster aboard the *Rising Star* not occurred, I wouldn't think of leaving the workshop early, but—"

Waving her hand between them as though erasing a chalkboard, Hillary said, "Hush. You are a beautiful and likable young woman, and perhaps you'll be a great writer one day. And if you learned nothing else at the conference in Paris, you must have gathered that to become a success in the literary world requires an immense amount of hard work and dedication."

She paused again, and Marnie could see she had an agenda. One that, Marnie feared, would be delivered with brutal honesty.

"I am not one to mince words, so I will get straight to the point." Hillary rocked back in her armchair. "I know quite a bit about your background—if what Graham and I found on the Internet can be trusted."

"The Internet?" Marnie stared at the old woman in disbelief.

"Of course. I take advantage of the Internet at times." She chuckled. "I don't do Facebook or that Twitter thing. But I'd have to live under a rock to avoid the advantages of today's technology."

Marnie couldn't get over her surprise. *Miss Hillary goes online whenever she pleases—and yet, with minor exceptions, I've been following Graham's rule like it was set in stone.* Like Bradford, Hillary had no idea of what it had been like for her to stop using email and the Internet for the past three months. Even these past two weeks had been a nightmare.

"It seems that for you as well as for Graham, life was no picnic in your early years. I hope one day you can share how your separate backgrounds influenced your future—and led you to writing."

Bradford's words echoed in Marnie's ears: *I did have a family once. A wife and a daughter . . . she was about your age.*

"How long have you known Graham?" Marnie leaned forward despite the sharp pain in her hip.

"Most of his life," Hillary said with a steady gaze. "Because I am married to my work, without Graham I would have no family. We've celebrated some incredible highs . . . and mourned some rock-bottom lows."

"Was he ever married?"

"That is not my story to tell." Hillary sighed. "As you may have gathered, there aren't enough hours left on my calendar to waste on frivolous conversation. I am ninety-three years old and nearing my expiration date. While I am in good health and don't feel my age, the fact is, I won't be here forever. My concern is the future, so . . ."

She beckoned to Marnie, who leaned forward still more.

"I find you to be a bright, decent, caring young woman—one whom Graham has a great desire to assist in reaching your dream." Hillary explained that while Graham has many admirers and acquaintances, his close friends are mostly married with lives of their own. "I would like to think that you will keep in touch with Graham once you leave London. You are young and doubtless have other important people in your life. However, you could have no better mentor than Graham Bradford."

Chapter
119

Sunday, May 24, 5:15 p.m.—London, England

Marnie stared at the computer keyboard, the glare from the screen stinging her eyes. In the past few hours, the only words she *hadn't* trashed were *Chapter Fourteen*. She knew the other students were in their flats or the communal area, endeavoring to write as she was. But in the quiet of this historic building, every creak became a distraction.

Liam, from the London office of Landes Agency, had come and gone earlier that afternoon. Marnie supposed her parents just wanted to check out things for themselves—that she was okay and not being held against her will or anything crazy like that. His half-hour visit had given her a small reprieve, but now she had no such excuse.

She'd been tempted to ask Bradford for more manuscript pages to type, but that avenue of escape was currently blocked. Bradford and Hillary were behind closed doors in sessions with the four other students in the workshop. Plus, he may not have any more yellow pages to be transcribed.

And yet she needed something productive to do. She had been experiencing writer's block since learning of Callie's amnesia.

Writer's block, my foot! What a feeble excuse, she chided herself. Did mechanics, secretaries, or any other types of professional workers complain of being afflicted by a "block" that prevented them from doing their job? Of course not.

Bradford claimed writer's block was merely one of three things: the fear of writing poorly, the lack of imagination, or pure laziness. So, despite the dull throb in her temples, Marnie forced herself to reread the first thirteen chapters of her novel. Though thrilled to find her initial chapters didn't suck, she'd failed to fully reconnect either with her characters or with the challenges and the obstacles they faced. That visceral connection continued to elude her. Try as she might to edit the paragraphs, the words wouldn't come.

Until she was with Callie and her family, her writer's voice would remain locked inside. To lift this weight, she would have to come to terms with a past she had no power to change. She had to apologize for what she'd put her family through. She couldn't allow bottled-up regrets to immobilize her.

Marnie knew in her heart that the time was not right to take advantage of all the Sloane Hall Workshop could offer. Every extra moment spent in London, she'd be spinning her wheels.

Saving the chapter heading, she shut down the computer. *Maybe a break is what I need,* she told herself. She knew her family would be arriving home from church soon. By the time she made a pot of coffee and took a long, hot shower to soothe her aching body, it would be after ten a.m. on the West Coast. *Maybe now is a good time to try calling home.*

Maybe it was time to speak to Callie at last.

10:35 a.m.—Long Beach, California

Following church, Ashleigh abandoned the idea of breakfast at Hof's. The girls wanted nothing more than cold cereal, so they could get to work on ironing out the kinks in their trio.

Upon returning to the beach house, Ashleigh lowered herself onto the edge of the king-sized bed, picked up the receiver on the landline, and made a quick call to Elizabeth. She was delighted to hear her report: There were no new wrinkles with Caroline, and they planned to be at the girls' dress rehearsal that afternoon.

Ashleigh quickly changed clothes, pulling on a pair of white pants and sliding a pale-yellow top over her head. She wondered if Marnie had gotten her message from Bradford. Would her wayward daughter call home this morning as she had requested?

The voice mail from Liam at Landes London had gone a long way toward allaying her fears. But as much as Ashleigh longed to see for herself that her precious child was alright, Marnie was an adult. The decision to come home must be hers. Whatever her choice, it was important she felt their love and stopped beating herself up.

Ashleigh knew Marnie was her own worst critic. Her poor decision had boomeranged in the most devastating way possible. What Marnie needed most was her family's love and support in moving forward. Neither she nor Conrad believed in rehashing mistakes or bad decisions in their business nor their personal lives. What was most important was setting up expectations for the future.

Slipping her bare feet into sandals, Ashleigh checked her wristwatch as Juliana's parting words replayed in her head: *Marnie won't be staying in London for two more months. I just know she won't.*

6:40 p.m.—London, England

Marnie headed toward the Sloane Square Hotel for the second time in a week. This time she was limping, however, and she looked to the right for a full five seconds before stepping into the street. At the hotel, she went straight to the reception desk and asked how to place a call to the U.S. from the hotel pay phone. Then she punched in the number Bradford had given her for the rented beach house and uttered a prayer.

Please, please, please be there.

She was about to hang up when she heard her mother's voice.

"Sweetheart . . ."

Chapter
120

Monday, May 25, 2:35 p.m.—London, England

Each footfall echoed off the walnut-paneled walls as Graham Bradford paced the length of the lower level of Sloane Hall. His concentration was shot to bloody hell. He couldn't bear seeing Marnie so at sea. Since she'd spoken to her mother, she'd been as skittish as an owl caught at the crack of dawn.

Apparently, Marnie had gotten up at sunrise and totally reorganized this lower level. It was now spotless. The bookshelves were dust free and evenly spaced. Nonfiction books were lined up by subject matter, novels were in alphabetical order by the author's last name, and the chairs at the conference table were neatly arranged, as if in a department store showroom.

Earlier, when she'd delivered a set of his printed manuscript pages to his flat, she'd planted a smile on her face, but her eyes were hollow. She appeared on the verge of tears, and uncharacteristically, she'd failed to ask a single question about his revisions. Instead, she'd announced her plans to take a nap. Then she had disappeared.

Being told her journey home was delayed until the following Monday seemed to have pulled the rug from beneath her feet. Her mother had informed her that due to her condition, they would need time to arrange for someone to accompany her on the eleven-hour flight—perhaps the Landes agent who had visited her yesterday. Her twin sister's own health issues, and her father's balancing act at a particularly difficult moment for his department stores, prevented either of her parents from traveling overseas right now.

Bradford understood the Taylors' dilemma. Yet he'd noticed Marnie had become more listless and depressed as each hour passed.

There must be a way to get her on an earlier plane for home.

Not for the first time, Bradford wished he could be in two places at once, but he couldn't just abandon the workshop. But without an escort, the grueling trip back would be pure torture for her—if not physically, then emotionally. There was no one harder on Marnie than herself.

If only . . .

That thought hung in the air for a moment before it was replaced by another. One Bradford could and would act upon.

"Blimey, Graham. You know I'd love to," Charlize said, "but I've worked my bloody head off all year to afford these two months in your workshop. I must get my novel in shape this summer. A round-trip to the U.S. would really put a crimp in my plans."

Bradford raised a smooth palm. "Charlize, please just listen. I anticipated your reluctance, and I admire your work ethic. But I have a plan. One that will benefit you as well as Marnie." He explained that he had spoken with her mother again, and that Ashleigh Taylor had expressed great relief at the idea of Marnie being accompanied by a friend. His description of the Taylors' personal and professional conflicts preventing them from travel drew a strong reaction.

"Jordon's?" Charlize cried out. "Well, I'm gobsmacked. Marnie never told me her dad was such a bigwig."

Bradford leaned in and continued as if there'd been no interruption. "I've not bounced this idea off Marnie yet, but here's the plan. The Taylors offered to reimburse you for your time. They would also be happy to treat you to a short vacation on the other side of the pond—following the workshop, of course, and at your convenience." Marnie's parents had also offered to reimburse Charlize for the workshop, but Bradford had decided that was on him.

"But Graham—"

Clearing his throat, he continued. "In addition, I will give you three extra one-on-one sessions when you return. Listen, Charlize. You'll be knackered, but the trip can be done in twenty-four hours."

Charlize's eyes widened as she tried to take it all in.

"Mr. Taylor had his secretary check flights on Norwegian Air. While she recommends that you stay overnight with them in L.A., you do have the option of returning on the same plane after about an hour's layover."

"Can I think it over for a bit?" asked Charlize.

"Of course," Bradford replied. "I realize this has caught you unaware." He had little doubt of her decision, however. And once she'd decided, all that was left was to bring Marnie into the loop.

Chapter

121

Monday, May 25, 8:15 a.m.—San Diego, California

"Conrad Taylor?" A petite young woman in a short purple dress and matching stilettos stood in the doorway of the green room, where Conrad waited for his interview.

"Yes." Conrad stood as the young woman introduced herself as the assistant to the host of Channel 6's *San Diego News in the Morning*.

"We're so pleased you took time out of your busy schedule to be on our show this morning."

"My pleasure," Conrad said, although it was a bold-faced lie. While he appreciated the opportunity to clarify the proactive way Jordon's had been coping with the current state of the apparel industry, the timing of this interview couldn't be worse. But the world didn't stop for his family drama. News of Jordon's shuttering twenty-five percent of its locations had hit the media from coast to coast. This interview was not something he could delegate.

The young woman was holding a small microphone and a battery pack. "I'll take you into the studio. But first we need to mic you."

"Fine." Conrad seated himself on the arm of the sofa. "I know the drill." As she clipped a small microphone to the lapel of his suit jacket, he reached for the battery pack and slipped it into his inside pocket.

"Follow me," she said. "Since this is hardly new to you, I won't bore you with the protocol."

Noticing the blinking red light outside the studio door, Conrad took light steps behind his guide, then took a seat out of the camera's view. When the segment ended, he was led to the news counter by the young assistant.

"This isn't Conrad's first rodeo," commented the host, Pat Davis. "He's a studio favorite."

"Nice to see you again, Pat," he said, stretching out his hand.

Taking advantage of the commercial break, she said, "Given the topsy-turvy state of the retail—"

Conrad held out a hand. "If you don't mind, Pat, I've developed an aversion to going over my interview topic prior to the cameras going live." He recounted his experience several years back, on CBS in Salt Lake City, when he had a terrific chat with his interviewer, but it had robbed the interview of spontaneity. "I'm not being difficult. I'd just like to give your audience my best overview."

"Alright," she said, her eyes troubled. "Well, I was sorry to hear of your personal tragedy. Would you mind if I mention the personal challenges you face in addition to the massive closure of one hundred Jordon's department stores?"

Conrad froze, although he was not surprised by Pat's interest in the rogue wave given how it had gripped the nation. Then he blinked and instantly regrouped. So far, he and Ashleigh had managed to maintain a low profile, and he had no desire to reveal any story-behind-the-story. "My personal life has nothing to do with the world of retail. Therefore, it's off limits."

Pat's dazzling hazel eyes widened. "I'm sorry. I just thought—"

"Apology accepted," Conrad said as two cameras rolled in.

At the flash of green lights, Pat smiled into the camera. "Welcome back. Conrad Taylor, CEO of Jordon's Inc., joins us this morning." She turned her head a fraction. "Welcome, Conrad. We're pleased to have you with us today."

"My pleasure, Pat." He smiled into the camera, prepared for whatever came his way.

"Given the state of our economy and the changes brought about by new technology, department stores have been rumored to be disappearing for more than two decades now. So far, you and your predecessors have proved those predictions wrong." With her head still tilted toward Conrad, the host continued, "Before we get into the dynamics of Jordon's shuttering twenty-five percent of their stores across the nation, I have a question regarding the overall state of retail."

Conrad ticked off a mental count of three following the anchor's sound bite.

Still smiling into the camera, Pat continued, "With the current surge of online retailers capturing larger and larger shares of the retail market, do you now foresee the demise of the brick-and-mortar department stores as an emerging reality?"

Conrad shifted on his stool. The question was not unexpected. "I most certainly do not. Just try to get a parking spot at your favorite mall." His smile widened. "However, we cannot overlook the rapid evolution in consumer and shopping preferences. The retail landscape has changed and retailers *must* respond to the changes in consumers' wants and needs. To succeed, we must be creative and remain open to change."

Conrad paused, but Pat waited, signaling that she hoped he would continue.

"Consumers have many options for shopping—by catalog, online, and in physical stores. With incredible competition for low- and high-quality goods, many consumers, particularly millennials, are taking advantage of the added convenience of targeting products through their phones. They decide what they want, where they want to shop, and how much they are willing to pay—all before heading to the store or making an online purchase."

"I understand Jordon's has a strong online presence," Pat added.

Conrad nodded. "We are now the third largest online retailer in the U.S."

"What effect does that have on your physical stores?"

"Most online sales are incremental. We feared a strong online presence might cannibalize our brand. We feared online customers would fail to shop in our stores. What we found, however, was that most were already Internet buyers. We don't care where customers are buying goods, as long as they buy from us."

Pat nodded her encouragement.

"The Internet is here to stay. And as I said, Jordon's has a strong online presence. The Internet is not king, however. Online sales surpass those in physical stores for some categories, such as electronics and books. However, in the categories we sell, eighty-five percent of all transactions occur in physical stores. Due to our strong online presence, thirty-five percent of our sales are made online and sixty-five percent in our stores."

"Last night, I caught a segment of Dana Telsey's retail predictions."

Conrad cut in. "She was on the mark. Retail cannot be painted with a broad brush. Business is booming in many individual retail categories, such as cosmetics and home furnishings. Nevertheless, department stores have faced major headwinds over the past twenty months. The holiday season of 2015, which was the hottest North American winter in a hundred years, had a devastating effect on shopping and sales."

"I remember it well." Pat rubbed the back of her hand across her forehead.

"That was a factor in the decline, but far from the only factor. The economy is good, and customers now have money in their pockets, but they are spending it differently. For instance, a great number of millennials have abandoned quality in favor of fast, cheap apparel, which they can discard and update often. Also, consumers no longer confine their shopping to one channel—catalog, online, or in-store."

"Is that right?" Pat urged.

"Statistics show that multichannel shoppers spend two to three times as much as single-channel shoppers do. Online shopping is here to stay. We need both. The harmonization brings higher consumer satisfaction. A consumer may buy online but pick up or return to a physical store."

"But aren't more sales made online?"

Conrad shook his head. "That's a misconception, Pat. Many consumers prefer to talk with an associate, touch, try on, and make sure the product is right for them. A few come to the store, and then buy online. Hopefully from us. Jordon's is diligent in keeping the competitive edge."

Facing the camera straight on, Pat said, "Stay tuned to find out if *your* favorite Jordon's store is on the chopping block."

"Ouch," Conrad said when the camera no longer focused on them.

"Sorry," Pat said. "We spent more time discussing the overall retail climate than anticipated. I'm delighted you were able to paint such an informative picture. But I had to make sure we didn't lose the passionate viewers who tuned in to discover the fate of their local Jordon's location."

"Understood." Conrad opened his mouth to express his pain, both personal and professional, over the vast number of store closings. His role was to quiet the predictions of gloom and doom for brick-and-mortar department stores and reassure the public of their longevity.

No, he decided. *I'll save it for the cameras.*

Chapter
122

Monday, May 25, 4:20 p.m.—London, England

Marnie tapped softly on Bradford's door. She was right on time. But when the door swung open and banged against the wall, her heart sank to her toes. She saw Bradford's tired, flushed face and puzzled expression.

What have I done now?

"What's wrong?" she asked, trying to control the tremor in her voice.

Raking fingers through the side of his neatly styled hair, he inhaled a sharp breath. "Marnie. You caught me at a bad time."

Her heart raced. "Did I get the time for our meeting wrong?"

"No, I'm sorry." His hazel eyes softened. "Please, come in."

The tray on his coffee table held a pitcher of water and two glasses. *So, he was expecting me.* She expelled a pent-up breath, wondering what had set him off, and lowered herself into her usual corner of the sofa.

Bradford didn't speak for a moment, instead taking a long pull of water. "Have you spoken to your Uncle Mike?"

"Uncle Mike?" she repeated. Then she waited, her fear tangible.

"He rang a few moments ago, to accuse me of . . . impropriety."

Oh, Uncle Mike, what have you done?

"I'm so sorry he upset you, Graham. He's a good man, just a bit overprotective sometimes."

"It's not your fault. I don't imagine he's the type of man to listen. However, he loves you." Bradford gazed unblinking for several long seconds. "I'm afraid I overreacted, let my temper get the best of me."

"I asked Uncle Mike not to call you," she explained. "I told him that everything was my fault, that I just couldn't turn down the opportunity you had given me." Her hotheaded uncle had been quick to jump to the wrong conclusion. But that didn't bother her half as much as what her mom had said . . .

"Had a similar incident occurred with *my* daughter," Bradford said, "my reaction may have been much the same."

Marnie froze, remembering his words from the previous morning. *I did have a family once. A wife and a daughter* . . . She sensed that her mentor was about to say more.

He did not continue for a few painful seconds. "They were killed on the A1. My wife and daughter. En route to the Isle of Wight, to celebrate Easter with my mother-in-law." He spoke in a staccato rhythm. "Laura would have been about your age by now. She, too, wanted to be a writer. You remind me a great deal of . . ." He shook his head, a puzzled frown playing across his features. "Her death was my darkest moment. My greatest shame."

"Shame?" Marnie echoed.

"Yes. I . . . I should have been with them. Instead I was caught up in my own selfishness. I bowed out of my family responsibilities, choosing instead to work on finishing my first Derek Duncan novel."

"But didn't you say they were killed in an automobile accident?"

"Logically, I know it's irrational," he explained. "But if I'd been with them, maybe the timing would have been different. Maybe I could have prevented the collision."

"I think psychiatrists call that 'survivor's guilt,'" Marnie said quietly.

"Perhaps. But it's still unfair that my wife and daughter are no longer here. I miss them. They mourned my rejections alongside me, never living to see the success."

Marnie totally understood. "Maybe if I'd been on the ship, Callie wouldn't have been in the same place when the rogue wave hit."

Bradford's eyes seemed sad. "As Hillary says, if hindsight were foresight, we'd all be living perfect lives. And there would be nothing to write about."

Marnie thought of her mother, who often expressed something similar: *To fully enjoy the sunshine, we must experience the rain.* "Miss Hillary told me she's known you most of your life," she said aloud.

He nodded. "Since I was nearly thirteen. She was my English teacher. Found me living in my dad's Ford Cortina. My mom was dead, and my dad was in prison. I was already working two jobs and still going to as many classes as I could manage. Unlike you, for me the greatest motivation was to *avoid* following in my father's footsteps."

Pressing the heel of his hand to his forehead, Bradford remained silent for what seemed like a long time. Then he said, "Hillary is the mom I never had. She's my moral compass."

The room fell into a comfortable silence. Bradford rested his head on the back of his armchair, his fingers interlaced behind his neck.

Marnie's heart went out to her idol. She became aware of every sound: the humming refrigerator, the thrum of cars passing on the street below—even the pounding of her heart.

She reflected on Bradford's willingness to share such a poignant moment from his life. She wiped her damp palms on the thighs of her jeans as Erica's words thundered through her head.

"My mother said I lack humanity," she declared.

Graham Bradford could hardly imagine the refined, kindhearted Ashleigh Taylor he'd spoken to on the phone would say such a thing to her own daughter. "Your mother said *that*?"

"Erica. My other mother," Marnie clarified.

"I'm sure that's not true," Bradford said. "Although on this particular occasion, perhaps she was right."

Marnie stared at him, the wound evident in her deep brown eyes.

He went on before she could respond. "Perhaps she was speaking of a lack of empathy. She is hurt that you didn't demonstrate enough care for how your decision to leave the *Rising Star* might affect those who care about you." He paused thoughtfully. "Empathy is a crucial element in storytelling as well as in life. In her lectures, Hillary often addresses the importance of the empathy gene."

"Empathy gene?" Marnie repeated.

"The ability to put yourself in someone else's shoes, to have empathy for their circumstances and problems. Unfortunately, we are not born with such a gene—it's a learned emotion. One can learn it through the school of hard knocks, which we both experienced in early life. Otherwise, fiction is an excellent source."

Marnie's expression remained quizzical.

"When we read and imagine stories, we build and exercise our ability to understand and interact with others. When we empathize, we write more engaging stories. We also have more effective conversations with those who cross our paths." He took a sip of water.

"I developed a love of the classics early in life, which Hillary cultivated. Stories were my salvation during the darkest periods of life."

"How did you go from the classics to commercial fiction and writing thrillers?"

"In college, I was a literary snob who read no commercial fiction. I earned a free ride for a master's in English literature. During my first year, however, I read two books that changed everything for me: Ken Follett's *Eye of the Needle* and Jeffrey Archer's *Kane and Abel* . . ."

Bradford paused, recalling the excitement and promise of his college days.

"While I felt I could write a good literary novel, I didn't think I could write a great one. Armed with that knowledge, I began devouring commercial thrillers—something I liked and understood. In our walk-up London flat, I set up my manual typewriter on the kitchen table and wrote every morning before work and every night. As most authors experience, my first novel was rejected. But following the success of my first Derek Duncan thriller, I rewrote and sold that inaugural manuscript, and it rose to the top of the charts."

Finishing his reverie, he turned to Marnie and saw that same light of excitement and promise rekindled in her eyes.

"Now, I am expecting Alexandre in ten minutes for our session," he said abruptly. "But I'd like you to leave the beginning chapters of your novel. We'll meet again tomorrow and go over what you've written."

Marnie got up slowly from his sofa as he picked up his diary and penciled in their next session. Tapping the pages, he broke out into a smile.

"Oh, and one more thing, Marnie. I have some good news about your travel plans . . ."

Chapter

123

Monday, May 25, 8:25 a.m.—San Diego, California

During the commercial break, Conrad uncapped his bottled water and took a long pull. When the green light flicked on, the numbers *3, 2, 1* flashed on the monitor, and the Channel 6 host welcomed back the audience.

As the list of Jordon's locations to be closed scrolled down the monitor, Pat Davis commented, "We can all release our collective breath over which department stores will survive the bearish culling of one hundred Jordon's locations." She paused deliberately. "At least some of us can. But while some will miss the convenience of shopping in our favorite Jordon's stores, what troubles us most is the massive loss of jobs."

Conrad jumped in. "That pains me greatly too, of course. Store closings impact people and communities. Jordon's is a vital part of every community it serves. Therefore, the loss of each job has a ripple effect."

"That is a substantial loss," Pat said, her voice filled with emotion.

Not wasting precious airtime on a verbal response, Conrad went on, "We shuttered forty-one locations a year ago, which failed to move the needle. The aggressive plan of closing another hundred locations within the next twelve months is healthy for the overall business as well as the consumer. The money we save will allow us to focus on our best stores, increasing staff and bringing in new technology, including digital and mobile."

He did not mention that many investors felt management should have acted sooner.

"Volume and profitability have steadily declined in the targeted stores. In others, the cost of remodeling exceeds their value. Saturation in real estate has tied up capital that could be put toward better use. With the closing of a hundred locations, we will retain a physical footprint in forty-nine of the top fifty U.S. markets."

"And yet you strongly believe in the viability of your department store buildings," Pat countered.

"Very strongly," Conrad insisted. "As I mentioned earlier, we're rethinking how customers shop. By getting in front of it, we can attract today's customer by being innovative. We can't offer what everyone else does. Currently, there is too much product and too much redundancy in the market. Brand is everything. By focusing on our strengths—concentrating on Jordon's brands and exclusives by key designers—we will bring consumers to us, since we offer brands you can buy nowhere other than Jordon's."

"Will those brands be available online as well as in the stores?"

"Absolutely. But, we find high-quality apparel, particularly ladies' fine apparel, is less likely to be purchased online. Discerning customers still prefer to see, touch, and try on clothing items. Today's consumers are reluctant to pay full price, which is unlikely to change. That train has already left the station.

"Department stores have hit a slump in the past twenty months, but we've seen this movie before. After facing the difficult times of bankruptcy, 9/11, and the 2008 recession, Jordon's came back larger, stronger, and more resourceful than it had been thirteen years before. The road to success is a business model that blends multiple buying channels. Even Amazon is building physical stores."

As the light on camera two began blinking, Pat again smiled into the camera. "Thank you for being with us today, Conrad."

"It was my pleasure."

"I believe we would all agree department stores are a vital part of our community," she continued. "Your view on their durability and longevity has indeed been enlightening."

When the commercial break began, Pat thanked Conrad again. "You covered a great deal of interesting ground in our four-minute segments."

Conrad smiled. "I tend to be a fast talker on TV interviews, but there was a lot I didn't cover."

"You covered more than most, and we hope you return. I wish all of our guests were so well prepared."

"Thank you, Pat. I could have done better. After all, the entire Gettysburg Address was delivered in two minutes," he quipped.

Outside the studio, Conrad raced to his rented BMW. Ashleigh and Callie had a 10:30 a.m. appointment at Dr. Martin's office. He prayed he'd reach Aliso Viejo in time.

Chapter
124

Monday, May 25, 10:10 a.m.—Mission Viejo, California

As they headed south on the 405 freeway in the diamond lane, Ashleigh was grateful not to be stuck in the bumper-to-bumper flow of traffic to her right. Her attention was already occupied by Callie in the passenger seat, asking a litany of questions about her twin.

"But won't we be at the dance convention when Marnie's flight arrives on Saturday?"

"Yes," Ashleigh said. "She'll arrive at LAX at three fifteen. It was the best we could do at such short notice. Jack has agreed to pick her up and bring her to our hotel."

She was thrilled with Marnie's decision to return home before the Sloane Hall Workshop was over. She and Conrad didn't want to prevent her from taking advantage of an important opportunity, but they had been hoping for that very outcome.

Callie frowned. "Mom, Jack works for an investigation agency. Is it fair for our family to be turning him into a chauffeur?"

"Jack offered his assistance," Ashleigh replied. "Why? Did he indicate to you that he was unhappy?"

Callie shook her head. "He's way too polite. "He told me he enjoyed the change of pace." Shaking her head, she said, "But it feels weird. He'd hardly take a chance of offending any of Landes's clients."

It was time to cut the idle chatter and stop ignoring the elephant in the car. "It seems like the two of you have hit it off," Ashleigh said.

Over the past few days, she had not overlooked how Callie's eyes lit up at the mention of Jack's name. She'd been relieved that her daughter had found a new friend—someone to fill that unique need for a confidant who was not part of her past. And yet she feared Callie was viewing Jack Kirkbride as more than a friend. Surely, she must realize that given her condition, it was far too soon to get involved in romance.

"We have," Callie said tentatively. "Is there something wrong with that?"

"No. However, you just met last week—"

"I know when we met, Mom."

"Of course, darling. Jack is a good-looking and very personable young man, and I think a great deal of him."

"But . . ." Callie said, her tone dripping with uncharacteristic sarcasm.

"Callie," Ashleigh said, noting her daughter's tone, "my concern is your present vulnerability."

"Then why did you keep throwing us together?"

"Darling, Dick Landes is the one who suggested Jack could help. Your dad and I agreed you'd be more comfortable with someone closer to your age." Ashleigh was grateful that Callie and Juliana had formed an instant bond. But she hadn't expected this young man to turn out to be someone with whom Callie might form an even deeper one.

"Okay, yes. I like him. But . . ." Flushed, Callie turned and stared silently out the car window.

A wall of silence radiated through the car's interior, and Ashleigh said another silent prayer that Conrad would make it to Aliso Viejo in time for the appointment with Dr. Martin despite the northbound traffic. She hoped Callie knew how hard her father was trying to spend more time with the family and still fulfill his responsibilities to Jordon's at this difficult time.

Ashleigh glanced over to the passenger seat. She needed to discuss this with Conrad. She feared her best-laid plans had gone awry, all because she hadn't imagined Jack to be so charming and good-looking. She'd never perceived a romance blooming between Callie and Jack. And that would be disastrous in her precarious state.

Chapter 125

Monday, May 25—Aliso Viejo, California

As the Mercedes bumped over the driveway to the large parking area between Starbucks and the medical building, I spotted Dad's rental car. My pulse thundered in my ears. Whatever I found out today might change my life forever.

Before Mom had a chance to switch off the engine, I threw open the door and made a beeline for Dad, who had just stepped from the BMW. I'd managed to hold back my tears for the entire car ride, but not a moment longer. The dam finally broke, and I felt tears running down my cheeks as I ran to greet him.

"Hey, sweetheart," Dad said, sounding a little surprised as he wrapped his arms around me.

Sobbing like a toddler, I wailed, "Oh, Daddy, what will I *do* if all my memories were washed out to sea and I have to start all over again?"

Dad simply let me have my cry until I could pull myself together. When I had quieted down, he said, "If that unlikely scenario played out, we'd all just begin creating new memories together. And look at us now! We've already begun."

I don't think I could have loved him anymore than I did at that moment.

"Callie," the receptionist called out. "Dr. Martin will see you now."

Conrad was about to get to his feet when he felt Ashleigh's gentle touch.

"Love," she whispered, "let's wait until Callie has a chance to tell the doctor whether she'd like us to be part of this meeting."

He watched his daughter walk into the doctor's private office. Letting go of his girls always felt like a new and unsettling experience. He was relieved when, only a few seconds later, Dr. Martin called out to them from his open doorway.

"Please join us."

In the office, the doctor pulled a third chair from along the wall and placed it beside the other two in front of his desk. Sitting on the desk was the colorful plastic brain he'd used to explain its various functions on their previous visit. On the wall to their right, Conrad noticed a huge diagram titled *Brain Functions*, with miniature drawings and labels explaining where the brain stored emotions, speech, motor control, hearing, and smell—as well as long-term and short-term memories.

The doctor gestured for them to be seated, his manner as warm as ever. "When discussing the brain, more than one set of ears is beneficial. I told Callie I'm delighted she feels comfortable with a family meeting."

Conrad found himself leaning forward, listening to every word.

"Fortunately," Dr. Martin said, "the PET scan revealed a healthy brain. No lesions or swelling."

"What do you mean, a healthy brain?" Callie asked incredulously. "I can't remember anything or anyone from my past. Not even my roommate. And I don't recall anything I've ever done with any of my family or friends. In conversation with anyone from my past, I have nothing to contribute." She blinked. "Did the scan reveal how long I'd be in never-never land, or if my memories are lost forever?"

The pulse throbbed in Conrad's temples as Callie voiced her fears.

"I'm sorry, Callie," the doctor said, "the PET scan did not bring the clarification we hoped for."

"Does that mean you don't know if the memory loss is temporary or permanent?" Ashleigh asked, her voice just above a whisper.

Callie did not lift her gaze from the carpet.

"I'm afraid we are back to square one," Dr. Martin said.

Conrad would need more than that if he was going to help his family get back on track. "So, where do we go from here?" he asked.

"I realize this is unsettling," the doctor replied, "but there are no other, more conclusive tests to administer. Only time will tell."

PART FOUR

May 29–November 22

Chapter

126

Friday, May 29, 12:45 p.m.—London, England

Even though Charlize would be flying to Los Angeles with her the very next morning, she and Alexandre had insisted on treating Marnie to this farewell lunch. Marnie had chosen a pub, and not only because it best fit into her new friends' budgets. Over the past few days, she'd grown addicted to the shepherd's pie at The Slug and Lettuce. No one, she'd discovered, made the dish like the English.

Her new friends tried to talk her into trying the steak and kidney pie, but the very thought of it made her cringe. When she refused even to try a bite, Alexandre and Charlize taunted her with a limerick—one she was sure they'd made up on the spot. "Only you two could think of anything so daft," she'd said, doubling over at the cadence of such nonsensical words.

"*Au contraire, ma petite chou,*" Alexandre said as he handed her a gift-wrapped box. "Charlize and I picked out something for you."

She tore off the paper and stared at a book sporting a blindingly bright yellow jacket and the title *Looney Limericks*.

"No writer should be without these lovely mood lifters," Charlize said, and guzzled the last of her beer.

They continued to the Duke of Wellington Pub for more limericks and another round of pints. It was after 5:00 p.m. when Charlize said at last, "Sorry we can't create more of this lyrical poetry, but we need to get you back to Sloane Hall for your farewell with Graham and Hillary."

Not much of a drinker, Marnie felt a bit tipsy as she left the pub arm in arm with Charlize and Alexandre. Her injured sides hurt from all the laughing. Good-humored teasing and the clinking of beer glasses had echoed off the walls throughout the entire afternoon. It was a delicious sensation—one she hadn't felt since she'd crept down the gangplank of the *Rising Star*.

Nothing could dampen her good spirits. The future looked as beautiful as a Queen Elizabeth rose.

After Charlize and Alexandre said their goodbyes and returned to their own flats, Marnie discovered she had less than twenty minutes to freshen up.

As she stepped across the threshold into Hillary's flat, she heard Bradford say, "You know I can never get enough of your blackberry crumble."

The old woman's face was still glowing when Marnie arrived in her sitting room. "I know," Hillary said, "but this is from the Harrods food hall. I don't think you will be disappointed."

A giant lump formed in Marnie's throat as she noted the time and effort Hillary had put into her farewell. A lace runner ran the length of the buffet table, bisecting a red tablecloth. The blackberry crumble had been placed in a shallow white dish, alongside a silver tea server and red-and-white cups. A small stack of red-and-white paper napkins complemented the china. On them were words to live by: KEEP CALM AND HAVE A CUPPA.

Hillary took charge of the conversation while Bradford poured the tea. "Now Marnie, don't allow the mess you've gotten yourself into to define you. You have learned a valuable lesson. Now it is time to let go. Take care of yourself so you will be able to give to others. Take care of your body. Your writer's voice will return—if it hasn't already." With a mischievous twinkle in her gray eyes, she added, "And when you return to London someday, always remember to—"

"Look right." Marnie's smile was genuine as she shifted her gaze between Hillary and Bradford. "I want to thank you both for not giving up on me."

"And you should never give up on yourself, Marnie. You are the only person who can effectively impact your future," Bradford said. "Be patient. Follow the writers' golden rule: Allow yourself to write badly. You must produce a great deal of rubbish before you produce prose worthy of publication."

She could almost repeat that caution in her sleep. Yet even after several productive days of writing, she still could not seem to turn off the editor in her head.

As they finished their crumble, Bradford cleared his throat and handed her another gift-wrapped package. This one, in shiny gold paper with a flat gold bow trimmed in black, looked very special.

"Thank you," Marnie said, not sure whether she was supposed to open it right away.

"Well," Hillary said, "perhaps you should see what's inside."

That was all the encouragement she needed. Carefully unwrapping the exquisite package, Marnie saw a rich blue, leather-bound book embossed with gold letters: *Great Expectations* by Charles Dickens.

She was helpless to stop the tears flowing down her cheeks. "Miss Hillary, I'm so grateful for the opportunities you've given me. I will never forget your kindness." She stepped closer to give the older woman a big, American-style hug.

"Take care," Hillary said, finishing the hug with a quick English squeeze.

Saying goodbye to Bradford was more difficult. Momentarily unsure of herself, she stuck out her hand and said, "I have learned so much from you, Graham. If there is anything I can ever do to make up for all the trouble I've caused, I hope you won't hesitate to ask."

He grasped her hand and stepped in to give her a fatherly hug. "What you can do for me is pace yourself. Respect your current physical limitations until you get back on track and regain your writer's voice. And don't make us regret taking a chance on you."

Marnie was determined neither to apologize again nor to display the emotions bottled up inside. She replied simply, "I understand—and I won't. When I get home, I'll finish my project and write something that will knock your socks off."

It was a promise made with confidence she did not entirely feel.

Chapter
127

Saturday, May 30, 2:05 p.m.—Los Angeles, California

Ashleigh checked in at the reception desk of the Los Angeles Marriott, leaving their overnight bags with the porter. Moments later, she headed for the lower level and peeked inside the main ballroom.

As students scattered all around her, she noticed Allison Dee talking with a couple of dancers from her jazz workshop. She had not spotted her girls but was pretty sure they would have attended the class. She was about to step out into the corridor when Allison called out to her.

Turning, she saw Allison dashing toward her. After a brief hug, Allison said, "Callie and I had a few awkward moments, but I'm pleased to see she has lost none of her dance skills." She explained that Callie had lost her inhibitions before the first hour of class had ended and was soon dancing full out. "The worry lines I noticed on her smooth skin have vanished. In the world of dance, she's in her element."

Ashleigh was filled with relief. She was reminded of how close the dance teacher had become with all her girls, particularly Callie. "Thank you, Allison."

"It was my pleasure." Allison glanced at the screen of her iPhone. "I need to dash upstairs and change my clothes." Her eyes filled with unshed tears. "Perhaps dance will help Callie release those trapped memories . . ."

As the double doors opened an hour later, music and lively chatter echoed loudly off the walls of the ballroom. Chairs had been set up theater-style, transforming the room into a showroom for the dancers.

Checking the program an usher had handed her at the doorway, Ashleigh noticed the large dance groups were scheduled to begin the competition. *Good thing Jack offered to meet Marnie.* With her mind on Marnie's impending arrival, Ashleigh took a seat on the aisle, at the back of the room, so she could step out without disturbing anyone in case her phone vibrated.

Although she knew fewer of the dancers' parents than in past competitions, she chose not to make eye contact even with those she did know. She hoped she and Conrad would be able to sidestep unavoidable questions about the girls' semester-at-sea program, at least for now.

Crossing and re-crossing her long legs in the uncomfortable folding chair, she checked her wristwatch again. Marnie's plane was due to land in the next half hour. Ashleigh longed to be there to welcome her, but Callie's well-being was her immediate priority.

Ashleigh wouldn't miss the girls' trio for the world.

Chapter
128

Saturday, May 30, 2:45 p.m.—Los Angeles, California

Jack parked the company car in the lot directly across from LAX's international terminal, unfolded his long legs, and climbed out. The car chirped when he locked it.

The moment he had learned Callie's twin was due to arrive at LAX Saturday afternoon, he'd racked his brain for a plausible reason why he should be the one to pick her up. This was the young woman who had turned Callie's world inside out. Meeting her rocketed to the top of his priority list.

Jack knew Ashleigh and the other girls would be tied up at the dance competition when the plane touched down, so he had called Ashleigh to offer his services. The drive would take no more than ten minutes, and he couldn't resist the chance of meeting the bad apple of the Taylor family. Bringing Marnie to the Los Angeles Marriott would also give him an excuse to see Callie's dance competition.

Jack felt Ashleigh's pain over not being the one to meet Marnie.

"Are you sure?" Ashleigh had asked again and again.

"It's really no problem. Besides," he had joked, "I'll have no problem recognizing her." He had hesitated before blurting out, "And maybe I could see the girls' trio, if I get there on time."

He didn't mention his ulterior motive: With Ashleigh's attention focused on Callie and Juliana, Marnie's selfish behavior might just be prevented from capturing all the limelight.

The plane's wheels bumped down onto the runway, sending Marnie's stomach into spasms.

The eleven-plus hours in flight had flown by, with little thought to what lay ahead. Marnie had tried to avoid touching on her reservations over facing family and friends for the first time. She and Charlize had spent most of their time discussing what it took to write the kinds of novels that would touch the hearts of readers—and how to get those novels into their hands. Charlize, being giant steps ahead, had talked about marketing being a necessary piece of the puzzle to success—and, of course, paying for a professional editor.

"You know we writers are too close to our work to be objective," Charlize had pointed out. "Graham is phenomenal, but after critiquing our work ad nauseum, he also lacks the needed objectivity. After all, even the great Graham Bradford has an editor."

"Right you are," Marnie said in her best English accent.

As the plane's engines silenced, she realized she must soon bid her new friend a safe trip home. "I hope you realize how much I appreciate you taking valuable time away from the workshop." With the return leg of the trip departing that afternoon, it would be a long twenty-four hours.

"Don't be a silly bugger," Charlize had replied. "A little break is just what I needed. Besides, with the extra cash and money I saved on the workshop, now I can afford a top-notch editor."

The seatbelt sign blinked off. Scores of boisterous passengers sprang to their feet to retrieve their belongings from the overhead bins. But Marnie remained riveted to her seat, waiting for the crowd to move forward.

She suddenly regretted leaving Sloane Hall. Another headache sent spirals of pain through her head. Her nerves took over, and she began rehearsing what she would say to Callie . . . to her parents . . . to everyone who knew of her mistakes.

Mistakes? she chided herself. *Mistakes are like forgetting to lock my car door, not turning the lives of people I love upside down.*

In her heart, she knew she didn't belong at the workshop—not at this point in her life, at least. The upheaval she'd caused on both sides of the Atlantic had catapulted her future into a tailspin. She belonged nowhere.

But Charlize's light touch on her forearm gave her a start. "You're back on your home turf!" Charlize said, and the moment of doubt passed.

When at last they exited the plane and entered the LAX terminal, the two friends embraced in a warm hug. "Will you be alright on your own?" Charlize asked.

"Of course," Marnie said, spotting the line for customs. "But I'm glad you were with me."

Charlize grinned. "Me too. Now, if you don't mind, I need a quick trip to the nearest loo and then a Starbucks. Thank your parents for me and tell them I'm looking forward to meeting them in August."

Marnie grinned back and gave her a final hug. "By then, this bum hip will be healed—and the two of us will have a blast running around Manhattan."

Craning his neck, Jack looked for Callie's twin amid the herd of passengers pouring into the terminal. His pulse skipped a beat when the outflow of passengers dwindled, and he had not yet spotted her.

There she is.

A young woman who was, in appearance, the double of Callie slowly made her way toward the baggage carousel, trailing behind the pilot and copilot from her flight. Clad in form-fitting jeans and a white cotton top with long sleeves, Marnie walked with a barely noticeable limp.

Stepping into her path, Jack called out, "Marnie Taylor."

Chapter 129

Saturday, May 30, 3:50 p.m.—Los Angeles, California

Marnie lifted her chin and stared up into the intense blue eyes of the good-looking man who was directly in her path. She took a step back. He was about her age and well over six feet tall. "Who are you?"

"My name is Jack Kirkbride. I work for Dick Landes. And you're Marnie."

"Yes?" She took another step back, her look of curiosity morphing into a frown of concern.

"Your mother . . . Ashleigh asked me to meet your flight and drive you over to the Marriott to meet her and your sisters at the dance competition. She would've been here if she could."

Marnie eyed him with suspicion. He sure didn't fit the image of any Landes agents she'd met. With his chiseled chin, thick, dark hair, and deep-blue eyes, he would stand out on any undercover operation.

Could even be a male model . . .

"So, Landes Agency now provides chauffeur services?"

"Not generally. But I'm happy to help."

As they walked toward the baggage area, Marnie's pace slowed. Her hip ached, and she wondered how much Jack Kirkbride knew. "How's Callie doing?" she asked.

"She'll be okay," was all he said.

Marnie got the distinct feeling that he disapproved of her. Or was she just being paranoid? Surely, he knew how terrible she felt about what had happened to Callie. And he had to know that she'd tried to communicate her plans for leaving the *Rising Star* to her parents.

Marnie tried again. "She's well enough to be in the dance competition. That must be good, right?"

Jack nodded but said nothing.

A man of few words, I gather.

Either that or he really, truly disliked her.

Jack loaded the luggage into the spacious trunk of the Landes vehicle, opened the passenger door, and waited for Marnie to climb in.

Does she realize the turmoil she's put her family through? Does she even care?

He slid in behind the wheel and backed out of the parking space, all the while listening to the idle chatter of Callie's twin.

On the short ride to the Marriott, Marnie asked about the dance competition and whether he had gotten to know her sisters.

"Yes," he said, "I've had the opportunity to meet all of your family over the past few weeks." He didn't trust himself to say more.

"Do you know if Callie is mad at me? About my not returning with her?"

Jack stared at her for a long second before turning his eyes back to the road. "You know your sister has amnesia, don't you?"

Her face instantly drained of color. "Of course. That's why I came home. I'm sorry I wasn't with her."

Well, that was your choice, wasn't it? he thought, but he kept quiet.

The curtain of hair covering Marnie's cheek fell back to reveal a nasty greenish-yellow bruise. "Have *any* of her memories returned?" she asked, her voice quavering.

"Her doctors are hopeful that Callie's memories will return eventually," Jack said. "As I understand, it will take time."

"How much time?"

He shrugged. "No one knows. A day . . . a week . . . a month . . . a year. Or her memories may be gone for good."

"I feel so bad when I think of Callie lying in her bunk, sick with flu, and then being hit by that monster wave," Marnie said quietly. "I keep thinking if only I'd been on the ship, in the cabin with her that day—"

"Hey," Jack interrupted, "no one holds you responsible for what happened. It was just a tragic act of Mother Nature. I can assure you that your entire family—including Callie—is simply looking forward to your safe return."

"Even so, what you've heard about me and what I've done—it isn't exactly good." She shifted in the seat, turning toward the window.

Jack knew he should say something like, *I haven't formed an opinion of you, one way or the other.* But that would be a lie. He'd formed an opinion of Marnie Taylor long before she'd stepped off the plane.

Chapter
130

Saturday, May 30, 4:10 p.m.—Los Angeles, California

Marnie crept into the ballroom. Onstage was a jazz group of five or six dancers. Adjusting to the light, she searched for her mother. When Ashleigh finally came into view, Marnie silently made her way toward her.

The music died. The roar of voices, followed by clapping hands, told her she'd missed the end of the number. The next number was just about to begin as Marnie slipped into the seat beside her mother. "Have they gone on yet?" she said.

Ashleigh turned and instantly wrapped her arm around Marnie's shoulders and pulled her close, giving her a light kiss on the cheek. "The girls don't go on until later in the program," she whispered. "At the end of this number, we can step out and we can get caught up."

"I'd like that," Marnie whispered back. This was working out better than she'd feared. Now she'd have a chance to talk with her mother before having to face the others.

In the darkened room, Ashleigh cupped her hand above her eyes and peered toward the doorway. "Where's Jack?"

"He's taking my luggage to the room," Marnie replied.

"Let me look at you," Ashleigh said when they stepped into the corridor. "Being told you stepped in front of a taxi, I didn't know what to expect."

"I should have known better," Marnie said, "but I was in a hurry to—

Ashleigh's phone pinged, and she reached into the side pocket of her handbag. "Hold on, love. Let me check my phone. It's from Allison."

Marnie's eyes focused on the burgundy swirls of the carpet beneath her sandals. "Allison must think I'm a totally horrible person."

"Of course not." Ashleigh frowned as she continued to read the message. "Oh no. Kaitlyn has twisted her ankle. Allison asked whether you're up to filling in." With a shake of her head at this change in plans, she continued, "Give me a minute to text her back, and then we'll go to lunch."

But as she began to do so, Marnie's hand covered hers. "Wait. I'll do it, Mom."

Ashleigh stared at her daughter. "Honey, you just got out of the hospital last week."

"I know, but I'm okay. We've got nearly two hours to practice. Kaitlyn took my part, and I remember the routine. If there aren't too many changes, Callie—I mean, Allison—can help me with the choreography."

"That's hardly the point, Marnie. It's your injured body that matters."

"I can do it, Mom. Please . . . let me try. Kaitlyn and I are about the same size, so her costume will fit, and probably her jazz shoes too. Please, Mom."

Ashleigh didn't respond right away. "Erica told us you were still getting headaches." Her face darkened, and she said, "Darling. I know you want to help your sisters, but it's too soon. Besides, broken ribs don't mend overnight."

Marnie stood firm. "Mom, I've *got* to do this. It's the least I can do."

Chills ran up Marnie's arms. Less than ten minutes home, and she had become the source of more stress for her mother. "Mom, please try to understand how important this is to me. Allison and the girls keep ACE bandages in their dance bags. I'll tape my ribs."

Meeting her mother's worried eyes, she continued, "If I can't do a good job without hurting myself, I promise I will stop. Dropping out would be better than my messing up with a lame performance. But the least I can do is try. Otherwise, the trio will be scratched from the competition."

"I wish you wouldn't . . . but it's your decision, and I understand." Reluctantly, Ashleigh gave her a gentle hug. "Take care of yourself."

Heading for the dressing area, Marnie prayed her body wouldn't let her down. She took a quick inventory and felt only a dull headache and a twinge of pain in her mending hip. She was determined to push through the pain. If she didn't screw up, she could show her family and others that she was willing to put herself out. She did not lack humanity. She had it in spades.

And there was another benefit she hadn't thought of when she'd volunteered to help: Throwing herself into pulling the dance routine together meant she could avoid, for the time being, the dreaded questions anyone who knew her might ask.

As Marnie walked swiftly toward the dressing room, she kept her eyes cast down—hoping to pass by unnoticed. Behind the curtain, off to the side, a few small groups and a couple of soloists ran through their routines—some without music, some with their music on Apple Beats or a similar device they listened to through wireless earphones. She couldn't escape the inevitable questions or backlash for long. She would have to face it—and get it behind her. But now was not the time. To pull this off, she must find the girls, tape her ribs, get into Kaitlyn's costume, and rehearse. This became the mantra driving her forward.

When she reached the dressing room and opened the door, the expected cacophony of excited chatter and pep talks greeted her. The enormous area was full. To her left, in the middle of the room, were portable tables, large stand-up mirrors, and rolling racks bearing costumes and other clothing. Dancers in various stages of dress were everywhere, and among them were a few family members and dressers. Street clothes were piled on the floor or had been thrown haphazardly on top of the laundry baskets used to transport the dancers' costumes, dance shoes, makeup, and other paraphernalia. A few dancers sat at mirrored tables applying makeup or fixing their hair. Others stretched, hydrated themselves, tuned into iPods, or chatted together.

Searching through the multitude of dancers for Callie and Allison,

Marnie felt her heart race, and beads of perspiration began to break out on her forehead. She heard someone call her name. When she spun in the direction of the sound, Juliana was weaving her way toward her.

The sensation of being in free fall took root in Marnie's stomach. But Juliana, clad in a royal blue and beige costume with matching beige jazz shoes, simply smiled and threw her arms around her. Then she took a step back and, looking Marnie up and down, said, "Are you *sure* you can do this?"

Marnie smiled. "I'll give it my best, Midget."

CHAPTER

131

Saturday, May 30, 4:35 p.m.—Los Angeles, California

My gaze shifted between Kaitlyn and Samantha as I stuffed Kaitlyn's tights into her dance bag. "What do you think about Allison asking Marnie to fill in at the last minute?" I couldn't help but ask.

The night before, I'd shared a hotel room with Samantha, my past and future roommate, and Allison. Talking about nothing but the dance competition, we had reconnected easily. They felt like old friends. As the thought drifted through my mind, I reminded myself they were exactly that.

"Well," Kaitlyn said, wiping her tear-stained face and holding her twisted ankle, "we haven't made many changes to the original routine. I think Marnie could do it, if she's willing."

Shaking my head, I said, "She just got out of the hospital. I don't understand. Was she always so reckless?"

Arching her well-shaped eyebrow, Samantha said, "If I'm not mistaken, you were in the hospital yourself less than two weeks ago. I guess it runs in the family."

"Touché. But from what Mom said, it seems crutches would be more appropriate than jazz shoes." Even so, I did want to reconnect with this person who was my mirror image. I had hundreds of questions that only she could answer. "What a way for us to meet."

"Just remember," Samantha said, fixing her tiara and adjusting her pink-and-white costume in the restroom mirror, "though you look and sound identical, you and Marnie are not at all the same."

"I know," I replied. "Everyone tells me that. But can she really do this? She probably feels awful about all that's happened and just thinks this is away she can help."

"Probably," Samantha agreed, "but she still has a lot to explain."

"It won't be the end of the world if we don't win platinum," Juliana said to Marnie. "We'd like to go for it, but only if you're sure it won't hurt you."

"I'll be fine," Marnie replied with a confidence she did not feel. "But where are Callie and Kaitlyn?"

"In the restroom. Kaitlyn's icing her ankle and changing out of her costume. Callie has extra tights, so you won't need to use Kaitlyn's."

Marnie knew the tights would cover the bruises on her legs, but now she worried about her arms. Rushing toward the restroom on Juliana's heels as briskly as she could, she confessed, "I still have some ugly bruises on my arms. Do you think we can cover them with makeup? I don't want to ruin the trio by looking like a train wreck onstage."

In the restroom, Juliana hurried to her friend and dropped down on the tiled floor beside her. Allison was with Kaitlyn already, attaching an ice bag to her swollen ankle with an ACE bandage.

Marnie drew up beside them. "Kaitlyn, I'm so sorry. How bad is it?"

"Hi, Marnie. So glad to see you." She sighed. "It'll be okay. It's my weak ankle. I've sprained it a whole bunch of times. Are you sure you're okay to take my place?"

"I'll give it my best shot." To Allison, she remarked, "I'm so sorry. You must think I'm a totally horrible person—"

Allison shook her head. "Thank God, you came home safely. We were all so worried. Are you sure you're up to this?"

"Is there a blooming echo in here?" Marnie chuckled, swinging her hair forward to cover her bruised cheek. "It looks a lot worse than it is, guys. And besides, what's my face got to do with my dancing feet?"

When Allison began wrapping the bandage around her ribs, Marnie winced.

Allison frowned and began to loosen the bandage. "Are you sure you want to go through with this?"

"Totally," Marnie lied as her hand shot out. "It needs to be tight. I was just being a wimp. It's okay. Seriously."

When Allison bent down over the bandages again, Marnie closed her eyes. *Please, God, help me do this. I promise not to ask for anything more.*

When she opened them again, Callie and Samantha were heading in her direction.

Callie was wearing the same royal blue and beige costume as Juliana. An extra costume was draped over her arm. Her blond hair fell past her shoulders, pretty much like hers. There was not a single bruise on Callie's smooth skin, only a barely noticeable, flesh-colored bandage at her hairline. She looked perfect—not what Marnie had expected.

Marnie had a fleeting thought that perhaps Callie's memory had returned, but she brushed it away.

They came to a full stop a few feet from Marnie. Samantha greeted her with a gentle hug and said, "So glad to have you safely home."

"Hi, Marnie," Callie said, her voice tentative. She stepped closer. "We all are. Now, let me help with your hair and a little makeup magic."

Chapter
132

Saturday, May 30, 5:25 p.m.—Los Angeles, California

In the dimly lit ballroom, Jack squinted at the program. *Just one more number before Callie's trio.* Ashleigh fidgeted in the aisle seat beside him, and he knew thoughts of her daughters further injuring themselves were probably repeating like a video loop in her mind.

"You made it after all," Jack heard Ashleigh whisper as she turned her legs to the side, preparing for her husband to pass.

Jack slid one chair over to his right, so Conrad could sit beside his wife. They exchanged greetings, *sotto voce*.

A hip-hop trio took center stage, their music echoing off the walls. Jack felt awkward and began to question his presence at this event. He wasn't part of the family, or even a family friend. He was an employee, and they were clients. And that was all.

What am I doing here?

He breathed deeply. What would Conrad think about him being there? Maybe the drama over Kaitlyn's accident and Marnie taking her place would keep the focus away from that very question.

Indeed, as Ashleigh whispered to her husband, his posture became rigid. While unable to hear what she was saying, Jack picked up two words in Conrad's response: *crazy* and *irresponsible*. Then Conrad shook his head and massaged his temples.

Applause sounded for the hip-hop trio, and Jack saw the next trio walk onstage. He swallowed hard. The Taylor girls struck a graceful pose as the strains of "Respect" filled the room.

It took less than a second for Jack to identify Callie on the left, the spotlight glinting on the slick surface of the small bandage at her hairline. Then their lyrical jazz routine began.

To Jack's untrained eyes, it was sensational. All three girls appeared to be in form. He felt sure no one would guess the twins were still recovering from separate accidents. Reluctantly, he had to admit that Marnie appeared to be saving the day.

Jack's breath caught in his throat as Callie continued to spin, and spin, and spin.

Conrad frowned. "Don't worry," he said, though he was shaking his leg up and down. "That's Callie's superpower."

"Awesome," Jack said, his eyes still glued to the stage.

As the music crescendoed, Callie took one last amazing leap, her long legs spread wide and her toes pointed, ending in yet another spin followed by a split.

Jack felt like clapping but knew he should hold his applause until the end of the number, so he restrained himself. Only when Ashleigh and Conrad sprang to their feet did Jack stand and shout, "Bravo."

It was then that he noticed Marnie was no longer onstage.

Chapter

133

Saturday, May 30, 5:30 p.m.—Los Angeles, California

In mid-plié, Marnie's vision blurred, and the room began to spin in a scary, unnatural way. *I've got to get off the stage before I fall and ruin everything,* she thought.

In step with the music, she danced toward the curtain and slipped behind it. Barely able to hold back tears, she took several long breaths, her arms wrapped around her ribs.

Juliana shot a quick glance in her direction but didn't miss a beat, instantly improvising and covering the floor space vacated by Marnie. Although not a dance major, her younger sister made it look as if this were part of the routine. Callie was center stage, captivating the audience with her endless pirouettes. She was a pro.

But if she has amnesia, will she remember how to choreograph on the spot?

A sensation of bile rose in Marnie's throat, and she forced herself to move in the direction of the dressing room. *Please let me make it to the restroom. I've got to loosen the tape around my ribs before my lungs burst.*

Weaving past several solo dancers who were practicing backstage, she willed the floor to stop tilting beneath her feet. Pausing at the doorway to the dressing area, she steadied herself against the frame before baby-stepping forward. A few feet inside the door, she made her way to the first chair she saw and collapsed upon it, closing her eyes.

"Are you okay? Are you okay? Are you okay?" The words echoed in her head as Allison, and then Callie and Juliana, ran up beside her.

Their show of concern opened the avenue for Marnie's tears to flow. "I'm so . . . so . . . sorry. I thought I could do it. I've spoiled everything."

Ashleigh rushed backstage. Marnie was not there. With a sinking heart, she chided herself for not being more persistent. It had been too soon for her headstrong daughter to try anything as strenuous as dance.

Not wasting a second, she headed toward the dressing room. Upon entering, the mixture of perfume fragrances, hairspray, and perspiration assailed her. Amid the expected cacophony of excitement, laughter, and tears of sorrow and joy, she scanned the packed room from corner to corner. She saw no one she recognized—neither her girls nor Allison nor Samantha. And, thankfully, no teams of paramedics.

She wound her way toward the restroom at the far end of the dressing area but stopped when she heard her name called out.

Kaitlyn rose from a bench at the entrance to the showers. "Marnie is okay. They're all in the restroom."

"Thank you, Kaitlyn. How's your ankle?"

With a shrug, she said, "Not that bad. If not for my dumb ankle—"

"It's not your fault. Accidents happen," Ashleigh replied. Stepping inside the restroom, she froze in place.

Marnie, now clad in Allison's model's coat, was sobbing uncontrollably. It was all Ashleigh could do not to rush to her side. Instead, feeling as if she were observing through a looking glass, she decided to let the scene play out.

Allison and Callie were trying to console Marnie, but Juliana stood back—head cocked to the side and hands on her hips.

"Whoa," Juliana said. "It's not the end of the world. Our dance didn't go as planned, but you tried your best. It's okay. Don't be such a drama queen."

Wide-eyed, Allison said, "Juliana!"

Callie's eyes shifted from Allison to her younger sister and then to Marnie, who was dabbing her eyes with a tissue.

Ashleigh held her breath.

But Marnie just straightened her posture and lifted her chin, meeting Juliana's eyes. "Well, Midget. Why don't you tell me what you *really* think?"

Juliana shrugged. "I'm not trying to be mean or anything. It's just that you need to get over yourself. No one's mad at you. We wouldn't have been able to perform at all if not for you."

A little smile began to lift the corners of Marnie's mouth. "Righto. Pip, pip, old chap! Time to move on."

"Oy vey," Juliana replied. "Nobody warned me you'd come back sounding like a character in a *Fawlty Towers* rerun!" And with that, all the dancers broke into a smile.

Taking her cue, Ashleigh stepped forward.

Marnie was the first to spot her. "Mom," she said, wiping away tears with the back of her hand. "I'm so, so sorry."

Ashleigh got no satisfaction in being right. She only wished Marnie had been as strong as she'd imagined. "Did you hurt yourself, sweetheart?"

Marnie shook her head. "If I hadn't gotten dizzy—"

"But you did," Juliana said. "You're not superwoman. That dizzy head was telling you so."

"Okay, Juliana, that's enough," Ashleigh said. "Marnie, perhaps we should have the doctor take a look."

Marnie started to shake her head, but stopped abruptly, massaging her temples. "Mom, honestly, I'm fine. The doctor said these headaches should disappear. I just need to give it a couple more weeks."

Of course she does, thought Ashleigh. *She was hit by a taxi less than two weeks ago.* Being here at the convention on Marnie's first night back had been all wrong. Why was it that only hindsight was twenty-twenty?

Chapter
134

Saturday, May 30, 5:35 p.m.—Los Angeles, California

Conrad left Ashleigh at the backstage door and returned to his seat. Not permitted to enter the dressing room area, he had no choice but to await news of Marnie.

The group dances had ended shortly after Ashleigh had darted backstage. The jazz solos were now in progress, but of course, his interest was elsewhere.

He'd been expecting to see Marnie sitting beside her mother in the auditorium—not Jack Kirkbride. And he certainly hadn't expected to first lay eyes on his prodigal daughter as she performed in the trio onstage.

What was she thinking? His impulsive daughter had stepped straight out of a coma and into a demanding dance competition. *Did she think she was capable of saving the day?* Yes, he realized, that was exactly what she thought.

Conrad glanced left at Ashleigh's empty chair and then right, at Jack, his leg bobbing to the beat of the music. Ashleigh had informed him the young man had offered to pick up Marnie from the airport. But why had he remained for the dance competition?

Callie.

Ashleigh had observed a growing attraction between Jack and Callie, but Conrad hadn't expected it to go this far. He would have to pull the young man aside. Romance was out of the question at least until Callie got her feet beneath her and a firm grip on her future.

By the time Ashleigh returned, stirring Conrad from his thoughts, the original cast recording of "Angel of Music" from *Phantom of the Opera* filled the room. Callie's roommate, Samantha, took center stage. The ballroom fell silent.

Unable to speak, Ashleigh formed an O-K sign with her right hand.

Well, at least Marnie's alright.

When the applause slowly died down after Samantha's stunning dance, Conrad turned toward Ashleigh with questioning eyes. "No real damage," she explained, "other than to Marnie's pride."

Following the last solo contestant's performance, while awards were being announced, Ashleigh suggested they step outside the ballroom. Jack followed the Taylors to an alcove paneled with flocked wallpaper. The couple sank down on a deep red velvet sofa, but Jack remained standing rather than sit in one of the matching chairs.

He had been right to feel out of place. They suspected his growing feelings for Callie and were going to ask him to back off. He couldn't blame them. It reminded him of what he already knew.

"Jack. We appreciate you stepping up to the plate over the past week or so," Conrad began.

Here it comes, Jack said to himself.

Ashleigh nodded in agreement. With a meaningful look at her husband, she explained that Kaitlyn and Marnie, of course, would be unable to take advantage of the next day's dance classes. And with a trio that ended up as a duo, there probably was no need to attend the awards ceremony, much less spend the night.

"This *is* a rather awkward place for a family reunion," Conrad said. "Perhaps we should just head back to the beach house this evening." Then he paused. "But how will Juliana feel about leaving early?"

"Juliana will understand. After all, she agreed to be part of the trio mainly as a favor to Callie," Ashleigh said.

"Right," Conrad said, "so if you agree, we'll drive back to Long Beach this evening."

At Ashleigh's nod, Conrad continued, "And Jack, your assistance would be appreciated—not as a volunteer, but back on the clock."

"I'm happy to help in any way I can," Jack offered. "There's no need for me to be on the payroll."

Ashleigh and Conrad locked eyes. To Jack, things could not have been clearer. This was exactly the slippage between personal and professional they didn't want to encourage between him and their family—especially Callie.

"On the contrary, there's *every* need that you be compensated as a Landes employee," Conrad said, his tone firm but not unkind. "Please be sure to submit a detailed record for the time you spend with our family from here on out."

Chapter
135

Saturday, May 30, 6:10 p.m.—Los Angeles, California

Ashleigh returned to the ballroom, leaving Conrad and Jack to work out the logistics of retrieving luggage from the hotel rooms and arranging everyone's transportation back to Long Beach.

Easing open one of the double doors into the ballroom, Ashleigh was met with a roar of applause as a group of dancers exited the stage, trophies in hand. Some rushed down the side steps into the audience, while others disappeared backstage. Amid the rush, she saw Allison descending the stage-right steps and heading toward her.

Allison's face spread into a wide grin. "The trio won a gold."

"They . . . they weren't disqualified?" Ashleigh stammered.

Proudly holding up the gold medal, Allison said, "Callie's amazing pirouettes and Juliana's improvisation managed to distract the judges and win their hearts." They hadn't deducted points for Marnie's early departure, perhaps not even realizing it was unintended.

"Thank you so much, Allison," Ashleigh said. "You saved the day."

"Actually, we owe it all to Marnie. Had she not stepped in, there would have been no trio."

"This is so, so wonderful. It's bound to lift Marnie's spirits. But Allison, we have a bit of a dilemma. This is not the right setting for the family time we need right now, so we're going to cut our time at the convention a day short."

"I understand." The perceptive young teacher smiled. "How about Samantha and I invite Kaitlyn to spend the night with us?"

"I hesitated to ask—"

Allison cut in. "Don't worry. It's absolutely no problem, and I'm sure Kaitlyn will understand your family's need for privacy."

A flood of relief flowed through Ashleigh's veins. Entrusting Kaitlyn to Allison and Samantha's care took a huge load off her shoulders on what might shape up to be a long and difficult night.

Marnie's headache must have been short-lived, because backstage she talked nonstop about her concern for me. She wanted me to explain my amnesia, yet she didn't give me a chance to do so. She apologized so many times, I longed for her to let it go.

There were more important things I needed to know—things only Marnie could tell me. I held back until the dressing area was nearly deserted.

"Marnie," I began. "Stop saying you're sorry. I know you are, and I understand you were chasing a writer's wildest dream—something you couldn't resist. But there is a lot I can't wrap my mind around. I need your help."

Marnie widened her eyes and took a break from her monologue.

"Following my accident, I didn't remember Mom, Dad, or Juliana. I remember nothing about them before the first time they came into my hospital room in New York. That was just a couple weeks ago. But it hasn't taken long for them to feel like family."

"Yeah. We have an awesome family." The tension in Marnie's face relaxed a little.

Not wanting to be thrown off track, I asked the question we all wanted to know. "What I'm having trouble wrapping my mind around is, why didn't you let anyone know of your plans to stay in England?"

"Didn't anyone tell you about my letter to Mom and Dad?"

"Yes. The one I was supposed to deliver. I don't know what happened to it. But that doesn't explain. You didn't need anyone's permission to remain in England. Why didn't you just tell them?"

"Temporary insanity?" A forced grin spread across Marnie's face.

"Seriously. I know you didn't expect the disaster at sea, but—"

"But it happened. I know. Maybe it was payback . . ." Marnie cut off. "Sorry. I meant payback for me. You didn't deserve . . . It should have been me."

"It shouldn't have been anyone. You didn't cause my accident. But I sure wish you'd been there when I woke up on the cabin floor."

"I wish I was, too," she replied. "After what happened in Southampton . . . Are you still mad about that?"

I looked at my mirror image, realizing she didn't have a clue about what I'd been through with my amnesia. "What happened in Southampton?" I repeated. But it was pretty clear. We must have argued over our opposing perceptions about how she'd handled abandoning the semester-at-sea program.

Marnie began retelling the story of my coming down with the flu and not making it to London, but I stopped her. "That's not what I meant. Mom and Dad found out about all that, mostly thanks to Ross Pocino." What I wanted to know was what Marnie had been thinking in the first place, how she had snuck through security, how she had ended up with my handbag . . .

As my questions continued, a look of horror arose on Marnie's face. It didn't take long for me to realize: Mom told her about my amnesia, but Marnie knew next to nothing of my mind-numbing days of attempting to be her and to follow her dreams.

Chapter
136

Saturday, May 30, 6:35 p.m.—Los Angeles, California

The moment Marnie saw her father in the Marriott lobby, and her eyes met his, all her well-rehearsed words evaporated. She felt as lost as the eight-year-old child who had been returned to her biological family . . . until he stepped forward, gently wrapping his arms around her.

She melted when her dad kissed the top of her head and told her how thankful he was to have her home safe . . . and relatively unharmed. Her heart swelled. But it deflated again the moment she stepped back. Disappointment was reflected in his eyes. His smile seemed forced. This was the calm before the storm—the one she'd feared.

The decision to leave the Marriott this evening sent everyone but Marnie to their rooms to pack. Ashleigh stepped away to call Elizabeth first, asking her to join them that evening at the beach house. Conrad instructed Jack to secure a bellman to help with all the luggage. Marnie watched Jack's retreating back as he walked to the reception desk.

Alone in the lobby, she sank down on one of the seats circling the round pillar. She replayed all that Callie had shared with her so far. Processing her sister's anguish over trying to mold herself into her writer's identity, Marnie felt hot shame surge through her bloodstream. She felt a thousand times more guilt-ridden and fearful than when she'd stepped off the plane.

Words, which were supposed to be the key to her future success, failed her. Her every expression of regret had fallen flat. Yet she felt a sense of guarded relief about driving to Long Beach in her parents' car, without the added challenge of her sisters' presence. At least she would get this dreaded conversation behind her.

The sight of her parents and sisters following a large brass luggage cart pulled her from her thoughts. She rose to join them. But a shiver shot through her when Jack Kirkbride's eyes met hers. Though he had been politely aloof, there was a certain coldness in his vivid blue eyes whenever they met hers.

Jack's eyes softened, Marnie noticed, when he looked from her parents and Juliana to Callie. He said something she couldn't hear, which made both her sisters smile. Marnie wondered if it was something about her.

What a surprise.

Everyone's heart went out to Callie, of course. As always, she was the golden girl—the one who could do no wrong.

Marnie could think of nothing she could say or do to regain the respect of her family and friends. She had a very long road ahead—one that was all uphill.

When the valet pulled Conrad's rental car to the hotel entrance, Ashleigh climbed in and Marnie followed. Jack brought over the girls' suitcases and dance baskets to put in the trunk of the BMW. With the problem of the luggage now handled, he and her sisters waved goodbye and headed for the Town Car.

Pulling away from the hotel, Conrad spoke over his shoulder to Marnie, in the backseat. "Mom said you've been craving good Mexican food, so we decided to have dinner at Paco's Tacos Cantina."

"Great. I love that place. Their tamales are to die for." Marnie feigned excitement while her stomach roiled. She would not have the chance to get the awkward conversation behind her until after dinner. "So that's where we're meeting everyone?"

"No," Ashleigh said, also turning to face the backseat. "Jack is driving your sisters home so that we can have some private time. We'll be together as a family when we reach Long Beach."

As usual, Conrad came straight to the point. "As you must know, we have a great many questions. We believed it best to talk before we reached the beach house."

Marnie tuned out. *Tonight's going to be a marathon.* Though unintentional, this was a course she had designed. She would draw on every ounce of her talent and commitment to the power of words to see her across the finish line.

Chapter

137

Saturday, May 30, 7:05 p.m.—Los Angeles, California

In seconds, Marnie's eyes had adjusted to the dim lighting inside Paco's Tacos Cantina, where the familiar earth-toned decor and Mexican artwork with aqua-blue accents covered the walls. The padded burgundy booths, with ivy peeking through latticework frames, were just as she remembered—only a bit brighter.

Recalling this was her dad's least favorite cuisine, she wondered if she should have suggested something else. And yet her heart lifted. Despite everything, her parents were trying to make her feel comfortable.

A waiter approached the table and set down three large glasses of water, along with chips and two small bowls of salsa. Looking straight at Marnie, the waiter gave her a smile of recognition and took their order.

Once he'd disappeared, Marnie took the plunge. "I wish I had the power to turn back the calendar—"

"We know you do, love," Ashleigh said. Her voice held no recrimination. It seldom did. And yet disappointment registered in her steady gaze.

Tears stung Marnie's eyes.

"No point in belaboring the *should haves*," Conrad said. "Those calendar pages are now behind us. What your mother and I need to know is why you had so little trust in us."

"I *do* trust you. I wish . . . I spent *days* writing and rewriting what I wanted you to know about the totally awesome opportunity that fell into my lap." She dropped her gaze. "If not for that freak wave, Callie would have handed you my letter and no harm would have been done," she ended softly. Meeting her dad's eyes, she quickly added. "But I am sorry about the way it turned out."

"Stop with the sorrys." Conrad's voice held little of his former tenderness. "No one could predict what happened at sea—or anywhere else for that matter. However, your actions threw your entire family and friends into a tailspin. Sneaking through the ship's security and abandoning your semester-at-sea—"

"I never dreamed I'd be reported as lost at sea for—"

"That's not the point. The point is the lack of trust your actions demonstrated."

Ashleigh took a sip of water, observing the dynamics between father and daughter. This first conversation was as awkward and difficult as they'd anticipated.

Conrad was doing his level best to speak to Marnie as an adult while also letting her know how disappointed they were and how much her irrational decision conflicted with their family values. However, it took only moments for her demeanor to escalate from contrite to defensive.

"When I heard about the rogue wave, I regretted not explaining my plan by phone, but I'd been afraid I couldn't make you understand . . ." She glanced across at Ashleigh and shifted in her seat. "When I told you about trying to win a spot in Bradford's workshop, you said I had enough on my plate and should wait. I was pretty sure you would get on board if you knew all the facts and understood it from my perspective," she continued, "so I wrote it all down."

Conrad leaned forward, his forearms on the table. "As I recall, you had a field trip to London before the ship sailed. You could have found a moment to call and speak with us then. Your rationale, should it come from any member of my team, would be cause to place them on probation, at the very least."

Ashleigh placed her hand on Conrad's wrist, wishing he had not made that analogy, but she remained silent.

Marnie blinked. "I'm not one of your executives. Under other circumstances, my—"

Conrad held a palm up. "Forget the circumstances. You are our daughter. There is nothing you have done or could ever do that would cause you to lose our love and support. You need to understand, though, the effect your lack of upfront communication had on all of us who care about you but were kept in the dark."

Marnie opened her mouth to speak, but Conrad continued, "We hope this poor judgment on your part was only a blip. No point running it into the ground. But don't defend it. As your mother is fond of reminding us, we all make errors, and that's why those yellow sticks called pencils are equipped with an eraser."

Ashleigh felt she had remained quiet long enough.

"Like your dad said, there's no sense going round and round about details and outcomes that can't be undone. We're happy to find you safe, so let's put this behind us. We want to learn all about your experiences during the semester at sea. And we want to talk about the future and how your connection with Graham Bradford might influence that."

When Marnie wiped the tears from her cheek with the back of her hand, it revealed her fading bruise. She appeared even more vulnerable. Ashleigh swallowed hard. The calendar marked her girls as adults, but they would forever be her children.

"Before you describe what you've been up to, we need to ask for your help with what Callie is dealing with. We fear she's facing a difficult road ahead. Until she regains her memory, it may take some time for her to reconnect with you. But remember, she's trying, and she needs all of us. While Samantha and Allison have agreed to do as much as they can, it's you who can do the most to help her on the road to recovery."

Marnie nodded. "It must be awful not to remember anything."

"I agree, honey." Ashleigh said. "I can't imagine having no memory of who you are. We are praying for a full recovery, but in the meantime, we all need to help her. We can start by going through photos of her with her friends . . . and our extended family. By relating shared memories—" She cut off midsentence.

Marnie was no longer listening, but fidgeting. Her intense brown eyes were damp, and tears were streaming down both cheeks.

"What is it?" Conrad asked, tuning into Marnie's discomfort.

"Callie said you didn't know I was the one who was missing. You thought it was her."

Taken aback, Ashleigh realized they had only briefly touched on the week of mistaken identity. During their phone calls while Marnie was in London, they had not discussed how that mix-up affected anyone other than Callie.

"That's right," Ashleigh said. "Callie was found with your handbag and your IDs, therefore—"

"No." Marnie blinked. "She had her own handbag, but my identification cards were inside." She fell silent as she processed this new piece of the puzzle. Her voice shaking with incredulity, she said, "So, you thought Callie was me?"

"We were thrown off by the amnesia. We didn't know what sorts of changes it might make to the patient's personality."

"So, you thought I had amnesia? And Callie was lost at sea?" Her eyes flashed between Ashleigh and Conrad. The intensity in her eyes demanded confirmation.

"For a very short time. Your dad and I were suspicious from the start, but passed off the personality changes as—"

"So the new Marnie had suddenly become a more acceptable member of the Taylor family?"

"Marnie!" Ashleigh and Conrad cried out in unison. "Of course not."

Marnie slumped back into her chair, muttering, "I bet you were relieved when you discovered it was *not* Callie who was lost at sea."

Chapter
138

Saturday, May 30, 7:15 p.m.—Los Angeles, California

I was hungry after the dance competition, but neither Juliana nor I wanted to stop at any of the fancy restaurants our parents mentioned. Jack suggested we pull through the nearest In N Out Burger on Sepulveda Boulevard. We each ordered a cheeseburger and fries, choosing three different flavors of shakes, and ate while sitting in the parking lot.

Afterward, Juliana fell asleep in the backseat, which gave me the opportunity to ask Jack what had been on my mind. "Did Marnie say or do anything to upset you?"

He glanced over at me. "What do you mean?"

How could I tell him? I had no road map for this kind of discussion, so I just blurted it out. "You're always so friendly. But not with Marnie."

"Seriously?" he asked. "Was I that obvious?"

"Well, in a single word, yes."

He hesitated. "Did you get much of a chance to talk with Marnie?"

"A little. I told her about how I struggled with adopting her identity. She was horrified."

"She should be." He must have seen the surprise on my face. "Callie, your sister went to such lengths to deceive your parents. I've only known them for a couple of weeks, but they didn't deserve that."

He was right, of course. "But I'm the one who hit my head and lost my memory. How is that her fault?"

"Callie." He paused, peeking at Juliana over his shoulder, and then lowered his voice. "You are blameless. What happened aboard that ship was an accident. But if your sister had been on the ship, things might have been different. Her presence could have changed the whole pattern for the day. Just think about all those stories of people who didn't show up to work in downtown Manhattan on 9/11 because of some fluke—something that saved their lives on that tragic day."

I thought about it. Sure, if Marnie had been with me when the rogue wave hit, things could have been different. But we wouldn't know for sure.

"So yes, meeting Marnie upset me. Knowing all the confusion and pain she brought about for your family, I prejudged her. But I'm embarrassed that I was so transparent. Do you think your parents noticed?"

I grinned. "Nothing much escapes their notice, but today they were preoccupied with their need for time alone with Marnie. I don't think they had a lot of time for observation."

When Jack reached for my hand, I felt no desire to pull away. "Had Marnie been on the ship as she should have been," he said, "neither you nor your parents would have had to endure the living hell she set in motion."

I shook my head slowly. "Why didn't she just tell our parents? I'm pretty sure we argued about it. And I bet they would have supported her decision if she explained it well enough. But she never gave them a chance." Headlights from the oncoming cars lit up the interior of the car. Gazing at Jack's strong profile, I said, "What I don't understand is why I covered for her."

"What makes you think you did?"

"I must have. Otherwise, she would have been reported as missing not long after we left Southampton."

"Did you ask her?"

"Not yet. We've only had a few moments together." I hesitated. "But Marnie is my sister, Jack. And that won't change, no matter what."

Marnie felt the green-eyed monster consuming her once again. Following her guilty role in her twin sister's kidnapping in Chicago when they were teenagers, she thought she'd finally put it to rest. But here it was, rearing its ugly head.

"*I bet you were relieved when you discovered it was not Callie who was lost at sea.*"

As soon as the words were out of her mouth, she wished she could erase them. "Forgive me," she said. "I don't know why I said that." It was a lie. She knew exactly why she'd said it. "I should just keep my mouth shut."

"No. That's not what you should do," Conrad said. "That helps no one and leaves problems unsolved. And *no*, we were not relieved. We would've been devastated if either of you were lost at sea."

"Your father's right, Marnie," Ashleigh added. "You three girls are very much alike in many ways and very different in others. All three of you have wonderful and not-so-wonderful traits, just as everyone does. There is no way we could choose one of you over the others."

Can she truly mean that?

"You don't have to say that," Marnie insisted. "Everyone has favorites."

Conrad folded his arms in front of him and sank back in the plush leather seat. "That so?" he said. "So, who is *your* favorite sister?"

That caught Marnie off guard. "That's different."

"How so?"

"Well, Callie's my twin and Juliana is my little sister, so they aren't expected to be the same."

"I see," Ashleigh cut in. "Marnie, love. Do you think any two people are exactly alike? You and Callie are as alike and as different as any two identical twins I've ever heard of. Twins are not carbon copies of one another. And what a dull world it would be if they were."

Chapter
139

Saturday, May 30, 8:05 p.m.—Long Beach, California

Jack pulled into the driveway, parking behind the Bentley. I remembered it from our drive to Naples the day we'd arrived in California—the first day I'd met Jack.

I'd heard about Elizabeth from my parents, Juliana, and even Samantha before I met our surrogate "grandmother" at the memorial service. I hadn't had much time to talk with her then, but her love for our family was evident in her eyes and body language. Her being here now for our family meeting came as no surprise.

And knowing she would be remaining here on the West Coast after my parents returned home to Greenwich warmed me all over. When graduate school started in the fall, I'd have someone to turn to for support.

As the thought crisscrossed my brain, I felt pathetic. Pretty soon, I would have to stand on my own two feet. Still, having another family member around would be comforting.

Juliana awoke when Jack slammed his car door shut and began retrieving luggage from the trunk. I stepped out of the car, then said, "Jules, I'll take the bags. Would you mind going on in and telling Elizabeth we'll be just a few minutes?"

"Ah . . . Sure thing," she said, raising a brow suggestively. "I'll bet she's made our favorite cookies."

As much as it hurt, this was a conversation I couldn't put off. "Jack, before we take the luggage upstairs, we need to talk."

———

When Callie said they needed to talk, Jack tilted his head and grinned. "Isn't that what we've been doing?" Then he noticed the intense look on Callie's face, and furrowed his brow.

What has she got on her mind?

They were interrupted by the beam of the BMW's headlights as it pulled into the driveway. Jack strode over to greet the Taylors.

Conrad lowered the driver's window, a questioning look on his face.

"Just leaving," Jack forced himself to say. "If you'll give me a couple seconds to turn my car around, I'll be on my way."

"Thanks for all your help," Ashleigh said, followed by Conrad's mumbled expression of gratitude.

"Thanks, Jack," Marnie called out tentatively.

Jack replied with his warmest smile and called back, "Take care, Marnie." After all, she was Callie's twin.

When he jogged back up the drive, Callie's luminous brown eyes took his breath away. He doubted that would ever change. "Feels like our time came to an end before we even got started. Tomorrow?"

Callie looked so vulnerable. "I'm not sure," she said. "It's important, but it will have to stay on hold till I know more about what my parents have planned for the next couple days."

He wished he could protect her. There was no telling what was in store for her tonight. Although it was an impossibility, he wanted to take her in his arms and make everything alright. Callie had an independent spirit—one he hoped would soon be free of all the unknowns in her life.

But right now, Jack had to move his car. His time was up.

Chapter
140

Saturday, May 30, 9:10 p.m.—Long Beach, California

The moment Ashleigh laid eyes on Elizabeth, her heart filled with love and appreciation. The family would not be complete without Elizabeth's grandmotherly presence. Pulling her in for a hug, Ashleigh thanked her for all she'd done for them.

Conrad stepped into the kitchen, lugging several suitcases over the threshold. A few steps behind, Marnie precariously balanced two laundry baskets full of her sisters' costumes and dance paraphernalia.

"Be careful, angel," Elizabeth called out.

Turning to Marnie, Conrad said, "Thanks, sweetheart. You can get your sisters to help you take these on upstairs. I'll get the others."

Although the baskets were not heavy, Marnie's face winced as she set them on the floor. When she straightened, the greenish-yellow bruise on her cheek was exposed.

Moving to embrace her, Elizabeth gasped.

"In this bright light, it looks worse than it is," Marnie assured her as she moved into Elizabeth's loving arms.

Callie and Juliana retrieved their baskets, with Marnie a few steps behind them. "Be right back," Marnie said. "Going to the loo."

"Hey," Conrad called after her, "you're back in the good ole' USA." But Marnie was already out of earshot.

Ashleigh reached out, placing her hand on his forearm. "Love," she said, "let's go unpack. It will give the girls some time to work things out on their own."

Conrad agreed. "We can play the rest of the evening by ear."

Ashleigh's gaze encompassed her husband and Elizabeth. "Although Callie and Juliana bonded quickly after the accident, I fear things won't be nearly so easy for her and Marnie."

"As always," Conrad added, "there's more than a hint of challenge in their relationship."

"While there are bound to be emotional obstacles," Ashleigh continued, meeting her husband's eyes, "I trust their innate love will get them through."

Elizabeth's smile was warm and her eyes moist. "Amen to that," she said.

Juliana and I ferried our baskets and luggage up to our bedrooms. I dropped mine on the floor beside my rumpled bed—and looked up to see Marnie standing in the doorway of the bathroom that linked our bedrooms. She held a damp towel, and her forehead was crinkled in a puzzled frown.

"Was someone staying in my room this week?" she asked.

"Just me," I said, flopping into a wicker chair next to the bed. "When everyone thought I was you."

"That makes sense." Marnie grinned back at me. "Well, you might not remember a lot of things, but you haven't forgotten how to turn a room upside down in a hurry."

"I thought I'd have time to straighten it up." I paused, not sure if she was upset.

"Don't worry about it." She raised the back of her hand dramatically to her forehead. "Everyone accuses me of being OCD."

Dashing into my room, Jules said, "And a drama queen," before flopping onto my bed. Just as quickly, she bounced back up. "Hey, how about I run down and get us some milk and a plate of Elizabeth's cookies? Fresh from the oven . . ."

"Sounds good," Marnie and I chorused. Jules took off down the stairs, and Marnie moved the other wicker chair closer to the spot where Jules had landed on my bed.

After all I'd heard about my twin, I'd expected her to be feistier and more decisive. She seemed a little shy around Juliana and me. I didn't want her to feel uncomfortable, but there was still so much that I didn't understand and needed to know—that only she could tell me.

Juliana reappeared, balancing a full tray and shaking her head sadly. "You two really wrecked my chances to enjoy eating raw cookie dough."

"What do you mean?" I asked.

"One time, you both had stomachaches after pigging out on the dough," Jules explained, climbing back onto the bed, where she perched Indian-style. "Now, Elizabeth's careful to leave only a teeny-tiny bit to scrape off the sides of the mixing bowl."

Marnie laughed. "I remember it well."

I didn't remember, of course, but it didn't bother me. "Well, I don't think that's one of the memories I need help filling in. There's nothing wrong with my imagination."

Chapter
141

Saturday, May 30, 9:45 p.m.—Long Beach, California

Although Juliana kept telling her to lighten up, every nerve in Marnie's body tingled. Try as she might, she just couldn't get comfortable. Maybe it was looking at Callie's untidy bed—or maybe things would just never get back to normal with her sisters.

At least her parents had finally moved past her faulty rationale for not announcing her plans upfront. "I should have realized the gods weren't with me when you came down with the flu before our London trip," Marnie said. "It gave us practically no time to talk."

"So, you think if I hadn't been so sick, I would have agreed to your plan?" Callie looked unconvinced.

"Well, yes and no. You would have wanted me to call our parents no matter what. But you would have at least listened. You wouldn't have been so angry."

Callie sipped from her glass of milk and stared at me. "Seriously?" She set the glass back down. "Let me get this straight. I was angry and sick with the flu, and yet I covered for you—told everyone you also had the flu. Even sent emails to your writing profess—"

"Hold on. I don't know what you did on the ship or how long your flu lasted. But you didn't send the emails to Professor Gaspar. I did."

Juliana piped up. "I think we've about run this topic into the ground. You can't unring the stupid bell. Just tell us how you snuck off the ship." She leaned forward, her elbows on her knees, her head propped in her palms in anticipation of an exciting tale.

"You couldn't have done it without Bradford, could you?" Callie asked.

Marnie did her best to explain, underscoring Bradford's reluctance over his role in her covert departure.

"Enough," Callie said, crisscrossed her hands back and forth as if to wipe the slate. "Jules is right. You've already explained that part of it. In the next few days, though, I want to hear all about the semester at sea."

Marnie nodded. "I'll tell you everything you want to know—what the classic novels call 'chapter and verse.' But Callie, although you don't remember, we exchanged some heated words. Words that haunted me from the moment I heard what happened at sea. And no matter what, I'll never leave you or Juliana again without telling you I love you. Because I do."

"Sounds good to me," Callie said. "I'll do the same."

"Me too. And we'll remind each other if we slip up," Juliana added.

"Now, we want to hear all about the exciting things you did in France and England," Juliana added.

"*That's* going to take a while." Callie's mouth turned up in a smile. "So, I think we should tumble on downstairs to let Mom, Dad, and Elizabeth know there's been no bloodshed."

The sound of six bare feet pounding down the staircase and a chorus of laughter met Ashleigh's ears all the way from the beachfront deck. The stars were sparkling in the clear night sky, illuminating the crashing waves below. Ashleigh smiled at Elizabeth and reached out to grasp Conrad's hand. "There appears to be a lull in our family storm."

Grinning, Conrad called out to them, "Out here on the deck."

The laughter grew louder until the girls appeared—not one by one, but all together. Looking out over the harbor and ocean, Marnie said, "I've missed you all so much. I know I screwed up, but there's no place I'd rather be than with all of you, here in this perfect spot."

Ashleigh wondered if their drama queen had rehearsed those lines, but it didn't matter. *Yesterday is dead and gone* . . . "The past is behind us," she said. "We've learned our lessons, and it's time to look ahead."

As her girls scampered down to the beach and across the sand to the water's edge, laughing and joking, all her pent-up tears began to flow. "You know," she said, "some people live a lifetime without experiencing this kind of happiness." There would be some inevitable bumps ahead, but the Taylor family was once again whole.

Chapter

142

Wednesday, June 3, 2:00 p.m.—Long Beach, California

Jack pulled into the driveway, cut the engine, and threw open the door. He spotted Callie rushing toward the car and thought, *four days is three days too long.* Clad in white shorts and a bright green shirt, her hair pulled back in a ponytail, she looked as beautiful as he remembered.

"Feels like I haven't seen you in a month," he said in greeting.

"I'm glad you could make it, Jack," she said. "I haven't been avoiding you. With family and doctor appointments, it's just been hectic around our house."

He smiled. "Seems like that's about status quo."

"Tell me about it." Callie's smile lit up her face, and as her perceptive chocolate-brown eyes met his. "I'm here on my own, by some miracle. Mom is helping Elizabeth get Caroline's house in order. Marnie is meeting her roommate after she drops Juliana and Kaitlyn off in Belmont Shore. And Dad left early this morning." She explained her father's crazy schedule, crisscrossing the country to meet with a bunch of executives and sales associates from Jordon's stores—the ones that would remain open as well as those on the chopping block.

Jack was confused. *Is this "the talk" she wants to have?* Her serious tone on Saturday night had left him unable to get a single decent night's sleep.

"All of you clearly have a lot going on." His heart beat rapidly. "So, what did you want us to talk about before we were interrupted the other night?"

She shook her head. "Let's take a walk on the beach. Maybe that will help me tell you what's on my mind, okay?"

She slipped off her sandals, and Jack unlaced his sneakers and placed them on the low wall in front of the house. Then Callie led him along the path to the shore. After a few minutes of silence, she drew in a deep breath and took the plunge. "Jack, you've been such a wonderful friend, but—"

"It's a friendship I value, even though we've known each other only a short time." Jack realized immediately that her words sounded like the beginning of a *Dear John* letter. He was determined to nip that in the bud.

They were now at the water's edge, the gentle waves lapping the shore. A few yards from where they stood, a large group of birds assembled as if for an all-staff meeting. He longed to take hold of her hand while they talked but didn't dare.

"Your friendship has meant the world to me, especially at this time in my life . . ."

Again she was using the past tense. He froze, a block of ice forming in his chest.

". . . but I think we need a break. Until I figure things out, I must learn to rely on no one other than myself. Besides, my family has taken up most of your spare time. And you haven't been able to work on the types of cases you signed on for at Landes."

Jack couldn't believe what he was hearing. "Callie, that has *nothing* to do with you or your family. Getting to know you has been a perk, not a disadvantage of this new job. And I *do* have new assignments. There's this tricky embezzlement case that will be keeping me pretty busy." A hollow sensation settled in his abdomen. "So my caseload will give us a 'break,' as you say, but there's no reason we can't be friends. Friends who talk on the phone . . . see each other now and then . . ."

"Of course not. You've gotten me through these first rough days, and I will always consider you a good friend. But until my memory returns, or I learn to cope better with the loss of it, I can't commit to any other type of relationship."

Jack breathed a sigh of relief and held her liquid gaze. "I get that, and I will give you the space you need." At least she hadn't shut the door on friendship.

Chapter
143

Wednesday, June 3, 2:20 p.m.—Long Beach, California

At the sound of my name, barely audible over the pounding waves, I pulled my gaze from Jack's.

Standing on the boardwalk in front of the beach house, Marnie motioned for me. Though I had not yet met my sister's roommate, I assumed the curly redhead beside her must be Brandy. Even from this distance, I saw my sister smile as Jack and I shortened the space between us. Marnie's timing couldn't have been worse.

Forcing a smile, I did my best to keep the quiver from my voice. "Well, I'd better let you get back to work."

I caught a glimmer of unease in the depth of his vivid blue eyes before he checked his phone. "Guess so. I've got a meeting in Newport Beach in an hour."

As we began our trek across the hot sand, my heart shattered. Jack had agreed pretty quickly that we should stop seeing each other. And why not? He was probably relieved. I had nothing to offer. With no memories, I was little more than an empty shell.

"I wish you fabulous success with your new job." My words were trite even to my own ears, failing to express how much his presence in my new reality had meant.

"Hey, Jack," Marnie called out when we reached the boardwalk.

"Hey, Marnie," he shot back.

"I'm not a complete monster, you know." She grinned. "Can we begin again?"

"Yeah, sorry. That awkward start was all my fault." Then, cocking his head, Jack stretched out his hand. "Hello, Marnie. Welcome home. My name is Jack Kirkbride."

"How do you do?" Marnie dipped down in a curtsy and made quick work of introducing us to her roommate. "Since it seems I'll be seeing quite a lot of you, it's best we become friends."

Jack shot a glance in my direction. Then he said goodbye to us all and headed to his car. He didn't look back.

Before Jack was out of sight, Marnie whispered, "Was that okay?"

She knew Jack wasn't a bad guy. He just didn't know the whole story, and he had been protective of Callie. *Nothing wrong with that.* If he made Callie happy, the awkwardness between the two of them had to end. Thankfully, Marnie thought he seemed ready to give her a chance.

"Sure," Callie said. Her brown eyes looked sad. "But don't worry. He won't be around."

"Seriously?" Marnie didn't understand. *That made no sense.* "What do you mean? He's hot, and he has eyes only for you."

Callie laughed a little, but it didn't sound happy. "He was assigned to deliver me to the doctors, and—"

"Apparently, an assignment he was totally on board with."

"—and Mom and Dad wanted him to get to know me a bit, help me feel comfortable with people again."

"You seem pretty comfortable with him."

Callie sighed. "Jack is a great guy. But he didn't sign on with Landes Agency to become a glorified chauffeur."

Marnie stared as though she had two heads. "Don't give me that. Has your amnesia blinded you, too? Don't you see the way he looks at you?"

"I'm afraid what you saw in his eyes was pity," Callie replied. "I need to get myself on firm ground. Jack is a terrific guy. I can't say I'm not attracted to him."

Well, that's obvious, Marnie thought.

"But it would be unfair to lead him on. He deserves a chance to meet someone without my baggage. Besides, I can't handle a relationship based on pity."

"Pity?"

Callie nodded. "That look I see in almost everyone's eyes. It tugs at my perception of a future."

Chapter 144

Monday, July 27, 11:55 a.m.—Long Beach, California

Marnie's heart swelled. She'd done it. She must have reread her short story twenty-three times, and it was darn good.

Both Callie and Juliana had read it, too, and loved it. They had also proofread the manuscript, cleaning it of typos, missing words, extra words, and so forth. And Marnie could be certain Juliana would have let her know if it sucked.

She was ready to send this draft to Graham Bradford. Although she knew her mentor was bound to find areas in need of improvement, she was pleased with this draft. In fact, the last scene was so pitch perfect, she had difficulty even believing she had written it.

In the two months since leaving England, she had longed to call Graham, and yet she'd held back. She couldn't call before finishing the workshop assignment—or until she could report significant progress on her novel.

The email was ready now, with the manuscript for her short story attached. But there was one more thing she must do.

Checking the time in the right-hand corner of her computer, she quickly calculated that it was just turning eight o'clock in the evening in London. With Brandy at work, she had their apartment to herself. The timing was perfect to place her call and bounce her life-altering idea off Bradford.

7:10 p.m.

On my way home from the dance studio I called in an order for a cinnamon dolce latte and drove through the Starbucks on Bellflower to pick it up. Since Samantha was working late this evening, I'd have the apartment to myself.

I'd moved back into the apartment after Juliana and Kaitlyn had returned to Greenwich with my parents. Over the past couple of months, I'd been reacquainted with old friends and made new ones. I didn't think my long-term memory had returned, and yet things my family and friends had told me now seemed like my own memories. The whole memory thing was fuzzy, but one way or the other, I was learning to cope. Now I was genuinely looking forward to next month, when I would begin my master's degree program in dance at CSULB.

I'd also reconnected with a couple of my former dance teachers, who owned Elevation Dance Studio and was overjoyed when they asked me to teach and choreograph dances for the four- to six-year-olds. These kids were so enthusiastic and adorable. It was a win-win. Samantha, who had filled in for me with the fashion director at Jordon's Westminster, said she'd love to continue for the summer. Everything had fallen into place.

Pulling up to our Belmont Shore apartment building, my heart jumped a beat. A royal blue Corvette was parked directly in front of the stairs leading to my apartment. Miraculously, I didn't need to search for a parking spot on one of the side streets. There was one on The Toledo—directly behind Jack Kirkbride's car.

After our conversation on the beach at the start of June, I had turned down a couple of his invitations for dinner. Sam finally had convinced me I was being silly. That's when I realized that my protective shield might prevent me from being hurt, but at the same time it could also prevent me from living a full life.

But after deciding I would accept his next invitation, I never got the chance. His phone calls had come to an end more than a month ago.

Swallowing hard, I tried to gather my wits as I prepared to get out of the car. I reached for the handle just before the door swung open, and Jack's eyes met mine. My mouth went dry, and my brain failed to function.

"Sorry to just show up," Jack said, "but I've been out of town for the past few weeks. I had to see you, so I took a chance . . ." His disarming smile rendered me speechless, as it always had.

"How long have you been here?" was all I could think to say.

"Not long." He extended his hand to help me from the car.

"Jack . . . How we left things . . . I don't know what to say." The last time we'd spoken was at the beach house. It was not the fondest of the relatively few memories I had.

His eyes locked on mine. "Our relationship can be that of good friends if that's still what you want and need. But Callie, I've got to be totally honest with you. I want you in my life. And I'm willing—"

"Oh Jack. I've got to be honest too. My memory *still* hasn't returned."

Jack shrugged. "That doesn't matter to me. I'm not attracted to your past. Can we go somewhere and talk?"

I nodded my head, then asked, "Would you like to come upstairs?"

"Sure."

I reached into the car to retrieve my handbag and latte, locking the car behind me. As he followed me up the stairs, I tried to assemble my thoughts. "Have you eaten?" I asked.

"Not yet. I'd love to take you to dinner."

"I had a very late lunch, but I can make you—"

"I'd rather just sit and talk, thanks."

"Something to drink?" I said, holding up my latte.

"Water's fine."

Inside, I set my latte on the coffee table and gestured to the sofa. Then I headed to the open kitchen at the opposite end of the room and set my handbag on the counter. The sound of the ice clinking into the glass seemed to echo throughout the silent apartment. Filling the glass with water, I wished I had a chance to check a mirror.

As I walked back across the room, Jack patted the cushion beside him.

I sat down but left a cushion between us. "So, you've been away?"

"I've been in Chicago for the past few weeks on a case for the agency," he responded. "Landes knows I'm from that area, so I drew the short straw."

"Did you see your parents while you were there?"

"I did. But that's not what I want to talk about." He took hold of both of my hands and looked into my eyes. "Callie, I can't get you out of my mind. You're there from my first thought in the morning till I fall in bed at night."

My body stiffened for a fraction of a second, then deflated like a balloon when you let go of the neck. "Jack, you don't have to do this. I understand completely why you stopped calling me."

There was hurt in his deep blue eyes. "I was trying to give you the space you asked for."

"Maybe that didn't come out right," I said. "What I was trying to say is, I feel I have nothing to give in a relationship. And we can't build a true connection on pity alone."

"Hold on." Jack's voice rose as he scowled. "*Pity?* You can't be serious. What I feel for you has nothing to do with pity. Not only are you beautiful, but you're bright and easy to talk with, and you have a great sense of humor—"

"But Jack, I don't know who I was before waking up on the cabin floor of the *Rising Star.*" I pulled my hands away from his. "I don't know what mistakes I've made in the past, so—"

Jack reached out and placed a gentle finger on my lips.

"For your sake, Callie, I hope your memory returns. Because it's important to you. But the past is behind us. Your life seems to be on the right track. Although the past may be a guide, during the short time I've known you, I've seen how you deal with what life tosses in your path. The situation with your twin . . . your aunt . . ."

He shook his head, his eyes never leaving mine.

"You're a compassionate, caring person. Memories of your past—your life before we met—are unimportant to me, other than their effect on you. I was not a part of that past, but I'd like to be a part of your future."

I felt dizzy.

"You can take all the time you need," he continued. "But we're so good together, and I think you feel it too. Please don't shut me out of your life."

I had no intention of shutting him out of my life completely. But he was right about one thing: I was going to need some time.

Chapter
145

Friday, August 7, 5:20 p.m.—Chicago, Illinois

Uncharacteristically ill at ease with her cherished Chicago family, Marnie felt as if she were walking barefoot on a floor made of shattered glass. To avoid hurting Erica and Mike, as well as Bill and Nelson, she'd rehearsed her words, writing them down and even revising them again and again. She had to put a positive spin on her decision. Let them know it had nothing to do with them.

So far, only Bradford was privy to the choice she had made with her career in mind. But no one she loved should be blindsided. They must know her plans. *Upfront communication* was her new motto. As Ashleigh had said, one must learn one's lessons—and then look ahead.

Marnie's early birthday celebration this weekend with her second family—including a special dinner at the Palmer Hotel—should make things a little less awkward. But one way or another, she was sure the delivery of her little speech would pack a punch.

In the living room of Nelson's comfortable historic row home, which he shared with Erica, Marnie announced, "I'm nearly finished with the fifth draft of my novel. It's called *No Return*."

"Fifth draft?" Mike parroted.

Marnie nodded. "It's bound to need even more. Jeffrey Archer usually does about seventeen rewrites. But I've done as much as I can without at least one set of objective eyes reading it through."

"I thought you said Callie and Juliana read and edited your manuscript."

"They did. But they're not objective. They're my sisters. Besides, they don't know what to look for." She explained that they mostly corrected spelling, typos, and missing or extra words. They didn't look for pace, voice, plot holes, and the more important parts of a novel. "I sent a hard copy to Graham yesterday."

"Isn't he flying in from London next week to attend your graduation party?" Mike asked with a note of incredulity. "Why not give the novel to him then?"

"Well, not exactly. He's scheduled to participate on a TV panel with three other authors in New York on the nineteenth, so I invited him to join us." She was hoping to qualify for his summer workshop next year and was sure that once her parents met him, they would have no further reservations. "But I couldn't ask him to lug my manuscript around during his visit."

"So, he's agreed to read your novel and give you feedback?" Nelson asked.

"Yep—the whole manuscript. I want his input on how to improve it before submitting it to an agent, a publisher, or even an editor."

Erica listened while Marnie explained her work, but she hadn't said much yet about Marnie's decision to use a pen name—or rather, to change her name altogether.

Mike, for his part, was skeptical. When Marnie told them what she was considering, he asked, "Was that the name your biological parents suggested?"

"Not at all," Marnie replied. "I wanted to talk to you first. The only person I've shared my plan with is Graham. And he likes the idea."

"I don't know about the name change, but you have an awesome mentor," Nelson said.

"As I understand it," Mike chimed in, "in today's world it takes a social media presence to get recognition and make sales of any commodity—books included. So, won't a name change—"

"You're spot-on, Uncle Mike. That's why I'd like to legally change my name rather than publish under a nom de plume."

"Isn't that going overboard?"

Marnie shook her head. "To be taken seriously by readers across the nation, and hopefully beyond, my writing must stand on its own. If I'm connected to past media attention, I won't know if I'm any good or not."

"But Marnie," Erica said, "couldn't name recognition also *attract* readers?"

"Probably. But in the wrong way, Mom." Graham had warned her that once she was published, PR professionals would encourage her to take advantage of her so-called notoriety. That type of hype could sell books the first time around. "But readers who were drawn in for the wrong reason won't necessarily buy my future novels."

Especially if the first one sucks, said a little voice in the back of her head.

Graham had also advised Marnie not to set her expectations too high. Other than the occasional fluke, a great readership seldom came before an author had at least three published novels, but usually more like five or six.

"So it's a good thing I enjoy working in the display department at Jordon's!" she joked.

"That all sounds daunting," Mike said.

"Graham says it takes a long time to become an overnight success. And I quote: 'The gold lies in a good backlist.'"

With a wistful look in his eye and a nod to Erica, Mike suggested, "Marnie, what do you think of the name *Chris T.*?"

Chris T.

Christonelli.

Marnie realized he and Erica were hoping she'd somehow retain their family name—the one she'd shared with them in her early years. Of course, she wanted to please the two people who had been the only parents she'd known for the first years of her life. But at twenty-three years of age, she was ready to claim her birth name.

Chapter
146

Monday, August 10, 1:20 p.m.—Queens, New York

After our flight touched down at JFK Airport, we were among the first to deplane and walk down the JetBlue ramp. Handing over our baggage tickets to Samantha, I said, "How about you and Brandy going to the baggage claim while Elizabeth and I check to see if David is here? That way he won't have to keep circling."

"What time did you say Marnie's plane was due?" Brandy asked as she pushed strands of curly red hair from her cheek.

I pulled my iPhone from Marnie's Juicy Couture handbag—the very one that had turned our family's world upside down. "Three fifteen. She may already be in the terminal. Keep an eye out for her at the JetBlue baggage carousels."

"Would you like me to help the girls with the baggage?" Elizabeth asked. It was so like her.

I raised a brow. "No, Elizabeth, but thank you. The girls can handle it. And David will load them into the limo."

Marnie headed straight to the baggage claim level, hoping she'd run into Callie and their friends. She wasn't too worried. If they were already out front, she'd just meet them there after she retrieved her suitcase.

Not having had a wink of sleep the night before, Marnie struggled to quiet the churning sensation in her gut. In Chicago, following some initial hiccups, her announcement had gone better than expected. It was not that which had kept her awake, but her fear of disapproval or even rejection by friends and members of her extended family—those whom she'd not seen or spoken to since the whole fiasco last May. That thought cast a dark shadow over the upcoming celebration.

"Marnie . . . Marnie." The high-pitched voices filtered through the cacophony of boarding announcements, rolling suitcases, luggage carts, and laughter. Stretching up on tiptoe, Marnie searched in the direction of the voices.

Brandy and Sam wound their way through the crowd toward her—with their rolling suitcases and handbags that swayed from their shoulders. Before Marnie could ask, Sam said, "Callie and Elizabeth are out front."

"There's my bag," Marnie said as she spotted it on the carousel. She made her way through the crowd but got there seconds too late. Rather than battling the crowd to chase her suitcase around the bend, she waited for it to come around again.

On the second round, as she reached for her bag, a tall, slender young man stepped in and grabbed it from the conveyor. She noticed a large camera hanging around his neck, secured by a wide leather strap.

Before she could tell him the bag was hers, he set it on the floor beside her. "Here you go . . ."

CHAPTER
147

Monday, August 10, 1:55 p.m.—Queens, New York

"Oh my," Elizabeth said as we spotted the tail end of the limo moving out of sight. "If only I'd moved a little faster, David wouldn't have had to circle the airport again." She sighed. "I suppose keeping our airports safe is worth a little inconvenience."

"Ms. Taylor?"

By now I was accustomed to the surprise of hearing an unknown voice. This one came from a vivacious young woman clad in jeans and a navy blazer. Her dark-brown hair was clipped back in a stylish sloppy bun. She didn't look familiar—but then again, who did?

"Yes," I said cautiously as she moved in closer.

"Could I have a moment of your time?"

I looked back toward the sliding doors at the baggage area. Neither Marnie nor Sam and Brandy were yet in sight. "A moment of my time for what?" I asked skeptically.

"My name is Terri Enders. I'm a freelance reporter." She handed me her card. "I'd like to speak with you and your sister. When it's convenient for you both, of course."

"About what?" I asked, even though I was pretty sure I knew.

She ignored my question. "Are you Callie . . . or Marnie?"

Just then Marnie bolted toward us, with Sam and Brandy close behind. Marnie shot a glance over her shoulder, then glared straight at the reporter. "Is he with you?" she asked, her tone accusatory.

In the next instant, a flash went off, nearly blinding me. A skinny guy pointed a professional-type camera at my sister and me and clicked one shot after another. He wore a satisfied grin.

The reporter's face drained of color. "Dennis. No. Stop!" she yelled at him. Refocusing on us, she said, "I'm so very sorry."

"Who are you? And what do you want?" Marnie asked. "If it's about the rogue wave and all that hype, it's old news. And you're fresh out of luck."

The reporter appeared on the verge of collapse, while the photographer stood by, unfazed.

"You may not use our photos unless we give you a written release," Marnie nearly spat at him.

"You think Princess Di signed a release on all those photos?" he shot back.

"My sister and I aren't public figures," I countered.

"Hey, free publicity is pure gold to—"

A quelling look from the reporter finally cut him short. She looked from me to my sister and repeated, "I am truly sorry for this invasion of your privacy. This was not what I planned." Looking directly at Marnie, she said, "And you are quite right about the *Rising Star* catastrophe. People stopped asking about it a couple of months ago. But I think they'd be captivated by what happened to each of you. And writing human-interest articles is my strong suit."

Marnie and I shook our heads vigorously, but the reporter kept talking. "I like what I've heard about both of you."

"Which is . . . ?" Marnie asked.

"Forgive me," Terri Enders said, and introduced herself to my twin. "I've heard very good things about both of you from a mutual friend."

Out of the corner of my eye, I saw David pull the limo up to the curb a few feet to our left.

"Great to hear," Marnie said as she started for the limo. Over her shoulder, she called back, "Have a great day, Terri."

"I'm sorry," I said. "But we are *so* not interested in any publicity. And we certainly don't want to relive the recent past. Our motto is, focus on the future. Bye."

Chapter
148

Monday, August 10, 2:05 p.m.—Queens, New York

David popped open the trunk before jogging around the limo to open the door, so Marnie and her companions could slip inside. As he quickly loaded the luggage, everyone climbed in. Once the trivial chatter died down, Marnie confronted her sister. "Why did you take that reporter's card? You can't be thinking—"

"Of course not," Callie cut in. "I just didn't think she needed the additional rejection of my refusing to take it."

"So, you don't care that she and her buddy were stalking us?"

"I don't like it any more than you. But she was only doing her job. Besides, couldn't you tell how totally devastated she was when the photographer started shooting photos?"

"Then why did she bring a photographer?" Brandy asked.

"Good question," Marnie shot back. "She said she was freelance, so she sent herself. And the bit about a mutual friend was pure fiction—the kind I'd never write, because it's bloody unbelievable. No friend of ours would send a reporter to buttonhole us at the airport."

"I agree," Callie said. "I didn't intend to keep her card."

"Didn't? You have a change of mind?" Marnie's voice rose in alarm.

"No! Why would I want to relive a past I can't even remember?"

Their mother had told her how their Greenwich home had been bombarded by reporters after the *Rising Star* disaster. They'd fallen off the grid for a short while when the family was in Long Beach, but a New York stringer had picked up their trail following one of her father's TV interviews and caught him after a Jordon's store visit. Eventually, their parents had reluctantly given a brief interview, but they provided little detail other than that Callie's recovery was going well. They had not mentioned Marnie's accident, only her elation over working with Graham Bradford.

"Time to forget about that reporter." Callie folded the business card in half and leaned forward to stuff it in the limo's ashtray. "We need to make plans. We have five days before the party this Saturday, so let's decide what we can do together and what we need to do on our own."

Marnie waited for Callie to begin throwing out suggestions. It would be a good test of what her sister could recall of her life before the lights had gone out on her past memories.

Every night, Marnie prayed for the return of Callie's memory. But she really couldn't relate to her sister's condition. They called it *autobiographical memory loss*—the kind where personal memories of the past were gone forever. But sometimes Marnie wondered . . .

Although Callie denied she was getting better, there were times when she talked about events with friends or family that, even without a major bonk on the head, had long ago slipped from Marnie's memory. But anytime Marnie pointed this out, Callie claimed it was something that had been filled in for her by others.

Marnie loved her sister, but sometimes she wondered: Could Callie be hanging on to memory loss so she could remain in the spotlight?

Chapter
149

Monday, August 10, 2:35 p.m.—New York, New York

As the representatives of the No Child Goes Hungry committee filed out of her office on the top floor of the Carlingdon's landmark store, April's eyes pooled with tears of happiness. Her heart swelled. Her hard work in qualifying this dedicated group for the generous Carlingdon's corporate giving program couldn't have been more rewarding. Every ten dollars of the sizable Carlingdon's gift provided one hundred meals for boys and girls.

Not only that, but today she might even get home on time. She could write her report first thing tomorrow morning, but she could hardly wait to tell Uncle Conrad the good news this weekend at the girls' celebration. She knew at this point, he could use some good news.

Slinging the strap of her handbag over her shoulder, April thought about the twins. She'd wanted to fly out to Southern California at some point during the past few months to see them and the rest of the family, but she'd managed only a few phone calls. There never seemed to be enough hours in the day, but now that her husband's eight-year-old daughter and the girl's grandmother lived in Manhattan, life was settling down at last.

Before leaving the office, April gazed out the window. Central Park and the bumper-to-bumper traffic defined Manhattan. *I love this city, and I love my life,* she thought as she headed for the door.

The phone rang, but she did not stop to answer it. Then, remembering her assistant had left early for a dental appointment, she retraced her steps across the carpeted floor and reached for the phone. "April Clark," she said.

Hearing the frantic voice on the other end, she tossed her handbag onto the armchair and leaned against her desk. The voice was familiar—that of a good friend with whom she'd worked at JJQ in Chicago.

"Slow down, please, Terri. It can't be *that* bad."

"It's worse. I am so, so sorry, April. I messed up."

"Okay. Just start at the beginning."

"I landed an assignment for the *Post*, to write a puff piece on Justin Trudeau and his wife, Sophie. They were flying in to JFK this afternoon."

"The prime minister of Canada?"

Terri began relating the details that led up to her disastrous first meeting with the Taylor twins. April's chest constricted, afraid of where this was headed.

"Since I didn't want to take a chance on missing the Trudeaus, I arrived more than an hour early. In the JetBlue terminal, I remembered you telling me the twins were coming in on that airline today, so I checked the arrival time of the Long Beach flight—"

"Don't tell me you approached them! I need to talk to them first."

"I know. I feel terrible. I royally messed up. Most people jump at the chance for the positive kind of human-interest story I plan to write. But the photographer I had with me for the Trudeau article—"

April felt a shiver run up her spine. "Did you tell them you were a friend of mine?"

"No. Not exactly. But I think I've damaged any chance—"

April's jaw clenched as she listened to Terri. She could visualize the scene and how it would have disturbed Callie and Marnie. That image shredded her insides.

"What can I say, Terri? Your intentions were good, and I feel the type of story you spelled out would be good for both girls. It could also inspire others. But considering how badly you got off on the wrong foot, I'm not sure I can persuade the twins to consider this opportunity."

As the receiver clicked into the cradle, April regretted having shared her thoughts about the twins with her caring friend. She hadn't spent time with either of the Taylor girls since before they'd left for their semester at sea. Perhaps her idea—about the healing power of getting their stories out into the world, in an article by such a talented writer—was completely off base.

Chapter
150

Tuesday, August 11, 12:45 p.m.—Greenwich, Connecticut

When I awoke, sunlight filtered through the shutters on my windows. I rolled over to look at the digital clock at my bedside. As the numbers came into focus, I shot upright. It was already one o'clock in the afternoon.

My sense of alarm waned when it dawned on me that we were on the East Coast and jet lag had taken its toll. Still, I hadn't meant to sleep so late. There was so much I wanted to do . . .

I hadn't heard a thing from the other bedroom. Were Marnie and Brandy still asleep? I climbed out of bed, finger-combed my hair, and headed to Marnie's room, still in my Cal State sleep shirt. Her door stood ajar.

Both beds were neatly made, and neither my sister's nor Brandy's handbag was on the desk where I'd seen them the night before.

I returned to my bathroom and washed up before deciding how to plan the day. Then I slipped on my model's coat, pushed my bare feet into pink slippers, and headed downstairs.

Everything around me now seemed familiar. I guessed that was because of the time I spent here after leaving the hospital. "Anyone here?" I called out.

"In here," came a duet of voices. When I reached the kitchen, Mom and Elizabeth were at the counter. Mom had a mug of coffee, and Elizabeth was drinking tea from what she often called "a proper teacup and saucer." They instantly abandoned their stools to give me hugs, and asked if I had slept well.

"Too well, I'm afraid. Half the day's gone."

"Don't worry about it. You must have needed the sleep." Mom's words were reassuring. "Marnie took Brandy to meet some of her old friends."

I remembered overhearing those plans the day before. David had delivered Samantha and Kaitlyn home, and Juliana was staying at Kaitlyn's. They would all return on Friday morning to help with the party preparations, and Dad would arrive later Friday.

Slipping into her former role, Elizabeth asked, "Would you like some eggs, pancakes, or both?"

"Thanks, Elizabeth. I'll just grab some cold cereal. Then I need to get dressed."

"You sure?" Elizabeth asked.

I nodded and thanked her.

"Have a wonderful day," she said, then left the kitchen.

"Mom," I said, "I told Aunt Paige I'd like to meet her before the party. Since everyone's gone, could we see if she's available today? Maybe we could all go to lunch."

"Well, you're in luck. She called this morning and asked about taking us to lunch. April also called."

I looked at the kitchen clock above the counter. "But it's after one already," I said, leaving my disappointment undisguised.

"I told Paige you were sleeping in. She suggested two thirty, after the lunch crowd. She tentatively made reservations for four, at L'Escale in the Delamar Hotel."

"Terrific," I said. "Is April joining us?"

"No. She works in Manhattan, so you'll need to go there to enjoy lunch with her before the party." She paused. "I overheard you girls talking last night. Since Marnie and Sam also want to see April, as well as Allison, perhaps you can coordinate a day together in Manhattan."

I nodded. "That would be great. If it works for them, maybe we could have lunch with April, then dinner or whatever with Allison the same evening." I took cereal from the pantry and poured it into a bowl. Mom had said a reservation for four, so I asked, "Is Elizabeth coming with us?"

"Not today. We'll drop her off at the Toddmans' to spend the day with Paige's mother. You and the girls call her Grandma Helen."

"I remember." *Did I?* "I mean, Juliana told me she has Alzheimer's but is sort of foxy and fun to be around."

"That's right. She's a wonderful woman and doing amazingly well after all these years. Some days are better than others, but she has sparks of wit and humor. April adores her grandmother, as we all do."

"So who's the fourth for lunch?"

"As it turns out, Mark Toddman can join us today."

This was turning out better than I dreamed. I would have the opportunity to get reacquainted with most of my extended family before the party.

Now, looking around the cozy kitchen, I felt totally at home.

Chapter
151

Thursday, August 13, 9:25 a.m.—Manhattan, New York

David maneuvered the limo through the Midtown traffic, then pulled to the curb at Carlingdon's on Lexington Avenue. Marnie and I scrambled out and watched David pull from the curb, heading for the Empire State Building with Samantha and Brandy. Mom and Marnie were right about having David drive us today. I wouldn't much like to be behind the wheel in this magnificent city. Even finding a parking space would be a nightmare.

We had a couple of hours to browse before meeting April at the odd hour of 11:20 a.m. I'd been conflicted when April asked to have lunch with just Marnie and me. Sam was looking forward to seeing her, and Brandy was always up for meeting new people. When I explained my problem, April quickly came up with a solution. She would get in touch with Allison, and they'd all have dinner this evening, if Sam would agree to take Brandy sightseeing. First stop: a tour to the top of the 120-story Empire State Building, which neither girl had ever taken.

Looking up above the entrance to Carlingdon's, and along the exterior of the landmark store, I saw our American flag flying beside the flags of other countries. "I love that," I said.

"You say that every time we've come into the city on college breaks," Marnie commented as we stepped onto the black-and-white art deco floor.

"Well, at least I'm consistent." I felt like Dorothy arriving in Emerald City. The store was magical and yet somewhat familiar.

"That you are," she shot back. "Callie, I think you remember more than you admit to." She seemed to be teasing, but I wasn't entirely sure.

I said nothing. I knew I had not been here since my accident. *Could a bit of my memory be returning?* I shut down that thought for fear of a big letdown if it turned out I was wrong.

In the past three months, I'd gone to Carlingdon's in South Coast Plaza in Costa Mesa and in Fashion Island in Newport Beach. Both had beautiful, upscale interiors. Perhaps that was why this amazing store felt familiar. But although they had the same art deco flooring at the entrance, I did not believe them to be half so grand.

"Callie? Earth calling Callie?" Marnie snapped me from my introspection. "Did you hear anything I said?"

"Sorry. Just thinking they sure don't build stores like this anymore."

"You're right about that. But all the Carlingdon's locations are first-class, and several steps above the norm."

We passed through Cosmetics on our way to the escalator, and I stared up at a magnificent gold-and-crystal chandelier in the shape of an inverted pyramid. *Do any of the thirty-nine other locations even come close?* Then I thought of the former Marshall Field's in Chicago. I wasn't sure if I'd been there, but I'd scanned photos in a book Sam had at the apartment. It, too, had been an amazing store.

As soon as we stepped off the elevator and began shopping, all thoughts of the grand interior evaporated. Marnie and I shopped separately but, as twins do sometimes, we both chose maxi dresses for the party this weekend.

We had just arrived at our meeting spot when Marnie spotted April heading our way. "Perfect timing," she said.

When April reached us, she drew us into a group hug, and we all laughed and exchanged our *It's-so-great-to-see-you.*

"Now, fortunately the owner has reserved a perfect table for us at Le Cirque. It's a little French restaurant less than a block from here," April stage-whispered. "To get any privacy, I need to get away from the store."

Chapter
152

Thursday, August 13, 11:45 a.m.—Manhattan, New York

A stocky, dark-haired Frenchman moved toward us as we stepped into the restaurant. "*Ma chérie,*" he said, taking April's hands and kissing her on both cheeks.

April's face reddened, but she returned his air kisses. "*Bonjour, Victor. Merci beaucoup pour le favour.*"

"*Mon plaisir.*"

April introduced Marnie and me, and after a brief exchange, Victor led us into a curtained alcove that housed a table for four. He said something else in French, then excused himself to officially open for the lunch hour.

I'd spoken with April soon after my accident and a couple of times since. I figured since April had some sort of agenda for our time together now, I'd hold off asking for updates on her husband, Kyle, and his daughter, Lindsay. Once we were seated, though, I did tell April about the lunch her parents had arranged with Mom and me on Tuesday.

April smiled and winked. "Then you know I was a pretty lucky girl to have been left at their doorstep."

I'd been told the real story, and I loved April's openness about being adopted. I also appreciated her genuine warmth. "Meeting your parents . . . well, I was captivated by both of them," I admitted. "They were such fun. I understand why our parents view each other as family."

"Don't forget, I'm not just their daughter. I've also been your big sister for nearly twenty-three years."

"Of course," I said, remembering that Marnie had shown me the photos of April's wedding. Just a few years earlier, I'd gone from being a bridesmaid to being maid of honor—after her best friend, Madison, was involved in a near-fatal accident on the eve of the wedding.

Marnie had told me about Madison's horrible accident, which had taken the lives of her abusive husband as well as their five-year-old daughter and two-year-old son. Only Madison and three-year-old Jena had survived. Lucky for her, a man named Bill had come into her life when she needed him most. But I couldn't help but wonder how you could possibly turn such a difficult start into a happy ending.

If such things had happened in my life, I wouldn't be so eager to regain my memories.

April thanked the waiter for their menus and started to give hers a quick glance, but Marnie wasted no time in getting down to business. "We're thrilled to have you all to ourselves, April, but what gives?"

Uncharacteristically, April felt ill at ease, even though she'd known Callie since the day she was born—and Marnie since she was Lindsay's age. "Let's order first," she suggested. "Today is my treat, by the way. Everything is good here, but my favorite is the *quiche au saumon et crevettes.*" She used her best accent, but French wasn't her strong suit.

"Sounds good to me," Callie and Marnie said in duet, then looked at each other and laughed.

"There are tons of other great dishes to choose from." April ran her finger down the menu.

"We love quiche and salmon," Marnie said. "And we're a whole lot more interested in what this private lunch is all about."

With all eyes on her, April gathered her thoughts. Resting her forearms on the table, she shifted her gaze from Callie to Marnie. "I want to catch up with all of you, and Samantha too, but I asked for this private lunch so I could apologize to you first."

Four identical brown doe-eyes stared back at her.

"Apologize?" Marnie blurted out. "For what?"

April sighed. "This is just so hard for me to explain, since my good intentions went so terribly awry."

"I know all about that," Marnie said, nodding her head sympathetically.

Inhaling a deep breath, April continued. "Your unfortunate encounter with the reporter at the airport—it was all my fault."

The twins said nothing, but their eyes spoke volumes.

"That reporter is my friend Terri Enders. I worked with her at JJQ in Chicago."

"Isn't that a TV news station?" Callie asked.

April nodded, glancing down at her intertwined fingers. She began filling them in on her conversation with Terri three days earlier.

"Can I ask a question?" Marnie said, but then she continued without waiting for a response. "You've been like a sister. How could you even think of talking to a reporter friend about us? We were relieved when the media blitz came to an end. Why would you think resurfacing everything would be a good idea?"

April gulped her water and looked from Marnie to Callie. The sense of betrayal in Callie's eyes was just as strong as the one in Marnie's—much worse than any words the twins might hurl.

Setting her glass down on the table, April lifted her chin. "I was horrified when I received the call from Terri. But I wanted to talk to you about it in person, not on the phone." She looked directly at Marnie. "Which is something I think you can relate to."

Marnie scowled. "But that's not the point, is it?"

"Please. You know I love both of you and Juliana like sisters. We're family. I would never do anything to hurt you."

Before Marnie could barge in again, Callie looked straight at April. "I'm sure you get that Marnie and I don't want to be at the center of more media attention. And we realize you didn't intend for your friend to ambush us at JFK. But I'm wondering why you didn't discourage her from writing a human-interest piece on us in the first place?"

Chapter
153

Friday, August 14, 4:30 p.m.—Greenwich, Connecticut

Marnie brushed the hair from her face and pulled her BlackBerry from the back pocket of her shorts. Ever since the marquee tent went up around noon, she and the other girls had been working with the event planners inside the huge, white octagonal structure.

Ashleigh had told the girls they were excused from all the setup—after all, it was their celebration—but they'd wanted to help. Besides, with everyone else lending a hand, Marnie couldn't imagine just sitting around and watching others work. They'd all had a blast most of the day anyway. All work and no play? Not by a long shot.

Over the past few days, Callie had seemed more relaxed and more like her old self. She laughed and joked about misadventures in the past, causing Marnie to hope her memory was returning. Coming back to the home they'd grown up in might have been just what Callie needed. But whenever Marnie "caught" her sister recalling certain memories from their past, Callie denied it.

"I wish that were true," she'd said yesterday, "but I'm unable to dig into real long-term memory. You've all done such a fantastic job of painting pictures of my past events and relationships, and they're beginning to *feel* like memories. But they're just images I formed from what I've been told."

Marnie wasn't so sure, but Callie's memory would have to take a back seat right now. Checking the time, Marnie saw that her dad was due within the next half hour. She would have to hurry.

Spotting Callie on the far side of the tent, Marnie cupped her hands around her mouth and raised her voice. "I'll text you!" It was time to sit down for another private pow-wow with her mom and dad.

As she descended the winding staircase, Ashleigh heard Conrad's key in the lock. She knew it was him since the rest of the family was here and accounted for. She dashed down and pulled open the door. Even after all the years and all the challenges they'd faced together, her heart still fluttered at the sight of him.

Dropping his bag at their feet, Conrad glanced around the empty foyer before pulling her into his arms, swooping her into a long kiss straight out of an old Hollywood film.

As he set her back on her feet, she grinned. "Well, I've missed you too."

He chuckled. Picking up his bag, his smile began to fade. "I got a text," he said, arching a brow, "from Marnie."

"Sorry about the timing," Ashleigh said, shrugging her shoulders as they headed back upstairs. Hitting him with the need for a family meeting the moment he walked through the door from a long business trip was not exactly her choice. "All I can say is it's nothing catastrophic. I promised Marnie I'd let her explain. I asked her to give you a call. She knows you're not a fan of texting."

Conrad shrugged. "I'm getting used to it. Texting isn't such a pain now that Juliana showed me how to use the speaker rather than type my messages. And with back-to-back store meetings, I now understand the advantage. I even find I'm saving time on business calls."

In their bedroom, he set his suitcase on the bench at the foot of the bed. Then he sank down onto the bed. "I'll have Juliana bring me up to speed on some of the new technology we're implementing for customers inside our stores. I understand the concept. It's phenomenal. But actually using it . . ."

Ashleigh's lips curved in a warm smile as she gazed at her travel-weary husband. Her eyes never wavered as she listened to her husband admit how he could learn from their youngest and tech-savvy daughter, her heart filling with love.

A series of light taps at the door brought their conversation to an end.

"Come in," Conrad called out. When Marnie appeared, he stood and pulled her in for a hug. "I understand you have an undisclosed agenda," he joked.

Marnie frowned for just a moment before breaking out in a smile. "I'm practicing my ability to create suspense."

"Well, you set the hook," Ashleigh said, gesturing to the round table by the windows. She walked over and lowered herself into the chair Conrad had pulled out for her.

As they listened to Marnie's rationale for changing to a professional name, Ashleigh was pleased with her daughter's thought process, yet she still felt conflicted. She trusted her husband would help put the situation in perspective.

Conrad did not interrupt their daughter.

Observing her husband apply the nonthreatening listening skills of an FBI hostage negotiator, Ashleigh's heart filled with pride and admiration. He paraphrased Marnie's words, showing she had his undivided attention and he understood her point of view—all while neither agreeing nor disagreeing.

"This is all very interesting, honey," he said at last, "and I know you've given this a great deal of thought. Your desire to change your Christian name presents no problem."

"None at all," Ashleigh confirmed. "On your official birth certificate, your name is registered as Cassie Lynne Taylor. Therefore, although that's never been an issue, Cassie is your legal name, not Marnie. And I love the idea of you using the name we chose for you."

"I sense a 'but' coming," Marnie said, with a quirk of her brow.

Chapter
154

Friday, August 14, 5:15 p.m.—Greenwich, Connecticut

Conrad reached for the pitcher of water on the table and poured three glasses before setting it back on the tray. He took a quick gulp from one. "So at this point," he began again, "you've discussed your plan with the Christonellis as well as Graham Bradford."

Marnie nodded. "I was afraid Erica and Mike would be hurt if I didn't make them understand first."

"I have no quarrel with you bouncing your ideas off of others," Conrad said. "You had to start somewhere, and since you and Callie returned, I haven't been around as much as I'd like."

The smooth skin on Marnie's forehead crinkled. "That's hardly your fault, Dad. You're been terrific. And I'm proud . . ." Her voice died.

Conrad picked up the trail. "I don't know what the others had to say, but here are my thoughts. Your desire to have your last name legally changed is not only unnecessary but not to your advantage, I would think." He paused. "Now, many authors write under a pseudonym."

"I understand that, Dad. You're not the first person to bring it up," agreed Marnie. "But today is different. With the rise of social media, pseudonyms are more difficult to pull off."

Conrad met Marnie's eyes and ran his fingers through his salt-and-pepper hair. "Let me understand. You want to abandon the Taylor name due to both the past and the more recent publicity. Also, you must establish name recognition as an author through social media."

"Exactly. Even though the interview you and Mom gave after the rogue wave was sanitized, photos and stories about Callie and me were splashed across the nation."

Conrad nodded to Ashleigh, signaling it was her turn to step in.

"Love, the public eye has a short attention span. By the time your novel is ready for publication—"

"I get that, Mom. I know most people wouldn't remember my photo even a day or so after it hit the press, but—"

Ashleigh went on, "In this day of fast and easy access to information, we're both blessed and cursed. Our family has lived a high-profile life, and the ups and downs of our history have been publicized ad nauseum. This shared history is inescapable, regardless of your legal name."

Marnie sighed. She sank back in her chair, her hands dropping from the table to her lap.

Ashleigh's heart went out to her daughter. She could almost see Marnie's strong convictions begin to unravel and dissipate. She decided to remind Marnie again of J. K. Rowling, author of the Harry Potter series. "Why not simply use a professional pseudonym, as she did when she wanted to write in a different genre? Why must you make it a legal change?"

"Well," Marnie replied, "it didn't take long for everyone to figure out who *she* was."

"Would changing her legal name have prevented that?" Conrad asked.

"She used the name Robert Galbraith, so unless she wanted to be called 'Robert,' that wouldn't have been possible." Marnie chuckled. "But I get your point."

Leaning forward on her elbows, she sighed once more.

"I guess I'm just a hardhead." She tapped her hairline, where the pale scar that matched her twin's had faded and was barely visible. Then she whispered, "If I don't write under an unknown name, I'll never know if I'm any good."

Her eyes drifted to the ceiling. "But if I haven't established name recognition for my pseudonym, no agent will want to represent me, since publishers no longer want to publish a novel by an unknown author with no platform for selling, no matter how much an acquisitions editor loves the story."

"It typically takes a least two or three years to be published," Ashleigh said. "Why not begin establishing a social media presence under a pseudonym?"

Marnie buried her face in her hands.

Ashleigh exchanged a knowing look with Conrad.

Suddenly Marnie's hands shot out as she lifted her chin. Her eyes flashing, she said, "Now, that's the conundrum of all conundrums." Not waiting for their reaction, she pressed on. "It takes time to build recognition on social media. It's more important to spend my time working on my craft, since no matter how terrific my pseudonym name recognition becomes, if my stories don't move my readers, I'll become a one-book wonder. There just aren't enough hours in the day for me to both write and promote myself . . ."

"Hold on," Ashleigh and Conrad said simultaneously. But Marnie was on a roll.

"Once I get the kind of recognition J. K. Rowling has earned . . ." Her eyes again shot to the ceiling, and she smiled for the first time, revealing her dazzling white teeth. "From my mouth to God's ear, as Elizabeth would say."

Ashleigh had to smile.

Biting down on her outer lip, Marnie continued, "But I won't care what anyone digs up, once I know for sure readers are loving my storytelling—not buying my first novel hoping to get some insider info about our family dynamics. At that point, I'll want everyone to know I'm part of the Taylor family. But if I use our surname from the start, even with changing my first name, I won't know if I'm any good or not. All of my friends and our family's friends will feel they have to buy that first novel."

"And that's not a good thing?" Conrad said, puzzled.

Marnie scrunched both sides of her hair with her hands. "Well, yes. A publisher will want to know what I can bring to the table in the way of readers." Graham had said a PR person would exploit her history, and she didn't want that. In the best of all worlds, she would love to have the people who knew the Taylors buy her books. "But I also want strangers to buy my books, just not because they're drawn to our family drama. Those people will be disappointed because my thrillers aren't based on any of my personal journeys."

"But aren't authors supposed to write what they know?" Conrad asked. A look of horror filled Marnie's luminous brown eyes. "You mean write a story about an identical twin being abducted from the hospital on the day of her birth?"

Conrad blinked as an expression of equal horror registered on his handsome features. "No. That's not what I meant."

Ashleigh realized it was a good time to jump in. "I don't believe your father intended to suggest you write a memoir. But it's my understanding that writers are most effective when they set their stories in a familiar background—"

Marnie nodded eagerly. "Yes, I write the kind of books I like to read. And I prefer familiar backgrounds, like for my thriller, which is set in Manhattan."

"And I believe it's just as important to draw upon the emotions they've experienced," Ashleigh continued.

"Exactly," Marnie agreed. "In fantasy and science fiction, writers create their own worlds, but they must create them in ways readers can relate to. Even elves and aliens draw upon human emotions."

Ashleigh couldn't resist a smile, and she saw that Conrad couldn't either. "We just hope you'll think a little longer before making such a life-altering decision," she suggested. "Be sure it's what you really want—and need."

Chapter
155

Friday, August 14, 6:10 p.m.—Greenwich, Connecticut

It was after six, but I still hadn't received Marnie's promised text—and I soon discovered why. The door to my parents' room was ajar, and they were seated at the round table by the window. It seemed Marnie still had their attention.

"I hope this isn't a bad time," I called out as I stepped cautiously inside.

"Please join us," Dad said. "We were expecting you."

Mom's eyes filled with love. "So, you'd like to discuss the human-interest story April's friend proposed."

"You already discussed this?" I said, taking in my twin's nonplussed expression.

Marnie tossed up her hands. "Not guilty," she cried out.

"Girls," Dad said in a voice sharper than usual. "April spoke to your mother—"

"When?" Marnie shot back.

"Monday evening," Mom said. "April was terribly upset over having her friend approach you at JFK. She wanted a chance to apologize."

"Yeah, she explained when we met her in the city yesterday. But she didn't say she'd already discussed it with you," I said.

"She told me after the faux pas at the airport. Not before," Mom said.

Incredulous, Marnie said, "And you think it's a good idea?"

"It's not our decision," Dad said. "It is entirely up to the two of you."

"We don't understand," I said. "We thought you'd be totally against more *family* publicity," I added as I slipped into the chair beside my sister.

"It depends," my parents said in one voice, before exchanging a smile. *A united team, as usual.*

I loved the way my parents always seemed to be on the same side, although not always on the same wavelength. They never failed to show love, respect, and support for each other as well as for us. Whether my memories returned or not, I vowed theirs was the only kind of relationship I wanted. No matter how long it took, I'd settle for no less than what they'd found.

As I tried to sort out my emotions about April's idea of a story about us, Mom and Dad voiced their opinions on the merits of such an article. Telling things from Marnie's perspective, they explained, could rescue her from the endless explanations she'd had to repeat on how she handled her decision to remain in England. But I couldn't imagine how sharing my story could help anyone.

"I don't know how my experience with memory loss might help others. I have no great insight. I'm just taking it one day at a time." I shrugged. "As far as I know, there are no support groups for amnesia victims."

Mom frowned. "Darling," she said, "I doubt the reporter plans to dwell on amnesia. I believe her interest lies in the ability to overcome a victim mentality."

"But we understand your reluctance," Dad was quick to add. "Why don't you sleep on it?"

When we reached the door to my bedroom, I guided Marnie inside.

"What's up?" she asked, glancing at her BlackBerry. "Make it quick."

With no preliminaries, I said, "It was you who invited Jack, wasn't it?"

With a shrug, Marnie said, "I knew you wanted him to come."

"Absolutely not," I countered. "I told you I didn't want to put him in that position."

Marnie rolled her eyes. "Be real. If he didn't want to come, he wouldn't have accepted."

She can be so maddening sometimes . . .

"Of course he would. He works for Landes." With our family as a long-term client, he had no choice. Now he had to give up his weekend, fly clear across the country, and then make nice with a whole bunch of strangers.

And to make matters worse, Marnie had seated him next to me.

"As Graham likes to say, no good deed goes unpunished."

I flopped down on my bed. "Graham says this, Graham says that. Enough already!"

It felt good to let my resentment spill over. I was tired of hearing about the amazing wisdom of Marnie's hero. She seemed to hope the English author would eventually become part of our extended family, but I just couldn't imagine it. Mom and Dad, and even Elizabeth, recently had managed to focus on Bradford's stature as a mentor, but I didn't feel quite so charitable. Especially right now.

"I moved Jack to the table with Landes and Pocino," I said. "I don't want him thinking this whole awkward invitation was my idea."

Marnie flopped down beside me. "Geez, Callie, I really thought it would make you happy. Does this mean you're already over him?" She looked far from convinced.

"There's no getting over him." I heaved a sigh. "Jack is a great guy, but I'm hardly ready for *any* romantic relationship. He deserves a partner who is, well, a whole person."

"Seriously, Callie," Marnie said, shooting to her feet, "if you keep this nonsense up, you'll totally shatter your future." She glared at me. "I don't have time for this BS. Graham will be here any moment."

"So you don't remember every person or event from your past? Well, neither do I. But if you don't register how Jack's eyes light up anytime you walk into a room, your short-term memory has also washed out to sea."

Marnie threw up her hands.

"You're as whole as anyone I know, Callie. More of your memories have returned than you admit, even to yourself. You're talking rubbish."

Chapter 156

Friday, August 14, 6:45 p.m.—Greenwich, Connecticut

As the taxi wound up the long drive, a thought passed through Graham Bradford's mind. This grand estate, though not ostentatious, would make a perfect setting for a second filming of *Gone with the Wind*. He had been filling his mind with such trivia throughout the trip in order to avoid dwelling on his first meeting with Marnie's family.

Despite her insistence that her parents had put their differences behind them, Bradford doubted the Taylors had truly forgiven him. He knew for certain they would never forget his less-than-admirable role in Marnie's subterfuge.

Nevertheless, the bond he felt with this talented young woman compelled him to reach out to her parents. The fact that he hadn't been there for his own daughter continued to haunt him. He'd been given a second chance when Marnie came into his life, though he hadn't realized it at first. If he could be a positive influence for her, perhaps he might regain a solid sense of purpose.

"Graham," Marnie called out, as she ran down the front steps to meet him in the driveway.

Stepping out of the taxi, Bradford froze. He wanted to wrap his arms around her in a protective hug, but he stood stock-still, afraid any sign of affection might be misinterpreted.

Coming here may have been a big mistake.

Marnie flew down the steps and threw her arms around her mentor. "I'm so glad you could come. I want you to meet everyone, but tonight it will just be my parents."

She quickly stepped back, her heart pounding in her throat. How could she have been so bold, so familiar? He was her teacher first and foremost—though at times he felt more like a friend.

His thick dark hair, sprinkled artfully with strands of white, fell rakishly over one eye. He looked so darn cool in his tight-fitting jeans and blazer. What she wanted to do was show him off to all her writer friends, but that was on hold until tomorrow.

"I'm looking forward to it," Bradford responded politely.

"You'll also meet my twin sister, Callie, and our little . . . I mean *younger* sister, Juliana. Oh, and a few of our close friends, but that'll be tomorrow at the party." She paused. "I hope that's okay."

His rigid posture seemed to relax. "Good," he said. "I'd like that."

As they headed into the house, Marnie peppered him with a multitude of questions about Hillary, Alexandre, and the others. Then she informed him that Charlize would be arriving the next afternoon. Although she was excited about the chance to see Charlize and spend time with her the following week, she was glad to have Bradford to herself after dinner.

"And your manuscript . . . ?" she asked.

Bradford explained, "I've been reviewing the final draft from my editor. My novel is on track for March fifteenth. It's Mothering Day in the UK."

"You mean Mother's Day?"

"Well, it's not the same date as the Mother's Day you celebrate here in the US."

"But it is close to St. Patrick's Day . . ." Marnie offered.

Bradford chuckled. "Not exactly a stellar day for publicity. But we have sufficient pre-orders, which has alleviated any major concerns."

As they neared the living room, where her parents waited to greet the British author in person, Marnie asked about his plans for his time in New York. She knew tomorrow everything was likely to be a bit crazy, with so many people anxious to meet the famous author.

"Since I must head to Manhattan immediately following tomorrow's festivities," Bradford said, "perhaps we can carve out an hour or so after dinner tonight to discuss your novel in depth. Maybe we can brainstorm some ideas for creating a more formidable antagonist."

It was just the answer Marnie was hoping for.

CHAPTER
157

Saturday, August 15, 7:25 a.m.—Greenwich, Connecticut

I rolled over, squinting at my bedside clock and not wanting to believe the illuminated red digits. I glanced over at Samantha, but with the blackout blinds drawn, I could barely make out her outline in the double bed beside mine. In the quiet of the house, I heard only the faint sounds of her breath going in and out.

Marnie had arranged to have Graham Bradford get acquainted with our parents over dinner the night before, so Sam and I had gone to dinner with Brandy and six girls from our former dance team. We had a blast, but we hadn't gotten to bed until after three a.m. After spending most of yesterday working on the decorating, followed by that evening of nonstop catching up—which I'd found less intimidating than I'd feared—I'd fallen asleep the moment my head hit the pillow.

I awoke the first time at 5:02 a.m. with Marnie's angry words hammering in my head: *You remember more than you admit.*

My mind was a jumble. I couldn't fall back to sleep, try as I might. I stared at digit after digit as the numbers clicked off. I just couldn't quiet my brain. The harder I tried, the more wide awake I felt.

I thought about the party and all the things Mom, Elizabeth, and everyone had done to make it special. I didn't want to sleepwalk through the day. But the writing was on the wall: I simply couldn't get back to sleep.

Slipping out of bed, I pushed my feet into slippers and reached for my robe, bumping into the bedside lamp. It fell on its side with a *crash*.

"What was that?" Samantha cried out as she sat straight up.

"Sorry," I said. "I couldn't sleep, so—"

"Worried about Jack?" She flipped on her own bedside lamp, rubbing the sleep from her eyes.

I blinked, shading my eyes. "A little. But that's not what kept me awake. Sorry I woke you. Go back to sleep. We'll talk when you get up. No need for us both to be zombies."

Throwing back the covers, Sam said, "I'm awake, so let's talk."

"You sure?" I looked at Sam as she rubbed her eyes.

She gave a sleepy grin. "We've gotten by with far less sleep on other occasions. But do you think we could sneak down to the kitchen and make some coffee?"

"Sure thing." I did need a sounding board. But after living with Sam for so long, I knew she was a night owl, not an early morning person.

We pulled on our robes and traipsed into the kitchen, where I popped two French Roast pods into the dual coffee maker and gazed out the kitchen window above the sink. The rising sun was visible behind the tent.

"Let's take our coffee out to the gazebo," I suggested.

As we trudged across the path, I recalled the last time I had come out here—to meet the Christonellis.

"Let me tell you what kept me awake," I said as we sat down with our coffee. "Marnie accused me of faking some of my memory loss."

Sam's mouth dropped open. "Why would she say *that*? Was she angry about something?"

"Not really." I flipped my hand from side to side. "She claims I remember some things better than she does. I don't think she was trying to be mean. She just seemed . . . frustrated."

"Frustrated?" Sam said. "I'd say you have a lot more reason to feel frustrated than she does."

I nodded, but my brain felt fuzzy.

"Well, we all forget things," Sam said. "But you have talked about things we did on the dance team when we were in kindergarten—things that I'd long forgotten."

"That's just it, Sam. My brain is scrambled. I can no longer tell if I recall something friends and family have shared with me since the accident, or if some of the things are actually from my own long-term memory." I took a sip of my coffee. "Since I've been here this week, there are things I think I might remember . . . Like Carlingdon's. It felt familiar. But that might have come from photos shown to me. I just don't know."

"Well, Callie, I don't know what to tell you. Last night, you were the only one to remember all the words to 'Cell Block Tango' from our dance routine in high school."

"Hate to burst your bubble, but that could be just because Juliana showed me some photos of us in the cell block costumes from the competition." Setting my cup down, I ran my finger around the rim. "That's the thing. It totally messes with my brain. I remember all sorts of random stuff."

Right after the accident, when I didn't even know my name, the words and music to "Seventy-Six Trombones" had run through my head. I had recalled *Alice in Wonderland* and related my feeling of disorientation to stepping through the looking-glass. And when I'd first looked up at my dad in the hospital, I had thought of James Bond. And yet I didn't recognize my parents.

Sam nodded. "That's not the first time you've told me about the random things people with autobiographical memory loss remember."

"That's right. I forgot. Do I have a short-term memory problem, too?" I looked at Sam and we broke out into giggles.

"I'm not sure we'll ever fully understand the mysteries of memory," Sam said. "But right now, I'm more interested in why you're stonewalling about another 007 lookalike."

I knew who she meant.

Chapter
158

Saturday, August 15, 2:05 p.m.—Greenwich, Connecticut

When I awoke with a start, it was after two p.m. Once again, Samantha was sound asleep in the next bed.

First too early. Now too late.

Sam and I had talked for a long time in the gazebo and then had breakfast. Then we'd decided to try for a short nap before joining the others to help with last-minute details. I had set my iPhone alarm for noon.

I reached over to check my phone, wondering what I'd done wrong. Siri had never let me down before. Checking my alarm setting, I saw a green circle lit up beside 12:00, but it was *a.m—not p.m.*

Juliana and Kaitlyn had planned to get up early to make sure everything was in order, and the caterer and event planner would be on hand well before the guests were due, so I let Sam sleep. Tiptoeing across to the bathroom, I carefully opened the adjoining door to my twin's room. Marnie had gone to bed by the time we returned last night, so I had no idea how things had gone with the famous author.

She sat hunched over her computer, which she'd propped on a pillow in her lap. There was no sign of Brandy.

"Marnie, is this a bad time?" I called out, just above a whisper. I knew better than to interrupt her in the middle of a scene, but we needed to talk.

"No. It's fine." She replied. "I was just spot-checking for typos and such."

"So you're really back on track with your writing?"

"I think so. Graham liked my ideas for the final draft, so I was up half the night inputting text, and again early this morning. This is my last edit before sending it to him again for one final review . . ." She smiled, her eyes dancing. "Landing Graham Bradford as my mentor is like you landing Twyla Tharp's or Bob Fosse's input on your choreography."

"If only," I shot back. My sister was either sky-high about her work or in the dumps. I liked this mood best. "I wanted to talk to you before April and the others get here."

"Good. I need to talk to you about my latest ideas about that human-interest article."

I nodded. "We're on the same page, then."

"Maybe not." Marnie closed her PC, setting it on the bed beside her. "I want to do the article."

"What?" I was stunned.

"Graham and I talked about it last night. Most of my friends are too polite to question me about why I jumped ship to stay in England, but I know they want to. April is right. The article could clear up a lot of unasked questions and put a positive spin on things."

"Hold on, Marnie. I thought the whole point of your plan to use a pseudonym was to distance yourself from the well-known Taylor name."

Marnie cocked her head. "Well, like everyone's been trying to pound into my head, I'm a Taylor, and all the drama on the Internet is baggage that I own. Instead of talking about kidnappings, rogue waves, and all that jazz, this kind of article will give me a chance to announce my commitment to becoming the best writer possible."

"So you're still going to change your name?"

"Yes and no." She hesitated as if trying to sort it out in her head first. "I'm going to talk to Madison about helping me on social media and with a blog that can establish name recognition for my pseudonym. But I'm not going to abandon my legal name."

Marnie explained that her queries to agents would all go out under her pseudonym. It would be the name on her novels until she had built a sizable readership, won some awards, and developed an active social media presence. She planned to announce it tonight.

"This way, I get the best of both worlds," she said. "It will take time before I begin picking up readers who don't know anything about me.

I'd be a fool to give up my built-in audience of family and good friends, but that's nowhere near enough to make me a best seller. That's where the social media presence kicks in."

She paused, her eyes locking with mine. "People can find out who I am if they try, but most won't look beyond a good logline. Once I know people are buying my novels based on their merits, I'll tie my pseudonym to my name. Like Nora Roberts, who Mom likes at lot. Everyone knows she also writes as J. D. Robb . . ."

I kept my thoughts to myself and just listened until Marnie wound down.

". . . and I know it's going to take time. But what do you think?"

"Well, maybe you'll be like Stephanie Meyer and start dreaming up whole books and become a best seller overnight."

"Not likely." The Twilight series was far from the norm, she explained, and just dreaming a story and writing it down would take half the fun away. "I like to discover my story as I go along. And I love having my characters surprise me." Her eyes narrowed as her forehead crinkled. "But we were supposed to be talking about the article. I'm so sorry, Callie."

I shrugged. "It's okay. You're just thinking about the future. You have a passion, and I know it will lead to success."

Marnie's frown transformed into a smile. "Thanks, sis. But if you're not comfortable with the article, I'll find another way to—"

I shook my head. "Let me think about it some more."

Chapter
159

Saturday, August 15, 3:50 p.m.—Greenwich, Connecticut

"You guys ready?" Marnie called out. She and Brandy stood in the corridor outside the open door to my bedroom.

"Just a sec," I called back as I buckled a strap on my stilettos. I took a last glance at my reflection in the full-length mirror. Smoothing the skirt of my unwrinkled sundress with my shaking hand, I headed for the door.

"You look fantastic," Sam said, tucking a strand of shiny blond hair behind her ear.

Sam's Tahari dress fit her slim body to perfection. This afternoon she'd indulgently stood by as I tried on one outfit after another, including the maxi dress I'd bought this week at Carlingdon's. While I loved the dress, it now seemed too formal. This simple sundress with spaghetti straps in an emerald green seemed perfect. I'd come across it in my closet—and yet it was new to me.

"Thanks," I said, meeting Sam's bright blue eyes, feeling as though I couldn't have a better friend. "I'm like a nervous teenager going to my first prom," I confessed, "not a twenty-three-year-old celebrating a birthday and a college graduation."

Reaching the tent, we saw flowers had been delivered, transforming the white marquee into a wonderland. A rainbow of wildflowers graced the center of every table, with more forming an archway over the entrance and lining the podium. "Made in the USA," backed by a five-piece orchestra, filled the air-conditioned interior of the tent as we stepped inside. The vocalist sounded just like Demi Lovato.

Juliana must have helped Mom with the playlist.

Several guests had already arrived. The majority were Marnie's writer friends, with whom she was immersed in animated conversation. Most were clad in sundresses like mine—not too dressy. Others wore maxis or just skinny jeans with a stylish top. Thrilled over the chance to meet the internationally known novelist, they'd arrived early. Other than Brandy, I wondered how many were privy to Marnie's planned announcement.

I scanned the rapidly filling tent but didn't spot Graham Bradford. It was unlikely he'd be among the first to arrive.

Across the lawn, I saw David pull up. When he opened the back door of the Town Car, a young woman with long, jet-black hair and a purple maxi dress emerged. As she drew closer, I noticed her alabaster skin and studded choker.

"Marnie," I called out, raising my voice above the clamber of friends surrounding her.

"Charlize," she cried, and made a beeline toward her English friend.

My heart leaped when I noticed Dick Landes and Ross Pocino step inside the grand tent. Diverting my gaze, I began greeting other guests and was relieved when I saw the Toddmans. A few steps behind were April and her husband, Kyle, and his young daughter, Lindsay. I assumed the older woman with the red hair must be Paige's colorful mother, Helen. Nora, Lindsay's other grandmother, had not been feeling well for the past few days and sent her apologies.

Lindsay held the hand of another little girl about her age, who I knew must be Jena, Madison's little girl. I didn't see Madison, but a guy behind the two little girls stopped to talk with Kyle. Taking note of his hazel eyes and sandy hair, and his good-natured manner, I figured he must be Madison's significant other, Bill.

Mom dashed over to greet the extended Toddman clan and to offer warm hugs. Dad and Mark stepped aside, most likely discussing the state of the retail climate.

"Callie," Mom said, and she introduced Helen.

"My pleasure," I said, knowing Mom had filled them in on the need for introductions.

Helen gave me a mischievous wink. "Your family has so many friends. It's no wonder you can't remember all of our names." Leaning in closer, she said, "I remember you and your sister. But I wish you had name tags, because I never could tell you apart."

"You're not alone." I gave her a warm smile. She seemed pretty with it for someone with Alzheimer's.

"Do you remember coming to our house to play in my granddaughter April's playhouse? I was the one who sat on the floor with you girls and poured the tea."

I smiled, visualizing the woman pouring tea and handing us cookies. *Was this a memory or something I was imagining?*

"Mom," Paige said, "Let's go find our table and give Ashleigh and Callie a chance to greet their guests."

I glanced around the tent again. There was April talking with Madison, whom I recognized from photos. There were Pocino and Landes, too.

I did not see Jack.

Chapter
160

Saturday, August 15, 3:55 p.m.—Greenwich, Connecticut

As the plane taxied into JFK, Jack Kirkbride readjusted his position. Impatiently waiting for the Fasten Seatbelt sign to blink off, he forced his foot to stop bobbing.

The ninety-minute delay at LAX hadn't been part of his plan, but at least he had finally made it. Although nearly certain it had not been Callie's idea to include him on the guest list, he appreciated the invitation. Maybe Marnie was not as unlike the other Taylors as he'd first imagined.

His heart quickened at the thought of seeing the strong, charismatic, vulnerable young woman who'd captured his heart. His brain had tried to tell him that Callie was right to wait, that it was too soon to pursue a serious relationship. However, his heart told him it wasn't so. He felt like a teenager, yet with the intentions of a grown man who knew what he wanted. Thoughts of Callie filled his every waking hour.

He hadn't wanted to arrive at the celebration as part of the Landes entourage. He had gotten that wish, but now he would probably be late.

When he was finally able to deplane, he wove through the crowd and bolted straight to the Hertz counter, hoping against hope that the traffic from JFK to Greenwich would be light. He didn't want to be the last person to arrive. The last thing he needed was to become a spectacle.

4:40 p.m.

Marnie felt buoyant as Bradford shared his tales of rejection for his first Derek Duncan novel. She'd heard this one while in his master's program upon the ill-fated *Rising Star*. Responding to scores of fans who'd expressed interest in learning more about his charismatic PI, he'd rewritten his original thriller on a blank yellow pad and resubmitted it to Harper Collins. His third published novel had become the prequel to his popular series. Knowing Bradford was in his element when talking with up-and-coming writers, Marnie asked Charlize to join her in greeting the other guests.

Buzzing from one table to the next, she began to relax. Although she knew some people were surely talking about it, no one asked about her questionable decision at the end of the semester-at-sea program. *Perhaps Graham's presence helps them make sense of it all . . .*

The guests were mostly her friends and Callie's, but as she gazed around the room, Marnie realized her extended family made a stunning fashion statement—Armani, Chanel, St. John, Dolce Gabbana, and more. Mom and Aunt Paige, April, and even Grandma Helen could always be counted on to show class and understated elegance. When she spotted her father with Mark Toddman, Marnie smiled. For this occasion, both men had chosen navy blazers and slacks rather than their customary Armani suits.

As she continued to float around the room, she spotted Ross Pocino. He'd been engaged in conversation with Madison, but it seemed she was leaving now. Marnie moved to follow Madison, but Pocino was motioning her toward him. Dick Landes stood by their table, talking to one of the few guests she didn't know—one of Callie's friends, probably. Marnie's eyes flashed around the area and beyond. There was no sign of Jack.

She floated nonchalantly in Pocino's direction.

"Hey!" he called out just before she'd reached him. "Well, how's our world traveler?" His grin was warm.

"I'm great, thanks. But Ross, I want to tell you again how sorry—"

Pocino waved off her apology. "Must admit you sent us on a merry chase." He chuckled. "But it motivated me to get off the dime."

"What do you mean?"

Pocino glanced around. "Can you keep a lid on what I'm going to tell you?"

Marnie nodded. She'd had many run-ins with Pocino, and he'd always had the upper hand. Sharing secrets did not seem to fit his MO. But agreeing was better than getting on his wrong side.

"I've got a buddy, a guy I grew up with in the Bronx. A middle school English teacher. For years he's been after me to collaborate with him on a crime novel."

Incredulous, she asked, "*You* want to be a writer?"

"No way, José. I'd be the idea man. I can't spell, and Buck says clichés are verboten. But your shenanigans gave me a wild idea for a plot."

"Ross," she said, panic slipping into her tone.

"Cool your jets. Our plot has nothing to do with college students. It'll be a crime novel set aboard a ship that encounters a rogue wave. That's all I'm able to tell you until my pal finishes the first draft."

"Whew!" Marnie let out a pent-up breath. "How about letting me read your first draft? I'd be happy to give you some feedback."

"Thanks." Then, taking her in from head to toe, he said, "You've got a good heart." He looked away then, seeming embarrassed by his admission.

When the orchestra began to play Halsey's "Castle," a group of girls took to the dance floor—and a few couples as well. Marnie noticed Madison standing near the wine bar, a glass of white wine in her hand, no longer engaged in conversation, so she drifted over. Madison looked fabulous, and Marnie told her so before drawing her in for a friendly hug. "I understand you're now doing social media work?"

Madison nodded.

"Well, since I'll be needing to build a platform, I was hoping you might spare a half-hour or so when I'm in the city next week, to discuss how you might help me begin building and maintaining a social media presence."

Madison said she'd be delighted, and that was that. Now Marnie could call tomorrow or the next day—and get started on the next chapter of her life.

5:25 p.m.

I'd told myself and anyone who'd listen how upset I was about Marnie inviting Jack to our party, but as I searched the room for the umpteenth time, I couldn't deny I felt deflated. I hadn't wanted Jack to feel obligated to come. But the fact that he had not shown up was a clear message: He was fed up with my failure to move on.

I slipped my iPhone out of my handbag and tapped on it to view my messages. There were none. Everyone was already here—except him.

While Sam and a bunch of other friends were having a blast dancing to Lady Gaga's "Marry the Night," I remembered that same song being blasted by the water's edge when Jack took me to the Pirate Invasion in Long Beach. Tears filled my eyes. I dropped my head as I made my way toward the house, intending to visit the powder room just off the foyer.

"Callie. Callie. Wait up."

I turned to see April rushing up to me. "I got something in my eye," I lied, brushing away the tears.

"Do you want to talk?" she asked.

"I'm headed inside—but yes, I would like to talk to you about something. Do you have a minute?"

I was glad for the distraction. And by the time we reached the foyer, my answer to her friend's request had changed once more.

Chapter
161

Saturday, August 15, 5:50 p.m.—Greenwich, Connecticut

My dad was the first to pull me onto the dance floor. Even though he teased about our selections of music, he fell in with the beat as if it were second nature. Neither my parents nor Mark and Paige Toddman were the least bit out-of-step with our millennial friends, either in dancing or in conversation. I couldn't imagine them saying things like *What is this younger generation coming to?* at tonight's celebration—or anytime, for that matter. Acknowledging our changing world, they accepted our differences. At least, most of the time.

Taking in the ambience of the well-balanced decor of colorful wildflowers and fashionable and funky attire, I realized I was blessed to have so many friends and family members who'd carved out time from their busy schedules—many traveling long distances—to make this celebration memorable. To show my appreciation, I planted a smile on my face and pretended I was having a fabulous time.

Fake it till you make it soon became more than a cliché. It was the truth. If Jack was moving on, so would I. And I wouldn't turn down a single opportunity to dance with my friends.

6:40 p.m.

The music ceased all too soon, and Ashleigh stepped up to the podium for a short introduction of the evening's events. She had carefully planned the short program to coincide with dinner being served at exactly 7:00 p.m., eliminating the need for food to be transferred to buffet-style warming trays.

As the champagne was poured, Conrad stepped to the microphone to make a toast. "Tonight, we have a quadruple header of family occasions to celebrate." Holding up one finger, he began, "The first is Juliana's graduation from Greenwich High. With honors."

Following energetic applause, Conrad held up both hands. "Thank you." Holding up two more fingers, he said, "We are also celebrating Callie's graduation from CSULB *and* Marnie's from UCI." After more clapping, he held up a fourth finger and thumb. "And last but not least, we are celebrating Callie's and Marnie's twenty-third birthday, though not official until next Wednesday."

Smiling at Ashleigh, he continued, "I'm told there is no time to tell you about their future plans. But feel free to have them fill you in throughout the evening." With a wink, he added, "Or I'll be glad to." His face lit up, and he lifted his glass of champagne. "And now let's all lift our glasses and toast to the continued success of the younger generation of the Taylor clan."

After tipping up her glass, Ashleigh laughed and pretended to reel in her husband with a hook.

He shrugged and parroted, "That's all, folks," before giving Ashleigh an air kiss on her cheek and surrendering the mic.

Ashleigh blew him another kiss as he returned to their table. "As you can see, we are very proud of our girls." Her words rang with sincerity. "Now, before dinner is served, Marnie would like to share with you, her closest friends and family, an important decision she recently made that will have long-lasting effects on her future."

6:45 p.m.

Marnie's knees shook as she stepped up to the mic. Standing tall, she lifted her chin and steeled herself. If she got weak in the knees every time she had to address a crowd, she'd have a short career. Gone were the days when writers could just write, while others took care of getting their books into the hands of readers.

Drawing in a breath, she began. "I don't think there's anyone here who doesn't know how much I want to become a published author. Not a middle-of-the-roader, but one who truly moves her readers. Once I'm published, I want people to buy my books because they love my stories, not because of my name. Therefore, at least for my first few books, I've decided to write under a pseudonym." Her eyes drifted to Bradford. "That name will be . . . Cassie T."

After quickly summing up her rationale, she concluded, "For those of you who don't know, Cassie is my legal birth name." She paused. "If you forget, I'll still answer to Marnie. But I'd love for you all to start calling me Cassie."

6:50 p.m.

As my sister took her seat, I stepped up to the mic before I could change my mind. It remained to be seen whether our friends and family would begin calling my sister Cassie. Our family had agreed to try our best. I wanted to signal to her that we liked the idea, although it would take some getting used to.

"While everyone's champagne glass is being refilled," I began, "please join me in wishing my sister Cassie a world of success."

When the applause died down, I continued, "And now I'd like to thank each of you for being here tonight and for the wonderful support Marnie . . . *Cassie* . . . and I have received from so many of you. I feel blessed. I'm grateful to be a part of such a wonderful family—one that extends far beyond blood relations. Not all the circuits in my brain have reconnected, and my memory may not allow me to recall all of your names." I arched a brow. "Even my sister's."

Everyone laughed, and I was able to relax at last.

"But I assure you," I went on, "that I want to make memories enough going forward to fill a hundred scrapbooks."

Chapter 162

Saturday, August 15, 6:50 p.m.—Greenwich, Connecticut

Jack quietly slipped into the chair beside Landes. He felt his boss's and Pocino's questioning eyes on him but couldn't explain until Callie left the podium. His heart had filled with love as he listened to her, noting the slight tremor in her opening remarks. He knew how hard it must have been for her to address a room full of people.

She is so brave.

"I've had a day from hell," Jack said in a loud whisper as Ashleigh stepped up to the mic. "The flight was delayed nearly two hours, no rental cars were available at the airport, and then my phone battery went dead." Getting an Uber all the way from JFK had cost a pretty penny—and he would need a ride back to the Landes Agency condo that night.

A crooked grin appeared on Landes's face. "Glad you made it for dinner."

As the guests were asked to take their seats for dinner, Jack discreetly took in the room in search of Callie. He spotted her at a table at the far end of the dance floor, sitting beside Sam and a group of other young women and men. He thought, but wasn't sure, he saw Callie glance in his direction for a nanosecond. Perhaps she hadn't seen him—or perhaps she had purposely averted her eyes. He feared the latter.

Jack knew his late arrival did not play well. He must apologize and wish her a happy birthday before dinner. Already, the awkwardness threatened to grow into too great a hurdle for either of them to overcome.

6:55 p.m.

When I saw Jack look my way, my throat went dry. Would he come over? It was only a fleeting thought, since he seemed to avert his eyes in the next instant. I hated the thought of his feeling obligated to be here. And I could no longer deny that Jack Kirkbride had captured my heart.

If only my parents hadn't hired him. If only he had come into my life after I got my feet firmly planted. If only . . . there weren't so many obstacles. This was not our time.

"Look, Callie," Juliana whispered in my ear, pulling me from my thoughts. "Mom said there were going to be some important announcements." I looked up to see Dad herding our extended family toward the side entrance.

My glance darted across to Marnie's table, where Graham Bradford and her friend Charlize had captured the limelight. Marnie had excused herself and was following the others. I did likewise.

"I bet I know one of the announcements," Juliana whispered as we gathered at the high tables on the lawn. "Maybe both." Her big brown eyes sparkled with delight, just like the glasses of champagne that covered the tables. Marnie's grin spread from ear to ear, hinting that she knew something too.

I had a couple of hunches myself. Judging from the delight on the faces of everyone else, many were already in the know. Looking clockwise from Grandma Helen, I took in the entire group.

We all knew Elizabeth was moving to Long Beach, so that wasn't it. Next to her were the two little girls, Lindsay and Jena, who shifted from one foot to the other as they giggled. They definitely knew something.

Madison and Bill, April and Kyle, Paige and Mark—they were all here. As my sisters huddled around the tall tables, Dad handed a champagne flute to each of us, so we could join in another toast.

At the center table, Mark tapped a spoon lightly against his glass. His gaze momentarily fell on Madison. "Please lift your glasses in a toast to Madison and Bill. May they have a long and happy life together!"

Bill beamed as Madison flashed her engagement ring.

"Paige and I have known Madison since she and April were in elementary school," Mark continued. "She's like a second daughter, and we couldn't be happier for her to have found the love of her life. Bill, you're a man we greatly admire, and we're proud to welcome you to the family." Mark held his hand out to Paige, who stood beside him. "Now, forgive me for going off script, but since we are with all our loved ones this evening, we would like to ask you two for the privilege of hosting your wedding."

Tears sprang to Madison's eyes. Bill pulled her close and looked both pleased and slightly puzzled.

"Please," Paige said, her emerald eyes moist, "Mark and I want so much to make your wedding a memorable occasion."

My eyes filled with tears of happiness. Madison's difficult life story seemed as though it finally would have a happy ending.

Following the toast, the waiters refilled our glasses. When all the tears and congratulations died down, Mark again tapped spoon against glass—a water goblet this time. "And now for the news I've wanted to share for a lifetime." He glanced over at his daughter and son-in-law. "You may have noticed that April toasted her best friend's engagement with a glass of water."

"I knew it. I just knew it." Juliana clamped her hand over her mouth, her eyes dancing.

April glanced down at her flat stomach. "Really?" she said, with a clear note of drama.

"Hey, Juliana, you're stealing my thunder," Mark chided, smiling broadly. "I never knew I wanted to be a father until April came into our lives, but becoming a grandfather has become the role of a lifetime." He reached across and ruffled Lindsay's silky blond hair. "And Lindsay told me she's ready—"

"For a sister," Lindsay shouted with gusto.

Mark chuckled. "Well, what if it's a boy?"

"Well, you told me there were no exchanges, so I guess it'll be okay."

Kyle rolled his eyes and April laughed. "Kyle and I are delighted," she beamed. "We'll be happy no matter whether it's a boy or a girl. What we pray for is a healthy baby we can make as happy as Lindsay makes us."

As we walked back to join our friends, everyone bubbling with the happy news, I glanced in the direction of Jack's table. I caught only a glimpse of his profile. It seemed impossible, but still I wondered: Would we ever make such an announcement?

Chapter
163

Saturday, August 15, 7:10 p.m.—Greenwich, Connecticut

Jack surreptitiously kept an eye on Callie's table throughout dinner. From all appearances, she was having a great time. Apparently, she'd overcome her fear of family and friends she didn't remember. Better yet, perhaps her memory was returning.

Dessert had not yet been served when the orchestra began playing "Believer" and the dance floor began to fill. Jack pushed back his chair, about to climb to his feet, when he saw Callie being tugged onto the floor by a guy with familiar movie-star good looks. Jack racked his brain but couldn't place the guy.

Deflated, he settled back in the chair.

Pocino guffawed and slapped him on the shoulder. "Go for it."

"Just waiting my turn." Jack forced a smile, attempting a lighthearted tone.

"You snooze, you lose," Pocino shot back.

Landes arched a heavy brow and shrugged. "Young love."

But Jack was no teenager. "Come on, Dick. Give me a break. I'm only three years away from thirty." As he'd feared, his late arrival was probably interpreted as a lack of interest.

"You could be waiting a very long time. Those Taylor girls love to dance, and there's no lack of willing partners. But neither Callie nor April would be upset if you cut in."

"April?"

"The former April Toddman. That's her husband, Kyle Clark—the man who's boppin' around the floor with Callie. They're family."

"Kyle Clark," he repeated. "The anchorman for *Eyewitness News*?"

"Affirmative," Pocino shot back.

Feeling an incomparable wave of relief, Jack got to his feet. Reaching the dance floor, he tapped Kyle on the shoulder and smiled. "Would you mind?"

Kyle locked eyes with Callie. Seconds ticked off before she nodded, and he stepped back.

"Nice of you to make it," Callie said once she was in his arms.

When she smiled up at him with her shimmering brown eyes, he vowed to do whatever it took to keep her in his life.

8:15 p.m.

Sarcasm was not my style, so I wasn't surprised when Jack didn't read it as such.

"I am *so* sorry for being late." He explained how Murphy's Law had haunted him all the way from Long Beach. Talking while keeping in step seemed to take some effort on his part, but I barely noticed.

"Callie," he said, "you weren't the one to put me on the guest list, were you?"

I said nothing but took hold of his hand. "Let's go out where it's quiet, and we can talk."

Leaving the tent, we walked a few yards to the gazebo, which was a dazzling white, the entrance bordered in tiny, twinkling lights. I didn't know if I was ready for this, but I desired nothing else.

Patting the cushion beside me, I lowered myself onto the bench circling the gazebo's interior. "You're right, Jack. I wasn't the one to add your name to our guest list. It was Marnie. Somehow, she read my scrambled mind. I did want you to be here. But I didn't want you to feel obligated to fly clear across the country to be with a bunch of strangers."

"You and your family are hardly strangers, my love. But that's not the point." Taking both of my hands, he said, "I care about you. I feel more alive when we're together. I've hated this distance we've forced between us."

Even in the dim lighting, he must have seen the moisture pooling in my eyes and must have suspected I no longer desired distance.

8:25 p.m.

Jack's heart thundered in his ears. He would not let her slip away again. He wanted her to be at his side, come what may. He'd fallen hard—as he'd never done before. He was in love with Callie Taylor.

Before Callie, he had no idea what people were talking about when they said they'd found their soul mate. He knew neither of them was ready for marriage, but his future included a family, and hers had become his role model. No matter what it took, he would win Callie's heart, and she would be his wife and the mother of his children. Long-term memories be damned.

Seeing her tears, however, he feared he'd gone too far. The last thing he wanted was to risk driving her away. He started to release her hands.

Callie squeezed his hands back. "I've missed being with you, Jack. There's no one I feel closer to. No one with whom I can share my fears—realistic or not." She paused, then straightened her back. "You're just beginning your career, and I'm still in school . . ."

He inhaled, fearing she was about to drop the proverbial "other shoe."

". . . but I want you to be a part of my life."

Taken by surprise, Jack found no words to express his feelings. Aware that he must take it slow, he resisted pulling her into his arms. Instead, he pulled her hands to his lips.

8:35 p.m.

I knew I should get back inside in a few minutes, but since I had no better sounding board than Jack, I wanted to share another decision with him. "Even though Marnie is now eager to work with the reporter," she said after explaining the human-interest story April's reporter friend had proposed, "I planned to tell April I wasn't prepared to participate."

"That's understandable, my love."

I heard the term of endearment. Was it accidental, or had he let it slip out on purpose? Either way, I didn't mind. It gave me courage.

"But I changed my mind," I said. "It might be good not only for Mar—Cassie and her future, but for me as well."

"How so?" asked Jack.

"By being forced to express how I'm coping, I just may unscramble my ups and downs, find balance, and move forward."

"As long as you're comfortable with the idea, I think it's great. Marnie's—or Cassie's—story could certainly drive home the importance of up-front communication. And your positive outlook would really inspire hope in others."

"Hi, Jack," Juliana's voice interrupted. "We thought we'd find you out here." Kaitlyn was just a few steps behind her. "Cassie, April, and Kyle have to get Lindsay home. She said you wanted to talk to her? But maybe now's not the best time . . ." Juliana wiggled her brows comically.

I laughed. *That's my little sister—always knowing just how to make me smile.* "Thanks, Jules," I said. "We were just coming in."

"Sure you were," she said, jabbing Kaitlyn with her elbow.

Jack just chuckled. And held tightly to my hand.

CHAPTER 164

Sunday, November 22, 10:05 a.m.—Long Beach, California

Our flight from JFK had landed fifteen minutes ahead of schedule.

As Jules, Sam, and I headed to baggage claim, I tried not to dwell on how much I'd missed Jack. I wished again that he could have joined us.

He'd called every evening over the Thanksgiving weekend, and we'd exchanged texts all day long, but I'd never missed him more.

During his obligatory trip to Chicago for Thanksgiving, Senator Thomas Kirkbride had roped his adopted son, Jack, into attending the type of political functions he detested. The Kirkbrides even had their Thanksgiving dinner in the fancy dining room of the Palmer Hotel with another couple, because Jack's father needed them to get on board with his political agenda. My heart ached for the man I'd come to love with all my heart. And yet his bumpy past may have contributed in some way to the man he'd become.

Trying to take my mind off Jack's past, I thought of our own traditional family Thanksgiving in Greenwich. We all had missed having Elizabeth with us, but we understood why she had stayed in Long Beach to spend the holiday with Aunt Caroline at New Beginnings.

Then my mind flitted to Cassie. She'd been walking on air over Graham Bradford joining us in Greenwich and his confirmation that the short story she'd written for her graduate program was deserving of an A-plus. He'd also given her a thumbs-up on submitting it to *Writer's Digest*.

Over the past three months, I'd become accustomed to calling her Cassie. Jules, Kaitlyn, Sam, Brandy, and even Elizabeth had done their best too. Perhaps my easier transition was due to the memory loss.

Occasionally, in the heat of arguing passionately in defense of our conflicting views, I slipped back to calling her Marnie. She even suggested, only half joking, that there was rhyme and reason to my choices: C for Cassie when she was feeling *compassionate* toward me, and M for Marnie when she thought I was a *menace*.

She no longer made a big deal over her name. She answered to both and was satisfied with introducing herself as Cassie. Our parents had said little about the name change, though I think they were pleased she'd chosen her birth name. But they also slipped up sometimes.

I loved my master's degree dance program. Jules had quickly adapted to college life. And Cassie, forever the drama queen, continued to have her ups and downs. On this first holiday break from grad school, Cassie had stopped off in Chicago for a second Thanksgiving with the Christonellis and decided to ask them to continue calling her Marnie.

We'd all be back in place in Long Beach this evening, and I couldn't wait to see Jack. We had a lot to talk about.

5:45 p.m.—*Los Angeles, California*

Jack had suggested I meet him out front of the terminal at LAX, but I wanted to see him the minute he stepped off the plane. So I parked the BMW—my college graduation gift—in the lot across from the Delta terminal.

Once inside, I checked the Arrivals screen and saw that the flight from Chicago was due to arrive on time. It dawned on me that Jack and Cassie both had reason to spend time in the Windy City—another point in common that would help them continue to develop their friendship.

I found the conveyer belt for flight 707, but the luggage had not yet begun sliding down the shoot. The plane had landed only moments before, but I turned in the direction of the ramp so I would see Jack the moment he appeared. When he did, my mouth flew open as he swept me into his arms.

When I came up for air, I said, "How did you get here so fast?"

"The senator booked me in first class," he said, using his favorite term for his father, "and I told the flight attendant I had a family emergency."

"You *didn't*." I laughed.

"I did. It was an emergency. You have no idea how much I've missed you." He stepped back to look at me before pulling me in for another kiss. "Please, please lock me in leg irons if I ever again consider spending a holiday with my pretentious parents. The only good thing about this trip is that it's behind me and my obligation is *over*."

He said he had missed me twenty-four hours a day. The feeling was mutual.

Chapter
165

Sunday, November 22, 6:10 p.m.—Los Angeles, California

When we reached the parking lot, I clicked the trunk open and handed Jack the keys. "I want to hear all about your trip," I said. "Then I have something I want to share with you."

He dumped his luggage, raising a well-shaped dark brow when I opened the passenger door.

"Just laying eyes on you has made my world a brighter place." He slid beneath the wheel and adjusted the seat before backing out of the parking space. "To be honest, the one terrific thing about my trip was this inspiring human-interest piece in *Reader's Digest*. Have you seen it?" he added playfully.

"Ha, ha." I tapped his shoulder. "What did you think? Honest opinion."

"Would you expect anything else?"

"No," I said, a bit too quickly. "Well, if you hated it, you'd spare my feelings."

"True," he said, reaching across the console to hold my free hand. "But I'd never lie to you."

"Fair enough," I said, and I meant it. But I knew the lawyer in Jack would find a way to give me any negatives in a palatable manner.

"I found it riveting," he said. "Honestly. As much as I know of your story and the rough road you've traveled in these past six months, I appreciated your candor. It gave me an even better understanding of the woman I love."

I felt moisture building behind my lashes and blinked it back. He'd never said it before—that he loved me. I knew he was attracted to me and we liked being together, but the word *love* had never been spoken by either of us. No response came to mind, so I said nothing.

"Thank you," was all I could think to say.

"So let me get caught up on your news." Jack momentarily took his eyes from the road. "What was it you wanted to share?"

"Well, the first thing was your reaction to the article. The other is my last appointment with Dr. Martin."

"Hmm" Jack replied. "When was that?"

"Last Wednesday."

"Before your flight to New York?"

Knowing the real question was why I hadn't told him, I said, "Yes. I didn't want to send mixed messages. I needed time to think things over before discussing it with anyone." Reaching for his hand, I added, "Even you."

And then I told him.

Pulling onto the 405 freeway, Jack was silent. Bringing Callie's hand to his lips, he kissed it gently.

"Sweetheart, I don't know what to say," he began. "Your long-term memories have no meaning to me. I was no part of your life before the rogue wave brought you to me. As I've told you before, I care about the return of those memories only because they matter to you."

For a few eternal seconds, Callie said nothing. Then she lifted her head from the back of the seat and turned to face him. "I'm sorry, Jack. I'm not sure what I think."

Forcing his eyes on the road ahead, he finally said, "Would it help if I fed back my understanding of all you've shared with me?"

She nodded, "I think I'd like to hear my thoughts outside my own head."

"You're frustrated and confused over the source of many of your memories?"

"Right. Since my family and friends have filled me in on so many events from my past, I no longer—"

"You no longer know if what you recall is a memory from the past or from what someone has schooled you on since the disaster at sea?"

"Exactly."

"Sweetheart," Jack said.

In the dim illumination of distant streetlights and passing headlights, Callie looked so damn desirable, he wanted to pull off the road, take her in his arms, and never let her go. But that could wait.

"Dr. Martin says your experience is quite common for individuals with strong support from family and friends, and there's no known test to sort that out. So, let's say you never truly regain those long-term memories. You're here. You're alive. You're happy. What, exactly, is the downside?"

That was a question I'd asked myself since returning to Greenwich last August. I had figured out my life is now and in the future—not in the past. And as I gazed across to the driver's seat at Jack, that future was looking darn good.

But I knew my greatest fear. "The worst part is not knowing what I don't know. You know, like that George Santayana quote: 'Those who don't remember the past are doomed to repeat it.'"

"Seriously?" Jack chuckled. "Where did that come from? For a million bucks, I couldn't dredge that name up from my memory—long- or short-term."

I had to smile at the irony. "That's just it. I remember all sorts of random trivia, but my memory algorithms are still all messed up."

"Whoa," said Jack. " You've lost me. In English, my love."

I shrugged. "It's an analogy I came across. What it means is, our brains are programmed to repeat certain actions to produce a certain result."

"I get that," he said. "And yet the inventive mind does not always accept what worked in the past. It may not work now—or in the future."

Pulling up in front of his apartment, Jack switched off the ignition and pulled me close. "Life is full of what-ifs, Callie. You said your greatest fear is not knowing what you don't know? Well that, I believe, is the condition of humanity."

Instead of offering suggestions, Jack had a unique way of just listening and giving me the opportunity to see things more clearly. I loved that.

"You are the most beautiful, fascinating woman I have ever met," he continued, "and one day, when we are ready, I will ask you to be my wife. I love you, and we'll figure out whatever needs to be figured out together."

As his lips touched mine, I had no regrets; I cared only about the future.

Author's Note

In this world of ever-changing priorities and values, I am often asked to comment on the long-range viability of department stores and shopping malls, as well as brick-and-mortar stores in general. While my passion and expertise are in the fashion department store arena, I have researched and will address all of the above.

Change is inevitable and necessary for progress. However, I strongly believe in the value of department stores, shopping malls, and brick-and-mortar stores.

Having been on the management team of one of the largest West Coast fashion department store groups (now a part of Macy's Inc.), I find my heart remains in the fashion industry. Therefore, I keep up with the daily changes in the landscape. Also, to create realistic stories based on real-life drama, I keep in touch with many of the passionate individuals who pour their energy, intelligence, talent, and creativity into meeting the ever-changing wants and needs of today's consumers.

The extinction of department stores has been predicted for decades. Yet I believe they are here to stay. Even so, the continual slashing of prices has created a population of consumers who are no longer willing to pay full price.

Gloom and doom for department stores prevailed following the fourth quarter of 2007, a time that many refer to as the Great Recession. Many department stores crumbled, as did other retailers, while others fell into bankruptcy and began shuttering multiple locations.

And yet following the recession, many major department stores emerged from bankruptcy. They sprang back, better and stronger than before. For example, Macy's and its stock prices were on a tear for more than two years. They were going great. Business was booming, and stockholders were happy. Despite the stock's recent tumble, many of Macy's investors have quadrupled their money.

For the department stores and other sellers of fashion apparel, the good time came to an abrupt end in the fourth quarter of 2015, when shoppers failed to deliver the expected sales growth. The hottest winter temperatures in one hundred years in North America attributed to this dramatic plunge, decimating the expected holiday sales. However, that was far from the only challenge faced by the sellers of fashion apparel.

Currently, the economy is good, yet shoppers with extra money in their pockets from greater employment and lower gas prices are not spending their money on clothing. Instead, they are spending on entertainment, restaurants, and durable goods. Many are buying new cars and homes. Home furnishings is another area that is doing well.

Millennials and others are opting for cheaper fashions that can be discarded and frequently updated, in lieu of quality. However, there will always be a quality market. For those with wealth that is not dependent on the current economy, there remains a quest for the best. And yet they insist on value, which is a combination of price and quality.

Terry Lundgren, former CEO of Macy's Inc., recently commented on the continual evolution in the world of retail, mentioning significant shakeups every five to seven years. He remains optimistic about the future of Macy's and department stores in general. Lundgren says, "Don't focus on what is happening now. It will clutter your mind. You may make a wrong choice. Think where you want to be in five years." While not always easy, that is a terrific motto for life.

However, he cautions that old ways do not work in today's retail environment because there is too much product and too much sameness in merchandise. To attract consumers, stores must concentrate on brands—merchandise the customer cannot get elsewhere. Macy's has several of its own brands and exclusives with designers, items you can find only at Macy's. Last year the company also contracted with

Bluemercury specialty beauty retailer and Apple for exclusive in-store boutiques. The plan for Macy's is to capitalize on, rather than run from, brick-and-mortar department stores.

For the past fourteen years, under Lundgren's leadership, Macy's has become the largest group of quality department stores in the U.S. and the third-largest online retailer. Currently, only Amazon and Walmart surpass Macy's.

Although I admire Terry Lundgren, whom I worked with at Bullock's department stores in the mid-eighties, and the entrepreneurial teamwork and creativity he's inspired at Macy's, I had not been a Macy's customer. My personal preferences for shopping have been Bloomingdale's and Nordstrom. However, as I was researching for this book, I discovered the vastness of the Macy's online site. You can search not only by category (which is common), but also by color and style for the item you desire. There may be other sites that offer this, but I have found none as sophisticated.

For different results, different actions must be taken. Therefore, Lundgren challenged his executives to find three things they plan to do differently than in the year before.

The closing of one hundred Macy's locations is a proactive step to benefit the remaining stores and, in turn, the consumer and stockholders. Lundgren points out the amount of retail space per capita in the United States is disproportional. Industrywide, we devote 7.3 square feet of retail space per capita, which compares with roughly 1.8 square feet in the U.K., 1.3 square feet in France, and 1.7 in Japan. While we in the U.S. are the greatest consumers, we do not consume two times as much as the three countries that come next—Australia, the U.K., and Canada.

In most cases, volume and profitability have steadily declined in the stores Macy's targeted to close. In others, the cost of remodeling exceeds their value. With the closing of 100 locations, Macy's will retain a physical footprint in forty-nine of the top fifty U.S. markets. The money saved will allow for a focus on the best stores, on increased staffing, and on bringing in new technology, including digital and mobile.

When asked about the impact of online retail sites, including their own, Lundgren said, online purchases have not impacted the apparel industry as much as other retailers, such as electronics and books. Customers still want to touch and try on apparel. Eighty-five percent of apparel purchases come from brick-and-mortar stores. Due to Macy's vast online presence as the largest seller of apparel, and the fact that merchandise can be returned to their stores, sixty-five percent of their business is in-store and thirty-five percent online.

Lundgren states it is vital that a department store maintain a strong online presence. At first, he feared the company's online sales might cannibalize those in the brick-and-mortar stores. He and his team had to rethink how today's customer is shopping—and get it front of it to figure out what they must do to have customers shop with Macy's.

What they discovered was incredible. Online business and its impact on brick-and-mortar stores was overblown. In fact, it is mostly incremental business, since many consumers were already online buyers. Lundgren believes in multichannel options for shoppers: in-store, online, and catalog. Multichannel buyers spend two to three times more than single-channel shoppers. He doesn't care how buyers purchase, as long as they buy from Macy's or Bloomingdale's.

Today, many customers shop first with their phone. They decide what they want and how much they are willing to pay, and only then do they head to the store where they talk to an associate, touch the product, and in the case of clothing, try it on. They make sure the product is right before purchasing. Some may leave the store and purchase online.

The one area where investors fault Lundgren is not getting into off-price retailing years ago, giving rivals such as Nordstrom and Saks such a large head start with their Nordstrom Rack and Off 5th. The Macy's equivalent, Backstage, is expanding, which will bring in incremental sales.

With department stores facing major headwinds for the past two years, Macy's is not alone in becoming more innovative and taking proactive steps to increase shareholder value. Many others are selling off real estate, including Lord and Taylor, Sears Holdings Corp., J. C. Penney, Sears, Saks owner Hudson's Bay Co., and BonTon—with some leasing back. Smaller apparel stores such as Abercrombie & Fitch, Ann Taylor, The Limited, Michael Kors, and many more are also closing many locations. Kohl's has recently made a deal to process Amazon returns and sell the tech giant's gadgets in-store. And Nordstrom is fighting back by venturing into uncharted territories, like Canada. The company is also experimenting with alternative store formats, such as small concept stores that will not stock inventory.

This downturn in clothing purchases is worldwide, with comparable department stores like Macy's in the U.S., and Edcon in South Africa, shrinking their footprint to focus on flagship stores.

Bernie Brookes, CEO of Myer, Australia's biggest chain of department stores, has a far less optimistic outlook for department stores than Lundgren. However, he agrees that the biggest problem for department stores such as Myer, Harris Scarfe, and David Jones—and their discount equivalents Kmart, Target, and Best & Less—is there are too many of them. "There needs to be radical surgery associated with a very different retail offer," Brookes says. "I don't see a particularly good picture going forward. There is still a place for them, but it's limited—fewer stores—and more important, it's for those with a unique offer and those that provide an experience."

Except for an online focus, I see little difference in the way these two superstar retail leaders view the current retail landscape. They voice the same problems and envision similar solutions. Lundgren is a great deal more optimistic, as am I. What a sad, lonely world this would become if we all did everything online.

Shopping center developer Scott Bell says while he believes the popularity of online shopping will continue to grow, he feels the effect on brick-and-mortar stores and shopping centers is greatly exaggerated. Currently, only 8.5 percent of retail sales are transacted online. The most savvy of the retailers at the Bell shopping malls embrace online shopping but know it is just one more way to serve the customer. Even Amazon is now investing in brick-and-mortar stores. Mall complexes adapt to shoppers' changing habits, forever striving to be a one-stop destination. Consumers can meet a friend while buying clothes they can look at, touch, and try on. They can also look over and purchase other merchandise. They can eat a meal, get their hair cut or styled, get a massage, and so forth. In many malls, there is also entertainment, among other options. That's why malls continue to succeed. If you doubt that, just try to find a parking slot in a mall on weekends—or even midweek.

According to Bell, Anthony Cafaro Jr., co-president of the mall complex's parent firm, has commented, "You can't meet your best friend for lunch on your smartphone."

Some of our beloved regional department stores that were taken over or driven into bankruptcy in the late eighties—Bullock's/Bullocks Wilshire, Robinsons, Riches, Foley's, A&S, I Magnin's, The Broadway, May Company, Marshall Field's, and many more—may never return. I say *may* since the fans of Marshall Field's, under the leadership of James McKay, continue to wage a battle in Chicago for the return of their beloved icon. Also, Strategic Marks CEO Ellia Kassoff prevailed in a lawsuit against Macy's for the brand names of I. Magnin, Bullock's, Foley's, Bamberger's, Jordan Marsh, and Robinsons-May. He has not given up on obtaining some of the others, such as Marshall Field's. He plans to deliver the essence of these brands online and with some smaller, pop-up stores. Kassoff successfully brought back the Hydrox cookie after winning that brand name in a similar lawsuit. What he will do with the regional store brands only time will tell.

And so, retail continues to evolve. The future landscape will not look the same as it does today, just as it is not the same now as it was when many of us were growing up. It has changed and will continue to do so.

Here are some of the changes I have observed: Stores were not open on Sunday before 1986. The first shopping mall opened in 1956 in Edina, Minnesota, near Minneapolis. Before that time, there were stand-alone department stores, mostly in the downtown areas. Home computers were not available before 1975, at which point they came in a kit; they were available in 1977 and became common in 1980. Amazon.com and eBay launched online shopping sites in 1995. With the advances of technology over five decades, our lifestyles have changed greatly.

While technology has made many things easier and more accessible, it has also somehow made lives more hectic and given us less free time. If offers both good things and bad. For those who grew up with or have adapted to technology, it can be a great time saver. It can also be a time waster.

However, among our aging population, technology can be a friend or a foe. For those who do not resist but instead have adapted to it, there are many new ways to stimulate their brains and occupy free time. Older people are also able to order food and other products they need when they're unable to get out to a store. However, for those who resist technology, it can be confusing and isolating.

I have often been accused of being a Pollyanna. This is a comparison I don't mind, since I prefer optimism. And my optimism tells me that none of us will live to see a world without department stores, brick-and-mortar stores, shopping malls . . . and books in print.

Where it all began . . . in the stand-alone Webs series!

Webs of Fate: In the high-fashion world of the mid-1980s, Ashleigh McDowell falls victim to a painful betrayal by Danielle Norman, a naive and vulnerable young buyer who is fighting to save her plummeting career. How high a price will both women pay in their battle over a grave secret?

Each step Ashleigh takes to uncover the truth about Danielle's actions and whereabouts, unwittingly expose her to a criminal mastermind as events spin out of his control. In her hunt for Danielle, Ashleigh discovers an unexpected ally in the handsome Conrad Taylor. Will he steal her heart—or break it?

In a race against both time and the emotions that haunt her, Ashleigh seeks—and finds—what fate holds in store for her.

This prequel—set in the golden age of regional department stores, and before the phrase "How much can you save?" became a status symbol—creates the background for the personalities and motivations that drive the Webs Series.

Webs of Power: In this raw, unsentimental portrayal of greed, manipulation, and relationships set in the excessive, insatiable retail industry of the 1980s, the dynamic characters find the courage to drastically reshape their lives in the face of crises and twists of fate.

When a hostile takeover of retail giant Consolidated is announced, the lives of three determined women, each linked to the corporate upheaval, are unexpectedly thrown off course.

Paige Toddman's marriage to Consolidated's West Coast Division CEO is threatened when she decides to step out of her fast-paced lifestyle to raise the unwanted child she is carrying—a choice driven by her secret past. The fabric of Ashleigh McDowell's life begins to fray when her fiancé, the president of Consolidated's West Coast Division, must move to Boston and her father figure faces a lawsuit that could wipe out his controlling shares of the company's stock. And the vain and power-hungry Viviana De Mornay will stop at nothing to become the wife of the man leading the takeover.

Twisted Webs: Out of love and desperation, a good, religious man takes fate into his own hands and commits an unthinkable crime that pulls at two worlds until they finally collide.

Hours after Ashleigh Taylor gives birth to identical baby girls, a parent's worst nightmare occurs: one of her daughters is kidnapped. In the eight traumatic years that follow, tightly woven webs of deception entwine two families. Suspense electrifies the pages of every short, fast-paced chapter as the mystery of the abduction of Callie's identical twin, Cassie—renamed Marnie by her unwitting adoptive mother—unravels.

With candor and sensitivity, Darlene Quinn probes the shock, despair, anger, and frustration of parents suddenly missing a child—and the long-term effects on a family wrestling with these emotions. Complementary storylines in this stand-alone sequel—Paige Toddman's reunion with her mother, Viviana De Mornay's secret, and others—tie into the redemptive theme of motherhood.

Unpredictable Webs: Betrayal, rebellion, jealousy, and a kidnapping gone awry are at the core of this ensnaring story. Marnie Taylor, who was abducted the day she was born and reunited with her family eight years later, is now about to turn sixteen. She is lonely and rebellious—fighting often with her mother, Ashleigh—and jealous of her popular, more even-tempered twin sister, Callie. Marnie finds a compassionate listener in Brad, whom she meets online. Spinning a web of lies to throw her parents off the trail, Marnie arranges to meet Brad—but she realizes too late that she has been targeted in a sinister scheme for ransom.

Quinn's vivid cast of characters returns in this high-tension, stand-alone sequel—but in this tale that discloses the darker side of human behavior, none behave as others might predict. "Cougar" Viviana De Mornay takes Chicago's fashion world (and "Italian Stallion" Gino Cabello) by storm. Tony Wainwright, who has paid his dues for a past crime and appears to have turned his life around, is catapulted to the top of the list of suspects. PI Ross Pocino is on the scene with his shocking insights into criminal behavior. And Paige Toddman's ailing mother, Helen, seems to grow younger every day. While some mothers can unintentionally do unspeakable harm to their children, Ashleigh's steel-magnolia efforts to wrest her daughter from her captor redeem the sacredness of that role.

Conflicting Webs: This stand-alone addition to the gripping Webs series explores love and loss, career and family, forgiveness and redemption. Fast-paced chapters propel unforgettable characters through the turmoil of overlapping and often conflicting commitments.

Wedding bells are set to ring. April Toddman, the darling of the Jordon's retail dynasty, feels blessed. Her handsome, amiable fiancé, Kyle Clark, is passionate and shares her dreams. No couple could ask for a more promising future. And yet just days before they are to exchange their marriage vows, their perfect world begins to crumble. Fate steps in and puts April and Kyle to the test. Will they successfully thread their way through the conflicting webs to secure their happiness?

With unfamiliar ground beneath their feet, April and Kyle must confront an unrelenting tsunami of obligations: to others, to their budding careers, and to themselves.

A child without a mother . . . A wedding without a honeymoon . . . A mother without a family . . . Beloved characters old and new weave secrets, mistakes, accidents, and lies into intricate webs of conflict as they strive to protect the next generation. Readers young and old will be held captive by the bold decisions these characters make to take charge of their destiny.

Available in all formats: Print, eBook, Audio.
View videos and read or listen to the beginning chapters at darlenequinn.net.

About the Author

DARLENE QUINN worked in department store management during a period of dynamic upheaval. Her first novel, *Webs of Power*, won the Best Fiction award from the National Indie Excellence Awards, and its follow-up, *Twisted Webs*, has generated interest in a film adaptation. A sought-after speaker and writing workshop leader, Quinn lives in Long Beach, California, with her husband, Jack.